H.M.S.
VANGUARD

H.M.S. VANGUARD

A Tale of Horror

John Conrad

**With illustrations by
C.J. Grzybowski**

To order additional copies of this book, contact:
Xlibris Corporation
1-888-795-4274
www.Xlibris.com
Orders@Xlibris.com
19468

CONTENTS

H.M.S. Vanguard

1 BOWSPRINT
2 FORE MAST
3 MAIN MAST
4 MIZZEN MAST
5 HULL
6 UPPER GUN-DECK
(CANNON: 12 & 24 POUNDERS BROADSIDE & CARRONADES ON THE FORECASTLE)
7 MIDDLE GUN-DECK
(CANNON: 24 POUNDERS BROADSIDE)
8 LOWER GUN-DECK
(CANNON: 32 POUNDERS BROADSIDE)
9 TOPSIDE SMALL BOATS:
A. PINNACE
B. LAUNCH
C. CAPTAIN'S BARGE
D. CUTTER
10 OUTBOARD BOATS:
ONE CUTTER ON EACH SIDE OF THE STERN.
11 WEATHER DECK
12 RATLINGS
13 RUDDER
14 BOW
15 STERN

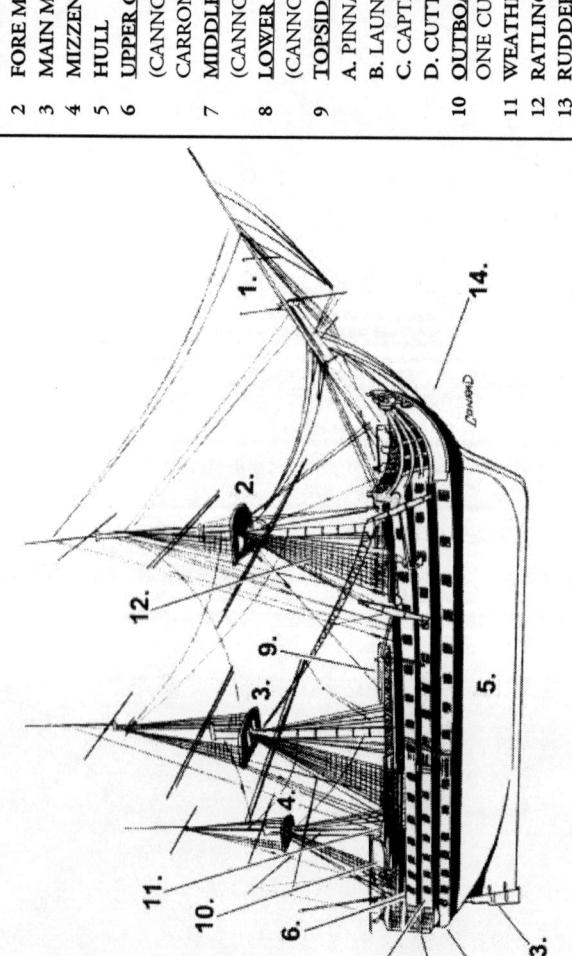

Bow of the H.M.S. Vanguard.

CHAPTER 1

Found

September 2003

HMS Vanguard
Portsmouth Harbor
September 16, 2003
0845 Hours

The crowds lined the shoreline and docks of Portsmouth. Some even dared perch atop the rock piled breakwaters, still slippery from the morning tide, crashing against their man-made walls.

In the distance to the south, the spectators could make out the low-laying form of the Isle of Wight, shrouded by a clinging fog. But, in the waters laying about the Harbor of Portsmouth the fog had moved off to sea. Its nearly still waters bore the deep chill of a cold September morning. The weather was cooperating with the recovery effort, the maritime townspeople and surrounding villagers, had come to witness.

To the delight of all, the meteorologists' forecasts had held true. The morning and day promised a tranquility, unaccustomary for the season and the coming winter.

The waters outside the harbor teemed with activity. Private boats of all sizes had taken up a circular anchorage, surrounding the scene of the expected activity. A British Royal Navy frigate stood at anchorage among the smaller craft. It was resplendent with hoisted flags and banners befitting the occasion.

Its dull gray sides dwarfed the smaller white pleasure boats and fishing craft. Its crew, like the civilian spectators ashore and afloat, listened to or watched a mixed assortment of radios and televisions, below or atop her decks.

The gathered spectators' attention lay on the sole large salvage barge, which had been anchored into position, atop a recently discovered shipwreck. A giant crane, more suited to lifting a giant bridge span or the prefabricated section of a modern skyscraper, rested silently atop its mounting, along one end of the gigantic barge.

An oceanographic research and salvage vessel, replete with a host of electronics and its own television equipment, nestled near by. It kept station near the recovery barge without the aid of anchors or chains.

The vessel's powerful thrusters, positioned fore and aft, allowed its helmsman to hover the craft, above and aside the shipwreck below. The vessel's divers had been below for nearly the better part of an hour, making the final preparations and checks for the crane to lift a section of the broken hull, rediscovered only this year.

The remains interred below in the soft silt, were those of the HMS Vanguard. She was a ship of the line, a man-of-war from Britain's maritime past. Her claim to fame lay in the fact, that she was sister-ship to the famous HMS Victory, Lord Horatio Nelson's flagship during the Battle of Trafalgar, perhaps the most famous and desperate of sea engagements, that had taken place during that age of civility and refinement, threatened by the dawn of revolution and dictatorial despots.

The sea battle, that took place on October 21, 1805, pitted a British squadron against a combined French and Spanish fleet, under the command of the French Admiral Villeneuve. The battle ended in a British victory, but at the cost of its greatest naval hero. Lord Admiral Nelson was wounded in battle, by a sniper's bullet, during the morning of the six-hour engagement and died later in the afternoon.

It ended any threat of the French ferrying an invasion army of 150,000 troops and 1,200 boats across the English Channel to invade England. The French fleet of thirty-three ships, that left the Spanish port of Cadiz, was attacked and defeated by Nelson's twenty-seven ship force, off the Cape of Traflagar.

But, unlike HMS Victory, now preserved and on display, as a floating memorial to Britain's seafaring past, HMS Vanguard had come to an ennoble end. Worse, almost two centuries later, she had been forgotten. Her memory clouded and dismissed from the minds of men and a once great nation.

There had been much justification for her name being stricken from the rolls of honor and hearts of men. She was from an age passed, its sailors gone on from this life, to sail heavenly skies and rest in peace, the trials of war at last put to rest.

Her name and past history had been slowly shrouded and forgotten as other ships, honoring her memory, assumed her name and took her place, surpassing her former valiant, but tragic history. The last among them was a great British battlewagon, finished in 1946. This post-war behemoth had a displacement of 42,500 tons and carried eight fifteen-inch guns. She boasted a speed of over thirty knots.

But, it was already obsolete at the end of World War II. A new generation of weapons, including the atomic bomb, rendered it an aging dinosaur of past naval strategies. The battleship was mothballed and scraped. The name and linage of the proud ships bearing the name Vanguard fell into oblivion.

More pressing matters had claimed the British nation's

attention in the decades that followed the loss of an empire's colonies and the twilight of a great nation. Two World Wars and the increasing industrialization of war turned fields and seas of honor and chivalry into vast killing grounds, for increasingly modern and deadly weapons.

Muzzle-loading cannons and swords, along with the colorful ornate regalia of battle uniforms fell away as the machinegun, aerial bombardment, camouflage, and a host of new weapons did for soldiering and the battlefield, what the assembly-line did for the factory's mass production.

In the tumult that followed, the survivors were content to lick their wounds and go about rebuilding their shattered lives and worlds. The regalia of past wars, no matter how valiant or noble, no longer held the romance and fancy of past military linages.

War had became more cruel and impersonal, if that had ever been possible, targeting soldier and civilian alike. It was a thing to be feared and dreaded. It was no longer a field on which a young man could test his mettle or prove his valor. War had become death, unsheathed of the false illusions of honor and a nation's pride.

But, still the past lingered, for those few, who would search it out and remember the sacrifices and honor of their forefathers.

HMS Vanguard had waited. She had waited silently in the cold waters between Porstmouth and the Isle of Wight. Her masts had long since faltered, collapsing into the fine silt, covering her beams and planking with layer upon layer, as the years hid her from the minds of men, like the sea hid her from their sight.

Alan Ward manipulated the pistol-grip control set atop the countertop console, controlling the ROV (Remotely Operated Vehicle), beneath the waters alongside the SS Reprise. The Oceanographic and salvage vessel, along with four divers below was ensuring the work, preformed days and weeks before, was ready for the final return of the stern section of the HMS Vanguard.

The monitors seated in the console before him showed the feedback from three cameras, mounted to the deep-diving ROV. The small remote-controlled submersible was an unmanned powered camera sled, designed for unlocking the mysteries of the deep, where the tremendous water pressure and great depths prevented man's incursion.

The sled's technologies and deep-diving capabilities were almost wasted over the final resting site of the HMS Vanguard. The shipwreck sat within 130 to 150 feet of water, well within the reach of experienced and professional deep-sea divers with their modern diving equipment.

The diver's below were clad in the modern diving suits, that had replaced the heavy bronze diving helmets and weighted shoes and belts of divers decades past. Their high-impact polymer helmets, linked by radio to the surface, resembled those of astronauts. Their light-weight, but insulated suits offered warmth and protection from the cold of the depths, as they moved about on the sea floor.

Ward watched, as the divers continued checking the series of lines and thick nylon straps, snaked about the exposed beams and sides of the remains of the shipwreck.

Shipwreck, the word seemed an enigma. The demise of the HMS Vanguard was still the subject of speculation among novice spectators and serious historians.

The Vanguard had reached home after her perplexing journey back from the southern coast of Spain and the Battle of Trafalgar. She reached the haven of her home port, only to disappear mysteriously, beneath the sea.

Several coastal observers, of the time, testified that they had witnessed a fiery explosion, before the sea swallowed the vessel whole. Their stories were balked at as fabrication, attesting to the disbelief, that a ship of the line of such magnitude and size, could have been dispatched to the bottom, so quickly.

And yet, adding to the lore and legend, that had preceded the vessel's demise, before it was forgotten among the pages of history as a footnote of the past and nothing more, was the startling fact, that not one man survived the sinking. A ship, of over 100-guns and over eight-hundred men, was gone without explanation.

Ward had read the writings of the naval scholars and historians, of the time, pouring through the historical archives and records, cherished with pride, by Britain's libraries and depositories, to her splendid maritime past. Many rationalized the disaster, claiming the ranks of the crew had been decimated, during the battle and little more, than a skeleton crew were tasked with sailing her home.

Many believed a tried and weary crew had blundered, igniting the great store of powder carried for her guns. Exhausted from battle and their lengthy return, a misplaced lantern or a carelessly struck match were suspect.

But, the truth was merely conjecture.

Some even suspected treason or subterfuge. A story still abounded, that a French spy, his government incensed by the naval defeat, was ordered to set about in a dinghy or other small craft, laden with explosives and tie it off to the returning heroic ship, to destroy by deceit, what could not be defeated in battle.

Such talk was the banter of pubs and angry men. But, the story persisted. It painted a face, though nameless, on the treachery of a known enemy.

Yet, the accounts were muddled. No memoirs or past logs could account or recall the damage suffered by the gallant ship and crew. No history regaled the French or Spanish vessels she engaged, though all thought she was in the thick of the fight at Trafalgar, as were all the ships in that outnumbered British squadron.

Her final location was relocated by only the scarcest of writings and memories of lore. Folk tales provided more reckoning of her final position, than the official records of the Admiralty's account of her journey, inventory, and stores.

Ward watched the monitor, halting the tethered ROV fifty feet above the divers. The sled's five small propellers rotated, holding the unmanned craft in a hover over the divers, checking the nylon straps snaked among the beams and under the broken hull, still stuck fast to the silt. The control room filled with the voices of the technicians monitoring the work of the divers, as well as, monitoring the telemetric equipment gauging the diver's heartbeats, blood pressures, and both tethered and self-contained emergency reserve air supplies.

The room hummed with the elated calliope of men on the verge of success, their dreams about to be fulfilled, after months of work and toil.

The recovery barge and the SS Reprise had employed giant vacuums, their suction carefully manipulated by the divers, over a period of weeks, to remove the silt and unbury the upper surfaces, of the Vanguard's stern.

Surprisingly, the ornate carvings adorning the stern windows of the captain's cabin and those of his officers were still intact. The cold waters and the covering silt had acted to preserve them from the decay of time and the ravages of the salt water the vessel laid in.

Ward backed the unmanned craft off, watching as two divers attempted to untwist a nylon strap, that had turned about on itself, during the night, as the unpredictable tides and currents had again tried to reclaim the wreck.

He could see the tiered decks or at least what was left of them. The remains justified the speculation, that a powerful explosion had ripped the vessel asunder. But, until the timbers were brought to the surface, where labs might test them for clues of the ship's fate, there were still no answers.

The forward hold and bow were gone, though there were smaller remains of splintered wood and a larger section, detected by sonar, further away from the original recovery site. They'd be a subject of study next year, when the salvage operations would renew again, in more favorable weather.

For now, once the stern was resurrected, the recovery at sea would come to a halt. But, it would take years for historians, archaeologists, and oceanographers to study the treasure, they were about to lift back up to the light of day.

Ward slewed one of the sled's cameras about, studying the

exposed stern. A few cannon were still buried among the broken remains. Their locations, along the buried decks covered with collapsed timbers or strewn debris were too dangerous to risk the life of a diver, in an attempt to lift them separately to the surface.

They had painstakingly recovered twenty-three cannon, along with the ship's bell. These early recoveries were done, as much to confirm the identity of the ship as to lighten its load, before they attempted to lift the stern from the sea.

Archeological technicians had cautiously removed the accumulation, encrusting the ancient weapons, before placing them in containers of fresh water, destined for the British Royal Museum and further study and preservation.

The Royal Crest and ornate lettered and numbered dates cast into the tops of their encrusted barrels, along with the foundry's own mark, left no doubt as to the Vanguard's identity.

Ward watched, as a diver moved through the blackness below. A stream of bubbles trailed from a valve and regulator, along the back of his helmet. A thick black insulated air-hose coiled and followed, his slow deliberate movements.

A light, mounted atop his helmet, illuminated the view before him. Churned up silt filtered through its beam. The diver's voice crackled over one of the control room's speakers. It was answered by another diver, out of sight of Ward's cameras.

Their voices seemed foreign and removed, high and tinny, as a mixture, of helium and other gases fed through their air-lines and filled their lungs, guarding against the pressure of the depths.

The scene below resembled the orchestrated movements of astronauts on a lunar surface more, than what the public envisioned as a salvage operation. But, unlike a moonwalk the scene was cast in a clouded darkness, devoid of stars or light.

"Reprise, we look good down," the lead diver's voice, came over the wall-mounted speaker in the control room, broadcasting the divers' terse conversations for all in the control room to hear. But, individual technicians were linked directly to the divers by their own headsets and microphones, as well as, the dive boss, pacing about the control room, behind the technicians monitoring the dive.

"I read you, Lead," the dive boss returned.

He studied the screen, before moving to a table and examining a plan of the shipwreck. A plaster model of the sea floor with the broken plastic hull of a model of the HMS Victory, standing in for the Vanguard, rested along the table.

The dive boss studied the lines drawn on the plan, a map of the location of the bits and pieces of the shipwreck and the almost intact stern. He studied the lines, that showed the placement of the nylon load-bearing straps, that would be used to cradle and lift the stern from the sea floor.

He returned his gaze to the monitors, showing the divers and the almost unfathomable stern, still partly buried in the silt, that had preserved it. The cameras of Ward's sled couldn't show him the detail, he wanted to see.

It was time for his decision. He had to trust in his divers and the abilities of the engineers and technicians, that had advised him on the placement of the straps forming the cradle. But, he wasn't going to be rushed.

Two members of the British Historical and Maritime Societies silently awaited his decision. They were observers and nervous ones, at that.

They were well aware of the spectators, along the shore and afloat. But, only one spectator remained foremost in their thoughts.

Prince Charles, heir apparent to the throne of England, was aboard the British frigate anchored, within sight of the recovery. His majesty, an officer of the Royal Navy himself, had developed a keen interest in the recovery operation. Or, more to the point, the goodwill and public relations opportunity, it provided him.

With the tragic death of Princess Diana receded from the headlines, but her memory still held in fond remembrance by the English public, there had been the slow acceptance of Lady Camilla Parker-Bowles, who appeared more frequently by the prince's side. With time, there had also arisen a growing acceptance of the prince's personal life and even the right of a member of the Royal Family to privacy and the right to choose his own path.

Despite, the tragedy, or perhaps, because of it, the prince had come to be viewed as a man, no more or less, than others. Though, he was a man pulled at by the conflicting demands of his own desires vying with the duties and responsibilities of the station in life he had been born into and strove his best to accept and adhere to.

The prince, guided by the queen's own public relations mentors, had taken to becoming more accessible, at least towards public events, charities, and acts of goodwill. The relationship, between monarch and subject, was still tender. But, traditional British reserve and a loyalty to the culture of the monarchy's past had restored a sense of civility and a penchant to embrace a monarchy more fashionable or vogue, than powerful.

A reigning monarchy upheld the pageant and grandeur of British tradition. It carried on the noblest heritage of England's historic past and honored the generations that had both reigned and served the Crown of England.

Besides, its pomp and splendor were good for the tourist industry, a staple of the British economy. The Queen's Royal Guard and palaces attracted a continuing stream of visitors, enthralled by a blend of the unique history of the past coupled to present, much as the event of the raising of the HMS Vanguard today.

And, so all did their duty as the members of the esteemed societies waited patiently for the dive boss to concur, with the men on the sea floor, that the lift was ready.

For his part, the would-be monarch waited inside the guarded confines of the steel and aluminum hull of the HMS Amazon. He sipped tea and exchanged platitudes with officer and seaman alike, courting favor with the common man, to pass the time before the recovery of the HMS Vanguard's stern.

The divers' voices crackled, the speaker filled with static and their almost comically strained high voices. The four men below talked among themselves, after checking the cradle for the umpteenth time.

The dive boss picked up an extra headset and talked guardedly with the lead diver, after a technician was ordered to cut off the public speaker. He held a clipboard in his hand and for one final repetitive time ran down the contents of his list, before falling silent.

"Okay, let's do it," the dive boss agreed. "Bring your people up!"

The room filled with anticipation. One of the members of the British Historical Society excused himself. His face was filled with jubilation as he headed for the radio room, behind the Reprise's bridge, to inform the HMS Amazon and its honored royal guest of the decision.

It would take up to forty to fifty minutes to recover the divers and ROV (Remotely Operated Vehicle). It would be an agonizing and tense hour or more, before the HMS Vanguard's stern was lifted from the depths.

"Ward, get your damn toy up on the surface!" the dive boss bellowed, across the crowded room.

"On the way!" Ward returned, already directing the craft's thrusters to crawl the machine to the surface in a slow spiraling climb, allowing the crew on deck to reign in its tether without fouling it or the ascending craft.

Starboard side of the H.M.S. Vanguard.

CHAPTER 2

Return to the Light

HMS Vanguard
Portsmouth Harbor
September 16, 2003
1023 Hours

Prince Charles was seated on the foredeck of the frigate. A white awning, usually reserved for the reception aboard the Royal Frigate Amazon of dignitaries at far away ports, had been erected between the superstructure and the forward gun mount.

Several chairs had been set up, their ornate wooden designs more appropriate to a chamber room, than the deck of a warship. The Amazon's captain and the prince sat amongst the presence of the gathered officers and crew not on watch.

Cameras flashed and clicked as crewmen and reporters vied with each other, to capture their Royal guest's momentous visit for posterity. The monarch obliged them in a manner quite uncharacteristic, of his earlier snubs of the press and his desire to guard his privacy.

His outward going generosity, even extended to rising from his seat, protesting a mirrored act by the ship's captain as he moved into the crowd of seamen and claimed pose after pose with the dress white clad sailors.

The press ate up the act of humility and good nature as the prince extended his hand to several mates and even partook of a shared joke. It was shrugged off as monarch and crew continued their expectant wait.

A shrill blast echoed across the water as the horn of the SS Reprise blared over the damp air. It was the signal for all surrounding the recovery site, that the lift was commencing.

The prince reclaimed his seat as all hands, that could, vied for a place closer to the rails. As one, they watched the operator of the crane engage its giant winch. Its roller struggled to turn as the powerful diesel engine, in the rear of the crane's cab, roared to life from the sluggish idle it had been held, warming and waiting.

Steel cables grew taunt as the slack was taken out of them. The barge actually moved as the cable drew tight, hanging down from the giant trestle-like boom, towering above the crane's cab.

Anxious eyes watched as the salvage ship slowly moved sideways, its thrusters redirected and pushing it away from the hover, that had held it positioned near the proximity of the wreck. It moved so slowly, that it made no waves or disturbance.

The wooden deck of the barge creaked and groaned as its hollow displacement bore the crane and the weight of the stern, being lifted below.

The blare of the SS Reprise's horn and the sight of activity on the barge roused a cheer from the crowds lining the docks and shore. Camera's flashed in a kaleidoscopic display of light along the breakwaters and the host of boats, ringing the scene.

The prince reclaimed his seat, accepting a proffered pair of binoculars. He studied the crane's cab and the small group of workers, standing along the barge's edge, one of them providing hand-signalled cues to the operator.

In the background, two television reporters vied with each other's sound levels as each informed his audience of the live broadcast, interrupting their normal programming.

But, for all the flurry of activity, atop the barge or along the deck of the Reprise, which was still busily set about recovering her divers and the ROV, now topside on her diving deck, there was little to see.

There was only the crane and the strain on its lines.

Beneath, the surface's cold waters the nylon straps pulled tight. Their flat webbed belts snaked underneath, what had been the critical lifting points of the HMS Vanguard's stern. The straps grew taunt and even stretched, under the unmoving weight of the waterlogged timbers and beams.

The silt had erupted into a blinding cloud, almost immediately with the displacement of the sea floor. There had been no point in leaving the ROV and its sled mounted camera behind, to monitor the ascent of the shipwrecked stern. In the floating cloud of debris, there'd have been no way to see the results of their efforts.

The cloud continued to grow, not only encompassing the wreck, but expanding outward, along the sea floor.

Several items, lodged inside the stern and held captive by rotted wood or fallen debris from the decaying vessel, moved about for the first time in almost two centuries. One cannon, deemed too risky to attempt to move before the stern's ascent, slid free.

Its wooden and iron banded wheels were locked stationary, frozen by years of silt welding them in place. It careened unseen out of the broken forward end of the stern's second deck, silently embedding itself, barrel first, into the sea floor.

A large iron box inched about, its weight steadfastly holding it in place in the depository of what was left of the captain's cabin. One wooden crate, that had defied time and retained its box-like form, despite its sides being reduced to the thin consistency of paper, collapsed from its own movement as the silt inside and outside of it shifted; turning it into unidentifiable debris.

Several small metal objects and dinnerware items tumbled from their precarious perches as their endless time was disturbed. They fell to the floor of the junior officer's quarters at the rear of the second deck.

Silt ran from the decks, rushing off towards the floor below as the rearmost part of the stern pulled taunt. It added to the madding mayhem of rising silt. It tested the power of the crane above the wreck, refusing to budge. The steel cables running through the pulleys, suspended over the water by the trestle-work of the crane, strained.

It seemed as if the copper-plated hull would remain forever locked in place, along the bottom of the sea.

Then slowly, the eroded plates surrendered. Some refused to release their grip from the sea floor, attesting to the craftsmanship, that had hammered and shaped them, along the bottom of the hull. Others surrendered their hold to the bottom of the HMS Vanguard, dropping off. The suction of the silt was too great to break, their simple fasteners having lost their hold in the rotten wooden bottom of the soft and aging hull, forced the plates to surrender their place.

The stern began to break free, held only in the grasp of the sea floor by the large rudder, that had pierced into it, decades upon decades past. The aging guide, of the ship's course, refused to release its grip to the bottom.

The unseen crane on the surface dipped in silent unseeing respect to this last hold of the sea for her victim. The iron bands, mounting the rudder to the flowing trailing lines of the stern, buckled. Their bolts came free or dropped away as the wood holding them could not retain its grasp.

In a sudden torrent, the stern broke free, leaving the rudder slanted, but upright in the bottom, it left behind.

The crane's operator wasn't expecting the lurch as the outstretched arm of the crane seemed to buckle skyward. The winch ran freely to his rear as the running diesel filled his ears.

The ship was coming up or at least, what was left of her. He slowed the winch. He'd been warned about the resistance of the suction, likely holding the bottom of the ship. But, he hadn't expected it to release, so unexpectantly.

If it hadn't been for the captured weight, still on the end of his cables, the crane's arm might have bounced rearward, sending it and its operator backwards towards the water, except for the metal swivel foundation and the track, it was mounted atop.

The barge had actually jumped in the water causing some dismay to the onlookers and guests. The guide, providing hand signals to the operator, was beset at once on his radio by demands to know what was happening, from the control room and bridge of the Reprise, floating nearby.

He answered curtly, unsure himself.

His eyes stared down at the taunt cables. They told him something was still there, suspended unseen beneath the waters. But, the wreck could have broken apart, the straps crushing it in their grip. He wondered how much of the stern was still intact, if any at all.

He watched eagerly, as the straining cable continued to be reeled out of the water. He prayed the bulk of the ship was still intact. His heart sank with thoughts of folly and disgrace, imagining the worst; that the cradle would be suspended in the air above the barge with nothing but splintered and pulverized wood to show for their efforts.

He thought of the disgrace to be born, before the presiding dignitaries and crowds. His eyes fell to the water, his lips silently praying their efforts were not in vain.

The cable continued its journey, water dripping off its steel woven lengths. Behind him, two men with hoses sprayed the surfaced cables with fresh water, washing away the salty brine, that would otherwise, slowly erode them.

He looked at his wristwatch. They were only ten minutes into the lift.

In the control room of the SS Reprise the crowd had gathered around the sonar operator. The round display screen, he monitored, was cut by a single oscillating electronic line. Its unfathomable wave told his unskilled audience little, but to him, it said everything.

The stern had remained intact for the most part. Several smaller objects had been cast aside, their signatures lost as they returned to the bottom of the sea floor. But, the HMS Vanguard or at least, her relatively intact stern was on the way up. He informed the crowd.

He received a welcomed pat on the back as the small room filled with shouts of success and joy. Elation and premature congratulations filled the room. But, the dive boss and the project's head were less, than pleased.

The stern was still at ninety-feet and rising. It wasn't over, yet.

An unexpected current, a change in the sea state's, even a gusting wind, along the surface could still make the difference, between success and disaster.

The sonar operator called out the depth as the Vanguard struggled towards the surface, still shrouded in the darkness of the depths engulfing her.

The Isle of Wight was acting as a buffer, sheltering the site from the strong September winds, that could easily turn the now peaceful waters, near the mouth of Portsmouth Harbor, into havoc.

"We're at eighty feet and going strong!" the operator sang out.

The stern was rising quickly. Perhaps, too quickly.

The project head leaned his head into the dive officer, guardedly voicing his concerns in shrouded whispers. The latter nodded his head, in confirmation and reached for the small handheld radio, linking him to the crane operator's boss on the barge.

He informed the man of the new depth the stern had risen to, mirroring earlier reports from when the warship's remains had broken free of the bottom. He advised the crane's superior to slow the ascent.

The fear was, that the stern would break the surface too quickly, even at its now slow crawl. The project head and crane supervisor agreed, that even this rate might be too much of a strain and burden, for the aging timbers and framework of the ship to cope with. The sudden rise to the surface and the cold air awaiting it, might prove fatal to the remains.

Their orders were received and the crane's winch slowed.

It was nearly two hours from the start of the winching, until the first signs of the Vanguard were seen on the surface. The crane's supervisor saw the ghostly dark outline of a large object nearing the surface as the barge tilted towards its captive load.

Its massive presence, so near the surface, took on a superstitious shadow, as if some menacing specter from the past lingered hauntingly below. Rather, than being lured to its nearness, the crane boss shied away. He stepped back, a shiver running up his back. He blamed the sudden and ludicrous feeling on the damp chill of the sea air and the slight breeze running across the water.

He tugged up the zipper of his jacket, but could not find any warmth or comfort in the act. His hands and fingers shivered, despite the leather work gloves, he wore.

He blamed the cold on his inactivity, forced as he was to merely stand about, watching over the edge of the barge. But, his companions, standing beside him, seemed to share the same feeling, though none of them said anything of it.

But, like him, they stood back. Perhaps, it was the awe of the moment and the hallowed relic, they had nearly wrested to the surface. The sea was an entity unto itself with a life and superstition of its own. Ancient mariners had feared it and worshiped it. Its bounty gave life. And yet, its capricious nature claimed the lives of both skilled and foolhardy seamen alike.

The outline of the stern appeared blacker, than the darkest night, below the murky green waters, off the Portsmouth anchorage.

"She's just shy, of five to six feet of breaking the surface," the dive boss's voice broke over the handheld radio, in the crane supervisor's gloved hand. The suddenness of the man's voice, startled the supervisor from his thoughts.

"We've got it!" he returned, keying his microphone.

"Hold her up there! We're sending over two Zodiacs with reporters and the project manager," the dive boss intoned, even as the supervisor motioned a cutting signal across his neck to halt the lift.

The dark shadow lingered, suspended beneath the surface. The water lapped against the side of the barge, as the crane's operator waited for his next command.

Three hundred feet away, two small groups of people alit into the small semi-rigid rubber boats. Their outboard motors sprang to life and the silver colored man-made fabric craft skimmed across the surface of the calm waters. They avoided coming near the suspended wreck and landed on the opposite side of the barge.

At once, the project director and reporters descended on the tilting end of the barge.

Again, cameras flashed and video recorders panned the water, taping the shadowy specter from the past. It was only moments away from being revealed again, to the world atop the surface.

The photo session was brief. It lasted only long enough, for the dive boss and project head to agree on their next course of action. Handheld radios squawked as a brief communique was heralded to the salvage ship in the background.

The crane started again.

To many the sight was a disappointment, though there had been rounds of shouts and cheers at the first appearance of the craft, upon the surface. Air horns blared and whistles shrilled, if only for a moment.

Overhead two news helicopters recorded an aerial view of the event, capturing the ship and the anticipating crowds, now lined up nearly a block inland from the docks.

They watched, expecting to see some semblance of the fanciful visions of Hollywood's interpretation of shipwrecks past. But, no such fare was present.

The dark shape of the stern slowly emerged from the sea. Perhaps, it was because of the agonizingly slow ascent, that the fanciful hopes of those ashore, waned so. The timbers and planks, that first broke the surface were sinisterly black, the wood soaked clean through. Water dripped from their porous wood.

Even the ornate designs, carved in the hard wood decorations of the stern about the captain's cabin, had lost their detail, eroded by the salt water and grainy friction of the silt dashing about the shipwreck, year after year.

But, still cameras flashed and those, that were there, made the most of the event. It was history in the making. It was history found. It was history brought back into the world of the living. It was the past returned to the light.

The timbers rose slowly.

Those nearest the surfacing remains no longer felt the fear or dread, the dark shadow of the ship had claimed as it lingered just below the surface.

Now, sadness seemed to grip those present as they recalled the graceful lines and splendor of the once great warship. The drawings and paintings, rendered by artists of the past, had etched an image of the grand man-of-war in their minds.

But, hanging in the air, still breaking the hold of the sea, the relic before them spoke nothing of valor or grandeur. It was merely a silent tombstone wrested from the sea, where it guarded the lost remains of its fallen crew.

The spectators, that had come, so filled with the promise of the event, retreated into a respectful silence, more appropriate to a graveyard.

Perhaps, the captain and crew of the Amazon summoned up the feeling, that was so pervasive among those gathered. At the shrill beckoning of a boatswain's whistle, prince, captain, and crew stood as one and rendered a silent salute to the remains, now swaying above the water as workmen rushed along the barge, beneath the dark suspended form, casting out guidelines and preparing for the crane to swing the stern atop the barge.

Officer and tar alike, stood rigid at attention.

The moment failed to be broken, despite the cameramen and reporters, aboard the Amazon, busying themselves with the opportune photo-op. Some wondered, whether the moment was staged.

But, none could deny the haunting chill of the sea-borne breeze running across the decks. The Union Jack snapped in the wind as if the country's colors recognized one of her own had returned.

Several boat-bound spectators trained their cameras on the sight. But soon, even they fell silent, their camera shutters halting as the dark carcass of the former ship cast a shadow across the waters.

The boatswain's whistle shrilled once more and a small ceremonial cannon, on the rear deck of the Amazon, let loose with its retort, attended by the stiff ritualistic steps and motions of an honor guard.

Across the water, a shore-locked red-coated uniformed band, of a nearby local military unit, struck up its rendition of "God Save The Queen." They marked the final ascent of the HMS Vanguard with the crisp solemn circumstance and pomp, worthy of the occasion.

At the conclusion of the rendition, the boatswain's whistle sounded once more. Again, the ceremonial cannon barked its loud retort, spewing wadding and smoke across the water from its blank shell.

The breech was pulled open by the brass handle at its top. The ceremonial guardsman stood at attention as the spent brass casing dropped to the deck and rolled towards the scutter, lining the deck's edge.

The Royal Marine Sergeant, overseeing the guard, barked

out his terse commands and the gun crew faced left and saluted sharply as the Vanguard's stern was delivered to the deck of the barge, the workmen below it scurried about with preformed lumber braces and supports to shore up the uneven hull.

As they labored to berth the remnant of the fighting ship, the ceremonial gun crew stiffly followed the commands of their sergeant, laying their field piece to rest. A cover was draped over tube and carriage. The spent brass was collected and stowed.

Four men clad in ceremonial uniforms, red coat and black collar, obeyed the commands of the sergeant as they came aline and turned as one. They marched away, disappearing below the decks of the Amazon.

Slowly, the Vanguard's stern was seated on the tresses and beams, meant to hold her fast. Dry nylon straps were carefully placed about her skeleton frame, lashing her to the oversized deck of the barge. Only when, the crane was freed of the cradle, that had lifted the Vanguard and the damp nylon straps removed and rolled away, did her operator lower the giant arm and trestled boom to the deck.

A diesel powered sea-tug was gingerly guided alongside and lines, lashed to the barge, were tied off to her. Slowly and deliberately, the HMS Vanguard was guided back to the port. The port she had failed to enter, nearly two hundred years ago.

Some of the crowds had subsided as the barge was guided on its short slow journey. The journey was slow, too slow for most, who had abandoned their earlier prized spots, along the docks.

The occasional camera flashed as the broken ship made its way slowly into the harbor. She was followed by the SS Reprise and the experienced salvage crew, who had made the unimaginable, possible.

But, the cold and the drizzle of a chilling rain quickly broke up the fanfare, that awaited the prize, claimed off the sea floor.

In the graying background, the HMS Amazon prepared to haul up anchor, framed by a darkening sky. The flotilla of small boats already plied the congested waters seeking to reclaim their berths and tie up, before the approaching rain burst into a torrent.

The sea's surface was peppered with the drops descending from above.

The workmen and crew of the salvage barge had donned their weather gear, but not because of the rain. To preserve the timbers and beams of the fragile ship, they steadily flushed her exposed wood with fresh water. They had to keep her wet and flush away the salt.

The darkening sky was a preservationist's blessing. The air would try to dry out her aging wood, soon enough, without the immediate help of the sun's warm rays.

Now, that they had fought to raise the Vanguard, they were faced with a host of preservation problems. They'd wet her down and cover her with a specially designed tarp to trap the moisture under it. A special preservative would be sprayed and painted sparingly on the wood in an attempt to buy more time, until the ship could be disassembled, her parts cataloged and numbered, for transport to a more suitable climate-controlled site for final restoration.

Ensign Robert Lewis' journal and its ornate container.

CHAPTER 3

Discoveries

HMS Vanguard
Portsmouth Harbor
September 16, 2003
1638 Hours

Alan Ward was content to return to the warmth and comfort of the control room. He still had several entries to update in the ROV's log from its deployment earlier this morning, along with a host of checks and inspections to ensure the unmanned device would be ready for its next dive, whenever that would be.

All about the Reprise the crew and guests had abounded with the adulation of success. A few had wrongfully believed the ancient warship would disintegrate at the first attempt of the cradle, stressing and straining its rotted timbers. To a man, they were all elated to have been proven wrong.

A combination of factors had come together to buy them success. Most important, had been the chilly waters plying the depths off the harbor of Portsmouth. The cold waters had acted as a natural preservative, despite the salt laced waters. And, the Isle of Wight had formed a natural barrier to the strong current running off the southern coast of Britain.

All in all, combined with the fine silt layering the shipwreck in a protective cocoon of earth, the HMS Vanguard had been protected from the very elements, that rightfully, should have destroyed it.

Alan Ward toyed with the light workload of closing down his station. He switched on an outside camera mounted to the deck of the Reprise, from another console and transferred its image to one of the screens in his own station.

The barge and its partly opened tarp-shrouded prize were framed in the color monitor. Only a skeleton work force still remained topside, hosing down the timbers exposed to the cold damp air. The water sprayed back in their faces, the earlier breeze now picking up momentum. They labored among several other hoses, whose sprinklers had been set to mounts along the barge to deliver a continuous unmanned spray about the undersides of the tarp covered wreck.

Their slickers glistened from the fresh water dripping or being blown back into them. A team of preservationists and archaeologists busied themselves with the treasures, that had ridden up to the surface in the intact framework of the stern.

Ward studied the grainy televised image, noting a large metal box, several smaller items, and a cannon barrel laid out atop a plastic tarp being doused with a continuous spray of water.

The smallest items were being immersed in a plastic water-filled tote to halt their rapid decay, upon exposure to the atmosphere. The larger items would have to take their chances, until the proper transport and containers could be provided for their relocation to the British Historical Society. Small pieced together frameworks of lumber and plastic tarps created shallow wading pools to soak the oversized items in, until then.

Curiosity got the better of Ward. He turned off the monitor and camera, his console falling black and lifeless. He exited the door to the rear of the control room, grabbing a dark blue windbreaker and his black knit hat.

The cold damp drizzle pelting the deck outside found him. It sent a chill through him, robbing his body of the leisurely warmth, he'd enjoyed inside the control room. He made for the diving deck, the lowest deck of the SS Reprise, along its stern and the only one sharing a gangplank running across to the barge, tied to the dock, on the ship's starboard side.

He held the handrail as he snaked his way across the narrow planking and carefully stepped aboard the slippery deck of the railing-less barge. His appearance from the Reprise drew no attention. After all, he was part of the salvage crew with every right to be there.

Above on the dock, three blue uniformed police officers stood guard over Britain's returned prize, plucked from the sea. Their job was to keep the curious and souvenir-hunters at arms length from the newly resurrected national treasure.

Mobile barricades and a roped off area kept all, but the authorized, from reaching the dock, directly above the barge. Several police cars and their occupants took turns relieving the officers on foot patrol in the dismal weather.

Their attentions were landward and no one paid any attention to the salvage crew member sauntering up to the cataloged items, removed from the interior of the stern.

Ward stood over the gray plastic totes seeking to identify the encrusted items within. He recognized the misshaped and caked forks and spoons, most likely, part of the officer's table settings. There were several tools, albeit absent their wooden handles, bathing in the fresh water of the totes. And, alone in isolation from the other treasures, lay a large iron box.

The large elongated container was nearly six feet in length. Its crude lid was securely seated and sealed. But, there was no lock present, nor any signs, of hinges or fasteners, along its exterior. Its purpose and presence aboard the HMS Vanguard escaped our archaeological team's knowledge and expertise.

The box was an enigma. The container's surface was pitted, giving it the look of some strange metallic porous skin. The pocked surface could have been the result of a less than skillful foundry, though the harsh environment of its internment in the depths had likely combined to erode, its original coarse surface.

There were several designs, that had been molded into its surface, but none were recognizable under the encrusted covering, that had caked in the folds and bends of their intricate shapes. Ward assumed, they were likely crude representations of some Royal Navy Crest or family coat-of-arms. He ignored their obscured designs and studied the hasty attempt to preserve the giant metal box.

A wood frame had been erected by his ship's carpenter and workmen. The frame with a plastic tarp seated inside it was filled with fresh water, resembling a crude bathtub. The lid of iron container protruded slightly above the tub's water, an oversight or mistake of the builders.

Correcting the flaw, two running hoses kept a constant flow of water running across the box's lid, immersing it almost entirely under their cascading waters and defeating the corrosive effects of the surrounding air and temperature.

The running water overflowed the captive confines of the tub and made the already wet barge deck, that much more slippery.

It was a makeshift attempt, at best, to preserve the large object, whose presence had not been anticipated. Special measures were underway, even now. A team of preservationists from the London Historical Society were due to arrive tomorrow with the special containers and equipment, needed to arrest any further decay of the large object from its return to the surface.

Several gulls shrieked making their presence known as they glided in circles above the barge. The light drizzle broke into a steady rain, forcing the police on the dock above to tuck the hoods of their raincoats, about their heads and uniform caps.

The workcrew tasked with hosing down the wreck turned off their hoses and retreated for the shelter and warmth of a nearby workshed, leaving only several archaeologists behind, as they tried unsuccessfully, to continue their cataloging duties.

They finally relented, searching out the shelter of the Reprise's galley and a hot drink. They left Alan Ward alone, paying him no attention, probably assuming he was part of the cataloging detail and silently passing along the responsibility for attending to the few items still laying about. Besides, the constabulary's presence was at hand and the treasures were already, by contract, headed for the displays and collections of several well-endowed British museums.

Ward left the sole cannon and the corroded trinkets soaking in their fresh water totes. He was drawn to the bulk of the ship, itself or what was left of the stern. The dark timbers and beams appeared black under the shadowy overcast of the heavy skies above.

A yellow tape was strewn about the interior of the stern, where a courageous or impatient soul had dwelled into the interior of the captain's and junior officer quarters on the second and third decks.

Unlikely, to have the chance of having the wreck to himself again, Ward cautiously mounted the slippery planks. The rain and the exposure to the air had left the inner decks slimy and almost unmanageable to cross.

And, any climb into the interior of the stern, was made the more perilous by the missing or rotted-away steps, now replaced with aluminum ladders, lashed about, between the rising decks of the ship's remains.

He braced himself along the low ceiling overhead and inched his way up, towards the second deck and its stern quarters or what was left of the ship's junior officers' billets. He carefully ascended one of the aluminum ladders, extended between the tiered decks.

He'd hoped to reach the captain's quarters on the third upper deck. But, the going was proving too treacherous and Alan Ward contented himself for a quest of the second deck's junior officer's quarters.

Despite, the tarp spread out above the third deck or what remained of it, like a tent's vaunted roof, the timbers dripped profusely with water. The unmanned sprinklers continuous spray was making his journey more perilous, than he had imagined.

The water pooled along the deck, he stood on and cascaded across the awkwardly slanted deck.

His arrival there was anything, if not disappointing. Like most of the stern, it was as if the ship had been gutted. The passage of time and the currents, siphoning through the interior of the sunken ship, had scattered most of its contents out onto the sea floor. A later search might unbury or uncover some of the lost artifacts. But, for now all that remained was the gutted shell of the ship's stern and those few relics, which had become trapped inside its interior, coming to rest, trapped against a beam or joint, that formed a ledge or lip, the object's size or weight refused to release from its new roost.

Ward was about to return to the lower level, he had scaled up from, lifting one foot and cautiously placing all his weight atop the other as he tried to turn around, atop the dangerously slanted and slippery second deck.

He slipped.

Fear welled up in him as he saw how high he was, above the deck of the barge, through the missing gaps of planking. His hands and arms flailed about, desperately seeking a handhold.

His other foot crashed down onto the floor, its knee buckling with the uncontrolled impact. But, his fall was not halted. In a final desperate act, his right hand lunged out at the curved upright shape of a crafted beam.

His fingers missed, clawing at the air. But, his palm collided with the wet wood. To his disdain, the wood gave way, crumbling inward as if wet cardboard. His fingers tightened on the new handhold, halting his fall. The act felt as if his arm would be wrenched from its socket. But, Ward held on. His fall was stopped.

He slowly righted himself, already regretting the damage he'd inflicted, upon the wide vertical beam. He looked in wonder at the jagged gap, not splintered, more pushed in or collapsed in the deceitfully thick beam.

It shouldn't have happened. The beam had probably been

made of the finest oak, British forests could have fielded, during the ship's time. As parts of trees were marked by their designers and builders to be cut out and carved. A tree's trunk became a beam. A trunk twisting about into a wide branch became a curved brace or support. All around him, similar beams offered no evidence of such disrepair or erosion. Yet, the beam, that had given way and saved him from a disastrous fall, had crumbled as if hollow.

Hollow, the word threatened to explain everything. Ward slowly returned to the beam, holding a tight grip on its handhold. He carefully studied the jagged, pushed in gap, his palm had inflicted.

The grit of silt and years of immersion had hidden the secreted cover, carved into the beam, lining the interior of the officer's quarters. He wondered if the cavity was placed there by design of the ship's crafters or at the mischievous hands of some junior officer, trying to hide some unmentionable contraband.

Ward came even to the hidden pocket and searched about it with his fingers. The water inside was brackish; despite the vessel being drenched in fresh water.

His fingers halted, feeling the ridged metal surface of some small unseen object. Its surface guided his fingers about its length as they tried to identity it, without seeing it. It was rectangular and thick, much longer than, the opening, it had been secreted away inside. It confounded him as to how the hollow had been made.

It had obviously not been made by the hands of a junior officer. The opening was definitely crafted, perhaps the handiwork of a shipwright or carpenter. Someone had wanted this treasure trove spirited away inside the beam. Its workmanship denied any unskilled hand or whimsical effort had carved the nearly undetectable hide.

Ward grasped, what edge he could. But, the elusive item defied his reach. He tried unsuccessfully to pull it free of its confines, several times, before finally, bringing its narrowest side into the restricted opening, rendered by his fall. Frozen fingers deftly toyed with its uneven metal surface.

It was a small metal case not much bigger than, a flask. Ward assumed, it was perhaps, some lessor officer's private reserve, a flask of rum or gin to offset the chill of a cold lone watch at sea.

Carefully, he pulled and tugged the small container free of the jagged opening. The disguised splintered wooden cover, finally ceded and dropped away to the floor, during his efforts. Before, Ward could stoop to retrieve it and attempt to place it back, the slow running water, across the deck he stood on, claimed it and ran it down along the slanted deck.

In horror, Ward watched as the artifact careened over the broken forward edge and down the deck of the barge, then into the cold waters of Portsmouth Harbor. A gull shrieked as if upon witnessing the act, he intoned some legendary specter to mark account of the deed and Ward's violation of the hallowed ship.

Ward unzipped the front of his windbreaker, the chill cold seeping inside his chest. He pocketed away the small metal box, clasped in his fingers, in the folds of his jacket, zipping it back up and securing the pilfered object away. He had no intentions of stealing it.

He was driven only to return to his shared cabin. With his bunkmate gone ashore, he'd privately peruse the contents of the box, if he could find a way to get it open.

His cabin partner had opted to partake of the celebrations, destined to last two or three days, across the coast of Southern England.

He and the crew would be hosted at several local hotels, laying claim to their new celebrity status. They'd be the honored guests of several historical societies and explorer groups. The festivities even included appearing on several English talk shows as the crew provided their own insights into the recovery.

His mind raced with the transgression, he was committing. He was tampering with an ancient relic.

He was failing to follow the proscribed procedures and methods to preserve it. He was succumbing to his own greed and curiosity.

Ward edged away from the beam leaving his crime behind and absconding with the hidden treasure.

Fortune was with him. The rains had driven the police officers above, away from the docks. Besides, what was there to see, save a large plastic tarp and a collection of dead wood.

Ward cast his eyes towards the workshed the workmen had retreated to, during the onset of the rain. A spiraling column of white smoke fought the rain to ascend skyward from the shed's stovepipe, only to be wafted aside into the stone of the dock, beside the roof of the shed as a gust of wind drove across the water.

He reached the deck of the barge and still no one was within sight. Only God and the gulls above had witnessed his crime. Selfishly, he clasped his chest, feeling the spirited away box.

He made for the gangplank, running between the barge and the salvage ship, crossing it at a run. He halted on the other side, safely aboard the deck of his own ship. His mind swelled with the trouble the simple act of larceny could befall upon him.

If the object was an antiquity, its value would be priceless. There might be all sorts of charges, fines, and imprisonment awaiting him for merely removing it, unauthorized, by the assigned technicians and archaeologists.

As Cain, eons before him, he turned in flight with the sudden realization of the fear welling up inside him. A conscious was a terrible thing, but it often kept men living righteously and justly. But, a belated conscious was even worse, the crime done, it plagued the transgressor with a guilt, that had escaped him during the moment of sin. It damned on relentlessly.

Ward disappeared along one of the side doors of the Reprise's superstructure. He disappeared from sight, leaving only the shrieking gulls harping above him and a discolored piece of water soaked wood, slowly descending to the bottom of the harbor.

Ward opened his locker and withdrew a gym bag, he kept his extra underwear and socks stuffed inside. He withdrew one sock of irregular shape, an oversized object stuffed inside it. A single overhead light lit the cramped quarters with two lockers, a small desk, and chair along with a set of bunk beds.

The door was locked, allaying Ward's fears of discovery.

He removed a small pint or bourbon, from the bag and unscrewed its gold plastic cap. He drank greedily, sitting atop his upper bunk, still in his wet clothes. His right hand greedily clasped the fold of his jacket and the small box underneath it.

He allowed the warmth of the bourbon to coat the back of his throat, rolling the fiery liquid around in his mouth, before swallowing. He rationalized, he still had time to examine the box and return it, to the remains of the wreck. Where wasn't important, he could even toss it into the remains from the deck of the Reprise or dump it into one of the plastic totes.

If he waited, until no one saw him, it would just be assumed an error, an item misplaced or erroneously cataloged. Yes, that was what he would do.

He unzipped the front of his windbreaker and removed the small case.

He stared in fascination at its workmanship. Its metal surface was constructed of two symmetrical halves forming a hinged hollow shell. But, its ornamentation and design must have been the extravagant work of a jeweler or metalsmith. It had a lattice grid work face folding in and about the exterior of each half. And, a fine clasp secured the tight fitting halves of the shell together, without the benefit of a lock.

The weight of the small box belied the truth, that something still remained, within its interior.

His chilled wet fingers fumbled with the clasp, trying to fathom its workings and unlock the secret inside. His first attempts failed and he sipped another mouthful of the bourbon, calming himself.

His heart was racing. It beat hard with the guilt of the theft and from the thrill the act illicited. He'd always been the trusted associate, the one known for common sense and good judgment. He'd been the cool-headed trustee and loyal crewman, the Reprise's crew had come to value, yet take for granted.

Now, he was engaged in an endeavor, totally out of character. Yet, far from damning himself, he craved the excitement and unknown pleasure of examining some long-forgotten treasure, only he'd been the first to reclaim.

The clasp opened.

Alan Ward slowly pulled the hinged halves of the metal box apart. They stuck together as if sealed by a vacuum, despite the opened clasp. His fingers pried at the metal edges, his fingernails digging under their rims. He was amazed at the craftsmanship of the lips, each having a set of inner rims, that set into each other in an attempt to make the small container watertight. The design had worked, no water dripped from the small box's interior, Ward tried to expose.

The box opened. Ward swore, he heard a hiss as if some venomous viper had released a damning warning of its presence. And, there was just a notion of a foul stench emitted from the box, if only for a moment, the length of a breath. It was as if some evil had been released from inside the hidden confines of the container.

Ward wiped his mouth and took another swig from the bottle, before replacing its plastic cap. His eyes were transfixed on the small leather-bound book, spirited away inside the container.

His fingers lifted it from the open box and set it reverently atop his bunk. He discarded his wet windbreaker, tossing it to the floor, less he damage the treasure before him with its dripping dampness. He dried his fingers, rubbing them in the wool blanket, tucked and folded across his bunk.

He opened the book's cover.

His awe and wonder fell away to disappointment as he noted the Old English text, written by a flamboyant and practised hand. The written word was in the style of ages past, the lettered combination "PF" had long since been replaced by "TH." "PFAT" meant the same as "THAT," and other words were similarly cryptically ciphered.

He'd gleam little knowledge from the words, at least not as

quickly, as he'd have liked. The small book and its contents demanded study and he was tired. He was spent from the day's events and his own larceny. He wanted only to close his eyes and rest, lured to sleep by the warmth of his overheated shared cabin and the bourbon calming his nervous heart.

Yet, he was intrigued, drawn to the flowing loops and flowering letters of the words on the browning paper. He began trying to read the author's hand, finding it not as difficult as he'd first imagined. Several words meant nothing to him. He ignored them, but lost nothing of the subject's gist or author's intent.

He rose up in his bunk. The book was no log or diary. It professed to be a true tale. A warning of some tragedy, encountered upon the journey of the HMS Vanguard and her crew. The letters and words written on the paper were made with a bold hand. The pen and charcoal that wrote them, nearly two centuries ago, had pressed deeply into the paper. The author warned of a secret, he had discovered.

The warning was written atop the book's first page and jotted across the inside cover as if added as a last desperate afterthought. Its charcoal written words were smeared and almost illegible as if the cover had been closed in haste. The charcoal-etched message was in contrast to the rest of the book's neat and flowing ink scribed penmanship. But, the hasty sentences could still be discerned.

> *"I and several of the crew have taken it upon ourselves to see that this evil does not reach our home shores. May God forgive me for the lives, I am about to take and not damn me for claiming my own."*

> *Ensign Robert Lewis*
> *HMS Vanguard*
> *November 2,*
> *Year of Our Lord 1805*

View of the Main Mast from the deck.

CHAPTER 4

The Night

October 14, 1805

HMS Vanguard
Portsmouth Harbor
Day 1

I remember that night well. I stood watch and fought its tedious boredom.

It was just before the midnight hour, the thirteenth day of October in the year of Our Lord 1805. I was yet a young Royal Navy Ensign, about to take on my fourth voyage aboard one of his majesty's warships. She was the HMS Vanguard.

She was as grand a ship of the line as any there be.

Her trim and railing, ye her doors and ornamentation vied

for sight and beauty against the noblest works of artisans past. Her handcrafted beams were made of strong oak. Her giant masts towered above the decks with all manner of block and tackle, or pulley and spar.

Her three thick masts were crafted in layers and wrapped with iron bands. Three peaking spires rose to the sky; the fore mast, main mast, and mizzen mast, while her bowsprint pointed straight ahead, like a compass needle pointing to Portsmouth.

She was a sister-ship to the HMS Victory, that famous ship of battle, whose claim to fame was assured as Lord Admiral Horatio Nelson's flagship. Like Victory, the Vanguard boasted the finest cannon, that British ironsmiths and foundries could craft. Their barrels rested behind the closed gunports of three decks. Their deadly broadsides were claimed by her ship's designers and drafters to lay any vessel, coming alongside, to the bottom with a single volley.

Her copper-plated hull rested heavily in the water that lonely October night, when the quartermaster, two hands, and I stood watch. The ship was fully loaded with provisions, shot, powder, and cannon.

Earlier in the day provisions and stores were taken aboard as a mismatched set of sacks, crates, and a large awkward iron box were brought to the dock by wagon and hauled aboard. The latter object caused much speculation among the crew assigned to berth it, in the hollows of the hold below.

Its locked contents engendered speculation, that a secret treasure or perhaps, a guarded plan of battle was stored within its sequestered confines. But, soon it was spirited away out of sight. And, all hands that had stowed it, had let it recede from the queries of their minds and curiosities. Such were the minds of men, given to simple pleasures and a last liberty ashore to partake in a final frolic, whence came the evening and their duties done.

But, food stuffs, limes, and barrels of rum, along with our mysterious box were not the only stores taken aboard.

A contingent of Royal Marines was on board, already fast asleep in the hammocks strung below the decks, among the guns.

Except for four of their number, two posted forward, at the bow and two at the stern.

The night was so dark, that I would not have even known, they were there, had not their presence been told to me. It was black as pitch, that late evening. So dark, that even the water beside the dock the Vanguard was tied alongside, could not be seen, save by the mere glimpses of the flickering flames of the streetlights vying with the fog.

We waited, fighting the damp chill of the waters, that lingered about the dock. The muster book still lay open, awaiting the late arrival of those seamen still intent of availing themselves of the liberties, that could be found among the taverns and inns of Portsmouth.

Only a few men had yet to return, before our voyage on the morrow. Fighting the boredom of an empty black night, we waited their return.

It seemed as if the watch would be froth with serenity and silence. Most of the crew was already on board, at this late hour. They took to safely resting in the comfort and warmth of their hammocks, sheltered from the rolling fog, engulfing both dock and ship.

Even the waters seemed to rest. Though their presence was made known, only by the lapping of the gentle waves, against our low-riding hull or the shrill shriek of a gull floating about below, its slumber disturbed for some strange reason.

The ship creaked and groaned as her timbers swelled with the dampness and she strained against her moorings, linking her to the dock.

I stood my post, along the open twin doors on the second deck. The ramp leading perilously up towards it, from the dock, was swallowed by the darkness. Three lamps lit the entrance, awaiting to receive the last of the tars, allowed the liberties of Portsmouth, before we cast off and sailed for a fortnight, patrolling the channel in a northerly and southerly route, guarding the coast of our beloved isle.

The duty was relished by officer and seaman alike. The

channel, even at that time of year, promised to present the ship and her company to a pleasant cruise, and being so near the British Coast, there was little danger of encountering the threat of Napoleon's French fleet.

It was our duty to protect against an apparent, yet never seen, invasion. But, all expected an inconsequential patrol. We envisioned a quick return to the delights and comforts of Portsmouth, after an uneventful sojourn.

We had learned, both officially from the Admiralty and from the wagging tongues of dock-workers and returning seamen, that the French fleet was massing to protect the boats and barges of a growing French army, intent on invasion of our isle.

But, their officers had not the mettle for a fight and had fled to the waters, along the coasts of Europe, sailing off to the safe anchorage of this or that Spanish Port. Where it was reported, they waited for the command to protect the French despot's beloved army from a counter-thrust by the sea, should they dare attempt a crossing of the English Channel.

Of these things the admiralty said little. But, returning seamen claimed to have seen the sight of an Armada near Cadiz, that warm-water port along the coastline of Southern Spain. Such a fleet had not been witnessed, since Spain contested our rule of the seas, an era ago.

They remarked in awe of the ghostly giants, French men-of-war, much like our own warships. These hallowed galleons bore stripes of red across their hulls in contrast to his majesty's and our own golden-yellow markings. The French masts and spars were claimed to stretch to the sky. But, such are the yarns and tales, that often drift across the sea, honed by bored minds and tongues spinning yarns of fancy.

And, it was claimed streaming atop those hated masts, the returning tars had sighted the tri-colored streamers and the daunting flags of the new French Republic.

Many a ship had sailed forth from Portsmouth, destined to some guarded journey, here or there. One did not speak of such destinations, we all were well aware of French spies among us or even of those, themselves subjects of the Crown, whose loyalties were suspect, harboring some greater desire for the rule of all men from a common body, as opposed to an unwavering belief in God and bless his subject, set above others to govern by divine right, the King of England, George III, in all his might.

And, so I stood watch on this black evening. In the chill and lonesome hour, I awaited the return of the ship's company from their frolic and depravities. To a man, they knew of their duty to return and the punishment of the brig or lash of the awaiting boatswain, should they dally or fail.

Beside me stood the quartermaster and two mates. And, as each man arrived and climbed the slanting gangplank, barely wide enough for one man's footing, his name was called for and checked against the ship's listing, among the pages of a worn leather-bound book.

At my concurrence, a check or mark was scribed beside each man's name, completing the roster of all on board, save a tardy few.

With a brisk chill wafting across the water, we stood watch. The night was pitch, save for the yellow flickering candlelight of the streetlights lighting the narrow gridiron cobblestone streets, bordering the dock and leading to the water's edge.

It was in this black void, that the last few stranglers came. I would not have noted their approach, save for the boisterousness of their voices. Their slurred tongues tried to recite the melody of some common folks' tune.

A deep baritone voice led the jubilation, though it could barely recall all of the lyrics to the melody. The small band finally came to within the reach of the flickering lanterns, mounted on either side of the ship's port entrance. I watched with a measure of detached resignation, as was my station.

In disorder, the first of the frolickers attempted to ascend the gangplank to the entrance, opened on the Vanguard's second deck. His left hand gripped the runway's sagging rope, pulling it taunt with his own misguided and reckless weight.

Only when it appeared, that he would fall into the water, did

I cast my eyes in his direction. But, a native son of England and born of the sea surrounding the isle, he righted himself and staggered upward with no mind to the precarious drop to the cold waters below or the steepness of the climb.

His path was soon followed by the others, their uniforms and seamen's hats askew atop their heads. More, than a few had their uniforms in a shatters. To a man all were in a disgraceful state, unshaven and foul, the stench of liquor upon their breaths. But, they were mates. They had left ship together and they returned as one. Though more, than one was none the better for it and was aided in their climb aboard by companions less ill.

I feinted my displeasure, though they had exercised their right. These were the occurrences and due folly of the common seaman. They had earned their right to abuse themselves, before we cast sail again.

The men had grumbled as their names were called and quartermaster made his mark. They entered the bowels of the vessel, each heading for his deck and the simple canvas hammock, that awaited him.

It was at this ungodly hour, when the night mixed with the netherworld's darkness of the coming morning, that I saw the strange sight, that continues to haunt me until this day. I did not know at the moment, that it was the beginning of a horror more gruesome, than the fiercest battle or an evil more vile, than the foulest image of an unholy spirit the gospels of church or mind could have imagined.

I saw the man first, that night. He was a frail character, pale and yellow as if gripped by some sickness. He was somewhat nondescript, devoid of any notable features, his hollowed face and cheeks lacking any distinction.

I thought perhaps, he'd succumbed to the demon liquor, the tars seemed to embellish drinking. Though in truth, his condition might have been from some ailment, jaundice or scurvy. But, he moved with none of the weakness of one afflicted by the latter disease.

In contrast, he had strength enough to aid a mate, who was surely more worse off, than he. They slowly climbed out of the night surrounding the dock. And, I found it strange, that the slight night breeze seemed to die away with their presence.

An ungodly stillness gripped the ship. It was like the quiet reckonings, that did intone a man to reflect inward to examine where he stood with his maker, tallying good deeds against past sins. The silence was eerie and foreboding.

Not a sound did I hear in the harbor, save for the steps of the two men's feet, threading the narrow plank ascending to the ship.

Not a gull squawked. Not a sound came from the streets nearby, that had surrendered the two forms, back to the ship awaiting them. There was a strange stillness, that seemed to beset the Vanguard.

It reminded me of the tales I'd heard from more experienced and practised navigators, who had sailed into the cursed bane of sailing ships, the silent unmoving lull's, where a lack of wind collapsed the sails and left them hanging suspended, dangling still from the masts. These windless seas left sails as lifeless sheets and damned a ship dead in the water.

I had been told on good accord, that these god awful afflictions could last for days. The haunting silence and inactive monotony afflicted the health and morale of the crew, as it left their ship dead at sea, adrift.

It was this menacing silence as if all life had fled the moment, that I felt the dread of.

But, the hour was late and I tired of the dull monotony of waiting at my post. Besides at this late hour, the mind grew tired and imagined things, where none existed. I stood my post stiffly as was due the responsibilities of my station. I waited for their names to be called out and for each man to affirm his return for the quartermaster's mark.

The seaman with the sickly pallor stood before the small ornate stand and the quartermaster with his book. He spoke his name. It was as if a whisper and yet, not.

His voice barely rose as he spoke a name I failed to decipher, though the quartermaster heard it and made his mark among the names upon his list. The moment was as in a daze, dream-like and surreal. But, it did occur. I watched the man report.

In the flickering light of the lantern atop the quartermaster's writing stand, I studied the pale face.

Unlike, the boisterous souls, who had returned earlier, it seemed void of life or should I better say a love of it. If he had engaged in merriment or even fornication, I could not tell. His thin lips were drawn taunt and showed no joy of debauchery or the common pleasures, suffered by the rest of the crew.

And, though it was perhaps, the failing light of the three lanterns at our post, his eyes were void of life. I saw only dark black orbs, though I searched out his pupils, devoid of the color or the essence of life.

He answered for his mate, the man standing at his side dumbfoundedly, before both retired to the interior of the ship.

I thought nothing more of it as my bones began to feel the dampness of the sea and the late hour. Already, it was the first hour of the new day, though all was shrouded in darkness. It was that odd hour of the morning, when even though I stood awake, my mind was predisposed of slumber, dulled by the monotonous stupor of our watch and far off thoughts, yearning to fall into the pleasant realm of dreams.

And, in truth, I was predisposed to the tasks, which would present themselves within a few hours. We would cast away from the dock and set out for the channel with the rising of the sun and I had many duties to attend to.

The lack of sleep and the dullness of my post had taken their toll on me. Yet, I had soon to put on my best pretense, before captain and men.

It was then, that I queried the quartermaster to see how many hands might still be ashore. The act, for my part, was fashioned as much as to discern the tally as to have something to do. I sought to pass away the remaining time of our watch.

I watched, as the quartermaster, clad in his red tunic and black leather hat, set about the task. The feather of his quill swayed about as the point lay beside the name of each seaman, who had departed ashore earlier and returned.

He halted, frustrated by his own inattentiveness. He was a

decade or more older, than myself and surely the late hour and damp chilly night had taken a toll on him. I watched, holding my disgust, that he was recounting, starting over once more.

Again, the man fell perplexed. His face fell blank in puzzlement as if fathoming some riddle.

"What say you, Quartermaster? What is the count?" I interjected.

"Sir, I must be in error," the man did answer me. "The count must be right. All that have gone ashore have returned."

"Then tell me, man, why must there be an error?" I intoned.

"As I said, sir, I must have made an error. I seem to have counted a mark twice. I thought a man too many might have answered our rolls. But, you were here and saw as I, all the ship's company have returned," he replied.

"Then all to sail are on board, Quartermaster?" I asked in confirmation.

"Aye, sir. All hands aboard!" he returned, in a guttural voice, whose briskness might have awoken those in the hammocks of the deck nearest the entrance, had not the rasping of his throat from the cold evening air straggled his words.

It was enough. At least, I thought at the time.

I turned and faced the dock, seeking to find the warm glow of a bedroom's window or some other sight or sound to cling to on the voyage, to remind me of land. It was a small concession I allotted myself, to frame some small comforting picture of shore in my mind for the days at sea ahead.

But, the darkness, shrouded in fog, offered me no object of comfort. If anything, I found the scene distressing, dismal, and even ominous. But, not being a superstitious man, I brushed the feeling aside.

The wonders of the expanding science of seamanship, the compass and the plottings of navigators, guided the course of men's lives. Man determined his own fate, not some celestial body or charted portent of seers or sages.

The evil wrought in our time was guided by the hands of man. The Frenchman Napoleon Boneparte was the living embodiment and proof of that. The reckless despot was wreaking havoc upon the civilizations of Europe and even the far shores of the Middle East as Boneparte's armies sought wealth and treasure of an expanding French Empire in Northern Africa.

The feeling of unease and of a fanciful mind, soon left me as the real dangers of the world and the responsibilities of the uniform, I wore, confronted my tired mind.

I stepped inside the port entrance, a shiver claiming me, despite the stiff high buttoned collar of my uniform. I ordered the two mahogany doors sealed, but the ramp left in place, until the command be given for our departure.

To clear my mind and reclaim the warmth of my circulation, I informed the watch I was going to make my rounds, inspecting the posted Royal Marine guard, fore and aft.

It was a short passage between decks, rising from the hold of the second to the third, along the steep wide wooden steps.

Once topside, I found the night no longer as foreboding. Perhaps, it was the spaciousness of the dark sky above. The overcast must have been heavy, for I saw not a solitary star.

Twas, as I looked skyward to the heavens, that it happened. At first, it was nothing more, than a blur, a glimpse of movement, the motion and not the object, catching the attention of my eyes.

It was a blur, a dark form careening from the masts. The form took on a shape, though I did not recognize the clawing hands and fingers, flailing out of reach of ratlings and ropes, leading to the mast the man had fallen from.

A tar had fallen from the mast.

I cannot forget the sickening echo as if a wet sack of flour had splattered to the hardness of the deck. There was no cry, not a sound. Except, for the low sickening hiss of the expelling of a final breath. And, despite the horrid sound of that body, crumpled upon the deck, I swear, that last breath ended in a willing sigh. It was as if its owner had found some heavenly release or relief.

My blood raced and my mind was afire, alerted to the tragedy. But, I could not find the words, nor the measure of breath to call out. I stood there frozen, staring at the misshapen form strewn upon the deck. Only when my thoughts collected, did I sally forth.

I stood over the lifeless body, its neck most likely broken from the twisted skewed position of the man's head. The body's limbs were likewise askew, twisted this way and that. And, one arm seemed jointed in a place quite unnatural, attesting to a break. A sliver of bone jutted through the fresh wound, evidencing the site.

Yet, strangely, there was no blood ushering forth from the wound. In morbid fascination, I studied the grizzly site. A novice of medicine and still to serve in combat, I would leave this oddity to the ship's surgeon to fathom.

The human body was a strange complication of parts and oddities as science continued to discover. There could be good reason for the strangeness of this calamity. In any regard, I was more, than happy to have turned away from the sight, after kneeling to the man and determining, he had expired and no breath was left about him.

My voice had returned and in quick measure, I shouted out the alarm. Strangely, on the top deck, it seemed, that I was the only soul, that had heard the fall and cruel landing. For, it was not until I had bellowed my alarm, for the second time, that I heard the footfalls of the Royal Marines fore and aft, coming to my aid.

And, then I thought I saw it. Actually, I know not what, my vision claimed sight of. It was like a wisp, a shadow of a dark cloud, a shadow to be precise. I thought I saw the movement of a figure descending from where the ratlings meet the deck's rail.

But, as quickly as I saw it, that maleficent specter had disappeared. I turned my head about trying to claim it with my eyes again. But, it was gone or so I thought, until my eyes fell to the hatch, leading to the bowels of the ship.

I started to call out and order it to halt, but was distracted from the task by the arrival of the forward posted marines. A lantern dangled from about one of their hands as they struggled to hold onto their slung rifles, at a run. When my eyes returned, the form was gone, if there had ever been one.

I heard no footsteps, I saw no face. It was as if a shadow had floated along the outer reaches of my sight. It defied me to prove it existed, if it was even ever there.

Matters were at hand, the two marines awaited, while their companions, being further astern, approached. I had ordered one to fetch the ship's surgeon, knowing it was to late and would not avail the corpse, laying twisted before us. But, it was my duty, protocol, and the way of things aboard our ship.

The good doctor would have to render his decision, though the death was obvious. The other marine, I sent to fetch another lantern. In the darkness engulfing us, I could not determine the dead man's identity. And, this I would need for my report to the captain.

Strangely, through all this calamity, the ship did not stir. I would have assumed word would have spread quickly. But, the fall seemed shrouded and hidden in the eerie stillness, about the ship. Even the marines' running feet did little to disturb the ship's slumber.

It seemed, as if some deity had cloaked a veil of sleep and unconsciousness over the ship and its crew. In respectful silence, a lantern was drawn up beside the dead tar. He wore a simple seaman's uniform. A full brimmed black leather hat, that was part of his uniform, lay not far away. His striped blue and white blouse, even his blue pants, showed no sign of blood.

Slowly, it had dawned upon my sluggish mind, dulled by the lateness of the hour, that this was the seaman, I last saw hauled aboard, upon the comforting comradely shoulder of his ghostly pallor-faced mate.

As I think back on it, there was a peacefulness surrounding the man's heaped shape as if death offered some strange release, we could not imagine the mystery of.

Yet, how had this man, so unable to stagger up aboard the

gangplank, have climbed the ratlings of the mast, towering so high above. What folly and blunder, for a man in his obviously drunken state to have claimed such heights, while so unsure of his own footing or surroundings.

Moments later, I heard the stir of the ship's surgeon, an aging man at that. He brought with him a leather surgeon's bag, despite the marine telling him of no need for it. But, like me, he followed custom and duty, reporting at the ready. I sent the marine, that had fetched the doctor, to report to the captain, detesting the ungodly hour we must rouse him from his slumber, with so much yet waiting to be done, upon the approaching new morning.

His arrival was delayed as he made ready his appearance, to be seen upon our deck. We stood in a stupor upon the deck, silently awaiting him. There was nothing to be done, but to receive his approval to remove the man ashore.

And still, despite the ruckus of our earlier activities and surely the pounding upon the captain's door, not a tar appeared at the hatches or the railings. Not one mate's sleep was disturbed, during the stillness of this late hour.

It was this inactivity, that marks my mind the most. The silent vigil over the still corpse made its mark upon me. The breeze, that had died away, left a stagnant fragrance, a foul scent of death lingering about the deck. Call it a seaman's legend or lore, but to a man, I believe the others felt as I, that death was still among us, finding our ship a place to plague as its temporary home.

And yet, mercifully, save for the good doctor, our four loyal marines and the approaching captain, none knew of the tragedy, that had befallen the Vanguard. Sailors are a wearisome lot, prone to routine and superstition. The breaking of their daily rituals would be enough, to give rise and suspicion of some ill-fated omen or portent. But, the death of a shipmate, so sudden and mysterious, would play havoc with their simple beliefs and superstitious minds.

When the captain arrived and was apprised of the situation, he agreed most heartily to the removal of the tar. More, he bid us not to speak further of it, among the crew and he would personally inform the rest of the officers on board, at his discretion.

I do believe the four Royal Marines were relieved, to be so lifted from the burden of our knowledge. Their silence was assured by the uniform they proudly wore. And, fortunately, unlike our own disciplined, yet lax tars, their tongues were not given to the idle gossip or speculation, that our own seamen seemed to relish in, to pass the time at sea.

Foremost, my captain commanded me to silently correct the problem, so no detriment to morale occurred. His voice was sullen, but firm in this matter. And, I immediately released the four marines from their post to transfer the body of the fallen mate ashore.

But first, I descended to the deck below us, relieving the watch from their posts. I awaited there, until alone with the glow of the three lanterns and table, absent the book of names retrieved by the quartermaster, I was satisfied, that no one would observe the stealthy procession of the dead seaman passing by.

Satisfied, there was no one to observe us, I returned to the upper deck and found the surgeon and marines waiting, for my command to move the body. More concerned with hiding the incident from prying eyes and protecting the morale of ship and crew, I ordered them ashore. I bid the surgeon and two marines to take the body to the nearest doctor, a healer attending to the needs of the local fisherman, nary three blocks away from our berth.

He was to be told nothing of the death occurring on our vessel. I left the details to the surgeon, ordering him to return two of the marines back to me, to finish the watch, after they assisted carrying the body down the plank. But, this later order proved folly as only one marine, fore and aft of the corpse, could negotiate the gangplank.

I amended my order. And, I ushered them ashore, retaining my original post from whence, I had begun the watch, at the top of the plank leading to the dock below. I saw the unease in the faces of the marines beside me for the first time, captured in the flickering candlelight of the three lanterns nearby.

Perhaps, it was the loss of a fellow journeyer or perhaps, the queerness of the unexplained death. I had done my duty and informed the captain, obeying his orders to correct the unfortunate matter. With pressing duties awaiting me in the morning, I blindly pushed the memory of the incident from my mind.

I remember last, a chilling rain, that beset our decks as the surgeon and his dead charge disappeared into the dark. Their shadows were cast by the streetlights below, disappearing in the descending shower, that raked the dock and the timbers of our great ship. The pouring rain drummed across the upper deck as if heaven had washed away our subterfuge.

At first, I claimed it as a blessing, even the heavens seemed to share our desire to keep secret the horrible and tragic demise of our undoubtedly inebriated crewman. But, in retrospect, I now believe heaven cried that night, as in our ignorance, we abated some horrible evil.

I did not realize it then, but it was an error, I have lived to regret. And, now I write down this testament, so that others may have record of the events that have plagued our ship and crew.

CHAPTER 5

Setting Sail

HMS Vanguard
Portsmouth Harbor
Day 2

The morning came with the suddenness of a fiery brightness, bathing across the deck. The men broke topside to the shrill whistle of the boatswain and the beat of the Royal Marine's drummers.

All thoughts of the events, that had occurred earlier, fell from my weary mind. As I look back, I wondered, how I could have so easily placed the death of a crewman to the recesses of my mind.

But, the darkness had been pushed away. The morning sunlight bathed us in the brightness of the noble task awaiting us. The roll of the drums, replete with the barked commands of our ship's master and his officers, summoned the men to their posts. Many took to the ratlings, climbing high above and edging out, along the spars to unfasten the ties holding our canvas bound.

The large sails unfurled, dropping earthward, only to halt in their captive reach, along the mast as the soft morning winds caught their flat surfaces and slapped their corners about, until lines were drawn taunt.

And, while the crew moved with deliberate haste to ready our vessel for sea, the marines, resplendent in their red and white coats, gathered in formation, all to the beat of the drums. It was as if the Vanguard had come to life, a large single living being. The individual was lost in the avalanche of excitement and fury sweeping across her decks.

A man's thoughts were swept aside by the incessant beating of the drums. Thoughts of home, family, or personal pursuit were gone. Our minds and bodies became as one. The drums more, than producing a beat or call to orders, harkened all to join in the common effort. More, than any other sole movement across the decks, they signified our purpose. They warned our foe and inspired the souls of our countrymen lining the docks, that we were a ship of war.

And, it was that same swelling pride and the sight of our might, that erased the haunting memory of the early morning hours from my mind. How grand and impressive, it must have been for those well-wishers and workers, standing on the docks, to have seen the splendid sight of our vessel towering three stories above the water. With her canvas set and decks manned the Vanguard brimmed with her own life and strength.

Her lines were cast, slipping into the water beside the docks with splashes of anticipation. Calloused hands, on the dock below, heaved the thick woven hemp out of the water, coiling it to dry and await the next arrival to claim the vacated berth. Other lines, tethered to our ship, were pulled aboard by crews at their stations, along the port side of the ship.

And still, as we prepared to make sea, two junior officers paced agitatedly about the deck. Their roving eyes were tasked to check, about this or that, ensuring redundantly, that all was well. The anchors, which had not been lowered as we berthed next to the dock, were checked to see that they were secured and their ropes and chains blocked.

For my own part, I instructed this man or that about. I was to ensure, that ropes were properly coiled and stored, that nothing remained underfoot, endangering the flurry of activity of the crew rushing about. I also monitored the shouts of those atop the main-mast. Should there be a need, I was to provide extra hands, from those loitering about the deck, be sent up to aid in unfurling the sails.

But, this proved unnecessary. Absent any inclement weather or gusting winds, unfurling the canvas above was more akin to a seaman unrolling his hammock and stringing it up, below deck for the night. Though I had been fretful of the duties, I was to attend to, earlier this morning, the new dawn had shown the worry an unnecessary expenditure of my time. None of my efforts proved pressing. And, the crew was well experienced in their duties, needing no encouragement or goading by me.

The helmsman cast an eye to the outer reaches of the harbor. Like every man present, he was anxious to be free of land, to feel the rudder answer the command of his hands.

And yet, we were plagued as if by the mischievous hand of some lessor malcontent or evil god. The wind, that had snapped about our sails and promised to billow them fully, departed as quickly as it had come.

The elation of the crowds about the dock and filled with the pomp of our own posturing was for naught. There we stood in all our glory, the ship in all her majesty, deadlocked beside our pier.

But, our captain was experienced in these matters, though his face frowned with the disappointment shared by all. His voice barked halting commands to the workers below, jolting them into action. Nearly twelve souls, hearty men of rugged persuasion, more noted for their brawn, than wit, answered his call.

They bore long wooden poles, twice the length of an oar. Their thickness resembled the spars of our masts. They were joined with dozens of others and pressed the tips, of the prolonged wooden shafts, against the hull of our ship.

To starboard, several large rowboats had been dispatched from those tied up beside the docks. Stowed lines were uncoiled at the captain's command and thrown down to waiting hands.

With three such boats afloat and tied off to our ship, the

order was given to all in unison, to push and pull the Vanguard free of her berth. Arms and backs strained as pole and oar joined with the little wind and conspired to clear us of land.

Yet, the grunting and straining of the robust hands ashore and on the harbor's water did nothing to set us free. The stillness was damning, mocking the power and might of our 103-gun behemoth.

The superstitious, among us, might have heralded this as an omen as if the ship, herself, harbored some reason not to sail. But, save for our captain, surgeon, and the four Royal Marines, I had summoned earlier, none knew of the disaster, that had befallen a member of our crew.

In the light of day and the warming rays of the sun, falling about my face, such thoughts mirrored those of fools. But, I cast my eye about the deck, seeking out the few, who knew our shared secret.

The captain offered nothing, except the model gentleman and seasoned seaman, his rank and tenure marked him to be.

I spotted the surgeon standing near the stern. His head was bowed, towards the water. His face had the look of a man, that fretted his occupation. But, I had seen that look before. Our good doctor had discreetly been known to visit the ship's store's, partaking of the libations, used to render the wounded eased of their afflictions. Wounded men were given several mouthfuls of rum and a measure of the strong alcohol was doused over their wounds, before scalpel and bone-saw took about their grizzly business.

I had been warned, our doctor had seen much of such medical necessities and their related horrors. He was no novice to the gruesome business of amputation.

His own weakness for the warmth of the ship's libations was overlooked. It helped him to forget the horrid work his hands had spawned. His sin had been to save a life, by whittling away a man.

Perhaps, last night had flooded his memory again, with the ghastly reality of his occupation. He looked much, like some of the seaman, I'd witnessed returning from their debauchery, while on watch.

But, unlike them, the doctor showed no boisterous merriment or rejoicing from his sharing of their vice for drink. He stared below at the cold waters, seemingly transfixed on the docile gulls floating about or taking to hovering, about the hull of the ship.

Again, the captain bellowed out orders. They were repeated by the ship's second officer. And, again, poles pushed against our vessel's heavy hull. Oars dipped in the water and muscles tightened, eager hands strained to pull the shafts held captive in their oarlocks.

My eyes roamed to the bow and found the red uniformed marines held stiffly at attention. Their tall black hats with short brims illusively made each man a giant. Unlike, our crewmen, they held a more professional bearing.

Their stiff collars and polished boots, along with the brass of their buttons and buckles glimmered in the sunlight. The ornate crests atop their tall black hats added to the flawless and poised display of their muster. Rifles paralleled the staunchness of their stance as they rested upright, buttplate to deck and barrels pointed skyward in each man's right hand.

I spied two of the four, that had been on duty, during my watch. One's eyes were staring forward blankly with the precision and obedient detachment, as was his lot.

But, I saw nervousness in the other's stance. He seemed to fidget about, if that was possible, within the stiffness of his uniform and his trained stance, his legs seemed locked within.

Yet, I saw the unease in the man. I knew it mirrored my own, though I believe, I did a better job of concealing it. I exhaled and breathed in, claiming the fresh sea air to alleviate my own feelings of apprehension.

The moment and its doubts were lost as new orders sounded across the deck. Several tars broke out cheering, standing close to the railings. They rejoiced as the heavy ship edged away from the dock for the first time.

The interceding heavens above saw our predicament and the

topmost sails billowed, catching the breeze, that had escaped them. The further we came away from the pier the more the wind and sea claimed us. Soon, we were no longer alee of the docks. We drifted upon the wind, towards the deeper channel waters of the harbor, out of reach of the poles, that had labored to push our hull aside.

The beat of drums and more commands saw more canvas unfurled. Hands pulled on lines and made them taunt as the blank sewn sheets of white filled and billowed. Lines were released and pulled in as the small craft and the hands, that had labored to tow us from the dock, now strained on the oars to move away from our wake. The HMS Vanguard was alive with the sea and wind beckoning her on.

A host of trivialities, small duties and tasks, that by themselves seemed to the unpracticed seafarer unimportant, were undertaken with a new urgency and haste. But, all of these lessor duties, when taken together, became a choreographed pageantry, making possible, the movement of our great ship.

With banners flying atop the masts and our ensigns whipping in the wind, the Vanguard moved with an ease, few of the uninitiated ashore could have fathomed. Wooden planks and iron guns, block and tackle, and rigged rope came alive to create an engine of war, powered by flesh and wind.

No eye could deny the magnificence of seeing our 2,162 ton vessel move silently through the harbor, save for the barked commands of her master and the answers of her crew. Gulls danced about her towering masts offering one final farewell, until we greeted the open sea outside the harbor.

Then our hull was caught in the great current, laying outside the protective breakwaters of the harbor. The wind, that had denied our sails earlier, picked up. Its gust drove our craft southward.

The Isle of Wight lay straight ahead, marked by the beams of a morning sun, piercing through the clouds above. Our captain steered straight for her, though the English Channel lay to the east. He sought deeper waters, before ordering our course to change.

The sails above leaned to the left, seeking out the wind, running west to east. When the order was finally given for the helmsman to turn the wheel over to port, the Vanguard banked and leaned so steeply, it threatened those, unprepared on the deck, with the loss of their footing. The bowsprit pointed due east as if pointing the way to the English Channel.

Wood creaked as the masts protested the strain full sails placed upon them. Waters rushed by on either side of the ship. They trailed into the foam of our wake. We paralleled the land to port, now distant and fleeting.

A few hands, their duties done, stood beside the railings. They viewed the shoreline with a last lament for the sight of a tree or the green of a hillside, that would escape their vision for the days and weeks to come.

The marines forward were smartly ordered through some drill or that, under the keen watchful eyes of their sergeants. Their officers stood apart, conversing among themselves.

One pointed his uniformed arm upward, towards our masts, outlining the high perches, where in combat his sharpshooters would be deployed. His men were tasked as marksmen and snipers, should we engage a French ship.

Their duties were not as honorable as those of the rest of the ship's company. But, they were no less important. From mast or ratling, our Royal Marine infantry were tasked with firing a deadly volley of descending fire, upon any enemy ship, that might come alongside.

Their orders were to target any officer, seeking to cut off the head of the snake. They were to sever our opposing captain from the controlling embrace of his own ship or if not the ship's master, those junior officers serving to relay his commands about the deck.

The men tasked with this wicked subterfuge were unfairly labeled as lacking in chivalry and any code of battle, though they had to contend with many difficulties.

Their weapon's, muzzle-loading flintlock rifles, necessitated loading pre-measured powder down the front of the barrel, while it was held upright and ramming their hollow conical round tightly down inside the weapon's barrel, while clinging to the side of our ratlings or perched high atop the masts.

Then, they must insert a small piece of flint and cock the piece, so that when their triggers are pulled through and the flintlock strikes the flint, it produces the igniting spark, that fires the powder, beside the touchhole, in the rear of the weapon's barrel.

All this must be done, while balancing atop the ratling's ropes, trying to hold their long swaying barrels atop their targets, while the ship rolls and sways about. Their task is viewed less romantically, than that of our shipmates and officers. Among the circles of our officers, these men are viewed as assassins.

But, to a man both officer and seamen are glad to have them guarding us from above, for French ships have similar men, skilled in the same deadly craft. And, though their own purpose mirrors ours, we take great comfort in the deadly talents and courage of our own marines.

And, one cannot underestimate their courage.

Before, our vessels can even close near enough, for the marines mounted in their aerial perches to come within range of rifle or musket, they will have been exposed to a hellish fire.

The only way to halt our large dreadnoughts is to deprive them of the wind filling their sails. And, to this end, both we and the enemy target each other's masts.

With shot and chain aimed skyward, volley after volley of cannon seek out the wooden spires from which sail and man are perched. Our craftsmen and shipbuilders have studied the dilemma and long since, began constructing the thick towering masts from many layers of wood, instead of from a single tree.

The wood is glued together and crafted as if it were from a single piece. Iron bands are heated and while warm worked by ironsmiths, wrapping them fast. The new mast's strength is unmatched.

I have heard that a round striking a mast in this way or that, has actually been deflected, bouncing off with no detriment.

Whereas, had a mast of the old style been in place, it would have cracked and splintered, raining a deadly shower of wood down upon the decks.

Worse, any men caught above in the masts, during this deadly hellfire, would have fallen to their deaths upon the deck or been lost at sea, if the mast had fallen overboard and had they survived to meet such a fate.

And, newer weapons and improvements still sought to wrest away this advantage of design. Our Royal Marines now have to contend with the threat of "chain shot" or as the crew have been given to the practice of calling them, "angels."

But, these weapons are of no heavenly hand or cherub. Two shot rounds are chained together, in the hopes, that fired from one cannon, their weight and force, combined with the wicked chain, will wrap around a mast cutting or smashing it with their force and iron.

Of a man, they would cut him cleanly in half.

These are but, some of the dangers faced by our marines, along with the volley and hail of French troops from the masts of their own ships. It is a wicked business, this.

I turned away from the drilling formations. And, found my heart calmed by the peacefulness of the sea.

I lingered beside the railing, watching several small fishing boats bobbing about off the coastline. Their occupants toiled to raise cast nets by hand from their unsure craft. There was a chop to the waves as the wind continued in its stead. The calm of the harbor was now behind us.

The fresh breeze at our stern had nearly erased all thoughts, of the start of this morning. Now, my mind was filled only with the journey ahead.

I lingered at ease, along the deck as we made our way for over and hour, then two. All along, the coast of England was readily in sight.

It was only later, that I was approached by the good auspices of the ship's surgeon. I had been so deeply ensconced, in my viewing, that I failed to hear his approach.

I had turned around to find him in the company of a seaman. The tar had, that tired look about him, that sailors who had served aboard ship, for year after year, were often prone to have. But, though his eyes were haunting and his face sunken from a stomach, that had turned tired of the routine rations of salted beef, porridge, or soup the man was fit and seasoned, an experienced salt.

The surgeon and I exchanged salutations, though I should profess the pleasantries were done, mostly upon my part. He swiftly dealt with the business at hand, entailing me, that the captain had ordered I assist him, more observer, than anything else, so that I might report the doctor's findings below deck.

"What is the problem?" I asked, recalling the dread of this early morning.

"Nothing fearful or so, I have been told," Surgeon Radford answered. "Two men failed to report to duty."

I understood the significance of his words. Failure to report to one's post was cause for review and discipline, most frequently a lashing. But, our captain was a fair and just man, such action and reputation bid him well by our crew.

The seaman, beside the doctor, had taken the first opportunity, that his duties would allow him, to report on the state of his mates below deck. Any officer would have rightly jumped to the conclusion, that yesterday's debauchery and drunkenness had been the cause of the two absent crewmen's malaise.

But, as I said, our captain was a fair man. He stood aside from casting judgment, until the surgeon could undertake an examination of the two and return a report, through me.

My role was, that of witness, to ensure the captain's authority was upheld and no malingering tar took advantage of the good doctor's generous nature. My words would have to be weighed carefully, when reporting to the captain.

A sharp tongue or rebuke from me, could rip the skin off a man's back or spare him the same amount of lashes.

And, so we set off to the berths, clustered among the beams of the second deck. We descended the steep stairwells. I did so with regret, knowing full well, that the coast of England would probably be out of sight, once I returned from this task.

I contemplated adding a remark, that would increase the punishment by a lash, if either man were proven to be laying claim to a falsehood of their afflictions. It was my right, indolence and laziness could not be tolerated.

The dampness, I had found on the second deck, where I had stood watch earlier, was gone. All about the hull, the ship smelled of the fresh air and salt, whipping about her.

I followed the good doctor as the seaman took the lead and guided us to two strung hammocks, sagging with the weight of their occupants. The white hammocks swayed about, counter to the movements to the ship, allowing their occupants to remain fixed and level, despite the lightly rolling sea.

I steadied myself, along the slanting deck as the tar stood aside of the berths and the still men in them.

One was an aging salt with a rough stubble of an early beard, about his face. He coughed a deep hacking rasp, far down inside his lungs. Its hollow discord evidenced a sickness, not likely pretended. A tough old codger, he tried to lift his head, upon the doctor's appearance.

But, his affliction had robbed him of strength and he merely remained swallowed up inside the enfolding embrace of his hammock, as the doctor took to examining him.

I saw the seriousness in the surgeon's face, enough to know, this man was no malingerer. Radford felt the man's head and told us there was a fever. He checked the old tar's pulse and confirmed the man ill.

It satisfied me enough, with regards, to what I had to report to the captain, of one of the men. I watched, as Radford bent down to the tar in the hammock below.

In contrast, the lower berth held a lad, a mere child. His face was unblemished, though quite flushed. Like the first sailor, the lad had a fever. And, from the sheen about his face, I could tell, he sweated profusely. Perhaps, because of his age, I would say barely sixteen, he did not bare the affliction well.

The doctor went about repeating his examination. He appeared more concerned, about the state of the young boy, who laid still and unmoving, through it all. The lad was almost lifeless, save for the slight rise and fall of his chest and the choking sound, about his lungs. He seemed to try to cough, but could not expel the breath from deep inside.

The doctor rose and stood perplexed.

His bloodshot eyes stared down at his two patients. There was no more doubt as to the authenticity of their ailment. But, there was much doubt as to the source of the affliction.

He bent down to the young lad again and removed the boy's blanket. The young man tried to protest, but immediately set about shivering. He clasped himself about as if his own embrace would restore his warmth.

The doctor tried to comply with the lad's sought after warmth, examining him, as quickly as possible, before covering him back up.

The surgeon motioned me to his side, a task I did not envy. I had never been one to attend to any bedside manner of the sick or ailing. It was an aversion, I readily admit was lacking in compassion for my fellow man.

I strode froth, halting several arm-lengths away. But, this was unacceptable to the surgeon, who grabbing my sleeve and uniform cuff, pulled me forth.

I stood over the young man.

"There. Do you see that?" Surgeon Radford directed, holding the young man's arm aloft.

"Those scratches?" I queried.

"Yes. But, they're not scratches. I suspect they're bites, rodents by the size of them."

"Rats?" I exclaimed.

"Aye. We've been tied ashore long enough. You'll have to tell the captain," Radford advised me.

I knew the significance of his words. The crew would have to be gathered from one end of the ship to the next, upon each deck. With lengths of rope, clubs, or whatever tool a man favored, they'd begin beating about the pockets and holds of the ship, searching out the rodents infesting it and driving them off the ship.

The rats would be beaten to death or driven topside to scurry over the side and into the water, save for those that sought the safety of the bilge. Among the ballast and barrels floating atop its slight waters, a rodent might find a reprieve from the human hands, seeking to extinguish its life.

But, rats were much like their human counterparts. Given to flight, they'd seek the decks and dryness above. If it was done properly, an assembled crew could rout the rodents, driving them off the ship or clubbing them to death.

"The illness?" I asked, hesitation in my voice.

"Some infection or ailment from the bite, likely mixing with their blood. I think it should be well deterred by seeing to it, these two are fed and rested. Allow the body to regain its strength, that is what I prescribe. And perhaps, an extra ration of rum to purify their blood and fight the infection," Radford added.

"This is not a plague, then?" I asked, failing to hide the worry in my voice from the tar, standing nearby.

"Plague? What books or stories have you been reading, lad?" the surgeon was morbidly amused with my question.

"Rats have always been the bane of seafarers. They spread disease. They foul fresh water stores. They pollute the foodstuffs, they break into, but they are merely a pestilence to be dealt with and forgotten, until the next port is reached and a new hoard of the long-tailed rodents climbs the mooring lines, starting it all again."

"No I've seen it before. And, I dare say I'll see it again. Let the captain know of the presence of the vermin. I'll attest these men are not malingerer's and charge them to my care," the surgeon said, waving the nearby seaman forward.

"And, with this stout man here, I'll have these two moved to an isolated part of the ship," he added.

"A quarantine," I asked.

"More a concession to morale. It's not good for the others to repeatedly see their mates afflicted. Besides, the sight of the rat bites would prove upsetting to the tranquil slumber of those sharing the same deck or quarters. The sooner, we rid the ship of this pestilence, the better. So, attend to your duties, lad. And, I'll attend to mine," he intoned me, with a gesture of his hand, waving me topside.

I hastened off, pleased to be gone from the sickness. And, in the end, I was pleased not to have to report to the captain, that two of his men had been guilty of malingering. I had no stomach to witness the deliverance of the lash, though I had seen it, only once before.

The punishment was a horrible undertaking, almost as heart wrenching to those forced to stand formation atop the deck to witness it, as to the flesh upon the back of the man, the blows were cut into. Though, I know the latter would prove me wrong.

Perhaps, it was just my youth and novice years as an ensign, but I found the act detestable with no redeeming qualities. I was suspect of its use to instill loyalty and obedience in a crew.

As I had looked about, that sole punishment detail, I saw only fear in the eyes of officer and seamen alike. In some, I saw compassion and sympathy for the bearer of the lash's marks. But, in many, I saw a deep-seated hatred, laying shallowly under stern set faces, forced to obediently stand witness to the distasteful act.

I was not one to deny a man, his punishment. In truth, all men sailing the sea, know a ship can have, but one master. Discipline must be maintained, especially on a warship, where all must function as one for the vessel to survive. Laxness and indolence cannot be tolerated.

But, I say better to confine the man in the brig, take away his blanket and rations, until hunger and the self-reflection of solitude, show him the error of his ways. Let him come round on his own. Or, if not, discharge him at the next port.

For the whip punishes not one man, but all. For they see, that they could be next. And, on some ship's, I have heard the lash is used far too arbitrarily. It has become the mistress of discipline for even the slightest of infractions.

I said a silent prayer along my ascent to the third deck, thankful that the doctor found no need for discipline. The afflictions were real and not related to the drunkenness and frolic of the seamen's last liberty.

I stepped up into the light above.

The captain stood silently along the stern. His back was to me. His eyes stared at the disappearing land, to our rear.

As I had suspected, we were leaving sight of land. But, I noted we were still traveling eastward, though the channel presented itself to our port side. I wondered, why we had delayed setting upon our patrol course, but made no mind of it.

I had matters to report.

The captain said little as I informed him of the matters below. He seemed comforted by the news, that the seamen were honestly ill. But, the doctor's discovery of the rat bites distressed him; though he did not say so.

With the French fleet in Spanish harbors and a French army along the opposite banks of the English Channel, hungry to invade, there were more pressing matters, than dealing with the lowliness of rodents.

Yet, the ship's company's health was of the utmost importance. A healthy crew bid an efficient and war-ready vessel.

I described the marks to him and informed him of the doctor's aim, to move the afflicted sailors away from the others.

Our captain merely nodded his assent.

Then, he bid me to collect the other officers, who by now, were enjoying their noon repast. A beating party would be arranged for each deck. I saluted and affirmed his request, watching the last shadow of land slip away in the background behind him.

I was about to turn, upon his salute and dash away, when he halted me with one more act.

"Also tell the men, I will be informing them of our new course," the captain added.

"Sir?" I said perplexed.

I noted silently, we were still heading due east.

"We do not sail for the English Channel," he told me, almost confessing. "The Vanguard sails for Lord Nelson's Squadron, laying off the Spanish Port of Cadiz. I received sealed orders, only moments before, we left Portsmouth, lest French spies or curious eyes and ears learn of our deception."

"You may tell the other officers the gist of it. I will provide the details later, along with a schedule of drills and exercises, to run up the ship's crew and prepare them for the battle the Admiralty expects of us," the captain's voice proclaimed solemnly.

"Aye, sir!" I answered and left him to the lonely vigil of his command.

I headed for the second deck and the junior officer cabins, along its stern. I wanted to claim one last glance rearward, perhaps to see no more, than the shadow of our shores.

But, the act seemed petulant and childish. I descended the steep wide stairs, along the center of the ship. War was to come to our ship. A new heaviness and urgency filled me.

The blight below decks.

CHAPTER 6

At Sea

HMS Vanguard
Sailing off the Coast of Southern France
Day 2-The Afternoon

The hours passed quickly. Those tars, not needed above deck, were set to the multitude of labors, demanding strong backs and dull minds below. The stores, which had been so lackadaisically strewn about the corners of the ship were sorted through and organized.

At the urgings of the boatswain or the direction of a junior officer, tasked with the responsibility of the inventory, a sack was moved with those already heaped in a pile. Or, a crate was stacked among those, bearing the same contents as others already lashed in place. And, so it went, as the ship fell into the monotony of routine, that marked the seaman's boring existence at sea.

Days would pass as we plied the sheltered waters along the

coast of Southern France and took up sight of Portugal. Twas the officers' duty to occupy the minds and lives of the crew, attending to it, that their hands had tasks and chores to busy them and save them from the mischief and larceny, that prevailed, when the men were left to their own devices.

Their efforts were aided by the boatswains. These veteran salts were wise to the temptations and schemes that could detract the average seamen from the path of righteousness, or cause them to lose sight of the King and Navy, they rightfully served and were indentured to by right of their enlistment.

Their mark beside the name, they gave on the ship's roll and the payment of fourteen shillings had bought them whole; body and soul, as the indentured subjects of the King's Royal Navy.

I left the comforting serenity of the upper deck, leaving behind full sails and a steady breeze driving our warship forward. I descended in the bowels of the Vanguard, my legs still moving with the unsteady heaviness of a man still more accustomed to land, than sea. I held the rope as the ship rolled, a solid wind claiming our canvas, lashed to the masts above.

The fresh salt air topside was replaced with the stagnant stench of dampness and the foul repugnant evidence of large numbers of men, working and living below. We were not even a day's journey at sea and already, the men's slop bucket's had found themselves readily used as the tar's paid the physical toll for their debauchery, the evening before and their stomachs' learned to cope anew with the rolling plunge of our ship.

Worse, soap was not part of the mens' ration or kit. It was deemed an extravagant expense not necessary to the good seamanship of the common tar. Therefore, it was not issued.

And, with soap not a requirement upon our ship, it was not purchased by our seamen, who had far more important, though unwise uses for the few shillings, that came into their possession. Besides, there would never be provision enough for the fresh water needed to cleanse the filth of over 800-men. Fresh water, in itself, was a scarce commodity at sea, deemed for satisfying the thirst of one's labors and little more. Except, where our officers were concerned. Our minority officer contingent strived to present themselves as a most grand display of ostentation, if only as an example to the crew and a reflection of the ship.

I moved slowly, despite the assault upon my nostrils. Still unaccustomed to the ship's movements, I balanced on the steep purchase, my feet claimed upon the ladder, I descended.

When I reached the lowest gun-deck, I heard the rushing waters lapping about the sides of the ship. The water's accompanying movement confirmed the fortunate winds, our sails had snared. The gunports were battened down, tied into place with their cannon lashed behind them.

It was not uncommon for a vessel of our size and displacement to run with her lower gunports dipping beneath the water. The waves of the open sea threatened to find any opening not lashed or battened down.

The large guns were plugged and tied to the iron fittings, lining the inside of the hull. The ropes, tied to the guns' low wooden and iron banded carriages, snaked through the blocks and pulleys used to run them up to the side of the hull for firing. Their wooden wheels were blocked off, fixing the heavy weapons in place, despite the changing slope of the lower deck, leaning to port.

I steadied myself, reaching a hand out to a nearby beam as the strong wind above drove the hull over again. I watched the tars walking about the slanted wooden deck at the bequest of the officer ahead. They stowed the last of the supplies, that had been left scattered about the middle of the lower deck, near the hold, that opened up through all three decks.

There were still several burlap sacks waiting to be moved to the rear of the hold. Two of the approaching tars were bending to claim the heavy loads, when the ship rolled.

I watched as the one tar abandoned his attempt to claim a sack and grasped the nearest beam, used to anchor one end of the stowed hammocks it accommodated for the men's slumber.

His fellow was left in a precarious perch, caught similarly by surprise, but with no handhold nearby. He lost his footing and careened head-first towards one of the lashed cannon.

Behind him, one of the sacks tumbled to the floor as the remaining bags shifted with the movement of the vessel. Its tied-off top came open and the brown-skinned potatoes spilled out of its captive confinement. In farcical reprieve, they rolled about the deck following the hapless tar, who had broken his fall and narrowly averted smashing into the iron barrel of the ornate cannon.

His mates to the rear of the deck laughed in humorous ridicule, mocking the misfortune of their peer. He cast them a damning gaze, before returning to his senses and finding no one to blame, but himself and the fickle motions of ship and sea.

Save for one step to the side, his headlong plunge would have profited him the Royal Crest, imprinted upon his forehead as he smashed against its raised design, atop the rear of the cannon's barrel.

Before, the ship righted from its sudden tilt to port, water found the gunports, now rushing beneath the waves. The partly submerged deck ran with the water, streaming atop its planks, before the ship came upright.

The water pooled, before finding the openings and cracks about the deck and seeking its way to the bilge, It ran down the interior, seeking out the lowest part of the ship, two decks below the waterline.

Our hull was a hollow framework. It was a unique and purpose-built design, answering the technological problem of its time; how to build a massive tiered warship, burdened with the weight of thousands of pounds of iron cannon and create a stable platform, that would not roll-over and capsize.

Past ship designs had tendered an almost primitive solution, though the deceptive ornamental exteriors, statuesque carvings, and the illusion of their sweeping lines and masts towering to the heights would suggest otherwise.

When viewed from the exterior, these ships with their tiered gun-decks appeared massive and solid behemoths.

In actuality, these vessels were little more, than giant floating platforms or glorified rafts, providing the massive deck space needed to float their colossal broadsides, but lacking speed and maneuverability.

Our ship's graceful lines and purposeful design were in stark contrast to these earliest designs, seeking to float towering monstrosities and broadsides of cannon, adrift upon the sea.

Those former elderly relics relied on hulls, whose bilges were nearly always filled with water, almost to the waterline, bordering its level outside. Some still served among our own fleet with Lord Nelson's heralded squadron.

Their buoyancy was ensured by their wooden construction and the hundreds of floating barrels packed beneath their lower deck, separating it from the waterlogged bilge. The buoyant barrels were netted together and forced their way under the bilge's water, two rows deep, sometimes more, their captured air pushing up in unison, against ship's weight.

The buoyant floatation of hundreds of trapped wooden barrels and casks created the lifting force, ensuring the vessel's weight was supported atop the water. And though the captive water of the bilge provided the ship with the stabilizing anchor, needed to keep the towering decks from rolling over in the heaviest of seas, without adding excessively to the depth of the vessel's hull, it cut down the ship's maneuverability and speed.

But, not so our prized HMS Vanguard. She was hollow and as buoyant as a cork, despite her massive size. Beneath, her upper, middle, and lower gun-decks, resided two more decks, secreted below the waterline with a bilge beneath the lowest for ballast and whatever seas might find their way inside our ship.

Her buoyancy and strength had created a massive vessel, willingly moved along by wind and current. Unlike the teetering and waterlogged giant floating rafts, masquerading as men-of-war, our ship was a true craft of the sea.

Her design combined the traits and features of a more maneuverable frigate or brigantine, though her sheer size still made her a difficult craft to maneuver with a maximum speed of only eight knots. But, the design was sound and a much better solution to the floating ornate rafts of the past.

HMS Vanguard was a formidable floating platform. She carried as many cannon as her designers could cram aboard her decks, matching and surpassing the ungainly galleons and men-of-war of the past.

The outside of the hull was plated in copper, as much, an attempt to strengthen the bottoms of such giant men-of-war, as to guard against the damage of an accidental grounding or an unexpected low tide.

But, in spite of the splendid magnificence of her design and structure, she was still an observant subject of Neptune's sea. Though slightly more maneuverable and able to out sail and tack, her more cumbersome opponents, she was still susceptible to the yawing uneasines of the rolling seas and oceans. This our spilled seaman would surely attest to.

I allowed the seaman to collect himself. I noted, he had miraculously escaped serious injury, his head just missing a headlong plunge, towards the cold iron of the stowed cannon. Only, his deft footing and the protective fold of his upthrust arms had saved him from certain peril.

As the ship rose, steading on her course, I released my hold on the beam, I stood aside and moved forward, having spied Ensign Higgins. It was with him, I would converse, informing him of the newest duties, directed by our captain.

As I approached, I noticed the sullenness with which, he went about his current undertakings. He did not share in the amusement of his men at their bedeviled and hapless colleague, still struggling to his feet and devoid of his sea-legs.

Like myself, Ensign Higgins had been made aware of our true destination. He wore the truth heavily across his brow. Like myself, he was untried in battle and no doubt fretted the encounter to come, along with dealing with his own doubts of how he might regale or disgrace himself in battle.

I spied the iron box, that had so fleetingly become the object of speculation and rumor among both officers and men. Its presence barely distracted me from my current duties and the heavy realities burdening my mind. Thoughts of our future sea battle seemed to dominate my every waking moment.

In the light of day, despite the battened gunports, I observed the details and craftsmanship adorning a portion of the iron container's cast lid. It meant nothing to me, at the time.

The design appeared more some artisan's whimsical intent to add some aesthetic flare or beauty to the metal box's ugly and ungainly coarse and porous surface. Its stylized markings meant nothing to me.

Though, among its many cast designs, some worn away or chipped off by the container's abusive handling and age, I thought I spied the raised surface of a cross, a simple design of two intersecting bars. One ran horizontal across its vertical mate, much like our Sovereign's own Cross of King George or the lofty relic, representative of the Church of England.

I would have not given the image a second thought, save for the small imperfection about its surface, that quietly suggested some blasphemy against God or church.

I would describe the image thus; among the raised surface was a depiction of a tiny cross, set in the center of two crossed horns or upright tusks. The tusks' tips pointed to an imaginary heaven, a field of whimsical stars and a crescent moon.

But, most disturbing among the image was a tiny bar, to the left of the small raised cross. It seemed like some ancient mathematician's sullied mark, negating the religious piety and mocking the reverence of the scared cross.

But, the box was old, its iron succumbing to the ravages of time. At best, its bulk and weight served us as added ballast, sheltered here in the bowels of the Vanguard.

Before, moving to my duties, my curious fingers lightly touched, its forbidden and alluring surface. They tested the seam, between lid and box, but found nary a gap among the well-crafted joint.

The tips of my fingers dug at what little lip the lid's rim presented. But, they found the container's cover unwilling to yield. I studied its surface as the men went about the final demands of their duties and my fellow officer's eyes noted my presence, for the first time.

The lid appeared locked. Yet, I could find no keyhole or even the makings of the hinges, that surely would have held such a heavy cover in place. From one end to the other, the box before me, was made of the coarse pitted iron denying access to the curious and hiding the mystery of the riddle hidden inside.

I turned away from the exotic oddity. There were tasks at hand to be accomplished as we continued preparations for war.

The tars had yet to be told of our true destination, though sailing any further south, would soon remove any doubt. Already, among those of the crew topside, guarded whispers had begun to spread the rumors of speculation, that something was amiss.

Only the strictest discipline and the threat of the lash kept the conjecture of their tongues within the confines of their small work details. But, soon, there'd be no doubt, that we sailed to join Lord Nelson's Squadron off the coast of Spain.

But for now, there were more pressing and distasteful matters at hand.

"Ensign Higgins," I interrupted the officer, more from his own brooding thoughts, than the count, he presumed to be taking among the goods stacked about.

He turned to face me as our ship continued its rolling progress south.

"Ensign Lewis," he returned, presenting the air of formality among the men.

"The captain has sent me to inquire upon your progress and to enlist the aid of your detachment in a new endeavor," I continued on.

"A new endeavor?" he questioned. "We've still to finish here."

"I fear you shall have to postpone these measures. The captain wishes our new undertaking to begin within the moment, in unison with those of the other hands on the decks above," I offered.

"Oh God," Ensign Higgins offered in mild resignation,

detesting the duty about to come. "It's those damn rats, isn't it? He wants us in the lower levels?"

He was well aware of my report to the captain of the affliction of our vessel. All now knew of the infested furry vermin hidden amongst our midst.

"We are the most junior officers aboard and the captain has decided ridding ourselves of these pests should be done, the sooner the better. The running of the ship has fallen into routine and now with the excitement of the harbor behind us, he believes, the appropriate time has come."

"And, us stuck down here on the lowest deck . . . the thought makes me shiver," Ensign Higgins returned, detesting the event about to occur.

"Not quite the lowest deck," I corrected, "there are two more, despite their cramped confines and low ceilings, below," I offered, sharing his disdain for the activity, soon to commence.

He and I would soon claim and divide those men upon our deck into two lots. Then, we would descend to the two lowest decks to ferret out the rodents, hidden in the labyrinth of its folds.

In unison, we would begin separating our own groups once more, upon one of the two decks below. With one group starting at the bow and the other from the stern of each, we would work our way towards each other in an attempt to beat the rodents from their hiding places.

The men would claim lengths of rope, pieces of board, or clubs, anything they chose to brandish, to beat along the deck or the secretive holds among which, the rodents might attempt to hide.

Walking in a line, they'd act as beaters on a hunt, driving the vermin from their hiding places and ahead of the two opposing groups of men. When they reached the center and the openings to the upper decks of our shared hold, the vermin would have no choice, but to remain and be clubbed to death or scurry up to the next deck.

The men were more accustomed to the drill, than Ensign

Higgins or myself, who would merely oversee their efforts. I suggested his men make fast the stores, they had already moved and leave the few other provisions and items for later, as the ship awaited for us to start this horrid business.

He agreed, though unenthusiastically and began to claim the upper of the two lower decks beneath us. He was intent on mustering eighteen men, enough to form two lines to cover the width of the ship, walking in a slightly dispersed and doubled line.

"I beg to disagree," I replied, "but, I favor the deck immediately below us."

"By what right, I claimed it first," Ensign Higgins protested, in disgruntled retort, "unless you would like to draw for it?".

"Sir," I mocked an authoritative tone, "I have no intention to draw for it. Gambling would set a bad example for our gathered crew. No, I claim the deck beneath us for myself, under the privilege of my rank."

"Your rank?" Ensign Higgins' words returned scornfully.

"Aye, sir," I returned stiffly, "I best you for command by a fortnight."

"Fourteen days, that's rot!" he exclaimed, in a disenchanted hiss, nearly audible to the tars behind him as he mused the dates of our varied commissions.

"No Ensign Higgins, that is my right and I choose to exercise it. I will claim the deck beneath this one, as soon, as one of the captain's officer's comes to relieve you of this one and you shall take up position with your men on the deck beneath me," I exercised my scant, though proper authority, to my fellow ensign's consternation.

No sooner, had our brief discussion concluded, then one of our senior lieutenants favored us with his presence. He was followed by another officer and a staunch gathering of tars, detailed to the lower gun-deck.

It was with deep embarrassment, that I was called to their presence along with Higgins. Both of us were ordered to descend to the lowest level of the ship.

I think our aloof lieutenants enjoyed the humiliation foisted upon me. I know they reveled in the disdain and dissatisfaction upon Ensign Higgins' youthful face. It was done.

We made our way down step or ladder, descending into the bowels of the ship, well aware, that as we moved, we crawled beneath the waterline of our mighty vessel.

I took a similar number of men, plus two extra hands for a total of twenty; whose misfortune it was to be seen by me as they loitered, atop the ladders, leading to our deck. After reaching the dark depths of our vessel the two groups dispersed and moved, one to the bow and one to the stern of the lowest level of the ship, just above our own bilge.

Our own bilge splashed about with some loose water, that had sought the openings of the ship or perhaps the worn gaps, between the pitch-chalked planks of our hull and gravitated below.

It was the source of the foul clinging dampness, that added to the stench of the ship and the smell of rot. But, our bilge was nothing like the generation of ships, that had preceded our own, though there were rows of wooden barrels bobbing about unseen, well below the waterline. Their presence was a testament to the slow changing minds of our shipwrights and the Admiralty, though their few barrels could scarcely keep our vessel afloat if our hull was breached by cannon or storm.

In a mirrored effort, both groups pushed their way, either forward or to the rear. The men gathered up this or that implement to beat about the planking or stowed items stacked about.

To a man, most favored the thick hemp rope, whose roughness and coarse-like fibers were like shards, held in their calloused hands. And, despite each length's thickness, each offered the flex and movement allowing its stinging hemp to lash into the narrow folds and burrows, a club's swinging movement would fail to thread.

With a nod or command by Ensign Higgins or myself the two groups began. The slapping of the thick cords of rope rose above the lapping of the water or the rush of our own ship's wake.

One man after the other took to the task with such relish and energy, that the din of their exertions soon filled the deck, assaulting the ears with their cruel whipping.

Like, the lower gun-deck, this lowest level of the ship was crowded with provisions and supplies spirited away in the depths of the ship's belly. It was not long, before the first of the small brown creatures was dislodged from its temporary home. It leapt from behind the stacked crates, that had sheltered it. Its long tail trailed behind, drawn out in a twisting line as the small mammal contorted about trying to find a new haven or asylum and escape the bloodthirsty line of beaters, approaching from behind.

But, its efforts were thwarted as it fell into confusion, finding a mirrored line of seamen ahead of it. It halted, frozen in confusion and fear.

Other rodents were driven from their hiding places and joined it in the open spaces of the deck.

Some of the beaters turned over the crates or stores lining the deck, while their mates stood ready with rope or club to slay any of the vile pests, that might be revealed.

The stench of droppings and rotting nests filled our noses as still more creatures, exposed and frightened, fled their uncovered havens. Nest after nest was exposed.

In panic, their denizens scurried away. Some dumbly tried to scale the near vertical beams, slightly slanted, as the ship continued to roll, only to drop down to the deck as the ship righted herself and they could no longer cling to the shear face of the escaping slope.

A few sought the nearest source of escape, a knothole or crack, that descended to the bilge. Some of the grotesque creatures dropped atop the hollow barrels, the floating ballast met to assure the buoyancy of the warship.

Others fell with an echoing splash of water as fate and chance conspired against them. They slipped through the narrow gaps of the barrels netted together below. As the barrels moved, ever so slightly with the movements of the ship, they were crushed between the gaps as they tried to slip through upon resurfacing.

Others would be trapped, beneath the bilge's waters, unable to penetrate the almost solid wall of barrels and casks, separating them from the surface as the ship continued to roll and trapped them from a life-giving gasp of air.

A few of the creatures succumbed to the well-aimed blows of a club or the lashing of a rope. The squeal of their tiny protestations and muted pleas filled the air in a sorrowful chorus. Their spoken and unspoken pleas fell upon unsympathetic ears.

A shrill cry from tiny frightened lungs marked the demise of one and then, another of their clan.

Not a single mate held back a blow or missed his mark. Instead, the incessant high-pitched squeaks and shrill squeals only seemed to enrage the beaters. Even the sight of the small creatures was apparition enough, to fill anyone witnessing the vile animals with revulsion.

One of the small creatures agilely reversed his course, snaking between the legs of the beater in front of me. With a swift kick of my foot, I sent him flying into the side of the hull.

A quick acting tar spun about and delivered the final blow with a splintered board. It crushed the ribs of the small animal, pressing the middle of the creature flat with the deck.

Its tiny paws flailed at the air. Its body and tail twitched in the horror of the final spasms of its agony. A second blow ceased its pain.

And so, the lines continued to move towards each other, the unnatural sound of the small creatures filling our ears as they were faced with capture and death in the center of our deck.

Ropes and clubs lashed out with the very real danger, that the men risked hitting their mates. In dumbfounded fear, some of the tiny animals froze, making easy targets of themselves. But, the more hearty and stronger among them continued their flight.

They raced for the steps and ladders leading to the next deck above.

But, unknown to them, they rose into the turmoil of the next deck's clearing parties. The men moved from bow or stern, ridding their own deck of the vermin, only to have more of the small creatures surface before their path. Their diminutive forms were dwarfed by the armed men above.

They scurried about only to roll among themselves in one massed ball of moving rancid fur. The sight was sickening, a moving wall of pestilence.

But, the beaters continued. Their ropes and clubs added to the unholy din, joined by the pleading chorus of small creatures seeking man's mercy.

But, there was none.

I remained below, until nearly the last of the rodents on our deck had succumbed. Then, I made my way to the deck above.

The sight on that deck was appalling. The pristine decks of our warship, were cluttered with the carcasses. They were littered with the remains of the dirty brown rodents or stained with the vile contents of their insides or blood.

Here and there, several tars continued going about the gruesome task of ending the life of this injured creature or that. But, the deck was nearly a mirror image of our own. The battle was nearly over. Any survivors had fled to the next deck above. They had scaled the ropes leading there or jumped the rungs of a ladder or the steps of the large double stairs, leading between the holds.

I continued through the other decks, intent on emerging topside to be greeted by the light of an otherwise serene afternoon, marred by the flurry of our grotesque activity. Uniformed men had lowered themselves to act as butchers, chasing about the scurrying tiny pests. The rout of the rodents was joined by the calliope of the shrill din of gulls, that circled about our masts.

The birds spread their wings wide, floating listlessly above. Somehow, their instinct or senses knew what was about. They watched patiently as our crew went about its bloody butchery.

A few of the rats proved quite nimble and despite the formidable bulk and strength of the lines of men awaiting them, they snaked through feet or legs and sought an illusive sanctuary. It escaped them.

They were soon cornered and dispatched to the howling

triumph of men, who had turned the folly of the small creatures into a sporting contest, twisted by its own gruesomeness and barbarity.

Even several members of our Marine contingent, resplendent in their bright red and white uniforms, joined in the fray to the consternation of their sergeants.

One committed the God-awful offense of clubbing one of the scurrying rodents with the polished brass buttplate of his rifle, slaying the rodent and dispatching a sizeable chip from the weathered plank of the deck.

But, such indiscretions were ignored. Ridding our vessel of the blight of the infestation was the order of the moment.

And, soon our victory was at hand. The small band of remaining rodents seemed to realize the folly of their inescapable situation. The moving brown wall, bedecking the planks, began to separate.

No longer content to remain as one, it burst forth in a flurry of motion. The creatures, most of them tiny, though some were ungainly large from undoubtedly raiding the plentiful bounty of our stores, tried to flee. They radiated out in all directions of the compass.

Some rats scurried for the rails, darting about their ornate trim, balanced three-stories above the water on one side, the other side lined with tars or marines, brandishing rope or weapon as they thrust a blow their way.

Several, of the creatures were merely stunned, lashed off their precarious perches. They fell into the sea, washed away by the waves or swallowed beneath to a cold and lonely grave.

Others made for the bowsprit, instinctively seeking its isolation, far out above the water along its wooden spar. But, other beaters were already there, contesting the creatures, who faced either death by clubbing or being forced over the side.

The hapless creatures hearts must have been filled with more fear, than they could stomach. In either fear or resignation, if their tiny minds could fathom either, they simply leapt overboard into the churning waters below.

Their tiny forms bobbed about the water. They were dragged under, only to reappear, then be dunked again, trapped within our ship's moving wake. Others simply disappeared, their presence aboard a memory as if they'd never been.

A few resilient creatures made for the ratlings and ropes, leading to the masts above. But, their tiny paws could scarcely out race the swinging clubs and ropes seeking them out. Some were returned to deck as a tar's blow knocked them free of their low ascending perch.

Other tars delivered the final blow, ending the withering creatures' agony and life.

And then, it was over.

To the rear of our wake, the white shapes of the gulls hovered over the water. A few birds dove down upon the hapless rodents, struggling to stay afloat. Mercifully, though in an act of vicious cruelty, one gull after another ended the misery and suffering of the small mammals still afloat and far from land.

They dove and pecked at the waterlogged forms, dispatching them to the depths as they tore and pecked a piece of flesh or the prized treat of an eye. Their shrill calls were a morbid death song as they went about the welcome feast.

A few birds lingered aside the masts, even setting down, to await the corpses of the vermin crushed along the deck. But they failed to approach.

The deck was filled with the inane shouts or bellowing taunts and curses of men, who had succumbed to animalistic butchery, more beholden to some tribal clan of savages.

Only when the movement of the small creatures halted did their own actions cease.

There was silence. It filled the deck above and descended down into the bowels of the ship. The eyes of officers and crew alike fell upon the remains littering our great ship.

The silence was born as much out of the sight of the small creatures, detestable as they were, as the sudden realization of the relish all had descended to, making sport of ridding ourselves of the vermin.

For all the pomp and ceremony of our departure or the regalia and ornamentation of our ship and uniforms, we had descended into the lowliness of the creatures, we sought to rid ourselves of.

A few faces among us harbored a look of shame, upon reflecting on the frail little corpses, they had abetted the demise of. Just being an accomplice to the act had soured my own disposition.

But, the act was a matter of necessity, ensuring the good hygiene and morale of our ship's company. It was a loathsome affair, but one that had to be undertaken, ridding our vessel of this typical, yet unwelcomed bane.

A few among the crew threw out this comment or that, seeking to replace the ungodly still silence with mirth and laughter, driving away the distaste of the sight filling their eyes.

The rats harbored and spread disease. Two stricken crewman below attested to that. Regardless, if we are all God's creatures and they too share God's good auspices of creation, they were still a blight.

But, one could not help harbor some slight sad emotion, raised by the sight of the helpless survivors of their pack. They lingered in their small pitiful agony, slowly succumbing to death.

One could not help but wonder, how slow and cruel death would come to those treading the waters behind us, so far from land with no hope of reaching it, no matter how desperately they paddled about, should they survive the onslaught of the gulls.

But, we fell back to order. The affair had created a new host of chores. The men, who had acted as beaters and slayers now turned to the grisly business of cleaning the ship.

Buckets of water splashed about the deck. Brushes and soap were brought out and holystones worked about. All evidence of what had transpired disappeared. Willing arms and backs set about the business of restoring the decks to cleanliness.

The small carcasses disappeared over the side, meals for the unseen denizens of the deep, a free dinner for Neptune's court. Cleanliness and order would be restored.

And, the men would sleep well in their hammocks, content,

that there would be no nocturnal visitations to either the ship's stores of flour, fruit, and meat or even their own flesh. At least half of our ship's compliment would enjoy the luxury of slumber.

Outfitted for war and bearing nearly a full crews' compliment, there was scarcely enough space, save for half our tars, to string up their hammocks or ferret out some corner about the ship. With nearly 821 souls aboard our vessel the crew had taken to eating and sleeping in shifts.

While half the men stood their watch the other half fell below. They attended to themselves and their personal distractions or went to rest in the comforting folds of their strung hammocks.

Then, at the hour of their own shift, they headed topside, attending to the never-ending toil, that kept our massive warship sailing, while those relieved, returned to the interior of our damp and dank vessel. These then claimed their turn in the hammocks, little more, than a discomforting fourteen inches wide.

I took a place at the rail as the ship drove forward, under a strong wind. The bow slapped the cresting waves as the sails above flapped and cracked with the running wind.

I calmed my stomach, still finding the whole matter quite detestable. I distracted myself with the vision of the French coastline, a distant specter, hidden in a light and illusive haze.

It was as I idled beside the rail that I thought of the seaman, lost in the darkness of the early morning. His passing was but hours ago, yet, it seemed like his death had passed into obscurity, fogged in the recesses of my thoughts.

Only the grimness of the bloodstained decks, now being cleansed of their foul harvest, had raised his memory. Perhaps, it was nothing more, than my lack of sleep.

Fatigue and long hours were prone to bedevil the mind. Long hours at watch and the tasks of the day could easily befoul one's thoughts, attaching too much emotion and significance to trivial matters, while at the same time, attaching too little thought and priority to the matters, that rightfully vied for one's attention.

Misjudgment and apprehension were the products of a tired mind and a weary body. Yet, now I saw the vision of our departed seaman. It was nearly as real as the first moment, I came upon his crumpled form.

The coastline my eyes stared ahead at unseeingly had been replaced by his still pale body, devoid of life and shrouded in a deathly pale pallor. I was bewildered, that I had not investigated further to find the cause or source of the man's death.

It was as if some untold spirit bid me, silently or unconsciously, to ignore the event or to place it to the back of my thoughts as if a dream, upon a fitful slumber, that was to be quickly forgotten.

And yet, I recalled the moment vividly with a clarity, that haunted my mind. By force of reason, I tried to force thoughts of his death away.

The seaman's death was an act of folly brought about by his own intoxicated state. Why should I look for some interceding hand, that had taken part in his demise, when the truth of the matter lay rightly, in the fact, that he had probably claimed his own life.

There was little doubt, he had climbed the ratlings seeking the purchase offered by the lofty masts in his bewildered and drunken merriment. He had simply forgotten himself and his place, perched so high and precariously among the lofts, only riggers and gulls dared to tread.

And, in his drunken rashness, he had fallen. A misplaced foot or a failed handhold, it did not matter. What folly and madness had enveloped him was unimportant, the end was the same. He was dead by his own accord and foolishness.

But, in silent shame, I admitted, I had found more compassion for the forlorn death of these rodents, than I had held in my heart for a fellow sailor. Until this moment, his passage beyond had been cloaked from my thoughts. It was as if it had never happened.

Only the violence and barbaric glee of the rejoicing tars, ridding our ship of infestation, had returned his memory to me. But, death at sea was not uncommon. A warship was a dangerous business even when not engaged in combat.

The towering peaks presented by our masts, the threat of storms, and unseasonable weather, or even the deadly nature of our ship-borne artillery invited disaster to the lax or reckless alike.

A fall from the ratlings or being washed overboard awaited the careless or distracted. And even, though our armories and foundries boasted the best workmanship of the day, our cannon were not devoid of hazard.

Too much powder or a worn and pitted barrel could spell disaster. Instead of sending ball or shot at the enemy an abused gun could explode in the hands of her crew. It was a dangerous business, we were embarked on, sitting atop a slow moving platform, which was loaded with powder and shot as we sought out battle.

I shook the thoughts of this morning away and counted myself lucky, that the unsightly task of ridding our ship of the rodents had nearly concluded, except for the cleaning of the decks and the removal of their last remnants. Their broken and dying population littered our decks.

I swallowed a breath of the salty air, already laced with the lingering chill of the evening to come. Several soft clouds billowed along the horizon. They passively intoned me, to forget the unpleasant start of our journey.

But, even as I left the upper deck and began the return to the junior officers' quarters, on the second deck, I superstitiously wondered, what omen the tar's earlier death and this ungodly infestation might portend.

A bucket's contents splashed along the deck, followed by the kneeling form of a seaman, brush in hand. He set to vigorously rubbing away the stain on the planks before him.

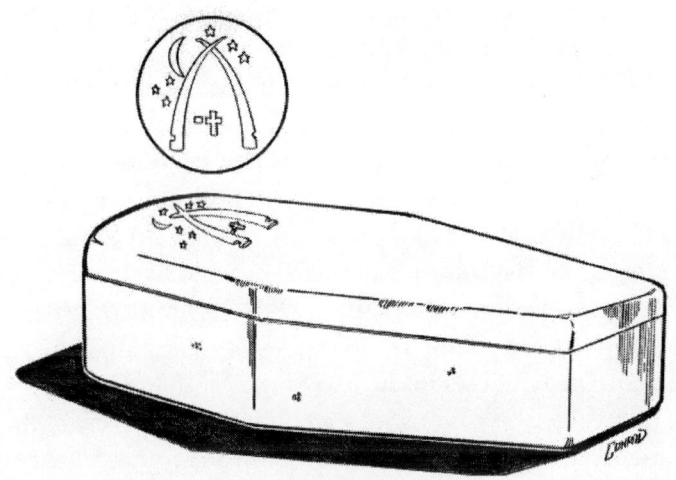

The mysterious iron box.

CHAPTER 7

Evening

HMS Vanguard
Sailing off the Coast of Southern France
Day 2-Early Evening

As was our captain's custom, the officer's joined him for our evening meal. The seamen acted as stewards. They had already transformed his cabin into the likeness of a spacious dining hall. Save for the low ceiling of the captain's quarters and the creaking of the ceiling from the footsteps of the watch standing duty above, we dined with an air of formality more accustomed to land.

Our dining table was a chart table, repositioned in the center of the cabin and serving as the platform for our banquet. Unlike, the tin cups and square wooden plates of the crew, we supped off fine china and had adequate tableware, fine silver borrowed at our captain's bequest from his doting and loving wife, wishing him some modicum of civility at sea.

A heavy wooden sea-chest with felt lined dividers housed the fine imported crystal, blown and hand spun by the artisans of Venice. Silver candlesticks and a fine linen tablecloth along with napkins completed the trappings of our posh and stately dining.

The only evidence to the uninitiated, that our formal repast was at sea, was the lantern hanging above and dangling with the swaying movements of sea and ship or the glimmering waves of the ocean's surface, framed in the background, through the panes of the ornate windows to the rear of the cabin.

Our diner was quite a formal affair. Officers were required to attend in full dress uniform, less swords, unless otherwise informed of more casual attire. But, the meal was much more, than the shared partaking of food.

Each shared meal promised to be a welcome feast, compared to the fare of our crew. Fire was a dreaded hazard aboard our wooden craft. There were few areas, that had been constructed and purpose-built to hold the fuels, that might release the warming flames to heat the contents of a pot or pan.

Even smoking was forbidden, leaving the tars to chew tobacco, such was the fear of fire aboard our crowded warship, laced with black powder along nearly every deck.

In resignation to their lowly fate, the majority of our crew ate their meals cold. Biscuits and cold salted or smoked meat or fish were their staple. All was eaten off the square wooden dishes, jokingly and sarcastically regarded by the men as a "square meal." Even a warm bowl, of the coarse mush, that passed as oatmeal, was a delight to their deprived tongues.

And sometimes, they were treated to the warmth of a cup of coffee, if that foul substitute masquerading for the rich aroma-filled beans could be called such. Their brew was nothing more, than hot water, that had boiled the burnt pieces of bread tossed into it. A foul and watery brew, it was heavily sweetened with sugar to the tars' tastes. Of it, I can say only, that it took the dampness out of their lives, but for only a moment.

The cabin's seating offered the pretense of formality. The captain was seated at the head of our table and the ship's second officer, upon his right. In due order, officers were seated along either side in order of their descending rank.

I sat across from Ensign Higgins. Both of us sat at the far end of the table with our ship's surgeon, the closest member of our ship's complement bearing the limbo-like stature of neither civilian nor combatant, seated at the end of the table, opposite our hallowed captain.

Captain Shefferd took the opportunity of our gathered presence to inquire into each man's progress. He questioned us, noting the status and completion of our assigned tasks and duties, albeit informally and with no intent to judge or decry our actions.

It was a gathering of the ship's officers, more in accord with the gathering of a family, than any pompous or contemptuous display of class or position. The master of the ship sought to know us and thus, gain our trust and respect. And, to a man we commended him for this civility, which gained him our loyalty.

And, in this hallowed exclusive group, he sought out our difficulties and problems. But, he did this not in judgment of our own faults or shortcomings, but as a mentor availing us of his experience and advice.

In this manner, our small band of officers became as brothers, not seeking to compete against each other, but working with our captain for the common good and welfare of both our men and ship. For many a time, did our master intone us, that without our tars and their loyalty and allegiance, our ship was nothing more, than the beams and iron of her framework and cannon.

Wood and iron were worthless of themselves. Only when welded with the will of the flesh did they make our vessel a warship.

The meal started pleasantly enough with the captain sharing a bottle from his private reserves with us. The generous act was his custom. The red wine was a notably sweet and full bodied port, whose liquid glistened against the candlelight with the deep burgundy richness, that came with the bottle's guarded aging.

As was our custom, we partook of the airs of civility. Some used the occasion to practice their manners and good breeding. French and Spanish tongues could be found wagging at our table as several of our more aristocratic officers sought to show off their education and worldly knowledge. I myself had to confess, I offered some knowledge and sampling of the Spanish language, though slight.

But, for the most part the demeanor was cloaked in good comradeship and a closeness, that I had rarely found, except among my own family.

The cabinboy assisted by several tars, clad as stewards, dished out proper servings of the soup, run up from the galley. Tonight would be a feast as was the standard of many sea journey's, when early out at sea, the perishable provisions were still quite ample and fresh.

We made the most of our abundance, knowing full well, the return leg of our voyage home would be dependent on the salted and smoked meats and whatever store of flour remained unspoiled by the salt water and dampness or the bugs and maggots, that would seek out our rations.

But, tonight was filled with rejoicing and the proud boastfulness of men determined to render service to the King and their chosen profession. Together, in camaraderie, we relished our eventual arrival at our destination, proud to sail under the banner of King George.

The glum and doubt, that some among us had shown earlier, upon learning our true destination, was lost in the support of our joined camaraderie. We sailed into battle, not alone, but as a ship's company.

It soon, became apparent to even the youngest and most untried among us, that we would not falter. False hopes and thoughts of valor and heroism were lost as we sat together in the mentoring presence of our tutoring master. We knew we would not fail or run from duty, no matter how perilous or distasteful.

The truth of the matter was clear to all. No man could flee the side of his brother officer, seated beside him. We were pledged to each other, our duty owed to each other. We were friends and comrades and we depended upon each other.

No man would shirk his duty and risk another to die in his place or await harm to befall his peer. Far more, than shame and dishonor, the force driving us to serve each other and our ship was the simple fact, that we knew each other well and were friends, a close-knit and reliant group.

Our captain only had to ask and we obeyed, such was our loyalty to him and our confidence in the good graces and judgment, his rank had continuously exhibited.

We greedily finished the first course of our meal, a hearty vegetable soup, more stew, than broth. The soup along with the comforting sips from our glasses of port warmed the belly and took away the chill and dampness, that were so customary to craft like our own.

During the day, even early fall, the decks took on the heat and warmth of the sun, drying out our canvas and men alike. But, with nightfall, the surface of the sea cooled quickly and the haunting drafts of cool air, soon found their way into the depths of our hull.

Not even, the warmth of a wool blanket could fend off the lingering dampness and the odor of wet and rotting timbers. Being afloat during the fall or winter was the most dreadful duty, I could have imagined. Several small stoves below decks or the open fires, contained in iron containers, above deck, offered the only reprieve to a man's freezing discomfort, save his winter uniform and blanket.

Sickness spread quickly about a ship's closed confines, forcing the conduct of war and strategy to bend to the dictates of warmer weather and a heartier climate, such as blessed us this day.

I barely paid attention to the ramblings of the others. As first, one officer and then, the next felt it was his stead to come forward in the conversation, invited by our captain. They added this or that triviality or some humorous comment making light of the eviction of our small furry residents.

A few expressed the proper and supportive comments

affirming their belief in England's domination of the seas. Or, they speculated on the prospects of the forthcoming battle.

Quite unaware, the table fell silent, while I chewed a morsel absentmindedly from among the contents of my soup.

"And, what of you, Ensign Lewis?" Captain Shefferd's almost fatherly voice inquired.

"Sir?" I responded, slightly embarrassed at my own lack of attention.

"What does our other ensign have to say of our departure?" the captain asked, before spooning another measure from his own bowl into his mouth and awaiting my reply.

I was at a loss to comment. I agreed with the patriotic reply, previously given. But, I did not want to appear the mindless boor by repeating it or even expressing my agreement. Instead, I sought to change the topic of our conversation. The subject of war and our own upcoming battle, already seemed to weigh depressingly heavy among all present.

I answered thusly, "Pardon my curiosity," I begged the captain's patience, before beginning, "but, I wonder if we are to be allowed some insight into the unusual cargo, we are carrying?"

The captain chewed and swallowed, before raising his eyes to meet my own questioning orbs.

Many of the others present raised their eyes at my impertinence, daring to question the captain on such a trivial matter. Our good ship's surgeon was not among them.

He continued supping on his thick broth, exhibiting an indifference to nearly all matters discussed at the table, even though, the point I raised appeared to have little to do with anything of a naval nature.

"And, what cargo does our young ensign refer to? The last I looked among the list of inventories, loaded at Portsmouth, I could scarcely recall one item from the other. I dare say, we have enough provisions to feed two small villages for months and enough powder and weapons to keep one of the King's regiments in the field for nearly four times as long."

The captain offered his words in friendly mirth, describing

the unfathomable stores, that were needed to put our ship to sea and make her the formidable warship, she was.

His words were greeted to comradely laughter and amusement, before I interrupted and asserted my own voice, politely above the group.

"Sir, I refer to the large iron box, stowed in the stern of the lower deck. I observed it being loaded, before we sailed and again today, as I made by way to join Ensign Higgins," I returned, seeing my fellow ensign avert his eyes and lower his head towards the table, unwilling to support my introduction of the oddity below decks into the conversation.

"And, why does this strange container hold such fascination for you," the captain questioned me.

I found myself at a loss to answer, when the truth was nothing more, than the fact, that it was locked and its contents eluded my inspection. I faltered for a thought or words, that would avail me of a response, more reserved and respectable, than just a mere child's curiosity.

"I spied its cover and several curious markings, crude art actually, cast atop its lid," I feinted an interest in the craftsmanship of the container, rather than its locked and hidden contents.

"So, our young ensign is a connoisseur of the arts," he remarked, expressing exaggerated dismay and wonder at the discovery.

"I've not seen this container, that's so peaked your curiosity, nor its crude artwork. But, I dare surmise, that like most of the crew, who have already seen it and have filled the corners of our ship with rumors of its contents, our young ensign is more curious of what secrets it holds, than any crafted depictions of the artisan, who crafted it. Would I be correct?" the captain replied, seeing through my deception with fatherly wisdom and insight.

"Aye, Captain," I returned, an embarrassed grin upon my lips.

Those seated around our improvised table broke into laughter at my subterfuge being so readily transparent.

"Not to worry, ensign," the captain began, turning his head

to ensure, that the stewards, who had served the first course of our meal, had left the cabin.

In the safety of our privacy, he continued, "I've not seen this strange vessel the crew and even my young officers seem so interested in. But, I assure you, it has nothing to do with the plans and orders we sail under. Nor, does it contain some brave new weapon or mechanization, developed by the fanciful minds of Britain's inventors or scientists."

"I am afraid, gentlemen," the captain dismissed the object, secreted below decks, "that, the upcoming battle will find us left to our own devices and the readiness of our crew."

"I hope to provide them with the space of two weeks time, during which we will prepare them and ourselves for the coming conflict," he continued. "I cannot stress the importance of our own self-reliance and the required proficiency of both men and weapons."

The captain partook of a healthy sip of port, washing away his distaste for the event awaiting us.

"We . . . you will be faced with a most unpleasant business. Some of you have seen conflict, though by your records and past histories, I know of none of you, who has been part to a major engagement. And, this is what we will be facing."

"Upon last report, I have learned from the Admiralty, through our spies and sympathizers in Spain, that the French fleet sits in the shelter of the Spanish harbor of Cadiz. A count of ships favors the French, who generously outnumber us," he added.

"And, worse I fear, there is a threat, that their Spanish allies might abet any attempt of the French fleet to sortie from the harbor. If the Spanish galleons join the French, Lord Nelson, despite his keen tactical skills and strategies will be hard-pressed to wrest victory from defeat. That is why we and several more British vessels, leaving from different harbors and points of the compass, are sailing to join Nelson's squadron, though the Admiralty frets, whether we will be in time."

The table fell silent. The lightness, I had hoped to interject into the conversation had escaped all. Even my own shame and embarrassment had receded into insignificance.

"I have been informed, that the French Admiral Villeneuve is in command, of the combined French and Spanish fleets. Our main advantage is, that he seems a timid man, more want and intent on living and enjoying the luxuries of his rank and status, than in contesting our heralded Lord Nelson for any sea lane or coast."

"It is his hesitation, contrasted to Lord Nelson's own boldness, that may save the day for us, unless the conflict falls to a contest of attrition, matching cannon for cannon and man for man. But, wars are never so obliging and succinct. They ignore the plottings of mathematicians and the science of numbers," the captain added, resting his ornate spoon beside the fine plate, his empty soup bowl sat atop.

"No, gentleman. Wars are won by cunning and tenacity. They are won by "will and fight." Mark those two words. The man, who will not accept defeat and refuses to let his foe beat him, despite the odds . . . if it is in his heart to win, fate and luck are often apt to reward him with victory."

"And, to that end, we shall prepare both ourselves and our men. I will expect nothing less from them. And, I will tolerate nothing less from you. We will enter battle as one. Ship, cannon, and men will be a single entity. All will share the common will to win," he paused.

"Am I understood on this matter?" he said, with a solemn voice expressing the gravity of our shared future.

"Aye!" answered one and then, another of the officers.

"No less!" responded another.

"Together, for King and Country!" came the proud retort of the captain's second in command.

"Victory!" exclaimed another, replying innocently enough, but invoking the name, dually tasked with that of success and of Lord Nelson's flagship.

"To HMS Vanguard and her crew," I exhaled the pride of my lungs, raising my half-filled crystal of port.

"Hear, hear!" proclaimed the captain, "to our glorious ship, then!" he raised his glass as did all.

We toasted our warship and our boisterousness and yet, unsecured success.

"Now, enjoy this evening. When tomorrow comes, there will be no laxity or rest. We'll press the routine of the drill, until I am assured everyone knows his duty and the ship is ready for combat. We've two weeks or perhaps, less if this favorable wind stays at our backs. But, we will be ready."

"And, as unpleasant as it might be, there will be no sparing of the lash. But, it will only be used, where there is plentiful or obvious evidence of a transgression. Those who've served with me, know I render its bite sparingly. It is one thing to instill discipline, but quite another to play the tyrant. But, we've no time to coax or cajole any sluggards among the ship's company. Though, I will be disappointed to find any about our ranks"

"If they'll not obey out of a sense of duty and honor, than by God, they will do so out of fear of me and the punishment, my authority can mete out. All I ask, is that punishment be dwelled out with justice and fairness. I detest officer's, who arbitrably resort to discipline and chastisement. Remember that."

"Discipline is one thing, but having a man's loyalty is the most powerful motivator, especially in our shared endeavor."

And, with those final words, our conversation fell away.

A warning knock, of a steward's knuckles upon the cabin door, alerted us to the arriving main course of our meal. I swore I smelled the aroma of roasted beef and potatoes, heavily seasoned and spiced, before the door opened wide and the tray, it sat upon, was delivered to the head of the table.

Our captain examined the fare approvingly, offering his compliments to the cook, spirited away in the galley, as he speared several petite and flavored roasted potatoes, bordering the sliced beef and lining the large serving tray.

I ate heartily, the long hours of my earlier watch and the tasks of the day fueling my appetite.

As I sliced the spiced beef into mouth-sized bites, fork held properly in my left hand, while firmly running the blade of my silverware's knife through its soft roasted juicy meat, the surgeon's voice vied for the attention of the captain.

Quite matter-of-factly, he requested one of the officers present, accompany him on his evening rounds aboard ship.

Before, assigning one of us, the captain wisely requested the nature of the reason for the escort.

The surgeon did not raise his eyes as he continued partaking of his meal. I and several other occupants of the cabin viewed his indifference as a slight, a gross sample of disrespect. But, the captain, by his response and manner, did not acquiescence our view.

Our master had long ago noted the indifference and disregard of our surgeon for the trappings of military pomp and ostentatious displays of rank. To the good doctor all men were as one, despite the epaulets, ribbons, and braids, they might wear about their uniform or the crests and plumage adorning their hats or headgear.

A man was nothing more, than the summation of his parts, a complex creature of limbs and bones along with organs and muscles, covered by flesh and subject to the dictates of nature and the abuse of man.

As I masticated upon a mouthful of beef and potatoes, the doctor explained he wanted to attend to the two men, examined earlier and confined to their hammocks, away from the other crewmen.

He decried, that he desired an escort, if only to send back word to the captain, using the officer as a runner and relaying the latest status of the two afflicted men. Or, in a worse case, the officer would aid him in administering to the tars.

The captain seemed surprised by the request as did I and the rest of those gathered. With the eviction of the rodents, what more cause or spread of affliction or disease could there be?

All expected a speedy recovery.

The request was granted, the captain bidding the surgeon to enlist the officer of his choosing. As always, the doctor chose among the lowest ranking officers, not wishing to test the patience of the more senior members of our body.

With a look to Higgins and myself, he made what I considered an arbitrary selection or perhaps, one made out of spite. I recalled, it was my request, earlier this morning, that had roused the good doctor from his slumber, beckoning him to give his judgment over the corpse, that had fallen upon deck, even though, I well knew the tar was dead.

So, this was to be the doctor's comeuppance, now keeping me from retiring early, after our splendid shared supper and the heavy onus of drills and duties awaiting me, upon the morrow.

I sat resigned to the extra and, as I thought then, uncalled for duty.

I ate my fill. But, the meal no longer held the same relish and taste, its flavors had possessed, when I had started it.

The surgeon availed himself of another full glass of port, the move befalling the disapproving glances of several of the senior officers. But, the captain did not deny our doctor. Instead, he ordered one of the stewards to bring forth another bottle from a cabinet, he had unlocked for this occasion.

The cork was pulled and his own glass topped full, before the steward made the rounds about the table, amply filling each officers' glass.

His service done, the nearly empty bottle was placed on the table, joining that already emptied by our surgeon.

As I had said earlier, our captain tolerated our doctor's weakness. It was a vice, engaged in after having endured much, witnessing the brutality and grotesqueness of battle and the suffering of the frailty of men's bodies.

The doctor had his demons, who even in his waking hours, kept recalling the past and the horrors of war. He had his fill of noble causes and the grandness of nations testing each other's wills and military strength.

I broke off a piece of freshly baked bread and continued my meal, detesting having to be in the presence of the afflicted later and on so full a stomach.

CHAPTER 8

Sickness

HMS Vanguard
Sailing off the Coast of Southern France
Day 2-Night

Our dinner concluded late. The captain had desired to share our company for the evening. And, with our stomachs content and sharing the warmth and good nature of the port, that had encompassed all seated at the table, we found the delaying invitation to remain a welcome repose.

It was probably, because of the battle to come, that our captain lowered the invisible, yet befitting wall his rank provided, seeking more, than ever before, to truly come to know his men. Perhaps, it was a sign of resignation.

He was a veteran of several major engagements, one of which I had been told, he had nearly lost all in. I had never seen the scars of that battle, but rumor and gossip spun a bold tale of a horrendous wound, that had nearly taken his life.

And yet, in spite of that wound, he was reported to have stood his ground, refusing to relinquish the deck to his second as he ordered his ship about. It was claimed two men replaced the slain helmsman, before they too succumbed to the deadly broadside of the 64-gun French frigate engaging his own brig.

Though his smaller ship was almost devastated by the Frenchmen's larger number of cannon, Captain Shefferd continued to fight, refusing to surrender.

Some say, those that served with him, that day, witnessed a madman. He was incensed, God's good senses having abandoned him, replaced only by a lust to dole out, that which was meted to him and his ship.

By some strange fluke, the Frenchie's broadside missed, most of its shot and chain firing into the water, its helmsman had misjudged the frigate's approach and she listed heavily to the side, her guns pointing into the water and not the smashed hull of the brig, Shefferd commanded.

Luck or tenacity, depending upon the teller of the tale, conspired to open the side of the French frigate up to the bombarding broadside of Shefferd's brig.

The skill of English gunners prevailed as the broadside found prized targets. The French ship's powder was set afire and a quickly following secondary explosion ripped upward through her decks and down through her hull.

Another cannon, loaded with "chain shot," found the multi-headed snake of the French ship's commander and attending officers. The heavy chain and shot, designed to tear down masts and splinter the heaviest of spars, cleaved brutally through flesh.

The tale I heard, envisioned the French captain's torso cut away and its remains dragged into the deep as the wicked links of this deadly "angel" wrapped about him. It was a damning embrace carrying him to the depths.

But, such tales are the yarns spouted from the bottoms of tankards of ale. Whatever transpired, it must have been an unspeakable horror. For, as veterans are prone to do, the captain and several of the crew, that had served that day with him, never spoke of the matter, nor the losses of their shipmates.

A silent reverence permeated that day, much like the silence, that ended our supper.

I believe, it was the captain's own way of celebrating our comradeship and silently noting, that many of us in that shared cabin might not be returning to our beloved England. It was a moment of reflection for those present and was meant to cherish the friendship and common bond, making us one with sea and ship.

It was the doctor, who left first. I excused myself to the good graces of the captain and my fellows. I dutifully followed the surgeon in tow, regretting the loss of not being allowed the luxury of staying as the captain's own hand. withdrew a bottle of prized brandy, but only upon the surgeon's exit.

I had duties to attend to, even if they were those of being a nursemaid.

The doctor and I approached a wall of strung-up blankets, procured from the ship's stores. The doctor had taken the precaution of moving the two ill sailors away from their mates, secreting them away in the bow of the ship on the lower gun-deck, away from their normal station, about the middle gun-deck.

Their hammock's were strung about, the massive beams, shoring up the bulk of our ship's thick prow. They were far forward of the other crewmen, sharing this deck, though most had been relegated to the upper decks, offering the almost exclusive privacy of this level for our charges and the stores cramming nearly every available space, that would not impede the operation of the cannon.

In truth, if we engaged in battle, this would be one of the safest points about our warship, save for the two decks further below. True, the waterline of any warship was always considered a viable target, but more so, were her masts, sails, and rudder the sole means of her locomotion and maneuvering.

There was a greater amount of safety in the lower bowels of the ship, free of the threat of splintering masts and the raking fire massed against an open deck.

Below, the massive oak beams were thick enough to withstand even the most savage bombardment, that cannon could throw against them. And, adding to their strength was the fact, that the shipwright's, in their haste to build the Vanguard, had been forced to use green wood in her some of her construction, when suitable and apt aged lumber and beams were found lacking to complete her mammoth design.

And, burrowed deep within the depths of the lower deck, there'd be less discomfort and exaggeration from the rolling movements of the ship.

The threat of war with France had sent the woodwrights and carpenters into the King's own forests with special dispensation, allowing them and their laborers to harvest, what mighty towering oaks, whose girth and bulk matched their needs and was required to speed our good ship's construction.

I held the lantern high in my right hand. The doctor walked slightly ahead, surgeon's bag in his hand.

Like the stern behind us, an empty space was laden with this or that sack or crate, a plethora of provisions and armaments as well as the daily necessities, of our life at sea.

The corridoned off hammocks were silent, engulfed in the darkness of the night claiming our ship, except for several lanterns, unsuccessfully lighting the blackness behind us and marking ladders and steps to the upper decks.

The surgeon pulled aside the blankets, creating a path to our two afflicted tars. I pressed forward, holding the lantern aloft as I thrust it forward.

Its glow magnified the paleness of the surgeon's wards. I found it a gawdawful pallor, quite disagreeable with the contents, of my full stomach, which set about churning at the sight.

There was no question of the sickness, that had stricken these two tars. There was no malingering hand to be found here. Before, one thinks ill of me or my aversion to this sickness claiming these members of our crew, I remind all, that disease was probably the worse bane, that plagued our ships.

Disease and plague were feared by every sailor, despite his

courage in battle or own prowess and strength. The sickness of disease could lay a healthy tar down against the deck as readily as any cannon or musket. True, any man of sense, feared the dread claim, that battle could take as he risked his life with those of his mates.

But, sickness came quietly and suddenly. It crept aboard with disregard of rank, status, or position striking the lowliest among us to the proudest and most dignified among our officers. For every ten men killed in battle, I could show you four-hundred, who had died of some disease.

Aboard the crowded and uncleanly confines of our vessel sickness could spread rapidly, quickly risking incapacitating the mightiest of warships by laying waste the health of her crew. Worse, unlike the French and Spanish foes, we could not see this dreaded foe to sail clear and circumvent it.

Once, it found us, it would bedevil us. The only cure was quarantine and isolation. It was a cruel and cold response, to an uninitiated outsider.

I stood my place, desiring not to go any further. But, our doctor took my arm, holding the extended lantern. His movement was so forceful, that it set the light swaying about, its flickering candle threatening to extinguish.

In that wavering light, he set his bag down on the deck and began his examination of the men before him.

I swallowed as we neared the man in the upper hammock. He was the doctor's eldest patient. Despite, the pallor of his cheeks, he looked no worse off, than when the surgeon had examined him in the morning.

It was the younger tar in the lower hammock, that distressed the surgeon.

He lay unmoving, his body slumped lifelessly within the folds of the hammock, like the sacks of potatoes or other vegetables, stowed along the stern of the lower deck.

And, his color . . . there was almost none. He looked like some ghostly white form, found laying in state inside the confines of a pine box, awaiting his final internment, after being viewed at a perfunctory wake.

The surgeon bent down over him, bidding me closer with a silent wave of his hand. His eyes looked up to me with disdain, shaming my tardiness to aid him in his endeavors.

Swallowing my own distaste, I edged forward, holding the lantern up against the upper hammock and bathing our young charge in its flickering light.

Despite, the dimness of the candle, the image was all too clear. The surgeon held the boy's left arm up, examining it for the marks, he had found earlier.

The small bites the rodents had taken of his flesh had dried, though no scab had formed upon them. And, the doctor detected several more, near the pale blue veins, running close to the surface of the lad's ghostly white skin.

"Damn!" the surgeon protested to anyone, who would hear.

He rolled the arm by its wrist. The left hand's fingers hung limp and nearly lifeless. He returned the limb gently to the warm folds of the hammock, covering the lad with the blanket draped over him, but agape.

The surgeon tested for a pulse, his alarm told me, that though present, it was inadequate. His hand moved to the youngster's forehead.

"The fever . . . it's gone," he offered aloud, somewhat surprised by the contradiction of the seaman's ailments.

"That explains, why he's not shivering or fidgeting about," the surgeon returned in prognoses as his hand moved beneath the tar's nose, testing for the strength of the young man's breath.

"Shallow, too shallow," he remarked, as the force of the young tar's breaths barely graced the top of his searching palm.

The doctor opened his medical bag on the floor beside him. He poked about, its organized contents, strapped about in its spacious interior or pocketed among several leather folds or holders.

He studied several small vials and jars among an assortment of containers. He withdrew one, whose thick brown glass ensured the safety of the bottle's contents, should it slip his stubby fingers and fall to the deck.

He removed its cork stopper and tilted the container, nearly spilling it contents. He dabbed a small measure of some powerful ointment about several of his fingers, before retrieving the tar's left arm and applying the healing lotion about the tiny wounds, that had most certainly been the source of the infection plaguing our young seaman.

He turned to me and bid me to fetch a cup and water. He returned the stopper to the bottle and deposited it back into the protective confines of his bag.

I left the lantern on the floor beside him, as I headed to the rear and the wooden cask of water and its serving ladle and communal cups, hung along a neighboring rack.

I sopped a healthy measure of the fresh liquid into one of the dented and worn tin cups, before threading my way back, using the light lingering about the floor ahead to guide my footsteps.

I spied the doctor pouring a measure of some dry white powder into his open left palm. He looked up to me, seeing my curiosity, though I did not speak, out of respect for his craft and to avoid distracting him from tending to the lad.

"Willow bark, crushed into a relieving powder," he remarked, seeing my perplexed face.

He lifted the palm and medicinal cure to the young seaman's lips as I lifted the lantern anew. In the light of its candle, I saw the young lad's lips were almost blue, his face wore the mask of death, persistently seeking him out.

The doctor forced the white powder past uncooperative lips, pushing down on the tar's lower jaw to open his mouth and expose his tongue. He grasped the tin cup from my hand, spilling a measure of water as he moved it to the unresponsive lips.

He tilted the cup and allowed a small amount of water to fill the lad's mouth, reflexively forcing him to swallow in his unconscious state. There was a hollow cough as the water threatened to choke him or find his lungs. But, the ministrations of the doctor succeeded. The bitter white powder was swallowed with the cooling water.

The surgeon stood.

"That's the best I can do for him," he exclaimed, his face filled with surrender, puzzled by the quickness of the ailment, that had beset our crewman.

"The powder, may I ask its purpose?" I inquired.

"The willow bark," he almost mused, "an elixir of the ancients, a staple of alchemists and doctors from ages past. The benefits of the powder are many, but mostly, it relieves inflammation and aches and has been known to reduce a fever, though the latter symptom no longer troubles our young charge."

"I saw the fresh bites," I remarked.

"Yes, as did I. Apparently, moving these lads further below and out of sight has only exposed them to further harm. The damn rats appear to have favored the lowest points of our ship, at least, until they were driven out," he added.

"With the rodents gone, will not, these two will return to health?" I inquired.

"If you'd asked me earlier, I would have answered, yes. But, now . . . it is uncertain. I dare to ponder on the disease our rodent intruders have wreaked, upon these two. I've never seen the likes of it, though I have read stories of plagues and similar afflictions, that have ravaged the body and even destroyed civilizations."

"I asked you, if this affliction be a plague, this morning and you dismissed my fears," I replied.

"True, very true. Still, I do not think there is anything to fear. The day nearly ends and these two are the only ones claimed by our mysterious illness. I suspected rats from the evidence of the small bites about these two. But, their illness could have just as easily been contracted ashore."

"Ashore," I answered in dismay.

"Surely, you are not as naive and innocent as your rank would suggest?" the surgeon returned.

"You've stood watch, when the liberty parties returned or their participants were dragged back from the excesses of their indulgences. Certainly, you are aware of the debauchery and women, they take their fill of, before returning to the dominating and isolating claim of their true mistress, our ship and the sea she rides upon."

"I am aware, of the common seaman's diversions," I replied.

"Than, just as assuredly, you know of the disease and filth, such women can breed and spread from their willing bodies. I've seen, such as these go blind, their bodies wracked with horrible sores and seeping blisters and all other matter of vile torment," he went on.

"If we'd been at sea any length of time, I'd prescribe to your fears. But, we have not, nor they. They returned from shore and quickly succumbed, likely having contracted the ailment there."

"No, there is little to be done, but to keep them rested, fed, and most importantly isolated from the rest of the ship's body. I will continue to administer to them, unless we come upon a friendly port and can readily relieve ourselves of the responsibility of them."

"You refer to Portugal," I responded, recalling the seaports and harbors lining the coast of Portugal. A seafaring people, the lives of the Portuguese were linked to their harbors and the seas. Their harbors heralded opening the doorways to India, the Far East, and other faraway lands for both ships of war and commerce. Their charts and maps continued to be coveted treasures.

"It is not off our route. Though, I can not say if we can spare any delay, in reaching Cadiz and Nelson's Squadron. I will speak of it to the captain. He may prove amendable. If only to allow us to provision the ship with fresh water and stocks. It would assure that we come to Nelson's relief prepared to stay at length. Besides, it does no good to harbor sickness on any vessel, when it can be safely placed ashore . . ." the surgeon added.

"And, forgotten," I added abruptly, speaking, without thinking.

"Sometimes that is best. There are many things not even a skilled surgeon can relieve. You'll learn that, once you get your first taste of battle."

I remained silent.

"If you survive your post come down to the infirmary. I'll show you the cost of the King's call to arms and glory. You can judge if the toll taken by bone-saw and scalpel is a fitting payment for England's prized national pride and adventurous profiteering about her far reaching colonies," he pontificated.

"I accompany you by the captain's order," I protested, "but, of your defeatism, I will have no part. Our duty is . . ."

"I've seen the likes of duty. I've seen one generation of youthful hearts, filled with dreams of glory and adventure, meet the truth. If fortune smiled upon their brow, they lived . . . though perhaps, missing an eye or limb. But, rather than, share the truth, they fell content to reside in the lies, extoling their own glory . . . when, if truth be told, in the confusion and din of battle, they could scarcely recall, who did what deed or whose heroism and self-sacrifice saved the day," he spoke in exhaled breaths, laced with more, than the wine, we had shared, as we supped.

"And, to what end?" he added. "Only to have another generation fill their boots and step into the next fray, promising great oaths and deeds to honor King and Country. No, I've seen it all come to pass and worse, play again and again."

He paused turning back to the two hammock-prone figures.

"There's the truth laying before you," he stated. "We're made of frail stuff and like that candle in your lantern, our time's far too short."

"And, what would you have me do, drown myself in a bottle, like yourself?" I spat back at him, proud of the uniform I wore and angered at his affront to it and my service.

"Ah, so our youngest ensign does have some fight in him and a sharp tongue, as well. Well, look at these two as I said, there lays your truth. Don't be so squeamish and step closer. If this disgusts you, you'd best learn to steel yourself for what's to come."

"And, no I do not wish upon you the solace and affliction of the bottle or strong spirits," he added, turning his attentions and administrations to the old salt laying in the top bunk. "I do not wish you to be tested by the same trials, I have had to endure. But, you'd better start learning to harden your heart and prepare for what's to come. There's no grandeur or greatness in our upcoming engagement," he continued, probing about the pale wrinkled flesh of the elderly patient and finding a new set of small marks marring it.

"You're as frail as these two, though you're strong enough to stand by your own stamina and will. But, you'd just as easily be claimed by an errant shot or splinter or the honed aim of a French sharpshooter, high upon his lofty mizzen mast. And, once crippled or better, dead, we'll see how long it takes for you to be pushed aside and forgotten, replaced by the lies and writ of rewritten history, extoling the valor of your battle, but saying little or nothing of its cost."

I remained silent. Holding my anger and merely remaining content to observe the doctor going through his final duties. I was an escort, nothing more. Perhaps, spirits had distorted the good doctor's sense of duty and honor.

Of common sense, I declared silently, it had escaped him.

But, more likely, the helplessness of his charges had returned memories, of the bone-saw and scalpel, that he dared to hold before me, looking in his own verbal platitudes for some reason or justification for such great loss of life and limb, that he had surely witnessed from battles long since past.

His excesses were inexcusable, regardless of his past service. But, I abided them, allowing him the grant of my tolerance. We were alone and not witnessed, by other officers or crew.

Had we not been in such self-imposed isolation, I would have surely reported his excesses and slanderous tongue, defaming Crown and Country, to the captain for formal reprimand.

As it was, his services were presently needed. And, a skilled surgeon's hands and his proven and trusted experience were the envy of any ship's crew, especially when faced with our upcoming perilous battle.

I was about to consider the matter forgotten, ironically marking the surgeon's own words, when he dropped to the deck, halting beside the lower bunk.

I had failed to hear the barely audible noise. But, the good doctor had heard the hiss of the young tar's wheezing lungs. I heard only the second emanation, before the young sailor's chest heaved violently, his elbows poking into the bottom of his hammock and threatening to throw him out of it.

His eyes opened as his mouth gaped wide. He looked as if he'd viewed some horrible specter.

The lantern in my right hand swayed about. Alarmed and startled, I took one uncontrolled step backward. Just as quickly, the tar's lungs emptied and failed to refill, in spite of the choking gulps, trying to swallow air.

He fell aside, only prevented from falling to the deck's hard planking by the strong arms of the surgeon, grasping his blight form and returning him back into the folds of the hammock.

His limbs shivered, shaking in an ungodly manner. His lanky hands and long thin fingers were skeleton-like in their gyrations. Then, just as suddenly as the spasm had arrived, it receded.

There was no more movement.

The doctor checked the tar for pulse and breath.

There was none to be found.

Except, for the violent fit of shaking, it was over. I could not rationalize the waste of it. The tar was not much more, than a boy. And, now with the promise of great adventure and a chance to prove our courage, he was gone.

I watched as the doctor's right hand descended to the tar's head, his finger's gently closing the lad's eyes, shielding the unseeing orbs, that stared up blankly at the beams and rafters supporting the deck above. He pulled the blanket up, uncovering the tar's bare feet and burying his head under its coarse dark blue wool.

"You best report this death to the captain," he requested of me.

"And, you?" I asked.

"I think I'll stay the night. It's best someone watch over our other patient and if nothing else, stand guard over the corpse, lest any vermin have survived the search of our beaters."

I nodded my agreement and bent down to leave the doctor the lantern, which I placed upon the deck.

I turned in a half-light of the shadows as the darkness cast from the beams and stores stretched out along the deck and its bordering walls. Perhaps, it was my own discomfort of the moment and the disturbing presence of death so near, but I swore

I saw a shadow move about as if cast from a solid form, a nearby man.

My eyes moved to search about and find the source of this specter. But, it availed them, not. Like earlier in the morning, after the death of the sailor, who had fallen from his drunken perch among our masts, there was nothing to be seen.

Yet, I swore, I saw a presence.

I ignored the thought and trepidation of my senses and mounted the ladder to the next deck.

Again, I was to be the bearer of unfortunate news to our captain. The fact distressed me, fearing it was sure, to earn me disfavor in the captain's eyes.

Only when I climbed to the next deck, did I recall the haunting vision of the iron box, entombed among the supplies at the stern of the lower deck.

What rot! I pushed away the coincidence and superstition fouling my mind. I had duties to attend to.

H.M.S. Vanguard (full hull view).

CHAPTER 9

Burial

HMS Vanguard
Sailing off the Coast of Southern France
Day 3-Morning

The drums beat in solemn unison, their crisp retort heralding the beginning of our captain's eulogy for the young seaman, whose body lay in state before us. A brisk cool breeze danced across the heads of those present, threatening to claim tar's or officer's hat, alike.

I removed my watch from its pocket and opened its protective cover. The silver timepiece was a status symbol of my rank. It was every bit a part of my standing and rank as was my uniform. Few of our tars would ever see the likes of it among their own meager possessions. And, I dare say, there were a few officers, who still lacked the expensive timekeepers, part mechanical marvel and part ornate jewelry.

I glimpsed the watch's face. It was the seventh hour of the morning.

My distraction with the hour ended as the ship's body came to attention. The act was most notably accentuated by the stiff clicking of the heels of our marine's boots and the dull thud of the brass buttplates of their rifles and muskets upon the deck.

The drums fell silent in chilling and haunting unison. They left the ship and her crew standing in eerie awe. Banners and flags whipped about the masts above their heads.

Our captive sails billowed full, driving our vessel southward. Only the helmsmen, lookouts, and officers of the watch went reverently about their business. It was as if they were in ignorance of the grieving burial detachment, that had brought our crewman to the upper deck.

The clouds were full. They moved rapidly across the sky, driven by the same stiff breeze, that hastened our own troubled journey. To the east a golden band still marked the distant horizon and the sunrise, now cloaked by the darkness of the gathered clouds.

The mood of the men and sky was somber, harboring both grief and dread. The dark full clouds appeared as if they had gathered to weep at the loss of our comrade.

The tars, that had brought our departed comrade topside went about setting his silent remains in state. Their own actions were to be relieved by the formal and ritualistic rites, performed by our captain and an honor guard detachment of Royal Marines.

In somber ceremony, the tars carried the young sailor's draped body, placed atop a plank. They set it over two great chests resting on the deck. Several lengths of twine were gathered around the wrapped folds of the heavy canvas of the funeral shroud.

Despite, their gentle movements, those of us forward of the gathered formations could not help, but hear the clank and rattle of the chains, beneath the shroud, meant to entrust our comrade to the depths of the sea.

We watched with dignified respect as the Union Jack was unfurled atop the shroud. One end was made tight to the upper end of the plank, where our seaman's head rested in final slumber. The tars performing this solemn duty were mates of the young lad.

They silently retreated from his still form as the Marine detachment stepped forward. The marines moved with the precise and exaggerated movements of a ceremonial guard.

Two Royal Marines, detailed with a row of their comrades standing beside the shrouded seaman, held the corners of the flag on opposite ends, lest the gusting wind rip our banner free. Not a length of our flag, touched the deck, despite winds pressing against it, trying to free it from the grasp of the marines.

As if in mirrored respect of the solemn moment, a bevy of gulls circled around our ship, choosing to remain among the heights and spires of our masts.

They were viewed with unspoken superstitious regard by many of the crew. Their presence was either omen or blessing, curse or fortune, depending on each man's beliefs.

To many, the winged creatures offered a final endeavor, heralding the passage of our seaman to the gates of heaven. To others the birds might as well have been earthly demons, sensing death and abandoning land to find our comrade, before he was laid to state and returned to the sea, that by tradition, we offered up our dead.

In the latter lore, the birds were kin of Lucifer, minions of the netherworld. They waited for us to release our comrade from our presence, so that they might snatch his soul, claimed for their master by past sins and debauchery. They would herald the sinner to the damning reaches of hell.

But, basking in the warmth of the sunlight, we stood formation in, it was hard to believe the harshness such lores would damn men by. In truth, the simple tar's life was filled with hardship and woe. There was more, than enough strife for him to atone for any transgressions committed during his brief life.

And, add to that the pain of the lash or a host of other

deprivations and punishments, that could easily befall his lot for the slightest of transgressions and one could scarcely believe the ancient lores, damning him yet, to further torment and suffering.

Besides, as I recalled the youthful face, that had been so masked in the pallor of death, the lad was but a boy. True, his young life was hard. And, to survive, such as him had no doubt committed their share of petty larcenies and crimes.

It was how many misguided lads had come to find themselves at sea, running away from the constables or sheriffs, that hunted them for their minor crimes and misdeeds.

But, regardless, of his past sins or the harshness of his existence, though brief, it may have been at sea, he'd surely atoned for any sins or wrongs.

The captain cleared his throat as he attempted to speak against the wind. The act intoned his second in command to order our formations to attention. Despite, my nearness, every other word, he uttered, escaped my ears. It was blocked out by the flap of the taunt canvas above or the moving air rushing along our deck.

In resignation and self-rebuke, I missed the young man's full Christian name. It floated away, brushed aside with indifference by a gust of wind. The billowing sails above stretched, then fell, before regaining the smooth roundness of the captured air.

I was not even certain of the sailor's nationality. Though, the bulk of the ship's compliment were Englishmen and proud of it, nearly a quarter of our tars were from foreign ports. Germans, Swedes, and a host of Europeans filled our ranks. And, I was led to understand the ship's muster book even included several Americans from our rebellious former colony.

Mindlessly, I heard the slapping of the waves and the water running alongside the smooth hull, decks below. The captain continued his eulogy, having not even known our departed seaman.

He offered a common lament for all those, who went down to the sea in ships. He extoled the hardships, all endured and the loneliness and sacrifice of our self-imposed exiles, so far from land and loved ones. His words could have aptly fit any man present, officer or enlisted.

The wind blew through ratlings and taunt ropes cutting the air noisily and filling in the pauses, between the words of our captain.

The Royal Marines stood about the flag draped shroud, their tall black leather headgear was held tightly atop their heads by cutting chin-straps. Their rifles, brandished ceremonial white slings and bayonets topped their barrels. The honed polished spikes of the bayonets glistened in the dimming light.

Their rifles were held upright, running beside the lengths of the marines' stiff bodies. Brass buttplates, pressed against the deck as the marines' eyes stared straight ahead at the humble shroud and our proud banner.

With the two marines at the ends of the shroud, holding our flag in place, the honor detachment bore the transfixed rigidity and inflexibility of a child's painted wood or tin soldiers.

One, could only marvel at the parade crispness of the Marines, clad in full dress regalia and presenting the polished stocks and glistening steel of their weapons. I allowed my eyes to rove over the sight and follow the pensive and somber faces of those gathered.

This was my first burial at sea. And, despite the morbidness of the occasion, its ceremony and rarity held a mixed sense of fascination and awe. We were strangely gathered together in a ritual of camaraderie, no shore-bound mortal would ever experience the like and mysticism of.

The captain ordered, "Uncover."

The order was repeated, barked by the shrill hollow voice of our second officer. Both our senior officers removed their dark blue felt chapeaus, trimmed in worn gold braid and adorned with the trappings of their rank.

With the act of respect completed, the captain withdrew a tiny prayer book from inside the pocket of his coat. His aging fingers thumbed about its pages, worn and bent with age, and discolored by frequent and reverent use.

"Lord Almighty God, your humble servants are gathered today, standing before You. We mourn the loss of . . ." he continued on, despite the assault of a growing wind.

" . . . we ask that You show our fallen comrade the mercy and compassion of Your forgiveness and grant him . . ."

I studied the faces of the tars, standing shoulder to shoulder, pressed into the tightly packed rectangular formations about our crowded deck. There was obedient silence to be found among nearly everyone. There was also dread, harbored by many, that the ship's luck and fortune had been jinxed or damned by some unseen hand.

It was the bane of the common seamen to fathom some superstitious reason for this or that occurrence, when science or reason would surmise, that for this cause, such result had been the response.

But, I saw it in their faces, having recognized their same worries in myself. In the early morning hours of the first seaman's demise, I recalled the specter of a shadow, that I thought was there, but was not.

And now, that seaman's body lay ashore, his death and silent form hidden from the crew, now standing about the deck, to release another of their mates from among the ranks of their compliment.

And, of the shrouded form before me, I remembered the shadow, that had twice eluded me. The last time it escaped my eyes was as I left this sailor's expired body to the lonely vigil of the doctor.

I wondered what that phantom specter might have been. Could it have been, I glimpsed the fleeting presence of an evil spirit or death?

I cast my eyes away, lest the ranks see my own fret and consternation. I did not believe in superstition or lore. Yet, I had no explanation, that would cast the light of reason upon speculation, resurrected by feelings and emotion.

Twice harm had come, to members of the crew. And twice, I had spied a fleeting shadow, only to search out the source of its presence and have it elude me.

A shiver ran up my back, despite the high buttoned collar and warm wool of my dress blue uniform. I blamed it on the growing wind and the dampness wafting over the water, claiming our southern-bound vessel.

An order was barked, stirring me awake from my thoughts.

My eyes returned to the flag-covered shroud before us. With rigid steps and exaggerated parade-ground movements, the Marine contingent had assembled about our deceased comrade.

As one, they lifted plank, shroud, and flag aloft, carrying it to the edge of the railing.

The captain's voice fought against the wind, towards the conclusion of the burial.

The plank was set atop the rail, precariously tilting halfway over its ledge.

" . . . thus, we bequeath our comrade to the sea," the captain's voice intoned, filled with somber resignation.

The sergeant, bordering the detachment, issued a tight-lipped whisper to his men and the plank was raised up high on its shipboard end.

The tightly wrapped shroud and our entombed sailor slid along the plank's smooth surface, until he reached the end of the wide board. His wrapped body fell from sight. A heavy splash gave witness to the body and chains plunging to the bottom of the sea.

"God have mercy on Seaman Christopher Jones' soul and grant him the joys of salvation and eternal peace. Amen."

"Amen!" broke out officer and men in a deep responsive chorus, joining in their captain's petition to the Almighty above.

The ship's bell was struck once. Its hollow tone resounded across the deck, echoing to our ears. Slowly, its metallic resonance died away.

The gulls above shrieked as if cheated from some bounty.

Several tars turned their heads heavenly, believing the ancient lore, that the birds tried to capture the souls of recently departed men. Grins marked several of the tars' faces as the gulls shrieked with displeasure. Malcontent, their actions reinforced the tale, that another soul had escaped, their loitering presence.

I recalled, how the deceased seaman had found his way among

our ship's compliment, his evoked name stirring my memory. Seaman Christopher Jones was one of the few Americans on board.

As I had heard his history, he had been snatched from aboard an American merchant ship, destined for a port in France. The supposedly unarmed trader had proved to bear several cannon as was the rash American custom of arming her privateers, small swift sailing ships, designed for the dual functions of commerce or war.

Her sleek hull and lines, coupled with her puny armament were no match for the patrolling frigate of his Majesty's Navy, set about enforcing the embargo and quarantine of the French port.

Seaman Jones was among those on deck as a British boarding party searched the vessel for contraband, that might aid our enemy. But, the boarding party had other aims, besides the inquisitive search about the ship's hold to surmise, what commitment America had undertaken in support of France.

The officer of the boarding party had orders to press into service any willing or unwilling member of the privateer's crew, that might round out the lack of crew upon their own ship.

This method of recruitment was protested as piracy and kidnapping by those countries, who had lost members of a ship's crew. But, there was little to be done about the abductions, since the Royal Navy had supremacy upon the sea.

I recalled the American's story, told to me secondhand, through a third party. It appears our young tar had stupidly admitted to his own mother's English heritage, when questioned upon the deck of the American ship.

That admission had been enough to welcome him back into the folds of his mother country, despite his protestations. The HMS Vanguard was the second British ship, he had come to serve upon.

Unlike, the sailors' that had enlisted, he was denied his fourteen shillings. More slave, than free man, he was indentured to His Majesty's fleet, nothing more, than a prisoner upon a floating prison.

The Royal Marines returned the plank from atop the rail, returning it to rest on the deck, before snapping to attention.

With halting commands and stiff steps, their sergeant returned them back into a line, that reeled about and faced the captain.

Our captain's head was now covered. With a nod of thanks to the honor guard for the sterling performance of their duties, he ordered his officers to dismiss the assembled ranks.

The formality, of the officers and the ritual of ceremony was broken by the coarse voices and bellowing of sergeants and boatswain's rousing the men to movement and breaking up the formations. Men were sent to duty or other business on their assigned decks.

I stood there dismally, content for the moment, to watch the ship's body break formation. Unlike, other gatherings, the men's dismissal was filled with bowed heads and lowered spirits.

Undoubtedly, some believed us jinxed. Others were already resided to the fate awaiting us, after the captain had informed them earlier this morning, that our much treasured Channel patrol was, but a ruse. They learned the truth, our destination was to join Lord Nelson off the harbor at Cadiz, Spain.

Whatever the reason, believing us jinxed or ruing the threat of the coming combat, the hearts of the men were heavy without having to bear the burden and loss of a fellow seaman.

I stepped up to the rail and searched the sea below. There was no sign of the body interred to it, not that I had expected such. The heavy length of chain had served its purpose well.

Our seaman sunk quickly to his final resting place. There was no threat of a bloated body returning to the surface to provide a meal for a gull or other scavenger.

The waters looked cold and desolate as they rushed along the side of the wooden hull. I saw only emptiness in their flowing foam and waves.

"Your first burial at sea?" the captain's voice replied.

Startled, I turned about to face him, having not heard his stealthy approach.

"Your pardon, sir. I did not hear your . . ."

He halted my attempt at formality.

"It's an oppressive thing, having to rid a ship of a body, to deny its return home to a man's family and loved ones. It means they receive but word or letter in place of his remains. They're forced to recall his image only in memories or the thoughts they might still harbor."

"It's an emptiness, I do not relish having to make them suffer. They gave us a man and we can only return news of his death along with the fabrication, that he was buried with honors and ceremony at sea. As I said, emptiness, nothing more," the captain lamented, quite uncharacteristically.

"I fear his family will not even have that," I returned, sharing with him the history of our seaman, in confidence. He had either forgotten or had not been informed of the seaman's past.

"Jones was an American," I said, trying to offer no offense at the revelation. "Gossip about the ship has it, that he was taken off an American ship, pressed into the King's service, because of his mother's English lineage."

"Then, I don't think his family will be informed of his death. The Admiralty will most assuredly not admit their culpability in his abduction. And, with the deep-seated hatreds still harbored between our two countries, I will not take it upon myself to write a letter, attesting to his fate."

He paused about the rail, before continuing. "It is a terrible thing, that his mother will not know of his demise and will still harbor thoughts of his eventual return. But, at least, she will have him alive and well in her thoughts. And, that is something, some small measure of compensation," he remarked sadly.

I merely nodded, my mind found no words to express the thoughts, I harbored. I had already admitted to myself, they bore a sense of foolishness about them.

"Have you told anyone about the loss of our other seaman?" he asked in confidence, referring to the drunken seaman, that had fallen from our mast.

I was slightly taken aback, that he might consider I had

breached the oath of silence, I had been ordered to observe on the matter. "No, Captain. I have said nothing."

He nodded his head. His action almost apologetic for even being forced to have asked the question of me.

"Well, it appears someone's tongue has been set a wagging. Though, I cannot say, I did not expect it. There are few secrets kept aboard a ship, even a military vessel. And, I fear these old sea dogs have tongues as sharp and spiteful as any old hags, that set about to gossip," he added, his voice despondent.

"Some of the men have set about talking, encouraged by the second death, aboard our ship. It seems superstition and yarns are still the fodder of His Majesty's lower ranks, even if their hands and backs are not idle."

"Is there some worry to be expected over the matter?" I inquired.

"No more nor less, than any other topic of gossip. But, keep your wits about you and your ears open. Being a junior officer, the men are more content to take liberties about you . . ."

I began to protest, this lack of confidence in my authority, but the captain waved it aside.

"I mean you no slight. But, the truth of the matter is, that before you and Ensign Higgins, and perhaps, a few of the younger officers, the mates are more apt to speak their mind. Once they spy the presence of myself or my second officer, their mouths clamp tight as vices and their eyes drop to the deck."

I listened silently, aware, that except for the watch and helmsman, we were alone on the upper deck.

"All I ask, is that you keep your ears open. If there is a malcontent or agitator among these tars, I will need to know it. A ship must be of one mind and one body."

"One, Captain," I returned in support.

"You understand, then," he added in affirmation. "It is especially important, that we rid our selves of any dissension, especially as we near our foe. If need be, I'll assign extra labors or drills to occupy these men's minds. And, as much as I detest the lash, by God, I'll use it freely to bring this ship to order and of one mind, mine!" he paused

"But, out of curiosity, who besides the doctor witnessed the death upon your watch?" he questioned.

"There were four Marines, two fore and two aft and possibly, the seamen of the watch I relieved. Some assisted in the removal of the body, returning it to the dock and the local doctor ashore."

"It will be an easy thing to find their names among the duty lists," he rued, intent on finding the loose tongue, spurring rumors aboard his ship.

The transgression was as distasteful as the man he hunted.

"I suggest for now, that you return to our good surgeon's side. I judge he could use some measure of relief. Perhaps, he would like to take some time to eat or take a nap or whatever vice, he favors to gain him some distraction or relaxation. And, return to me with a report on our other ill sailor's health . . . though, I pray he is making a recovery."

"As you wish, sir," I replied sharply, pushing away from the rail and heading for the hatchway, leading into the ship's bowels.

The captain took my place along the rail, removing his hat, lest it be claimed by the wind and cast upon the waters. He continued my lone vigil and the mindless task of staring out along the emptiness of the waters. His back was to the coastline of France, off our port side.

CHAPTER 10

Relief

HMS Vanguard
Sailing off the Coast of Southern France
Day 3-Late Afternoon

There was a sullen silence as I passed between the decks. Men loitered about in their own select groups as was their natural custom, each man among friends or companions as the late afternoon dulled the flurry of activity aboard our ship.

The topics of their guarded utterances escaped my ears. But, questioning eyes and faces were prone to suspicion, leaving no doubt, each was trying to fathom the demise of our young crewman. No doubt, they wondered what strange affliction had claimed his life and confined a second comrade to the lower reaches of the ship.

I made my way down along the wide slanted steps of the hold, joining each of our three decks. My form fell among the shadows of the lifeboats, lashed atop the giant rafters, spanning the breath of the hold above.

A few men noted my passing presence. But, it was as the captain had said, though they were more, than apt to observe the respect, due my rank and uniform, they still conversed among themselves. Only their guarded tongues and whispers prevented my learning the subject and nature of their gossip.

But, their faces told all. They harbored no mutiny or shred of malcontent. I saw fear residing in their faces along their wrinkled brows.

Their ages varied. Some were young tars, this their first or second time at sea. Others bore the leathered faces and wrinkles of wise old salts, who had known no other trade and had lived at sea, nearly all their lives.

Their calloused hands were marked by blisters, some filled grotesquely with blood from handling the coarse hemp rope of our rigging or sewing rips in the thick canvas of our sails.

Others bore the horrid ulcers, that plagued their skin, attesting to their long life at sea and the corrosive effects of salt and brine, that ate away at our ship's wood and copperplate, along with the flesh and strength of our crew.

But, all held the silent fret and discontent of a ship, that had befallen misfortune, let alone still sailed to war.

I descended to the next deck, until I came upon the isolated planks, leading to the doctor. To the stern, I thought I detected the creak of some aging hinges, their metal protesting the movement of their rusted joints.

The sound halted almost as suddenly, when I stopped to try to discern the low sound.

I began to turn rearward, facing the stern of the lower gun-deck, when the surgeon's voice entreated, "Who goes there?"

My keen hearing and pricked ears lost the low sound of hinges and metal, now gone flat and wanting.

Despite, the morning hour, the lower gun-deck, its gunports battened, was cloaked in the semi-darkness of candles in hung lanterns and the thin beams of light penetrating the cracks and seams of the gunports.

I began to step forward, when the surgeon started to call out again.

"Ensign Lewis," I bellowed my name in answer, allaying his concerns, which seemed apprehensive and unjustified.

I moved along the deck, I had walked the night before, when the doctor and I had checked on his two charges. My nostrils were again assaulted by the scent of rotting wood and the lingering dampness, permeating the lower gun-deck.

As I neared the blankets, strung across the deck ahead, I smelled the odor of sickness. I immediately recalled, last night's foul scent and the death of our young seaman. And, now it seemed as if the moment was repeating itself.

I slowly pulled aside the makeshift curtain, expecting to find the doctor administering to the remaining tar.

The sight before me, filled me with horrid surprise and dread. I had expected to see the lower hammock empty, while the surgeon tended to his remaining patient.

Instead, the berth was slumped heavily to the floor, a new patient was claimed by the sickness, that had befouled our ship. And, beyond those tars, two more hammocks were strung.

The upper canvas was filled with a newly afflicted sailor, whose disposition and haunted color seemed to match the pallor of original survivor. The surgeon sat in the center of the lower hammock, his feet set apart on the floor, trying to steady himself among his uncomfortable perch, which threatened to move and sway with the rolling movements of the ship.

The lantern, I had guided him with the night before, sat along the deck. Its wide candle still burned, melted down to nothing more, than squat short remains of itself. The flame engulfed the drooping wick, captured in the center of a pool of melted wax.

As the ship rolled, another stream of melted wax escaped the confines of the pool and traced a streaming path along the side of the candle, it had spilled over.

It just as quickly hardened, resting in a jagged trail as the ship returned upright and even.

"Another two men have taken ill," the doctor offered, in obvious resignation.

"From this deck?" I asked, fearing the ailment of the surviving crewman had infected a mate on this level.

"No. This seaman was standing watch the night before on the upper deck. He was far away from our afflicted friend," the doctor motioned towards the old salt, laying unaware of my presence or our conversation.

"It defies explanation. He was topside, breathing only fresh air. And, though the night was chilly, he was well clad, warm enough in his wool coat and leather hat," the surgeon added, in puzzlement.

"Could he be suffering some cold or ailment attendant to his duties on watch?" I asked.

"That is what I thought or at least, had hoped," he continued, his voice perplexed.

He slowly stood up, after hefting his own bulk out of the restraining folds of the hammock.

He turned to the prostrate form in the upper bunk, pulling aside the sheltering warmth of a covering blanket. He removed the man's left arm in a mirrored performance of the young lad's the night before.

He beckoned me forward with a silent wave of his hand.

I bent down. My eyes searching for the spot, his hammy fingers pointed out. There, along the inside of the arm, close to the surface, where fat blue veins neared, were the tell-tale marks, we had both witnessed before.

"The rats?" I said in disbelief.

"What else? But, how?" he returned, bewildered as I.

"But, we drove them from our midst. You saw, the same as I. They were beaten from the lowest deck and clubbed, where they stood or chased topside to be driven overboard."

He merely continued pointing at the scarred limb and the two fresh sores, evidence to the contrary.

"So it is some sort of plague, assuredly transmitted by the bite of these rodents. Some have survived. Somewhere or somehow, they have escaped our eradication," I remarked.

"I don't know?" he returned. "I don't know?"

There was a marked pause between us. The evidence was before our eyes. But, what to make of it? And, even our humble diagnosis was left lacking, providing us with an enigma, a vexing riddle, that defied our explanations.

"But, look!" the doctor intoned, pointing again to the uncouth marks.

I picked up the lantern and its nearly extinguished candle off the deck and held it near the limb.

"See, here," he said, pointing at the mirrored marks.

"If a rodent was responsible for these scars, why did he assail the same arm and in nearly the same place as the marks afflicting our deceased comrade or that old salt, over there. Look!" he directed, puzzled beyond the reasons of his science or the known dictates and behavior of the small rodents' nature.

"You surely don't believe, that rodents with their insignificant minds and humble nature, that has them feed and scavenge by instinct, would lead them to attack the same limb, nearly in the same spot on all four men?" he tested the beginning of some odd hypothesis.

"I have no knowledge in the feeding habits or predilections of rodents," I returned.

"Even, if that is true, the odds, that a nearly mindless creature would favor the same limb and location to afflict its tiny bite seems an absurdity. Would you not agree?"

"It would appear to stretch the imagination and test the limits of the abilities of such small mammals. But, who is to say, that these tars did not favor dangling the afflicted limb outside the protective cover of their blankets, exposing the same limb, within the reach of the rodents, doing so not by design, but by coincidence," I sought to reason.

He returned the limb to the comfort of the hammock and covered the seaman, who shivered at the slight draft finding his sweating body. Like the others, he was now succumbing to the ravages of fever.

"What to do? What am I to do?" the doctor pleaded almost silently, perplexed and unable to fathom a solution to the riddle confronting him.

"Perhaps, that is all it is, a coincidence as you dare say," he mulled my words over.

"Perhaps, they favored relieving the same limb from the restricting confines of their hammocks. And, as you say, the rodents merely fed upon the limb, that was offered," he appeared, to be trying to make himself believe the suggestion, I had offered.

"But still, the rodents favored the inside of the limb and chose the veins, that were near the surface, easily exposed under thin skin . . ." he replied, falling silent, still doubting the evidence before his eyes and the teachings of his profession.

The candle flickered and a drop of melted wax spilled beyond the small pooled liquid puddle atop the candle. It dripped along the base of the lantern, before slowly stretching in a melted fall to the floor.

"You'll have to inform the captain. This bane has spread to two new men," the surgeon offered.

"Sir, the captain bid I relieve you. Perhaps, you could inform him yourself, breaking to attain a hot meal and perhaps, the comfort of your berth, while I attend to these two?"

"No, no, no!" he returned, without turning around to face me, still studying the tar before us. "I've no desire to leave these two. I've other measures to try, elixirs and ointments, that might relieve their symptoms and perhaps, halt the encroachment of the fever assailing them."

I turned to view the elder seaman, unmoving in his hammock.

His condition looked no the worse, than the previous night. He lay in state, still afflicted, but no worse. His condition had not degraded like the young lad, who had failed to survive.

Perhaps, it was because of his age and hardness, that the blight or plague had spared him.

Regardless, he might hold his own. But, the newest seamen to succumb were showing the same difficulty and intolerance to the disease as the young lad, so recently departed. One seemed to be deteriorating more quickly, than the other patients.

I understood the surgeon's desire to remain and attend to his patients.

"If you wish, I will return to the captain and report this new outbreak," I began, "And, I'll see to it that some provision is made for your comfort and that of your patients. I'll have the stewards send some hot soup or other rations to help break the hold of this clinging dampness. Dare I say, the chill and rot down here may alone be enough to be responsible for the illness."

"No, it's not the rot or chill . . ." the surgeon returned, shaking his head as he bent to his open medical bag, resting on the floor.

His hands probed through its contents, searching for some illusive vial or bottle, while he searched his mind for some lesson or journal, that might shed light upon the affliction stumping his therapies and doctoring.

As he hunted for the illusive item, the seaman, in the upper hammock, gagged. His body convulsed as if he could not find the air to breath. He jerked upright so sharply and unnaturally, that it was hard to believe, he had been soundly asleep, during the doctor's examination of his arm, only seconds before.

His mouth broke out in a deep coughing spasm, before spitting the foulest of bile across his chest and over the side of his hammock. The brackish fluid barely missed our good surgeon. Yet, it found the sides of his worn black leather case, laying about the deck.

The tar's mouth filled with the burning bile. The seaman panicked, unable to claim his next breath, drowning on his own vomit.

The doctor stood and quickly rolled him about, so furiously, that I thought the seaman would spill from his hammock and collide with the floor. But, our surgeon held him captive, pointing his head over the side. He kept the man's head facedown as another stream of the repulsive liquid sprang forth.

I felt my own stomach protest the act. The sight of content's of the man's stomach, likely paled the pallor of my own complexion.

I swallowed, hoping the simple act would hold down my own stomach, which the sight of sickness and the rolling deck, now seemed to similarly threatened.

""Get it out, lad!" the surgeon ordered his patient as the haunting cough returned.

The man could say nothing. He still struggled to regain his breath. His coughing turned to rasping as his throat and lungs burned from the bile coating his desperate breaths.

He clasped a hand to his mouth, ashamed at his own infirmity and weakness. His eyes showed his own revulsion at the wretched contents coating his fingers and drooling uncontrollably from the corners of his mouth.

He gasped, like a man just pulled from beneath the waves. His eyes watered and stared wide with the fear and the realization, that death might be near.

His elbow poked a sharp fold in the underside of the canvas hammock, when he tried to reclaim some measure of control about himself.

The doctor gently returned him back into the restful comfort of his hammock. He checked for pulse and breath as the seaman closed his eyes and accepted the reprieve of his restful recline.

Soon, the doctor was about his bag, searching for the illusive cure or preventative herb or tonic, that might halt the spread of the seaman's ailment.

He shot me a glance, silently begging me to depart and leave him to his duties. Worse, I saw in his eyes, despite not a word being uttered, that he had no clue to identifying the affliction or its treatment.

I saw only despair.

One of several giant carronades mounted on the forecastle.

CHAPTER 11

Drill

HMS Vanguard
Sailing off the Coast of Southern France
Day 3-Evening

The drums beat incessantly. Their din's short retort summoned the crew to their stations. The call had been given to "clear for action." Now, the drums beat their unbroken rhythm, droning "beat to quarters," urging the men to rush beside their guns and clear them of any obstruction to their operation.

There was a flurry of activity as men abandoned their dinners. They left the odd square wooden plates, they ate off, running for the ladders or steps to make ready for war.

I stood topside behind the captain and the second officer as the drill commenced. It was sixth hour of the evening and the ship had become lax, its crew already preparing to seek the simple comforts of their hammocks or the camaraderie of a deck of cards.

Now, they were stirred into action, tested by our drill. Its progress was marked by both senior officers, each noting the time from when the drums commenced to the point our crew reached their places, beside cannon or rail.

Other officers stationed upon the lower decks mirrored our own actions. They witnessed the response of the gun crews, falling to their knees beside the mixed batteries of 24 or 32 pounders, relegated to the lower decks and the lighter twelve pounders topside with us.

Our marines seemed the most at hazard. With the continued roll of the drums, they climbed awkward perches along the tops of the rails, before scaling the ratlings to their aerial sharpshooters' perches, atop the fore mast, main mast, and mizzen mast.

They were burdened by slung rifles or muskets and the restraints of their stiff uniforms and belts. But, to a man they skillfully climbed upward with an agility, I could only marvelled at. Their daring movements rivaled the acrobatic feats of squirrels, beset amongst the high trees of a park.

And, like those small brash creatures, our marines showed no fear of the lofty heights above them nor the rolling disposition of our ship.

Some marines stood about the gun-decks. They took up the positions, they would guard in real battle, stationed behind the gun crews. Their duty was less noble, though no less necessary. They were set about the gun crews, their only task to ensure none of the untested tars broke and ran, during the horrors of combat.

It seemed unnecessary to me. But, experience was a wise teacher. And, those, who had survived the brutal combat of our age, knew that many a man would fall upon instinct, once he found his mates dead or horribly wounded and his own turn next on the cruel anvil of war.

It was the natural state of a man to save himself. And, the instinct of flight was as strong in men as in the beasts or lessor animals. We had many untried hands, novices of war, like myself.

And so, our marines were positioned, so that any man would reconsider, the hazard of failing to do his duty, when faced with the awaiting rifle and bayonet of our unforgiving and merciless marines.

I had reported to the captain, informing him of the doctor's decision to deny himself any measure of relief, though I had dutifully offered it, as I had been requested.

I also informed our master of the newest case of the blight befouling our crew. I tried to report its revolting symptoms as tactfully as I could, if only to relay the seriousness of the plague or illness besetting our ship.

And, almost as an afterthought, even though I had no medical background or experience to draw upon of my own, I discreetly expressed the doubt, that the affliction might be beyond the good surgeon's ability to deal with it, but insisted supportively, that he was trying.

It was not, that I did not have faith in our good doctor, nor that I held any spite, for his own weakness with the bottle. It was only, that I thought the captain should know the truth.

Besides, the decision to change our course, even slightly to a Portuguese harbor, was solely the captain's. I knew our journey had progressed rapidly, we were well ahead of the generous schedule, provided for us to reach Cadiz.

But, the decision to detour our route and stop for any length of time, no matter how short, was our captain's. I knew not, how pressing the Admiralty's demands were, upon him. But, I hoped a detour, to a friendly port along Portugal's coast, where some of our own forces were present in the fight against Spain and the French, might meet with his approval, if only to relieve ourselves of the burden of our sick.

I had no idea, how far the illness might progress or even, if it would claim more of the crew. But, I felt it best, that he should know the seriousness of it. Then, upon his discretion, he could amend our orders, putting men ashore, lest we bring some sickness to the squadron, we were to aid.

I was well aware of the yellow flags and paint, that marked a plague ship, though I had only heard stories and tales of such vessels. And, most of those tales resounded with the misfortune of prison ships or warships, that had been forced to endure a cruel winter with their prisoners or crews left afloat in a forlorn harbor, fighting the cold of winter and the ailments accompanying it.

We watched as men fell to their knees behind the low carriages of the guns. Others readied cannonballs or held aloft rammers or buckets, ready to do their part in servicing the guns. Powder was broken out and the men were well ready, to ram it home, until the order was given for their efforts to halt.

The main guns on all three decks were manned. The 12 and 24 pounders of the upper deck, awaited only powder and shot. The middle deck with its 24 pounders and the lower deck with its massive 32 pounders were all reported ready, as flesh and muscle rolled and hauled the weight of iron cannon to face the sea, beyond our broadsides.

Even several gigantic cannon, nicknamed by the crew as "Smashers," but officially dubbed carronades, had been wrested to face about by their laboring and straining crews.

The men stood ready. Had the command been given, they would have filled the menacing barrels with the cartridge bearing powder, ramming it to the rear. Then, after straining to lift the heavy shot into the barrels and force it rearward with the rammer, they'd have filled the powder hole and on the order, fired it with a slow match or flintlock.

Had this not been a drill, the gruesome business of arming and firing the guns would have repeated, until the target ahead was devastated or our own crews had been found by the enemy's deadly broadsides.

Under fire, men would wield the "worms," that would snake out and remove the burning cartridge fragments, clearing the way to load again, but not until, a damp sponge had swabbed out the interior of the barrel, extinguishing any sparks, that might fire a new cartridge prematurely.

Buckets and barrels of sand were broken out. In combat, the

sand would have been spread liberally about the decks. Its gritty surface served two purposes. It was meant to retard any fires, that might break out. And, it was meant to sop up any blood from the vicious wounds, that were sure to come from any contested and hard fought engagement.

Already, a few tars' keen and experienced eyes had taken a brief glance about the sea surrounding us and had quickly surmised, we were the only vessel about. But, dutifully and with practiced haste, they continued doing their part in the drill.

The second officer was the first to spot a sluggard's performance. One of the mate's appeared unduly lax to our senior lieutenant.

He'd noted him slow to man his station beside one of the twelve pounders, already pushed through the narrow opening of its opened gunport by the rest of the gun's crew.

Now, he sluggishly leaned along the length of a rammer as if the drill was of no importance.

Before, the captain could halt the second officer, he had left our presence and moved forward, taking angry strides past the two helmsman, one to either side of our behemoth ship's wheel.

The unfortunate tar ahead was unaware of his approach. We watched, while the sluggard dallied about, lost to everything going on about him. He was an older seaman and should have been more appreciative of the demands and routine of our drill, to say nothing of its importance.

The second officer halted, his uniformed right hand lifting and stretching out to the offending tar's lax body, still leaning upon the rammer and completely unconcerned.

He grabbed the seaman's shoulder, startling the middle-aged tar.

The second officer's voice boomed, damning the tardiness of the sailor and the laxity, he still exhibited. All hands about the upper gun-deck, fell silent. They halted their own actions, ceasing to stow the cannon, securing the pieces, from our drill.

Their eyes cast fearful glances at the man, who had enraged

the ire of our second officer. They looked away, lest his anger find new marks for his bombastic retort.

Unsatisfied, that his words stressed the proper import of the necessity of all to heed the demands of our drill, he uttered a damning verdict. As was his right.

"Five lashess . . . no, ten lashes," he bellowed, "if your wits can't bring you to understanding, then we'll try your back," our second officer barked, in anger.

The tar before him still stood still, bent slightly as he rested upon the rammer. He offered no defense, though he slowly stood upright and erect, accepting his punishment with the quiet dignity of a veteran, who had sailed before the mast.

His leathered brow faced the second officer almost emotionlessly. His eyes met the officer's own, not in defiance, but in silent resignation. Unlike, the tendency of the younger seaman, he made no protestation nor plea for lenience. The die was cast.

Once, the second officer had uttered his sentence, it was the law of the ship, unless the captain choose to intercede. But, that was unlikely.

Had the offense and swift judgment been made in some isolated quarter of the ship, perhaps time and cooler heads might have reassessed the rash verdict, delivered in the heat of anger.

But, the tar had been dressed down in front of the ship's compliment. Worse, the sin was laxity and lateness in the performance of a drill, which had it been an actual combat could have placed his mates in hazard, while they served his assigned gun.

No, it was done. There'd be no intercession or appeal by the captain. He would uphold the rights and authority of his subordinate. He had to support and uphold the chain-of-command.

Ten lashes would be delivered.

There was a deadly silence along the deck, broken only by the sea and wind. Even, our stiff and proper marine contingent seemed to hold their breaths with the rest of our crew.

All knew the severity of the whip and the tearing wounds, that could easily rip down to the bone. To our captain's credit, I had yet to see the lash uncoiled for any offense aboard our ship.

Many other ship's captains arbitrarily used the leathered mistress of discipline for the slightest infringement.

The lash was looked upon as an inescapable and reliable instrument to assuring obedience and toughing the backs and hearts of the men, turning them like some caged and tormented dog into spiteful and unmerciful fighting men.

Many of our tars had been pressed into service, stolen from about the pubs and taverns of the English, Welsh, or Irish sea towns. They had been forced into service by press gangs, seeking to add to the ship's ranks.

Iron-handed discipline, at the hands and whims of almost indifferent and autocratic captains, was seen as the key to producing a splendid fighting man. No dandies were these hard-living men, our navy pressed into service. They were filled with spite and fight, before being forcefully enlisted into the service of his Majesty's Navy.

They were defiant and aggressive, many disobedient. It was the lash, that transformed them into the superb seaman, the hallowed British Jack Tar with his clay pipe and ready penchant for a fight.

But, not all aboard were Englishmen. The muster book showed only 430 of the Vanguard's crew were Britain's son's, proud and true. 50 were Scots and nearly a like number were Irishmen. 22 were Welsh, 4 were Shetlanders, and 1 was a Channel Islander, rounding out the bulk of subjects from his Majesty's kingdom.

And, there were foreigners in our ranks. The muster book listed a jaded blend of sailors from foreign ports. I knew not whether the press gangs had merely hauled them aboard, while in a drunken stupor or if they had joined of their own volition, simply seeking to find a ship and return to sea or flee some law or punishment, they'd violated in their native land.

Despite the insurrection and disloyalty of our former colony,

America and its ungrateful citizens of the Crown, 26 Americans still served aboard, some were undoubtedly pressed into servitude, like our seaman Jones.

There was also a sprinkling of 3 Dutch, 10 Swedes, 6 Italians, 2 Maltese, and 5 Frenchmen. The latter, I viewed with some suspicion, though I was told, they were eager volunteers, apparently having lost everything in their native homeland, through some disfavor or infraction with the new revolutionary government.

Our ranks even compromised the likes of Germans, Swiss, Portuguese, Danes, Norwegians, Russians, and several dark-skinned natives from Africa and the West Indian Islands.

When faced with such a varied lot, that barely fathomed the King's language and knew not, but their own native tongues, there was no easier means of soliciting the desired response, than the motivating bite of the lash.

It was favored by aloof and autocratic officers, content to quickly gain obedience to their orders with the least resistance and effort, on their own part.

Our good captain was not prone to being among their ranks. He'd preferred to gain the men's loyalty, through example and deed. He was resolved to show his own commitment to our vessel and thereby, intone the best in others to mirror his undertakings.

But, times had changed. We sailed to war. There was no time to coax or cajole the lax or slow-minded. Performance would be had as quickly as possible. The life of our ship and crew depended upon it.

I felt the unease of the men's stares. Several turned their gaze silently towards the captain, suspecting his intervention. I witnessed the second officer's disdain, that they would even think, his own judgment would be challenged.

The captain was being placed, between his own officer and the crew. It was not to be.

"Boatswain!" the captain's voice bellowed, "I'll not allow our ship's compliment to endure any disorder or disruption to our drill. If the second officer says, this man was late to his station and lax about his duties, I concur his punishment."

The boatswain nearly ran from his own post to report several lengths away from the captain, but well within his sight.

"Aye, sir!" he answered, "I'll take the man to the brig . . ."

"Nay, boatswain!" the captain returned. "Administer the punishment now. We've no time for ceremony or decorum. Tie him fast to the main mast."

"Sergeant!" our captain entreated a nearby marine and his contingent, positioned along the rails, practicing for the eventuality of repelling boarders as part of our drill's exercise. "Form up around the main mast, for the administration of punishment!"

The sergeant came to attention and returned a crisp obedient salute, before it was returned by the captain. The marine verbally badgered his men to isolate the space about the base of the main mast.

The boatswain moved towards the unlucky tar, after claiming two short lengths of rope like those used to tie down hatches and loose objects, when the ship fell upon heavy seas. He ordered another seaman down into the bowels of the ship to retrieve the almost forgotten whip.

Then, he fell upon the tar, claiming the man's right shoulder as he guided him about and led him, through the encircling square of marines.

The tar offered no resistance. He was strangely resided to his fate.

The tar halted before the mast and removed his wool jacket, dropping it in resignation to the deck. He even stretched his arms around the mast willingly. The act of submission seemed as if he meant to caress its smooth roundness.

The boatswain tied him fast about the wrists, making the knots tight.

A second length of rope wedded the man's feet to the mast, tied about the ankles.

"Guard, come to attention!" the Royal Marine sergeant barked. "Fix bayonets!"

The Marine drummers fell into accompaniment with his orders, adding formality and ceremony to the hastily proscribed punishment.

The silence of the deck was broken. It was filled with the simultaneous din of the sharp spikes being removed from their holders, about the Marines' belts.

"Present arms!"

The brass buttplates of the rifles thumped along the deck, before the high-collared Marine contingent hefted their weapons in one flowing movement, bringing their rifles up in front of their proud chests.

The boatswain stood back, his actions guarded and protected by the armed detachment of Marines, standing with their rifles held as if on parade. He stepped back slowly, watching the sight unfolding with a dream-like quality, though he was an active participant, albeit unwilling.

The sails snapped and filled as the wind grew.

The boatswain halted well beyond the length the whip would travel. The instrument of discipline had yet to arrive. He studied the unresisting tar before him, knowing him by name from several other shared journeys.

The boatswain would do as the captain ordered, but he would not relish it. His mind filled with the burden of the pain, he'd be forced to inflict on another, all in the name of duty.

Captain Shefferd had never been one to allow the indiscriminate use of the lash, aboard the HMS Vanguard. And, except for the hothead and quick temper of their second officer, it might not even be uncoiled now. But, it was too late for that.

The captain was bound by tradition and necessity to bolster and support the decision of his second officer or for that matter, any of the officers in his command, less his own authority be diminished and that of his officers be lessened.

The sailor sent to retrieve the whip returned. His thin form seemed almost timid as he pressed through the drawn ranks of the marines, standing in formation about the main mast. He fell under the silent, but damning gaze of his mates, even though he was only doing as ordered.

He held the whip up to the boatswain, his eyes filled with shame and guilt, for being the one to turn its wicked braided leather over to its cruel artisan.

The boatswain took it silently. He was skilled in the instrument's use, though in truth, he had been elated, that he had not had to prove the expertise of his deft handiwork, until now.

Now, that had all been pushed aside.

His right hand grasped the whip's wrapped handle as he let its length uncoil to the deck. Its leather failed to lose its round shape, a testament to the days it had hung out of sight, coiled, bound, and unused.

The second officer walked about the square formed by the marines. He entered it, well behind the boatswain. He stood out of reach of the stretch of the boatswain's arm and whip, waiting for the punishment to commence.

The captain approached the tightly formed square, studying the deck and witnesses about him. He was silent, no doubt feeling the heavy burden of the punishment, awaiting his command.

"You there!" he engaged the tar, that had returned to deliver the whip, "make that man's back ready for the lash."

The tar obeyed, moving unwillingly to the back of the seaman, tied to the mast. He gripped two handfuls of the man's shirt and yanked his hands down along the tar's back, ripping and pulling away the cotton material, that offered little protection from the lash.

The act was meant to expose the severity of the lash, offering a sure reminder to the fate awaiting the next offender or any, who failed to meet the demands placed upon them.

As the boatswain prepared himself to deliver the full measure of the wicked tip of the lash, the second officer ordered the tight square of marines to begin to separate. Their dispersal still kept the other tars at bay. But, it allowed all on deck a view of their comrade, tied about the mast and of the gruesome lashing to come.

Each section's officer or boatswain ordered the men's eyes

upon the mate, standing to take his punishment. And, each man obeyed, less failure to witness the dispensed justice be viewed as an infraction, enough to find themselves following in their mate's place.

The wind blew steadily. It held the cool briskness, that those upon deck would have enjoyed, savoring its freshness and the simple pleasure of being at sea. But, that was reserved for another time, a time now forgotten and that seemed strange and distant.

"Boatswain, you may begin," the captain directed, without any emotion or fret in his voice.

The boatswain's eyes fell to the deck. They studied the whip in his hands, before lifting it to find the back of his mark. Perhaps, the most dreadful part of flogging, for both the man suffering its punishment and those ordered to witness it, was the painful silence and waiting for the strike of the whip.

One knew the outcome, but it was the delay between each blow and the preparation and force with which it was delivered, that played with the mind and unnerved one's soul. The morbid anticipation and waiting weakened even the strongest hearts and resolutions. Each strike was separate and new, no sound or strike was the same and all stung at body and will.

I saw the tar strapped to the mast prepare himself, taking in a deep breath. But, instead of holding it deep inside his lungs and bearing for torment of the lash's bite, he released it and the tension of waiting for the arriving blow.

The air cut with the sickening sound of the lash growing taunt and being thrust forward. Staring eyes barely saw it snake through the air, its braided leather unfurling, its wicked tip cutting, slicing ahead.

The crack of the whip snapped, just as the tip of the lash reached the exposed flesh of the tar. His muscles and limbs tensed as if he would be thrown forward from his own movements, save for the obstruction of the mast, holding him firmly in place by his bonds.

The boatswain had taken a full step forward, throwing his body's motion and weight into the blow. Our eyes were rewarded by a crimson red streak, running diagonally down the tar's left shoulder and towards the center of his back. The skin was filleted cleanly open.

It was as if the wound had been wrought with the delicate sharp blade of a surgeon's scalpel, though not wielded by a surgeon's skilled light-handed touch. No slight given to our own good doctor.

But, the blow had been masterfully delivered. It received the silent approval of our second officer, whose eyes gleamed at the wound and awaited the delivery of nine more blows.

The whip cracked sharply. Again, bare flesh surrendered to its wicked sting, splitting and gouging the open back in an elongated gash.

Eyes turned to the boatswain to find him steadying himself from the forward throw of his body. His swung arm nearly touched the deck, the whip running its full length.

The bound seaman shook within his restraints. His shuddering body fought to absorb the pain. His mind tormented him with the apprehension and fear of the eight lashes to come. Any fight or will, he still possessed had nearly abandoned him, though he still fought to accept the lash in silence.

In the stillness of the gathered formations, men and officers alike, could hear his pained breath slowly exhaling from his lungs as he fought to keep from crying out.

The third lash was errant. It missed its intended mark as the ship rolled, while the boatswain stepped forward.

The tip of the leather whip struck the back of the tar's head finding the soft and tender flesh, covering the rear of his left ear, before crossing down the nape of the seaman's neck and down along his right shoulder blade.

The tar screamed out in agony, the lower half of his left ear nearly sliced off. Myself and several of the younger officers were appalled at the grizzly sight.

One even looked away to the consternation of our second officer, who glimpsed the lack of fortitude and resolve as a damning weakness, before our gathered crew.

The tar's legs collapsed from beneath him. His knees bent as his body caressed the mast. His face turned to the left, his right cheek and lips pressed to the towering spire.

His eyes closed as he gasped in pain. Three lashes proved the measure needed to break his defiance. His nearly fallen form was held in place, captive by the bonds holding him fast.

The humble supplicant awaited the remainder of his punishment. His now crooked back offered a wide target for the unfurling ship.

The whip cracked. The fourth lash delivered its full force into the hunched back and its sheltering shoulders. The seaman's body withered with pain as a cry was forced beyond his tight lips.

In quick order, the fifth and sixth lash were delivered. The fifth found the tar's body unprepared. He tried to drop to the deck, but was shamefully held about the base of the main mast in an undignified squat. He shuddered with the bite of the fifth lash.

But, there was no movement from the sixth.

"Hold your place!" the second officer ordered the boatswain as he prepared to take up the lash and fling it again.

The captain's second was displeased with the disgraceful slumping form of the collapsed tar. He strode forward indignantly, studying the six crimson gashes along the man's back.

He'd expected to find, the seaman's pleading eyes, begging for some reprieve. But, he found only a still form, unmoving and unresponsive.

He turned about to the inquisitive looks of the marine sergeant, who was in charge of the detachment around the mast. He ordered the sergeant to have two men break their loose formation and heft the tar upright.

The tall black leather hats of two marines bobbed about as clad in their red and white resplendent uniforms, they moved on the "quick," slinging their rifles and dropping to the tar.

They pulled him aloft, despite the tugging restraint of the ropes binding him. One held him fast to the mast as the other secured a new length of rope and tied it about the tar's waist, fixing him upright.

The tar offered no resistance to their handiwork having passed from consciousness. His head drooped backwards in unresponsive resignation, his was mouth agape and eyes unseeing.

"Continue!" the second officer ordered as the marines quickly left the mast and took their place within the ranks of the loose square of men formed about it.

"Stop!" the single word was issued from the damning lips of our surgeon, who had left his post attending our sick. He had come as soon, as word of the punishment detail had reached the lower deck.

With black bag in hand, he pushed through the marine formation, making his way to the main mast.

The deck was silent and tense. The doctor had disputed the rank and authority of our second officer's lawful order. Worse, the boatswain waited in fearful remission, heeding the doctor's temporary pardon of our tar.

The surgeon dropped his bag at the foot of the mast, while the sails cracked and billowed above our heads. He felt for a pulse, before searching out the tar's forehead.

Before the others, I understood, what he had spied there. His face bore the same fear as mine as he slowly moved his hand away.

He said nothing. But, he set about examining the arms and limbs of his patient. I saw the confirming and disquieting resignation in his eyes and knew at once, he had found the marks, both of us had linked to the pestilence plaguing our ship and crew

The surgeon moved away from the tar and strode towards the boatswain and the second officer.

In puzzlement, officers and men watched as he tore the whip out of the hands of the former, curling it in his tight angry grasp.

He ignored the second officer and made his way to the captain, a little more past him, before halting.

"He's dead!" the doctor hissed vehemently, fighting to control his anger and the tone of his voice. "And, it was not only the lash that killed him . . ."

"He was slow to report to quarters and once there, he was lax in his duties . . ." the second officer joined us and barked his dissatisfaction with the doctor's intrusion and failure to recognize the proper chain-of-command and respect of his own rank and position.

"He was tardy and lax, because he is afflicted. With the same pox, that has claimed the life, of Seaman Jones and has left three more in their hammocks below. If you don't believe me, examine the marks on his arms. They are the same as the others," the doctor turned about, coming face-to-face with his detractor.

The second officer began to protest, but the captain interceded, aware of the eyes and ears of the crew upon us all. The crew said nothing, but their eyes and faces held the resentment and spite of men, who believed their shipmate wronged.

The captain sought to defuse the moment, halting the biting words of our second officer and speaking in guarded confidence to the doctor, heeding his words and advice.

But, as I eyed our stern-faced tars, I saw our ship divided into factions, which I had never seriously contemplated before. True, as in life, there were classes of people, after all, every man has his place. There were commoners and lords, much as there were seamen and officers.

Each class served its purpose and had it own responsibilities and duties to administer to. Neither entwined with the other, which would prove reckless folly and the undoing of civility. Each had its own unique tastes and manners, likes and dislikes.

Each lived in their own separate worlds, determined by the accident or the fickleness of birth. And, each was bred and reared to accept their place in the likes of the civilized world and society.

This I had always taken for granted, being keenly aware of my own place and the prospects for my own success within the guarded framework, set about me. But now, I saw the grim reality of such separation and division. Our small band of officers stood at the head of over eight-hundred crewmen, though only a small number were topside and bearing witness to our folly. But they were already intent, beset in pre-judgment, that we had wronged them, through one of their own.

But, discipline and duty are strong ties. Their norms bind men to inaction, allaying their own anger for the norms and dictates of duty. Though, the body of men before us seethed quietly, they stood in formation, in resigned acceptance.

Our captain moved to quickly allay their anger and calm the situation. He ordered the second officer away on some made-up or meaningless duty, removing the source of the men's anger from our midst. It was as if with him out of sight, their calm would be restored.

Then, he turned to the doctor, commiserating with the surgeon's announcement and apologetically delivering the truth, that none present on deck knew of the man's plight.

This he did in a strong clear voice, not in any offer of being right, but to show to the formation, that rightly or wrongly, ignorance and the failure of the tar to present his own disposition had led to his own unfortunate demise.

Rightly, our captain returned the ship to some semblance of order, seeking the comfort and station of his own rank and authority along with the rules and routine, that governed our body.

In short order, he had the tar removed from the mast. The good doctor officiated, supervising the release of the penitent into the arms of several of his mates. Despite their grief, I saw the angry scorn in the men's faces and their guarded movements.

Only our good doctor's compassion and the solid hand of the captain, banishing our second officer to the nether reaches of our ship, had prevented any incident from frothing to the surface of the men's hearts.

I witnessed a gentleness of heart, I would not have expected from the cold rough and weathered forms, that moved beneath the main mast. Their rough calloused hands treated their deceased comrade with all the reverence and respect, one would expect upon some hallowed ground of a cathedral or monastery.

And though, I doubt they had forgiven the arbitrary indifference of our second officer, they handled themselves in a stalwart manner as if somehow above his foul intransigence. They had taken the higher road, stepping apart from the entire incident and the death of their companion.

I studied the removal of their friend and comrade, watching their rhythmic motions. I could not say, there was a holiness about their actions. But, there was a tenderness, quite unnatural to their efforts. Yet, its presence seemed demanded. It was the least, that they could entail in a final salute to their shipmate.

The formation was dismissed, only after the body of the tar was ferreted below decks. In those awkward moments, the ship's company waited in silence.

Only the flapping of our canvas or the sound of the waters frothing breath reached our ears. Each man was lost to his own thoughts or hatreds, depending on his predilection.

As for me, my thoughts returned to the strange marks upon the arms of the afflicted men. I wondered how long it would be, until another of the crew succumbed to the plague, that sought to cast itself about the Vanguard.

CHAPTER 12

Around the Point

HMS Vanguard
Sailing off the Coast of Portugal
Day 4-Evening

I could not say things had returned to normal. But, for all good intent, the morning and afternoon had found us free of any further outbreaks of the affliction, that had so quickly disrupted the peace and routine of our vessel. In the seventh hour of the evening, all was peaceful. Or, so we had thought.

The topics of our gathered dinner group would prove otherwise. But, other matters preceded that revelation. No less important among them was the mood of the men and the readiness of our ship

The mood of the men and the uneasiness finding our ship had risen like froth from the discipline, that had been so harshly delivered, upon the back of a seaman. It belabored our minds, if not our tongues.

As the captain had instructed, I kept an eye and ear about as I went about my daily duties. I noted some of the men had fallen silent, disgruntled or soured by the death of the seaman, disciplined by the lash.

A few hands bantered about this or that discomfort, they endured at sea. But, these jaunted topics of their discussions were the common grievance of the seaman and despite their voiced dissatisfaction were quite normal.

They griped of the mold growing on the dwindling supply of biscuits or loaves of bread. Or, they complained of the tasteless toughness of a ration of salted beef. They lamented over the rock hard biscuits awaiting them in barrels as the last of the loaves of bread drew near and similar dislikes. All were common dissatisfactions and the fare of routine topics.

In fact, I was somewhat elated to be able to report a measure of normality, back to the captain.

The meal was much shorter this evening. There had been an uneasy tension about the table. The openness, with which the captain customarily addressed us and entreated our own thoughts and conversations, was lacking.

Perhaps, it was the cold silence, between the captain and his second officer, that made our gathered presence so ill at ease. We knew, without it being said, that our master would think the latter's previous day's actions had been too quick and arbitrary, compared to his own manner and method.

Our captain would have fathomed some reason for the seaman's failure to perform. He'd have questioned the cause of the man's tardiness and laxness and only then, allow himself to fairly mete out a just punishment.

But, not so our rash second officer.

Regardless, eyes were cast down upon plate or fork, content to find distraction amid the portions of our meal, rather than look up and search out the piercing looks of faces and eyes, willing to delve out blame and judgment for what had happened.

It was done. And, now all officers, seated at our table, must make the best of it, come what may.

Far from seeking the unity our captain had desired of our warship, while we prepared to meet the French foe, our ship's body had fallen into division. Yet, such division fell upon clear lines, enlisted parted from officer. But, that was as it should be.

There was still the authority of rank and uniform to lord over the seaman and the now ominous presence of the lash. Its leathered bite had found our decks. And, in doing so, had destroyed the trust and loyalty, our captain had labored, so hard to instill.

Our ship was mastered by the dictates of the captain as always. But, his unquestionable authority was now joined by the spiteful discipline and physical punishment of the lash. We were no different, than any other ship-of-the-line. The message was clear and the change in the common seaman's plight was all too apparent.

In an instant of anger, our second officer had changed everything.

But, there were other more pressing matters upon us. Including those reported regrettably by our doctor, when he joined us late for supper.

At supper, we learned the dreaded affliction had raised its head anew, after a short reprieve, that had made all think the sickness was behind us. The reprieve, we had assumed, was found in the morning and afternoon, escaped us.

It had been thought, that the illness had been confined to the lower gun-deck, where the doctor had sequestered himself and our ill tars. The rats had sought out the protection of the lower decks and their shadows with their secretive nooks and crannies. They had spirited themselves away, until our beaters had driven them to the light of day and over the side.

But, at our dinner, we learned from the doctor, that others had fallen ill, though they showed only early signs of the sickness. In truth, our doctor could not say with any certainty, that the affliction was the same one, plaguing the men he had placed in quarantine.

Three men on the upper gun-deck and another six from the middle gun-deck claimed some discomfort or malady. All had carried out their duties aptly enough during the daylight, eating heartily, and consorting with their mates for a game of cards or dice, before retiring to the simple comfort of their hammocks or a cold supper.

But, all now bore some infection or symptom of whatever illness had found them. I was to assist the surgeon, who we now learned was overwhelmed by the number of cases.

Each man's symptoms were different, depending on his age and the constitution of his body.

Some merely resided in a restful stupor as if in a daze. They were too tired and fatigued to even rise from their hammocks. A cold or indigestion had been their first thought and that, of the officers or boatswains, they had confided in.

At the hour of our supper, others had become violently ill, similar to the young lad before them. The contents of their own supper were uncontrollably released upon the deck. More, than one was threatened with choking upon the fluid and undigested morsels of his vomit. They were too weak to fight the confining folds of their hammock or to turn their heads over its side.

To a man, some were like helpless children. They depended on the doctor or the compassionate hand of a mate, willing to chance the risk of infection, to aid them in their time of need.

Mop and bucket ruled their berths. And, strong lye soap, our only disinfectant, were liberally applied to the staining remains, found upon the wood of each deck.

The isolation of the temporary infirmary upon the lower gun-deck was proving ineffective. The threat of illness still continued. It was unabated by the doctor's administrations or his attempts to separate patients from those among the crew.

With the threat of the illness spreading ship-wide, it was required to hastily move the afflicted to the forgotten hollows of the lowest decks. The temporary infirmary would be moved two decks further below, hidden beneath the Vanguard's waterline. This new measure was prescribed by the doctor, himself.

It offered nearly total isolation, the only reasonable alternative to his failed potions and elixirs.

Now, the doctor dared not prescribe fresh air or risk chancing leaving the men on their assigned decks. Moving their hammocks apart from the crowded haunts of the rest of the crew, such as he had on the lower gun-deck, profited us little.

To some measure, it appeared, that this might work. We hoped for as much.

We also learned, that some of the afflicted seamen's flesh was still marred by the small little nicks or bites, that had been blamed upon the rats. It defied reason and logic to all.

We had rightly assumed, the vermin had been disposed of. Yet, fresh marks were present. So, the doctor informed us.

Not all the marks were in the same place on each tar. Some had the tiny scratches about their arms, like the earliest victims of the ailment. But, others had the nicks upon their legs or about their shoulders, near the neck.

All had the tiny wounds near some vein or artery, running close to the surface of the skin. And, to a man all harbored the same pale pallor and lack of color, that would have alarmed any, who saw or witnessed their ghostly faces.

I stood upon the railings. Silently, I chose to spend as much time topside as I could after dinner. In truth, I was avoiding the sickness, even though, it was my new found duty to assist our good surgeon's needs, providing for rations or hands to aid him.

Night had come early, more in answer to the thick heavy clouds claiming the sky around us, than the setting of the sun.

I was not on duty and availed myself to the colorful hues of a distant vista, watching the coast of Portugal, barely a line along the horizon, off our port side.

My mind was filled with all sort of thought and emanation. It was joined, by the lightness of my head, spurred from the wine, I had partaken of during our captain's routine evening meal.

Our vessel was rounding the tip of Portugal, nearly finished on its southerly journey and would soon, be turning eastward.

In moments, the navigator would order the correction of the helmsmen's course, turning our warship to the east and towards Spanish waters, laying beyond the tip of Portugal.

Despite, the illness plaguing us, the drills continued unceasingly. The drums had beaten incessantly, for several days.

They sometimes called the men to their stations, three times a day. The short retort of the drums' din was etched into our lads' minds and echoed in their ears.

Upon only the first few strikes of the drums, summoning the crew, they abandoned their current tasks and undertakings, dashing for their guns or posts.

My heart and thoughts felt the worst for our marines, repeatedly scaling the ratlings to take a sharpshooter's perch about the mizzen mast or some other awful height.

But, all did as they were required. I preferred, to think it was pride, rather than the threat and sting of the lash, that drove them to excel. But, it mattered not. The sole goal of our exercises was to prepare our men and ship for battle.

Their tireless efforts now, might assure that we succeeded in the upcoming battle and that, fewer of our lot would perish.

I rested against the rail, turning my back to the coast of Portugal and studied the nearly empty deck before me.

Ensign Higgins had the watch. He stood beside the two helmsmen manning the wheel, linked to rope and chain, that moved our giant rudder. The rudder was a massive thing. The oversized steering mechanism was nearly four-stories tall about the stern, with most of its length beneath the water.

At eight knots, turns were still slow and distant, though a skilled captain could aid and hasten our maneuvering with the positioning of our sailcloth. Skill and seamanship along with our vessel's design would see, that we outmaneuvered our foe's ancient galleons.

But perhaps, wheel was a poor choice of words to describe the two joined spoked wheels, linked to the wooden yoke that allowed the two helmsmen to wrest the rudder about.

In heavy seas, two men would find themselves strained and hard-pressed to turn the giant wheels, linked to a central hub by their spokes. Four to six men might find it a test of their manhood and strength, trying to even coax the rudder towards their intended destination in foul weather.

But now, in the mild waters we traveled, the two helmsmen

merely stood beside the wheel, awaiting any command of the officer on watch. Two ropes held the wheel in place, lashed to ply us straight ahead.

The wheel's watch was also supervised under the attentive and observant eyes of a veteran boatswain. A practiced hand aboard our ship, I think the boatswain's presence was at the bequest of the captain, seeking to keep a wise watch over young ensigns, like Higgins and myself.

The tip of Portugal was slipping past our port side. But, we would journey still farther south, keeping our vessel away from any prying eyes, that might be trying to spy our presence.

We ran without lights in the darkness, lest we announce ourselves to those ashore or the occupants of the bobbing lights, marking the fishing boats returning home with the approach of darkness and their nets full.

It seemed strange, that we had seen so little traffic in these tranquil waters. There were barely any merchants of commerce and only a few fishing boats present. It was known, that many ships had regularly plied these waters and should have contested or joined our presence, sailing along this formerly well traveled coast.

Even the gulls, that had ushered our ship to sea, when we left Portsmouth or when, we had provided the waters a feast of rodents, had left us. I found their absence distressing. It was like some omen or portent of an evil, yet to come.

So close to shore, the gulls should have been readily about us, if for no other reason, but to follow our progress and feast upon the garbage discarded from our ship.

The last, I had seen a gull, was at the burial of the young seaman. I recalled the lore and yarns of dead men and the passage of their souls. But, I did not believe the birds had awaited to claim the young tar's soul, when we released his body to the sea.

Nor, did I believe they cursed us for denying them his flesh, dragged beneath the surface by the heavy chain wrapped about his legs and hidden beneath the shroud, bearing his lifeless form.

Ensign Higgins went about studying our position. He held a

sextant in his hands, but the object might as well have been a trinket, adorning his uniform, for the blackness of the night. There were no stars or heavenly bodies by which to fix our position.

The only shimmering lights were those of the shore and fishing boats. But, the loss of sight of the stars above in the inky clouds of blackness, blocking the night sky, did not matter.

There were charts below and Higgins knew our course and the upcoming maneuver, ordered earlier by our captain. Our ship's master had seen to it, that all his officers knew our course and his intent.

In the darkness, I saw Higgins turn and move toward the port railing. I assumed he was making one last quest to mark the coastline, assuring he was well clear of the tip of Portugal.

He stood silently alone, allowing our ship to continue south, a good measure further, insuring our clear passage of the coastline, before returning to the wheel. In the semi-darkness of the unlit deck, I could not tell, if Higgins' stern face was set for want of doubt of his next order or his self-satisfied ego, finding the satisfaction and enjoyment of being in command.

Like I, Higgins was taking a measure of satisfaction and pride in his supervision of the watch. It was not only the trust of being in the most temporary of command of our great vessel, but the chance, however slight of exercising the knowledge, we were learning.

Though, Higgins' and my own rank entitled us to the same indifference and aloofness, shown by our captain's second officer, it did not demand it of us. Our young careers allowed us some indiscretion, though not outright fraternization among the men.

We were viewed by the men and officers alike as more akin to candidates for our hallowed officer ranks, serving about sea. And though, our uniforms were of the same material and cut of the higher ranking officers, it was well noted that we were merely the students, learning by deed and observation, those things academy life and formal schooling could never teach.

And, this made myself and Ensign Higgins approachable by

our crew. We were placed in charge of the most irrelevant duties, if only to learn even the smallest details from each man, noting how life at sea was conducted aboard our ship.

And yet, for all the aid and mentoring of our boatswains, eager to informally tutor us in why, this line was pulled taunt or that man was sent back up to man the canvas, there was a limbo-like world to our existence.

Our senior officers, only several years elder, than us, had little time to assist us in instruction or questioning. They had pressing duties to carry out, leaving us to learn our lessons by ourselves or at best, through the observation of the crew, under the charge of our boatswains.

Repetition and rote, these were the methods of our learning. We gained experience by watching and doing. There were no practice lessons or tutorages. The captain ordered an action and we did it, ordering the crew about. When in truth, they were often times more familiar with his dictates, than ourselves.

We studied their actions, learning at the captain's bequest, what order would summon his desired action or response. With time, we knew what was expected and instead of trying to learn the action, we came to anticipate it, having learned it in the doing.

Among the watch, if Higgins gave an order, it was obeyed as readily as if he was the captain. I watched as his ego glowed in preparation for his next momentous maneuver, be it ever so slight and insignificant.

This was a time of growth for both of us. We felt our way about the novelty of our newly chosen careers.

But, I knew that Ensign Higgins, like I, held the dread of committing an error. Though our commands were accurate and rightful enough, we gave them only after some hesitation, giving ourselves time to search out their correctness and assuring that they placed neither ship or crew at harm.

Unlike us, the captain and his second officer issued orders instinctively. They knew or sensed by feel of the deck or the flap of our sailcloth, what proper order or maneuver was to be undertaken. They had no doubts and there was no procrastination or hesitation in their decisions. There was no doubt or fret.

But, having surmised the state of things, I could see our other ensign was ready to confidently issue forth his next order.

"Unlash the wheel!" Higgins ordered, his voice raised.

He mirrored the commands of a captain. He practiced his orders, during his own brief moment in command of the deck and watch.

"On my order, commence our turn to port!" he said with crisp authority, watching as the two helmsmen released the ropes, holding the wheel fast.

Two men atop the mast, serving as lookouts, gave his orders only slight attention, keeping their eyes peeled along the lit coast or the dark horizon, searching for the lights of an approaching ship or threat.

Somewhere, near the bow as well as along the stern, a duo of marines walked their post, while two more walked amidships. Other tars busied themselves about the unending tasks, that kept our ship at sea.

"Turn to port!" Ensign Higgins ordered, sending the two mates pulling the spokes and handles of the wheel, bringing the large rudder about and slowly turning our behemoth ship to the left.

The turn was barely noticeable, except by the banking of the ship. In the darkness, there was no way to measure the width of the maneuver. Above, the stars and moon were blotted out by the clouds, bathing us in stumbling blackness.

Only the lights of the fishing boats, near the shore and the few fires upon land guided our ensign, ordering the Vanguard onto its new heading. He ordered our rudder straight ahead, once his eyes had fixed upon some distant light along the coast, safely informing him, we were running parallel to the southeastern coast of Spain's neighbor.

Like I, he soon spotted lights running high atop the water in the distance.

"Lookouts, stay sharp!" he bellowed, through cupped hands, pleased to have beaten the tars to the first sighting of the unknown vessel. He ordered the watching boatswain below, tasking him to inform the captain of the vessel's approach and to claim several more tars for duty about the ship.

The darkness promised to deepen and he wisely chose to bring more eyes topside to search the night. Though, the ship ahead was lighted, there might be those, who like our own, moved under the cover of the night's blackness.

They might not only be cloaking their presence, but their identity. I spied the gold trim, adorning our captain's headdress, marking his return topside with the boatswain.

His brass telescope extended along its telescoping length and pointed out towards the coast, studying our position, before slewing about and locking upon the lighted ship.

Despite, seeing her lights running high above the water, our captain's voice showed no alarm. His experienced eye marked the craft as a merchant ship, likely carrying spices or goods to the western shores of France or even our own isle.

His voice instructed our other young ensign, pointing out several other lights, hung about her bow and stern. The craft lacked the towering hull of a warship. It had the low draft of a merchantman, its hold likely full and weighting it down in the water.

The weight of its load slowed the merchantman's progress. It seemed to be running slower, than our own larger vessel, merely drifting off the coast as it pushed against the natural flow of a southeasterly breeze.

The captain took the time to share his knowledge, adding other observations, that likely described the identity of the ship approaching us, though well to port and bathed in darkness.

I assumed, he welcomed the distraction from the incident the lashing had nearly incited, save for his own intervention. I left Ensign Higgins and the captain, choosing to visit the surgeon, before retiring to my quarters.

I moved across the deck, without incurring an inquisitive look of either the watch or our captain. I sought the escape, provided by the steps and ladders, leading down the hold, beneath our stowed small boats.

As was the want of the common seaman, after a day's labors, they had retired about the corners and spaces of the ship. They sought out the small islands of privacy, where three, four, or more might gather to play cards or otherwise wile away the time, before claiming their hammocks.

A few small bands talked in rambling conversations. Their words offered little thought or depth, harboring neither resentment or malice. Their discussions were those of friends and mates, offering only the reassuring comfort of camaraderie. I judged these men and their small groups of no concern or threat.

But, several small bands and even single tars loitered about. They cloaked themselves in an uneasy silence. These I fretted, because of the thoughts, they likely harbored, though guardedly to themselves.

They did nothing more, than cast their eyes away at my approach. Though, a few held their heads up, their eyes defiantly following my path with distaste and disfavor, almost daring challenge or conflict.

I continued my downward journey.

Lieutenant Samuel Isaiah Loydd.

CHAPTER 13

Personalities

HMS Vanguard
Sailing off the Coast of Portugal
Day 4-Evening

For the most part, the tars had taken to their hammocks. A few played simple instruments, biding away the last few hours of the evening, before all turned to sleep. But, in the eight hour of the evening, some men still sought some refuge or distraction.

A handcrafted wooden flute joined in accompaniment of a small concertina. The squeezebox raised an awful din, accompanied by the shrill pitch of the homemade fife. Neither musician seemed to recall all the notes to the next stanza.

Accompanying voices droned on with the song's lyrics, adding to the amusement of the participants.

A few tars munched about on rations, they had withheld from their evening meal. But, for the most part, the sights and sounds, that filled the lower decks, heralded the coming of a restful night, after a trying and unwelcome day.

Still other tars' exposed backs or arms became the willing human canvas for the artistic skills and talents of a few of their creative peers. Their flesh was the canvas of tattoos.

They gritted their teeth and bore the pain as tattoos remembering a loved one or sweetheart were pricked into their skin with a needle or sharp sliver of wood. A mixture made of ash or ink was then, rubbed into the wounds, making the image permanent.

One tar, a veteran of many voyages, had almost every space along his back covered with this or that, dizzying image. His flesh bore the likeness of every ship, he had served on. And, there were the names of several women from long forgotten ports.

The skill was crafted from those mates, who had returned from expeditions to the Pacific Isles, the likes of James Cook's adventures. The craft was mirrored, after being learned from the islanders, pleasant natives knowing little of toil or guilt, but living life freely among the beautiful islands, they were blessed to inhabit.

I passed along, finding no more sailors prone to silently demonstrating their anger. Most knew, there could be no good to come of it.

But, had our second officer traveled my same footsteps, I readily believed more, than several of our crew would find themselves up before the lash by morning.

For had those stern gazes directed my way, befallen him, he would have certainly found them an affront and dealt with them most severely. But, that was partly hand-in-hand a blessing of being a junior officer. I could overlook perceived or imagined slights, provided they were not open demonstrations against my authority.

The music and a calliope of conversations retreated behind me, when I left the middle gun-deck and came upon the lower one. It held a similar assortment of gatherings.

Though, the deck's tars were not as talented or musically inclined as their brethren on the deck above, they joined in their own brand of revelry. They sang or mouthed the offensive words of some seaman's ditty, before it was followed by a ruckus chorus of laughter and amusement.

I quickly transited the lower gun-deck, seeking the lowest of the two remaining levels below. I sought passage by way of a lantern, I had claimed from the lower gun-deck. Unattended lanterns were forbidden and there seemed to be no sign of anyone or any light further below.

The two lowest decks seemed dark and grim. They appeared abandoned by the healthy. They lacked the sounds of laughter and merriment. It was like passing from a world teeming with life to one harbored in death. I found darkness about me, in spite of the half-light of the lanterns below, coming into view from the lowest of the two decks, below the waterline. The dim light was emitted from the infirmary.

The bowels of the Vanguard were engulfed in the quiet and solemnness of a crypt. It was hard to believe this underworld existed inside the haunts of our ship.

I searched out the new infirmary, set up by our doctor and holding his afflicted charges.

Far forward, I again found the blankets hanging limply, off the strung lines, meant to intone some isolation to our afflicted patients. Despite, moving the infirmary further below, the quarantine was still ineffectual. But, it had the desired outcome of separating our ill tars from the rest of the ship's healthier compliment.

But, any benefit it might have obtained as a morale boasting measure had been lost. Our second officer's penchant to unleash the disciplinary power and bite of the lash had crushed the morale and goodwill, our captain had labored so hard to instill.

Still, it was something. And, I think the good doctor's

empathy and concern for our crew, especially with his almost conflicting intercession a day earlier, though too late to benefit the tar being disciplined, had endeared him to the crew.

Surely, his daring to brave the wrath of our second officer, standing up in behalf of our deceased seaman, had shown him a champion of the men. It was a fact, that had surely set the second officer against him for the rest of our voyage.

And worse, it would merely exasperate matters, between the two, since the captain's second officer was already predisposed against our good doctor for his lack of self-discipline, regarding his drinking and his less, than proper respect for our military bearing and protocol.

I moved the blanket aside and found the doctor seated upon an empty crate, pulled up under the glowing halo of a lantern's candle. He poured over the pages of an opened medical tome.

It took my own eyes a moment to adjust to the dim light, making me wonder how he could even read at all, in the semi-darkness, offered by the single lantern nearby.

He did not acknowledge my presence, but chose to continue scanning about the pages of the thick medical volume. He searched its listing of ailments, diagnoses, and treatments for some cure, that might alleviate the pox weakening his patients. A cure escaped him.

The surgeon appeared intent and studious. He mirrored a younger university scholar, incensed with preparing for some forthcoming examination to test his recitation and knowledge.

His eyes peered, through the delicately framed reading lenses set about his head and balanced precariously atop the ridge of his nose. It was the first time, I had seen him rely on spectacles. They belied his age.

Despite, his tired eyes, he allowed himself no reprieve. His right hand's index finger marked his place and moved down along the page. His lips moved silently as if in incantation or conjuring.

But, his heavy brow showed, he had not discovered any magic elixir or remedy, let alone an enlightening clue to identify and battle the affliction.

I found his devotion to his profession and to finding a solution
to mend his patients commendable, even after our harsh words
earlier and his outspoken and defeatist attitude towards our war.

As time went on, I would continue to find the doctor a man
of splendid character and integrity. Perhaps, there was truth in
the old adage, that one could not judge a book by its cover.

It applied aptly to our surgeon.

From the outside, his slovenly appearance and his almost
disrespect for the formalities of rank and military etiquette were
offensive and distressing. They wrought only disfavor and
displeasure from a more proper and staunch officer, say such as
our captain's second officer, Samuel Isaiah Loydd.

Lieutenant Loydd was every measure the aristocrat of good
breeding and more. He was a proper and God-fearing Christian.
To him, there was almost no difference, between serving his
Majesty and the teachings of the Church of England.

A vicar's gospel to strive to do one's best in one's position or
duty, attempting to honor the Lord, was equally a call to do
one's best to serve our monarch. It was as if serving the King to
the best of one's ability meant serving God, as well.

And, there was nothing wrong with setting a standard of
performance to be met, if not for other's, than for one's self. Few
men can say, they have strived to some success or profit, without
having established some goal or aim, for its attainment.

And, few among our small band of officers doubted, what our
second officer's goals were. He meant to obtain a captaincy and ship
of his own. More, he wanted to obtain both in the service of the
Royal Navy, despite his family's vast wealth, which could have easily
purchased him several ships of a private merchant shipping line, thus
placing him in command of a private and purchased flotilla.

But, merchant ships and commerce lacked the regalia and
stature, that our Lieutenant Loydd coveted.

Our second officer treasured the wealth of respect and
adoration, his uniform and rank could purchase him in the closed
courts of the Dukes and Earls, which his family entreated with
their money, buying power and favor.

He had yet to earn the coveted medals and ribbons for his chest, that would capture the eyes of the ladies of those galas and courts, he regularly departed to, once we returned to port. But, he was on his way.

And, he would not let us stand in his path. Nor, would the backs of our seamen or even the generosity and gentleness of our captain prevent him from achieving, his desired success.

In truth, I believe, he judged our captain a weak man for wanting to provide for the benefit of our crew over his own ambitions.

I found our second officer a lonely man, at least, while we were at sea. When not forced by the order of the captain to attend our informal dinners or to be upon deck to administer to his turn at watch or other proscribed duty, he was to be found in the self-imposed isolation and exile of his berth.

He seemed to prefer the solitary reprieve of a book to the camaraderie of his fellow officers. Though, "officers" was probably a poor choice of words to describe his colleagues and shipmates. For, I believe he had none, subscribing to the apt belief, that he deemed himself superior and did not judge us to be his peers.

At first, I thought his standoffish attitude might be to place some distance between himself, as a senior ship's officer and ourselves, because of our novice standing. But, the longer I sailed with him, the more I found his disaffection borne out of aloofness and his own self-superiority, real or imagined.

The doctor turned a page, his face showing no promise from having gleemed the information printed there. His finger began moving again. It followed the tiny print, almost unreadable in the dim light, that harbored sleep for his patients and beckoned even the doctor to succumb to its seductive entreaties.

He closed the book, the pages of the thick tome clapping shut and threatening to wake his charges, one of whom stirred with its dull din.

He looked up.

"Never mind them. None of these have awoken for the past two hours. It's like they're half dead or don't care anymore," he surrendered in failure.

"The prognoses is not good and I can't make any mind or sense of this affliction. None of them has eaten, though I did try to spoon a measure of soup into each of them with the aid of the tar assisting me. It makes no sense!" he added, in bewilderment.

"If they don't eat . . ." I began.

"I know, I know . . . they're only going to get worse. What little strength their bodies have is slowly being ebbed away. But, I've been here with them for two days, save for when I came topside . . ."

"The lashing," I interjected.

"Yes, that fool business. That bastard Loydd is worse for our ship, than this pox. And, mark my words, he's just as deadly to the health and well-being of our crew. In one moment of anger, he's undone all the months of work and trust, our captain has earned of the men."

I turned slightly, to ensure a measure of privacy, lest any of our misplaced ill crew, berthed in the hammocks about, try to fathom our conversation.

"Don't tell me you approve of the lash?" the doctor questioned, mistaking my reason for turning away.

"I approve of whatever ministration our captain deems necessary for the good the our ship . . ."

"Rot! That's rot and you know it. I saw your face and the face of that other young ensign about to lose his lunch. You may have attended the lashing as mandated, but your heart wasn't in it, nor was our captain's, I'd wager."

"In truth, I did not relish it. And, I agree with you, that neither did our captain. But, he will subscribe to it, if it is necessary to prepare our ship for what awaits us," I returned.

There was a moment of silence. The doctor studied my words, seeking the meaning, I had laid there.

"I see," he expelled the words as if slowly resigning himself to their import. "So our ship is to be ruled by expediency. Whip the lads into shape, since time rises up against us, just like the French."

"We will do what is necessary, no matter how distasteful. A

ship has only one master, one captain," I replied, recalling an earlier discussion with the captain, when he bid me to watch about the crew for signs of malcontent.

The doctor merely nodded his head. "It never changes. You'll use these lads up with no regard, just to assure yourselves a victory or success, than forget, it was they who paid the greater price, gaining you all. They'll bring you your ribbons or medals. And, when its done, you'll replace your losses in the muster book with a new generation and start about this horrid business, all over again."

"We sail to war, Doctor. We are bound by restraints, that must be answered and dealt with," I returned.

He smiled and studied my proud face, doing so with some self-centered satisfaction. It was as if he was secretly amused at my stern loyalties and convictions.

"Just remember, lad," he began, "they'll spend you, just as easily in the bargain. You may come to pay the price for our second officer's quest for glory as readily as these tars, the backs of whom, he'd just as soon, whip raw."

I fell silent, acknowledging the truth of his words and readily agreeing with his assessment of the character of our second officer. But, I was not able to voice, as much.

I was fully aware of the implications of our second officer's thirst for victory and success. But, I shared his self-interest. For in advancing his cause, my own welfare and career was advanced.

While we were forced to press our tars into service, there was no problem attracting gentlemen to the ranks of our officers. Like myself, there were many willing recruits, who queued up to enlist in His Majesty's Navy. Some were even as young as fourteen, plying to become midshipmen and seek out a career of adventure and fortune.

And, to a man, fortune was what drove us. A career, if one plied oneself dutifully, would lead to rank and wealth. Prize money from captured ships stood to make a man rich. Bounty from the smoldering ashes of a foe's wrecked merchantman or warship was divided, according to rank, easily according even the youngest officers a wealth, they might have never have imagined, if they could survive the trials of combat.

With my family not having the advantage of our second officer's position and wealth, the lure of prize money was inducement enough, for me to leave the safety of shore and the mundane tedium and boredom of my father's shopkeeper's life.

Not, that his lot was without respect or standing in our community, a neighboring borough of Portsmouth. But, what could vie with the proud banners and heralded sight of the King's mighty warships.

As a child, I had raced to the docks to see this or that giant man-of-war regally ply the harbor's waters, either sailing to some faraway destination or returning to port, after a victorious encounter.

And, I had witnessed the valor and reward, due even the common sailor, who sauntered down the gangplank to the arms of sweethearts and well-wishers, waiting in the rejoicing and gathered crowds.

No, I was well aware of our second officer's intention to seize fame and renown, should it fall within his grasp. In truth, despite our different natures and his vile disposition, we were more alike, than I would admit to the doctor or even myself.

But, there was one difference, that could not be overcome. Despite, wearing the same uniform and sharing the same brotherhood of our navy, I would always be deemed the lessor in his aristocratic eyes.

Where I sought fortune and spoils, our second officer sought more fame and distinction. He sought to match the past greatness of his father and a generation of others before. Perhaps, Lieutenant Loydd was more abusive and expectant on the men, because he was thus or more so, harder on himself, trying to meet the expectations of family and some imagined goal, whose impossibility perplexed and confounded him.

It did not matter. Our ship's compliment was drawn and matched together, as it was. We would do with what was at hand, all mastered by the firm hand and judgment of our captain.

I returned to the matters at hand.

"I came to check on the condition of your charges and to report back to the captain. Or, tender any aid, you might request."

"My charges . . . just look about you. These men are near death's portal!" he answered in disgust, waving his hands towards the slumping hammocks.

Save for the shallow breaths of the sailors spirited deep inside the hammocks' folds, the men were lifeless.

"And, as for tendering me aid . . . if you can bring me a cure or even tell me, what this cursed affliction is . . . that, is the aid I require. This business escapes me. It is like nothing, I have seen before. It is not plague or pestilence. Yet, it is some affliction, beyond description. Damn, how it escapes me." he offered in resignation.

"I can have others bring food, broth or soup and assist you in feeding these men. Forcibly, if need be," I offered.

"No, not yet. Perhaps, if I let the illness run its course, matters might correct themselves. I fear my own administrations may complicate matters or worsen their condition. The elixirs and salves, I have administered or applied, have come to nothing. Success and a cure eludes me, though I don't know how I could make matters any worse. I fear quarantine is our only recourse," he added.

"As you wish. I'll make your report known to the captain and arrange for hands to bring food or assist you, at your will," I returned, before bidding him good-night.

I shuddered, at the imposed isolation the good surgeon was condemning himself and the tars to. I suspected, he would have liked to keep them about one of the gun-decks, where even in their semi-exiled state at the bow, they might still reap the benefit of fresh air, flowing on the drafts, that easily found the interior of our hull.

But, we could not risk further contamination of the crew. Isolation was the only measure we had to avail ourselves of the affliction. There was no choice, but to reside the ill tars to the dank and nearly forgotten lower decks. They were a stowage place for extra lines, blocks, and tackle, and all manner of implements, that required a storehouse of parts and tools, just to keep us at sea.

The lumber for the ship's carpenters and woodwrights resided in their dark narrow haunts. There were even several large timbers, that would be used to repair our warship's battle damage, bracing or shoring up her mighty beams, after the shattering rebuke of an enemy's broadside.

I made my way towards the upper decks.

CHAPTER 14

Darkness

HMS Vanguard
Sailing off the Coast of Portugal
Day 4-Midnight

To my utter dissatisfaction, the officer meant to relieve Ensign Higgins, had taken ill of seasickness or indigestion. With the senior officers already engaged or asleep in their quarters, his watch duty fell to me as I reported to the captain with the news of our patients.

If for no other reason, the duty of the midnight watch was mine simply because, I was at hand in the captain's cabin, when news of our ailing officer was brought to him.

I cursed my bad luck, slamming a clenched fist's bottom against the top of the railing, I leaned against. I watched the lights of Portugal sliding away off our port side. The lights dotted the hilly terrain lining the sea. They marked the fishing villages at their lowest points and the farms along the heights of the bordering hills.

There were even several campfires, positioned along the lonely isolation of the hills and cliffs. I wondered whether they were the attempts of shepherds to guard against the cold chill, coming across the sea or if some French spies loitered about on their lonely heights, posted upon some vigil to search out our presence and report it to Napoleon.

Again, I was faced with a lonely vigil of my own, during the dead hours of an early morning, when wiser men knew better to seek the comfort and rest of a good-night's sleep and the fanciful reprieve of their dreams.

I turned to check on the boatswain and helmsmen at the wheel. All was well, as I knew it would be.

The merchantman, our captain had pointed out earlier, was long gone. Even in the distance, her running lights could no longer be seen. It was as if she had been a phantom, appearing and disappearing from our sight and thoughts. She had been like a whisper in a growing wind.

The wind, I turned my head skyward and studied our rigged sails.

Our sails were alive giving life to the ship, even though more, than half our compliment were crammed below decks in a fitful sleep.

One set of the Vanguard's rigged canvas was made up of thirty-seven sails, nearly 5,428 square meters of sailcloth. And, like the extra wood and lumber ferreted away below decks, we carried another twenty-three sails. These were replacements and spares.

They would be used as weather and combat would see fit, necessitating repairs and substitution.

I had been told, on good advice, that it took the better part of eighty-three days and the labors of twenty skilled men to sew together a complete set of sails. By hand, they sewed our sails out of 58,240 meters of canvas. The tallied cost of their efforts was set at 1,300 pounds.

I studied the full canvas, capturing the wind blowing from the northwest. It pushed us eastward and easily kept us away from the coast, which our captain wished to give a wide berth.

The sails flapped and whipped, despite the lines holding them taunt.

Like many of the parts of our ship, the sails had been manufactured elsewhere, coming together in the great summation and effort, that had been required to launch our vessel upon the seas.

Most sails were made in Dorset, Northern Ireland, or Scotland, where the flax plant, from which our canvas was made, was plentiful. The flax was woven into bolts of canvas and these were in turn stitched together, forming a sail. Their strength was reinforced by nearly over a hundred stitches per meter at each joint.

The light wind captured in our square sails, hanging from the fore, main, and mizzen masts, did little to test the strength of our canvas, laced to the horizontal wooden spars of our yards.

Even in the darkness engulfing our ship, the sails and rigging were a wondrous sight. Like our tars, they were the life of our vessel. Over twenty-six miles of rope rigged the Vanguard's masts, snaking about their towering heights or returning, in their wandering journey, to the deck.

The largest rope vied the thickness of a woman's waist. It measured nineteen inches round.

Drawn taunt, the ropes played a haunting melody of their own devices as the wind, that filled the sails, strummed or cut through them in a musical chorus. Those, that knew only land would not understand the mystery of the line's tune. They reasoned it, only the wind cutting itself against the rope's tautness or some other logical reason, feinting ignorance.

But, to one who had been at sea for years, the ropes were like a siren. The wind played about them, creating the seducing tune, that mirrored the lonely vastness and isolation of the sea. It was as if Neptune's court had graced those, who answered the alluring call to come to sea with the ungodly melody only one's ship could sing.

The sails flapped as a gust retreated, then rushed forward once more, filling them full. I marvelled at the cleverness or the lines and the nearly seven hundred and sixty-eight pulley blocks, used to operate the yards and sails.

Weighty things, these blocks were crafted from elm, beech, or ash. They may have seemed small and insignificant from the heights, they were hung or strung by, but they added to the massive weight of our ship.

The ropes, used about our ship, were of two kinds. They were either tarred or untarred, depending on their use and function.

Untarred ropes were natural coradage, used to raise and turn the yards and their sails. I was still set upon learning all their different names. There were lifts and ties, then jeers, halyards, and braces. Each had its own purpose and design.

And, there were two sets of rigging. "Standing rigging" consisted of the black tarred ropes used only to support the masts. Of these, there were three types; shrouds, backstays, and forestays.

The second set of rigging was the "running rigging." These were untarred ropes used to set or furl the sails. They were known as sheets, tacks, leechlines, clewlines, and brails.

I had thought my grandmother's knitting a complex undertaking. But, having come to know this tangled mass of ropes, I dare say, even she would find her yarns and needles a comfort, compared to what our seamen must fathom, just to hoist a sail aloft.

I returned my gaze downward, having heard the approach of two marines patrolling our deck. Several tars went about pulling on this rope or that, tending to the knots, that held our sails and rigging taunt.

I ignored them, intent on watching the blackness of the water.

The men knew their duties. Each man kept busy, according to his assigned tasks and the needs of our ship, that had become second-nature to her crew. I left them to their work.

I peered over the railing, bowing my head in resignation to the waters flowing past below.

And, there I saw it.

It was a shadow, that accursed shadow, I had sworn to have seen before. Yet, I could never focus upon its shape or form. But now, it could not escape me, hanging from its precarious perch along the planking of our hull.

It was unnatural. It was unreal. I thought, it was human, but its shape lacked definition, swallowed up by the darkness engulfing our hull and the water rushing beneath. I blinked my eyes in damning disbelief. But, there it was and still remained. I leaned forward, so treacherously, I heard one of the approaching marines call out in alarm.

I ignored him, meaning to keep my vision locked upon the formless specter, that until now, had eluded my observations.

The shadowy form clung to the oversized wooden rungs of the ladder, built into the side of our port hull. The precarious climb lead to the middle and top decks from the lower deck and waterline. The specter moved as if swirling about. It had heard the alarm of the marine, who had called out.

It crawled with the agility and ease of a spider or fly. It danced with an eerie grace along the near vertical surface, despite the roll of the ship. I could not ignore or deny its presence. But, I could not describe it or tell what it was, if asked.

It left the handholds of the hull's built-in ladder and clung to the smooth planks along the side of the ship. The ghost-like form defied the dictates of gravity and the principals of science.

My breathing ceased. I was filled with a strange mix of wonder and bewilderment. Rational thought and reality escaped me. There was no explanation for what I saw, save for the legend and lore of sailors describing sights, they had witnessed, but could not place to words.

A gunport raised along the middle gun-deck, after this ghastly specter's hand reached down towards the lip of its heavy planking. Despite the rope lashing it tight, to prevent the intrusion of the sea, a shadowy limb ripped it upward. I heard the tied rope snap and release its binding restraint upon the cover.

The marines came rushing up beside me, one pressing a supportive hand to my back and anchoring me against the rail, lest I tumble overboard. His mate, leaned over the side, expecting to find me ill of seasickness, relieving my stomach of its churning contents.

But, my eyes sought only to watch the shadowy specter, both

marines were ignorant of. As the marines faces joined mine, the shadow vanished, witnessed only by my own eyes.

It was gone as suddenly as it had come. Thrice, I had glimpsed its presence. But, only now, could I confirm its existence with the certainty of my observations.

No sea creature was this, no playful dolphin, or bird running beside our ship. I shivered silently. I feared, what I had witnessed and was afraid to tell of it. For what did I see?

I saw something. But, what? It was a shadow, but not. But, I could not say, it was a man or a woman. I could not claim it was human. It seemed endowed with limbs, resembling arms and legs. But, there were no distinguishing features to identify it as a member of the crew. And, what man in his right mind would leave the safety of our stout decks, treading along the vertical reprise of our steep towering hull, lest he fall and be set adrift, claimed by the sea, so far from land?

Despite the coastline and its lights still within distant sight, we were far from land. It was doubtful, those few tars, who could swim, would even be able to make the distant shore, if one were to fall overboard.

Likely, the currents would drive a man farther out to sea, until he succumbed to the fatigue of his struggling body and found the waters' bottom, joining Neptune's court.

But, though I could not describe, what I had seen or even accurately recall the sight of it. There was now evidence about.

I had heard the snap of the rope, that secured the gunport. It would be an easy enough task to go below and search out the physical evidence for examination. It would confirm my story, such as it was.

But, what could have entered below? And, what creature, in its madness, would dangle, from the threatening side, of our ship?

"Are you all right, sir?" one of the marines beside me asked, after studying my transfixed face, still locked upon the middle deck.

I pushed away from the rail to his welcomed relief. My hands grasped the security of the rail's firmness. I noticed both my hands were shaking about the wrists. I clamped my grip upon the rail tightly, hiding the shameful reaction and swallowed any fear or apprehension. I gave answer to my would-be rescuers.

"I'm fine. All is well," I replied, lying to hide the truth, I could not explain.

"We saw you bending over the rail . . ."

"It's nothing," I interrupted, trying to allay the marine's fears.

I rose to the rail and bowed my head over it, not leaning forward, so threateningly.

"Did you see anything amiss . . . near the middle deck?" I questioned.

The two marines were taken aback, having seen nothing more, than my own form, balanced awkwardly over the side.

"No, sir!" the first shot back.

"Nay," answered the second.

"I suspect something is amiss," I entreated, offering the observation as the reason for my own actions. "I want you two to come with me. I want to inspect the middle gun-deck."

"Boatswain!" I called, "I think something might be afoul on the middle deck. I intend to search it out to ensure all is well. You will note my absence from the watch and take command, until my return. And, be about you, I am not certain, what has happened below on the middle deck."

"Aye, sir!" the aging boatswain returned, seemingly thinking, I made too much of nothing, but allowing me the discretion of my youthful rank.

I turned about and made for the steps of the hold, claiming a lantern as did one of the marines from beside its rafters.

We descended to the middle deck as silently as we could. Around us, a maze of hammocks was strung about. Sleeping men rested in ignorance of our passing, while we sought the widest aisle through their presence and made for the port side of the deck.

I counted off the cannon from the hatchway to the ladder, mounted to the outside of the hull at the middle deck, where I'd spied the shadowy specter. From the large ornate double doors, it would be the sixth gunport to the left, where our specter had re-entered the ship.

The lantern swayed in my outstretched left hand as I strained to see in its flickering light.

Three, four, five, . . . we came upon the sixth cannon from the entranceway set to the middle gun-deck. The sixth cannon was bound fast, its thick rope tied off to the blocked gun carriage, pulled away from the gunport.

I bent down and lowered the lantern. In its dim light, I found the gunport undone as I had expected. A section of thick hemp rope was still tied to the heavy wooded gunport door, that hung agape. A damp sea breeze penetrated through the gap.

The door swayed in and out, closing flush, then opening with the constant roll of the ship.

My right hand stretched out and examined the thick cord. Its ends were frayed and loose as if some giant force had been exerted upon it, which its thick cord could not bear the weight of.

But, I had seen no tremendous weight or bulk, only the wisping shadow of the specter's thin outstretched limb, if it was that at all.

But, here was the evidence, before my eyes. The rope was broken, torn apart. Its other end littered the deck and mirrored the damage of the first.

"Sir, how did you know the gunport was undone?" one of the marines asked.

"It doesn't matter," I replied.

"I have to return to our watch. Make this fast as best you can. I doubt we'll be hitting heavy seas. Still, its best to set things right. I'll inform the boatswain to ensure a new length of rope is provided to do the task right tomorrow. When you're done, return to your duties topside," I ordered.

"Aye, sir!" came their whispered response in unison.

I left them to the gunport and turned around, studying the dancing shadows, feeding off the flickering flame of my lantern's candle. In amongst the cast silhouettes of the hammocks, I could see nothing, save the sleeping forms of our harried tars.

To the rear of the deck, lay the junior officer quarters, well out of reach of their presence. Stealthily, I strode forward on guarded footsteps, seeking to pass through the sleeping sailors and reach one of the two doors to the junior officers' shared quarters.

I found myself alone, my only companion the weak light of my lantern.

I peered inside our quarters, where Ensign Higgins and two other officers were quartered on the starboard side of the stern. Casting the lantern about, I found Ensign Higgins body surrendered to the pleasantries of his dreams and a deep sleep.

Similarly, the other two officers, both lieutenants and responsible for the lower gun-deck, were fast asleep. None were aware of my presence or the oddity, that had been sighted on the port side of the hull.

But, the room was strangely different.

Perhaps, it was the lateness of the hour or that, I had become accustomed to the cool breeze, that found our deck topside. It took me more, than a moment to realize one of the large multi-paned windows was unlatched and opened to the sea.

Only the rolling sway of our vessel, alerted its presence to me as it swung out on its hinges, then returned once more, just short of closing. I stepped into our cabin passing the shared writing desk and its tiered shelves, each allowing every officer sharing the cabin, a space for his correspondence or books.

Of my own shelf, it contained a bible with a small silver-plated cross spirited away inside it. The sacred book and reverent cross were bestowed as gifts, given from a mother to a son. They were meant to protect me on my journeys, while facing the hazards and uncertainties of the sea.

There were also, several well-read and worn books. They were trivialities really, writings and authors by which we wiled away our lonely off-watch hours, while far from sea and family. The dimness of my lantern's candle, did not intrude upon the gentle slumber of my comrades.

I made my way to the open window. I was sure, that none of those present had intended to leave the window's ornate frame open and ajar. The chill and dampness entering the cabin were appalling and could easily leave the cold draft to inflict some sickness or ailment, though no more serious, than the common cold or a sore throat.

I poked my head out the window, after removing my uniformed hat, lest it be blown into the trailing wake several stories below.

There was nothing, but emptiness behind our ship's wake. Even the Portuguese coast was lost from sight, swallowed up by some fog, that even blocked out the lights of beacons and homes bordering the seaside.

I grabbed the metal handle and pulled it inward, drawing the window up tight within its frame, before locking it securely. I did this as quietly as I could, attempting not to disturb the slumber of my fellows.

But, our Ensign Higgins stirred in his berth to such a degree, that I thought I had awoken him. Yet, he did not rise. He only parted his lips with a moaning sigh. It was the sort, one heard from the labored breaths of the elderly, who were at the twilight of their years, but still refused to meet the grim reaper, though life held few pleasures and almost little hope for them.

I turned around and prepared to extinguish the flame of my lantern's candle, less its dim light wake my colleagues. That is when I saw it.

Our young ensign's left arm thrust out, free of the warmth of his blanket and the softness of his dow-filled bunk. It was the paleness of its color, caught in the faint light about the cabin, that froze my heart in fear.

His arm was almost white. It had a sickly pallor far worse, than that of those tars quarantined to their hammocks below. In morbid curiosity, I strode closer. I feared what I would find.

They were there.

The cursed marks, that had scarred the tars earlier, now marked our ensign's flesh. Nothing more, than little nicks, they could easily be mistaken for the bite of some small animal, a rodent or some insignificant vermin.

I was halted in place. My legs and feet were unbelievably heavy, almost unable to move, despite my will. It was fear welling up inside me, but not the fear of some ailment or disease.

No, the hour was late and I was tired, but not that fatigued. I knew what I had seen. I had found the elusive shadow, I had only thought I'd glimpsed two times before. Now thrice having witnessed it, it had led me to another victim of our doctor's so-called plague or ailment.

I bent to the outstretched arm, listening to the labored breathing of our ensign. His pained breaths sounded as if he had been afflicted with some grievous wound. But, he remained ignorantly silent as if nothing had happened.

His eyes were closed, still in slumber. His lips parted, sucking air, but expelling some repressed pain held deep within him.

I examined the small marks. They had occurred recently, unlike the scabbed over marks of the tars below. They still boasted fresh seepages of blood, though their was little of it. The wounds were moist, nothing more. It was as if someone or something had sopped and dried the two small marks of their crimson fluid.

Underneath, the glow of the candle, I saw the marks were again close to veins, running just beneath the flesh's surface.

My mind raced in speculation, but I had no explanation to ease my fears or rationalize the cause of it. And what could I say or to who could I speak of what I had seen? There was no sense to it.

I saw a shadow, but what to make of it?

I found a gunport's lashing torn away, but who was to say the cause of it?

Dare I speak, of some unknown phantom or ghostly specter?

No, of course not. I could not. Such rot would leave my own faculties open to speculation and my career and credibility suspect and the target of ridicule.

I gently eased our good ensign's arm back under his blanket, amazed at the loss of his youthful healthy color.

Rest, I would let him rest. And perhaps, I might be able to speak to the doctor. If I chose my words carefully and remained guarded about my suspicions, I might entreat his advice and counsel.

For now, I was on duty and must return to my watch. I left the cabin, closing the door silently behind me. I crept along the deck, heading for the nearest ladder topside. I harbored the fears of past legends and lores.

The ones that spoke of the darkness and the ghastly things residing in it. I returned topside to await the approach of dawn, still hours away.

I was like a child awaiting the glowing warmth and light, that would drive away the imps and sprites, that a small one knew, beyond reason and sense, shared the confines of his sleeping chamber, crossed with shadows and a haunting darkness only the sun could push aside.

One of the Vanguard's cutters rowing out
to pick up the Spaniard.

CHAPTER 15

Morning

HMS Vanguard
Sailing off the Coast of Portugal
Day 5-Morning

The sun rose early.

Five hours into the new day, it found our ship surrounded in
a thick fog, that denied us even the knowledge of the presence of
the waters running alongside our ship, except for the lapping of
the waves caressing our hull.

Despite, the high-buttoned collar of my uniform's jacket and
its wool's warmth, I shivered from the dampness, no garment
could dissuade. The tars on deck were no worse, than I. Cold
fingers and hands plied at the wheel they held, keeping our course
straight and far away from the coast, we could no longer see.

There were no landmarks to guide us or stars above to make
a plot, guided by their heavenly markers. We steered by dead-

reckoning and compass, having known our last position and that we paralleled the coast of Portugal before the fog set upon us.

Though, the winds were at our back, we fought a strong current, reducing our speed to no more, than five or six knots.

I wondered what the sight our massive hull and towering masts would have appeared like to any resident of the coastline, had they spied our slow-moving vessel protruding through the thick fog like some mythological behemoth.

But, the fog was so thick, that even the swipe of an outstretched hand did little to move it, providing vision only at arms length. All on deck were shrouded in its misty haze as if somehow our upper deck had dared reach up to heaven.

Though, my eyes could follow the thickness of our masts, our lookouts above were blurred from sight. They were merely hazy shadows. They were indistinguishable from the ratlings and ropes, feeding to the spires above.

Only occasionally, did one call out, having glimpsed some sight of a light, most likely burning along the coast, too far away to be another vessel.

I noted their warning, marking it against our relative position as best I knew it. The riddle of the ghostly shadow or apparition, I had spied hanging about the side of the hull earlier, fled to the recesses of my mind. New fears filled my thoughts. I feared coming too close to the shore and its rocky hazards or colliding with some unseen ship, sharing the fog cloaked waterway with our own vessel.

About the deck, we were bathed in the strange glow of the early morning sun. It glistened on the fog surrounding us, reflecting a golden glow, that blurred or blinded one's sight, brightening the whiteness of the fog.

Lieutenant Loydd arrived on deck along with one other officer. They were the next watch, come to relieve ours.

He made for the port rail, studying the fog and searching for the coastline.

I left my post and made for him, intent on turning over the watch to my superior.

I halted slightly behind him, merely making myself available to be relieved at his convenience. The act was meant to show him the due respect of his rank and station.

As was his custom, our second officer deliberately ignored my presence, physically asserting the superiority and privilege of his rank.

But, I was accustomed to his slights and arrogant behavior. I found myself content to wait on tired legs. Despite, the cold chill, we both searched for the masked coastline ahead.

The wind blew, not a gust, but noticeably perceptible, compared to the light wind, that pushed our vessel steadily onward. I fought the urge to tug at my collar, seeking the warmth, that continued to elude me, during the tedious and boring routine of my watch.

"Ship to port!" a voice yelled down, from the mizzen mast.

Our second officer's back straightened, his upright form casting his gaze abeam of our ship.

My eyes followed his as did those about the deck, searching for ship called to our attention.

"Where away?" our second officer called out.

The answer was ignored as we saw the spars and masts of a ship, smaller than ours, emerge from the path cut by the wind, that had graced us.

It banners flew from atop its two masts. Its sails were full as she ran with only part of her canvas rigged, much like ourselves.

It was obvious from the height of her masts and cut of her sails, that she was a smaller craft, than our own. She also seemed to sail slightly faster, being lighter and unencumbered by our own size and bulk.

Like us, she ran without lights, despite the thick fog.

The second officer and myself claimed lenses, extending their telescoping brass lengths fully, before raising them to an eye.

Our search was rewarded quickly. We laid the polished optics upon the tops of the ship's masts and quickly fathomed her identity. The banners bore the colors of Spain, stripes of red and yellow.

"Ensign Lewis, I have the deck!" our second officer ordered, taking command.

I surrendered the lens to his accompanying officer and prepared to dismiss the men, who had stood watch with me as their replacements were at hand.

"This is an opportune bit of luck. We'll call the men to stations," Lieutenant Loydd suggested, his telescope still fixed upon the vessel to port.

"A splendid opportunity. It will give our tars the reality needed to reinforce the importance of their drills," his companion returned.

"I don't believe they've spied us. The advantage is ours, if they are unaware of our presence. I say, we might even make a prize of the Spanish vessel, if we don't give her the chance to run," the second officer said aloud, as if considering his own words.

"Ensign Lewis, leave your hands here and report to the captain. Tell him of our discovery of our Spanish friends. And, have the each deck's boatswains rouse the men silently. I want no drums or shouts. It is my intention to sneak up upon our sleeping Spaniards, if they'll continue to oblige us with their laxness," he instructed.

"Aye, sir!" I replied, turning around and heading for the boatswain to order him below to pass the order, while I sought out our captain.

I saw Lieutenant Loydd raise his head, his eyes studying the sailcloth above.

Before, I exited the upper deck, I heard him issuing commands, that the stays, triangular sails extended between the masts, be rigged in an effort to increase our ship's speed.

I descended below.

The captain and I returned to the upper deck. It was in a flurry of activity. Men moved about their stations as silently as they could. There were no damning shouts to "clear for action," nor were the whispered orders accompanied by the drums heralding "beat to quarters," calling the men to their cannon.

They were goaded and prodded by their boatswains and officers to move silently, in all haste. Some were only partly dressed, having been ejected from the comfort of their hammocks to man the guns and make ready for war.

Our second officer had words with our captain, describing the details of the vessel, that had appeared off our port.

The Spaniard was gone, once more. The fog had claimed the smaller warship, entombing her within its damning mist. Our helmsmen held the wheel fast as our two ships, one hunter and one hunted, blindly stumbled about in the fog.

Above, our lookouts strained to reacquire the haunting silhouette of our foe. It eluded us in a silence, broken only by the flap and crack of our canvas and anxious whispers.

Our officers scanned the port side, while listening for any sound, that might betray the ship, we hunted. Our muted crew prepared for battle, their guns ready and eyes turning towards officer or boatswain, awaiting their next command.

The crews' forms were half-hidden by the fog, that claimed our deck. It rolled and wisped about the masts as if devouring our ship into its damp white abyss. There was nothing to do, but wait in the silence.

Men fretted or prayed silently, that the advantage, we had held so fleetingly, would again be ours.

The fog continued to bedevil both our ships, closing around us. Than, it opened just enough for us to find and hold her in sight.

Our second officer had already made the subtle course change, that would lead to our interception of the Spanish vessel, most likely judged a brig in Lieutenant Loydd's experienced estimations.

The captain concurred.

Our orders where to join Lord Nelson's Squadron. However, nothing was said, of taking advantage of an opportune moment to claim the smaller foe, blundering into the sights of our broadsides.

The brig must have been a picket for the Spanish fleet, safely tucked away in the shelter of Cadiz. So far from home, she was probably sent to patrol the coasts, tasked to alert the Home Fleet of any intransigence of our own navy's approach to bolster Lord Admiral Horatio Nelson.

Yet, with our nearness certain, her lookouts and watch were indifferent to our presence. Asleep, indifferent, or exhibiting the Spanish penchant for wine, their failure would cost them dearly. If we could close the gap between our two vessels, before they spotted us and likely turned and ran, they would be ours.

The water slapped along the hull as men finished making the cannon ready. Powder held in reserve, during the drills, was filled in the ornate iron powder holes as cartridges and shot were rammed home in the forward lengths of the weapons' barrels.

Lines were pulled and block and pulley's squeaked as the guns were pulled through open gunports along the port side of our ship. The haste and stealth topside was mirrored on the middle and lower gun-decks as the 24 pounders and 32 pounders were made ready.

Topside, our twelve pounders were loaded with a mix of solid shot and the deadly "chain shot" or as the tars loving nicknamed them for their lethality, "angels."

The smaller vessel could clearly outrun us, if she were given the chance. An alert lookout or officer of the watch might still chance upon the opportunity to flee.

We meant not to give them the occasion to evade us.

Aloft in the masts, the marine sharpshooters were joined by tars, making fast the unfurled staysails. Headsails were rigged to jibbooms as more canvas searched out the driving force of the light wind.

I judged our own speed had been increased by as much as two knots. The eyes alone attested to the increased speed as the brig's masts loomed ever closer.

To our benefit, the fog still engulfed us, clearing towards land and our foe, but still claiming the cool waters out to sea.

Our captain and second officer continued in their guarded

discussions. Our tactic was simple enough, we'd have one chance to come alongside within the range of the full measure of our port broadside.

The goal was simple enough, to lay upon the Spanish foe, such a devastating fire as to slow or halt her in the water. Then, with her advantage of speed stolen from her, we would come about, finishing her off with the freshly loaded batteries of the guns lining our starboard broadside, if needed.

Though, I am certain our captain and second officer sought only to incapacitate the Spanish ship, leaving her defeated hulk seaworthy enough to be claimed as a prize.

All that was required was that the Spanish remain ignorant of our presence.

Several 12 and 24 pounders had been wrested away from their normal place about the upper deck. They'd been moved about to face as far forward as they could. They would be the first guns to bear upon the Spaniard ahead.

Four guns in all, loaded with the deadly "angels," would do their best to try to find our target's sails, should she be alerted to our presence in the final lengths of our approach.

The deadly carronades, two large and oversized cannon mounted foward, were deemed too devastating to be used against the small target ahead. We wanted to halt and capture the brig, not send her to the bottom.

The giant guns, the largest aboard the Vanguard, were loaded and made ready. But, their disappointed crews were ordered to stand aside, deliberately instructed, upon the pain of the lash, not to intercede in the upcoming melee.

Our captain and second officer were intent to claim a prize-ship.

The crews stood by eagerly. Short match and flint awaited the command to fire, to strike the spark or light the flame, that would unleash our deadly barrage.

As we neared the farthest reach of our cannon's range, the captain had the helmsmen turn the ship to starboard, halting the direct line we traveled to intercept the brig and bringing us parallel to her.

At that moment, the sun glared. Its approach in the sky climbed higher. And, with the coming of its light, the winds shifted in unison, fanning the fog about. Our canvas sagged and flapped as the direction of the wind changed.

The wind left our sails, then filled them, once more.

Exposed ahead of us, we saw the brig. Two Spanish lookouts made their way along the ratlings of the brig's main mast. One had his back to us and continued in ignorance along his lofty path.

The other halted in disbelief at the sight of our massive man-of-war, bearing down upon their own humble craft. His voice broke the stillness of the shrouded fog, screaming out in alarm to his officers and crew below. His cry traveled across the water, his hurried words reaching our ears.

As the shifting wind continued, we found a hapless group of men standing dumbstruck about the brig's upper deck. They were ringed about the ornate ironworks of a potted fire, the likes found on Spanish vessels.

Both officer and crew had availed themselves of the fire's warmth, fighting off the chill of the early morning. They had been serenely content and confident, that they were the only vessel about in the godless early hour and plaguing fog.

We watched as the officers below turned about. They searched for our hull and masts, still befuddled by the fog lining their deck.

A shrill whistle was blown by their boatswain, while another mate clanged their ship's bell. But, it was too late.

"Order the bow gun's to commence," the captain ordered the second officer.

The two-masted Spanish brig's sails fell into clear sight, their canvas teasing our gunners.

"Bow guns . . . fire, when you have your target!" the second officer's voice blared, the need for silence and stealth having escaped us.

One of the 12 pounders was the first to unleash its deadly projectile. Its deafening boom brought all men present to the reality of the grim business underway.

The gun had been moved clear of its gunport and fired from the openness of the bow. Its barrel and shot, just cleared the rigging, leading to our massive bowsprint. After its thunderous boom, its unchecked carriage rolled rearward, despite the restraining weight and arms of the tars, seeking to hold it fast.

The solitary shot screamed through the thin damp air. It sang with the metallic length of chain, joining two solid rounds of shot as they were lobbed upwards, straining to claim the masts and rigging of the brig ahead.

There was a silence aboard our ship. All held their breath as one. We waited and willed our unholy round to find its mark.

And, then it struck. A length of canvas was torn, the sail losing its fullness. A spar cracked as the chain entwined in a damning embrace about it, the weight of the second ball splintering its light pine wood.

As it fell, the shot and chain snared about the rigging, ripping and dropping the remaining sail.

A second cannon added its retort and was quickly followed by two more. The guns were positioned to take advantage of the spacious width of our bow. The second 12 pounder's crew misjudged their aim, their deadly "angel" sailed high of the targeted mast and came to fall with a resounding splash, landing on the other side of the brig.

But, not so, the two 24 pounders, that had unleashed their fire.

One had aimed too low, nearly sending their lobbed projectile towards the deck. Its chain cut away part of the ratling, one of the Spanish lookouts still clung to, before finding the large square surface of the lower sailcloth, tethered to the brig's main mast.

The large sail crumpled loudly, mirroring the snap and toss of a chambermaid fixing her mistress's bed. The drive of the wind was forced from her sail. Loose shards of sailcloth were sent flapping along the light breeze.

The other 24 pounder found its mark, snapping the top mast of the two-section fore mast. Its banner and sails dropped aside to starboard and dipped into the water.

Still connected by rigging and lines, the canvas acted as an anchor on the starboard side, actually slowing the brig and turning her inward, towards our approaching path.

Her speed lost, the Spaniard was ours for the taking. Too late, the Spanish ship's crew began to respond, pushing her cannon through their gunports and trying in haste to meet us. There was no way for them to catch up or to reclaim the advantage, our surprise had won us with the benefit of the fog, that had cloaked us, yet revealed them.

Anticipation and fear were replaced in the eyes of our officers and men alike. We had succeeded in our subterfuge and stealth. The prize was among us. Thoughts of victory and prize-money awaited as our ship continued to edge parallel to the crippled brig.

The winds gusted and our sails billowed. Our ship was moving at eight knots, despite the current, it had fought earlier.

The captain and his second debated on what fire to unleash, but there was little time to change their tactics as the first guns of our port broadside came even to the brig.

Already, the Spaniards summoned from below their decks had reached topside and crewed their guns.

"Fire at will," Captain Shefferd offered in resignation, unwilling to allow the Spanish the opportunity to fire one round against our own vessel.

"Port guns, fire at will!" his second barked.

The din was thunderous as twenty-five or more of the forward guns along the port broadside opened fire. Their kinsmen to the rear, still not acquiring the brig, held their fire and waited their turn. The guns on the middle deck had been aimed to rake the brig's masts with a mixture of solid shot and our devilish "angels."

Their rounds tore through canvas and splintered wood, that fell atop the Spanish crew on the unprotected upper deck. Men collapsed or were horribly torn apart by the debris raining down upon them.

Their screams were masked from us by the deafening retort of our broadside, still continuing its deadly fire.

Our lower gun deck's 32 pounders were aimed at the brig's

hull. The long barrels of the heavy cannon found an easy mark, firing nearly straight ahead, devoid of any trajectory or lobbed path of the smaller guns, that had fired.

Their solid shot drove through the brig's planks, splintering and crushing wood and bone. No sailor, standing in their path, would find any mercy. In disbelief, we watched, astounded at the power of our weaponry.

One of the 32 pounders had pierced the brig completely, its shot crashing through her starboard side and exiting to port to splash into the sea.

The brig came to a halt in the water, turning towards us as her rudder went unanswered, her helmsman and officers reposed in the silent slumber of death.

Our captain was the first to see the folly of our actions. He moved at once, to halt our deadly cannonade to save the remains of the prize our gunners had obtained for us, yet still targeted.

The second officer barked the command to have all guns cease. But, it was to no avail. His words went unheard, drowned under the thunderous din of the next guns on our port side to have the helpless brig float into their sights.

The boatswain was quick to act, dropping down the hold. The middle deck fell silent with one last retort as word continued to the lower deck.

One cannon, then the next, released its fury as others fell silent or never fired.

Only the solitary retort of the 32 pounders of the lower gun-deck, continued to drone on as the harried boatswain fought his way towards the stern, trying to halt their gunners.

The brig continued to shatter. Overmatched, she could only absorb the attack set upon her. Planks were cast aside or thrown skyward as wood splintered and released its hold. Pitch and caulking weakened or released its bonds, allowing water to find the interior of the small craft's hull.

The bulk of our fire raked her stern, where her officer's quarters and any bounty might be found. She began to settle down in the water, her rudder disappearing from sight.

Amidships, where the open fire had warmed the officers and men of her derelict watch, the coals had spilled to the deck and set the littered canvas ablaze.

Our eyes watched as every seaman's dreaded bane, fire, threatened to spread across her deck.

In haste, our second officer was already assembling a boarding party, intent to loot, what could be taken and perhaps, extinguish the fire to claim the brig as a prize-ship to be taken into tow.

One more 32 pounder, towards our stern, fired.

Eyes rose to port and anxious hands clenched the rail. The solid round flew straight and true, aimed for the hull and the brig's vulnerable waterline.

It was an excess, the ship was done, already raked with a devastating fire, that found her decks devoid of life, except for the few wounded seaman, making their way up from the lower decks.

There was an unnatural crack, so sharp and piercing, it defied description. And then, the brig erupted in a mighty roar, flame ripping upward through the center of her upper deck. The brig lifted in the water.

Her powder stores had been found, if not by intent, then by fortune's hand. Splinters showered the water, radiating out from the center of the blast and pocking the waves with their deadly shards.

It reminded me of a heavy rain, while tied up in the tranquil waters of a harbor. A host of tiny splashes pelleted the surface of the water, still misting with fog. The rain of deadly pieces of wood and metal drummed across the surface of the lax waves.

Men's mouths fell open in mortification and disbelief. Our prize and the promise of its wealth were wrested from us in an instant. The hull of the brig twisted, tearing itself in half. The already heavily waterlogged stern was swallowed up by the waters first. Its decorated carvings and trim vanished beneath the waves.

Her main mast lingered as the deck pooled and the bowsprit fell beneath the sea. The remainder of her deck slowly flooded, releasing only barrel or plank to bob up and float atop the waters. Her place was marked by the debris of a once proud vessel.

A piece of canvas, wood, or a facedown corpse was all, that was left to mark her existence. Our second officer's face flushed in rage, his victory unfairly taken from him. Cheated, his anger rose. He dismissed the marines of the boarding party gathered about him, fuming with disgust.

Our captain fell along the rail, leaning against its firm support. His eyes compassionately sought out the remains of the brig, watching its sole surviving topmast retreat beneath the waves.

Its sodden banner licked across the top of the water. Before, it too was pulled under. It was as if the brig refused to allow it to escape their joined fate.

Several of the crew cursed our misfortune. Luck had been with us, we had sighted the foe. Yet, we had not been sighted. We had claimed surprise and advantage, disabling the Spaniard and besting her.

But, we had overpowered her in our eagerness and greed. We had defeated her and her crew. And, we had cheated ourselves, as well. Our gunners had delivered the full measure of their skill and deadly aim, only to rob us of the laurels, that could have been.

I came up to the rail and studied the grim flotsam, swaying atop the waves. There were still eerie wisps of fog swirling about, beside our hull and atop the waters.

The sunlight brought witness to our deed, framing several floating corpses and the scattered debris. There was nothing, but silence and the lapping of the waves.

And, then we heard it. It was an almost muted plea.

It was a voice. A survivor, from amid such devastating destruction.

Our captain searched the waters, his own telescope extended to port. He was joined by others as the officers and boatswains ordered all to silence. Keen ears listened for the call, trying to locate the adrift seaman.

And again, we heard the mournful plea of a seaman lost atop

the waves. His Spanish tongue was foreign to us, but not his plight.

"Over there!" insisted the captain.

"By that planking," he pointed to the driftwood, littered about among a clearing patch of fog.

"I see it!" the second officer joined in.

"Shall we pluck him from the sea, Captain?" he added, in his cold heart wanting nothing more, than a souvenir or evidence of our victory.

"As you wish, Lieutenant Loydd. But, be quick about it. Our Lord Nelson is awaiting this ship's presence," the captain relented.

"Aye, sir!" came our second's crisp reply.

"Make ready a boat and eight able hands at the oars," our second officer ordered.

I watched as the tars moved to the lashed down boats. They undid the ropes securing a cutter in its blocked perch, while others used blocks and tackle, stretched about the masts, to hoist the boat skyward and manhandle it, towards the port side of the ship.

Lines guided the craft's progress as a complicated set of lines and pulleys were moved about, positioning the craft over the heights, three-stories above the water.

Two tars climbed into the boat, one fore and one aft. Their willing hands controlled opposite lines as other tars used their muscles to gently lower it, towards the water below.

Within minutes, they were away with one of our officers and a marine guard joining them to ferret out the survivor, again hidden by the fog.

Their oars dipped in the water as the boat's crew pulled in unison. They rowed about the waves, that bobbed the small craft up and down.

The cutter's bow bounced, as they listened for the Spaniard's tiring cry, now fallen to little more, than a pleading whisper.

The boat reversed course and plied for a sheltering bank of fog. The officer at its bow held up his hand, demanding the oars to halt and that silence fall upon the boat.

An oar bumped hollowly, disturbing his straining ears as the water slapped about the boat's hull.

"There!" the officer commanded, stretching out his uniformed arm and the ornate gold-braided cuff, surrounding the sleeve of his pointing and extended hand.

They found the survivor stretched out, clinging to two joined pieces of planking. He clutched the wood threatening to submerge under his weight. His breath was pained as the salt water licked the burns across his back.

The sight was repulsive, despite our distance from the boat. As the Spanish tar was pulled free of the clutching embrace of the waters, we saw his raw back.

A cry fell over the waters as he protested the arms and hands, that bid him well, pulling him into the safety of the cutter.

Foes one moment, our lads fell into the silence of shame, seeing what they had inflicted upon the frail figure, that clung to life.

I watched one of the tars break out a blanket from among the boat's stores and drape it about the Spaniard in a tenderly act, more akin to that of a brother or father, than a combatant.

The man accepted it willingly, offering no curse or rebuke. Though, he was now a prisoner, he had survived. And, that was by nothing less, than a miracle.

The bow of the boat below turned towards our imposing port side, whose black and yellow striping attested to our identity and the greatness of our empire. Oars dipped upon command and the tiny craft labored against the current, trying to push it away and past our stern.

But, the eight hands at the oars were practiced seamen. Guided by the small rudder astern, the small boat quickly returned, tying up alongside the ladder leading to the entranceway along the middle deck.

While two tars awaited the lines being dropped from above, the officer and marine guard began climbing upwards. The Spaniard was aided in his climb by two tars. They escorted him along the perilous slope of the ladder's surface.

CHAPTER 16

Revelations

HMS Vanguard
Sailing off the Coast of Portugal
Day 5-Mid-morning

Our ship had become burdened with loss. Our tars exclaimed our passage to be jinxed. Perhaps, some malcontent spirit or sea deity had been given offense by our actions and sought a cruel repayment for our transgressions.

Aboard, we harbored death. Three tars were now dead. Though, one death had been hidden from most of the crew. And, we had become a haven for illness. Some plague or affliction bedeviled our good surgeon and escaped his efforts to cure his patients.

Now, we had borne the loss of a true victory. The prize we sought, a Spanish brig, had been sent to the bottom by eagerness and a fool's folly to bully his helpless opponent. It seemed a fit punishment for showing such a mismatched opponent no mercy or quarter.

Whatever wealth or booty the small Spanish ship's officers and crew possessed had slid to the bottom of the sea, relegated to

Neptune's plentiful treasure coffers and the myriad of shipwrecks, already befouling his ocean floor.

And, now I had learned Ensign Higgins was no longer in our midst. Before I had been relieved of my watch and duties, extended by our encounter with the Spanish foe, his ailment had been discovered and he was removed to the bowels of the lower decks. There, he joined thirteen other crewman, now under the care of our surgeon and suffering the same affliction.

It had already been decided by the captain, goaded by a little encouragement from the doctor, that our ensign and these seamen would be set ashore at Portugal.

If we were to be tried by the fates, we would raise our own hand to contest their capricious whims and tests. The ill among us would be released from duty. They would be removed to the safety and comfort of shore, where they might once again grow strong and rid themselves of this cursed affliction.

But oh, how we did want to sail victoriously into a friendly harbor, a defeated prize-ship in tow behind our illustrious warship, attesting to the skill and valor of our crew.

It was not to be.

All we had to show for the encounter was a half-drowned Spaniard. And, he was not even an officer, at that. He was a simple seaman without a shirt upon his back. So much, had been his haste to report to his station and later, abandon his ship, that he had nothing, but his trousers. And, by the marks along his back, he was one, who had fallen victim to the lash for more, than one infringement.

Despite the burns, along his back, one could still see the horrible scars of a flogging, embedding a diamond pattern across his back. The men mused at his disfigurement.

They found the lash's scars closely resembling the pattern known aboard British ships as a "checked shirt."

The doctor had been brought topside to attend to the Spaniard on deck. He gave him ample time to dry out and become accustomed to his new home, before being relegated to the dark confinement of the brig, deep in the bowels of our ship.

I heard on good account, that the prisoner was a religious sort, despite the scars of many a whipping, that attested to ample sins and transgressions.

He called himself a Catholic, evidenced by the simple chain and crucifix hanging from his neck. And, after bearing his pain with the relief of an applied ointment by our good doctor, he blessed himself profusely.

He kissed the crucifix and rose to his knees to give prayer for surviving the disaster, that had claimed all, but him.

One of the men had thought to steal the charm or relic, dangling about the Spaniard's neck, but thought the better of it, after witnessing the man's devotion to the miniature replica of the savior, fixed to the metal cross. Besides, the metal was neither gold or silver and lacked any plating. It looked like some nickel or iron, cast, hammered, and filed into a crude representation. It was nearly valueless, except to its wearer.

One could scarcely argue, that some divine intercession or favor of the fates had saved the Spaniard, when the rest of his crew was lost. The odds defied explanation. Even the man's small and weak stature made one question, how he, above all the others of his ship, had survived.

The Spaniard was a small man, lanky and thin. He barely reached the shoulder of one of our statuesque marines. He seemed more, than content to accept his captivity among us. It was as if being in the hands of his British foe was the least of his worries.

It was one of those strange quirks of fate, that he, the least likely of all candidates, lacking strength and fortitude, should be the sole survivor of his dead ship. But, that was the way of life. It moved not at the hand of man, no matter how much men would seek to control life or twist it to do their bidding. It moved of its own accord, providing all with surprise and awe.

Our Spaniard wore the thin mustache and tightly trimmed beard, customary to Spanish nobles at court or the lowliest peasant. Of fashion and taste, our Spanish counterparts were of one mind, dull and boring. I should say, they seemed lacking of any individuality.

But, there he lay, atop the upper gun-deck, draped in a worn wool blanket as wind and sun dried him out. He was our prisoner, our sole souvenir of the encounter. What a sorry prize fate had bestowed upon us.

But, I think his presence was good for the morale of our men. The act of so easily sinking the Spaniard's brig had some merit and reward. It bolstered the men's confidence and showed demonstratively, that our foes were not invincible, despite their greater number of ships.

Nothing tastes so satisfying in one's mouth or is relished and savored as sweet as victory.

Yet, some aboard showed pity for the Spanish tar, likely finding us guilty of claiming the unworthy laurels of an unfair fight. Regardless, right or wrong, the encounter was a good exercise and drill for the men.

It allowed the novices aboard, including myself, to sample a taste of what was to come. It acclimated us to the din of our guns and the smell of burnt powder. We'd no longer be startled or apprehensive at their retort. We knew what was to come.

Or, so I had confidently thought at the time.

And, we had witnessed the true cost of defeat; the loss of life and ship. No man would settle in his heart for anything short of victory.

No, this encounter had best brought home the realities of our mission, that no drill or practice could ever impart.

We saw, that our lot was as one. If one man failed, all could die. Men and ship would share their defeat together.

Had the Spanish lookouts not been so lax to descend to warm themselves and had their commanders not been so generous and undisciplined as to permit that excess of privilege, than they might still be of one ship, one body. They might have survived, using their brig's greater speed and lightness to have escaped our coming onslaught.

The lesson had been rammed home, more so, than any bantering shouts of a boatswain or officer. The men had seen the price of failure.

I had returned to the warmth and comfort of my shared cabin, intent on closing my eyes and resting. But, sleep escaped me.

Too much had happened. My heart still raced and my mind was filled with the images of our engagement. I relived our approach and our first shots, that robbed the Spanish brig's mast of her canvas and brought her still in the water.

It was not the noble and exultant battle, which had I to confess, I had daydreamed of. Nor, was my place in it anything like I had fantasied, extoling myself in some great heroic measure or feat.

No, my first combat had just happened, quite by chance and serendipity, almost by accident. There had been no grandeur or valor in the engagement.

It had fallen into a simple act, a dueling contest, where our weapons and the men manning them went blindly about their duties, feeding their weapons and discharging them, with the detachment of a laborer in some cruel foundry or industry.

And, when their labors were over, instead of some rendered product, there was only death and destruction, witnessed by the flotsam cast atop the waves.

This was the true measure of my chosen profession. The grim reality of it haunted me. I had become as guilty as the men, who had fired the cannon that had sent the Spaniard to the bottom. As an officer, I was not merely an accomplice to the death of two-hundred or more men aboard the Spanish brig, I shared an active part in it. I was as equally damned as the captain.

I threw my feet onto the floor, finding my narrow berth uncomfortable and my mind troubled. I had thought, I had acquired a significant amount of wisdom for my early age, twenty-three.

But, now I found I knew nothing, not even of death.

My eyes screwed up to the bookshelves above the writing desk, between my berth and that, which was our Ensign Higgins'. I stood and stared eye-level at the worn brown leather cover of a bible, I rarely opened.

I had some measure of religious instruction in my youth, but it had long since fallen by the wayside. Still, I reached out my hand to that good book and clutched it in my grasp, descending back upon my berth and opening its hallowed covers.

A simple red ribbon had marked a page chosen by my mother. Its words were meaningless, when I had first read them to myself, out of respect for her treasured gift.

I could not bring my eyes to them now, fearing, that somehow I was less worthy, than a religious zealot, who revered and worshiped the sacred text.

I thumbed through the pages and noticed the gap between them, formed by the thin thickness of a silver-plated cross. Another gift, imparted to keep me safe upon my journeys. My fingers stumbled to pluck it from its resting place, removing it from the imprint, pressed into the bible's pages as it sat trapped inside the folded and closed covers.

I held the cross before me, marvelling at its simplicity of design. It was simple, its workmanship austere and basic. But, its sight was comforting and offered me some mild manner of relief, if only as a link to my now distant family.

I placed it beneath my pillow, intent on keeping it close to me.

Standing awkwardly as the ship commenced to roll, I returned the bible to its place on the shelf, reserved for my few treasures and distractions. Then, I sat back down atop my berth to reflect again, on all that had transpired.

I decided, I would try to fall asleep again, despite the din outside my cabin as guns were still being cleaned and stowed back in place for when next, their use would be called upon.

A boatswain's shrill bark and tongue lashed out at an inattentive tar, motivating him back to work, less he find himself the next victim of the lash.

I closed my eyes as I reclined in my berth, covering myself in the warmth of a deep blue woolen blanket. The waters slapped and licked about the stern soothingly.

I unexpectedly found slumber.

CHAPTER 17

The Decks

HMS Vanguard
Sailing off the Coast of Portugal
Day 5-Afternoon

I awoke at three in the afternoon. My sleep had been deep and restful, in spite of the din outside the junior officer's cabin. Again, I heard the booming voice of a boatswain, demanding obedience from the crew, outside the shared quarter's thick door.

I coughed hollowly, my throat the victim of a cruel draft, cutting about the cabin from beneath the closed door and seeking the closed windows, through which it could not escape.

I cleared my throat and rose on my elbow, finding my mouth dry and throat scratchy. Swallowing seemed to relieve the temporary discomfort. But, nothing could rid the cabin of the awful chill about it. With my blanket thrown aside, I desired only the warmth of my uniform.

I rose from my berth, making it quickly, though we had several cabinboys about, whose duty it was rightfully, to attend to the officers' needs in the manner of a servant or valet. But, I detested disorder and was certain, that by this late afternoon hour,

our other officers had found many other tasks to busy the young hands, they seemed to relish abusing.

Clad in the regalia of my uniform and its stiff collar, I prepared to exit our quarters.

I opened the door. At once, my nostrils were greeted to the strong odor of paint and turpentine. About the middle deck, this tar and that busied themselves, more slopping, than painting the middle gun-deck.

Brushes or rags were dunked into buckets of liquid crimson and slopped about the heavy wooden planks of the deck. The planks glistened as if some ghastly murderer or fiend had borne out his hideous crime upon their surfaces.

But, there were no victims about, except for several inept tars, who wore as much paint on themselves as was applied about the deck. I studied the glistening application, searching for some dry path, that might lead to ladder or step, allowing me to climb topside.

The boatswain, who had just rebuked the sloppy work of one of his charges, saw my impasse.

"Here, sir. We've left a dry corridor through here," he offered.

"Thank you, Boatswain," I returned, carefully passing behind a kneeling tar, who slopped the thick worn bristles of a round paint brush about as if it was mop. Red droplets splattered, flying through the air, threatening to find the dark royal blue of my uniform.

"You there, stop what you're doing and let the officer pass!" the boatswain's voice boomed, before being answered in instant obedience.

"These blokes are willing enough, but none could earn a living as a painter's apprentice or tradesmen," the boatswain offered, in apology and disdain for the shoddy work of his charges.

"No problem, Boatswain. No harm was done. But why are our decks being painted red?" I inquired, indisposed to show my ignorance.

"Sir, we're preparing for battle," he answered.

"Preparing for battle by painting the decks?"

"Aye, sir . . . as the second officer has ordered. It makes perfect sense, once you think about it," he returned, moving closer to me, so that the men would not hear the truth of our conversation.

In a low guarded voice of a deep throaty baritone, he informed me, "custom and prudence dictates, that we paint the decks red to hide the sight of blood from the men, like the sand we toss about to sop it up. They see their mates' insides splattered about the deck and it makes them skittish, less apt to fight. We need to keep up the lads morale, stiffen 'em up!"

I stood there silently, pondering the truth of his statement and viewing the wet red finish coating the deck.

"Keep up their morale?" was all I could offer, finding the painting detail wickedly absurd, but quite logical and correct.

"Aye, sir. Bucking up their morale, that's the ticket," the boatswain, returned with a wide grin.

"And, this takes place on all three gun-decks?"

"Aye, sir. Especially topside, the upper deck is always the center of the storm. What with sharpshooters shooting down from a mast and rigging at our officers and hands, not to say anything of shot and chain and all manner of munition aimed topside at our sails or at our helmsmen. It's a wicked thing, our business," he lamented, with the low tone of a man, who had seen it all before.

"How many such encounters, will this be for you?" I asked.

"It will be four. Five, if you count that mismatched fight with the Spaniard's brig," he returned, looking away as if I had forced him to recall some long ago act or event, he would rather leave undisturbed.

"I meant you no discomfort . . ." I started to make amends.

"None here, sir. I survived. There's no discomfort in that," he said, nodding away my concerns.

"I was at the battles of Ushant and Cape St. Vincent," he offered. "I served with Admiral Keppel, though I doubt, he'd know me from any other tar about his flagship."

I nodded, in tribute to his service, offering a simple "thank you," as I passed among the sailors, kneeling about the floor.

Several halted with my passage, not wishing to chance splattering the blood red pigment about the legs of my uniform.

Their subservience heralded the quiet resignation, that the reappearance of the lash, aboard our vessel, had commanded. I fretted for their own worries and apprehension, having preferred the cheerful banter and openness, that was once found among every deck of the Vanguard, before that wicked leather mistress's head was reared.

But, necessity drove us and the lash, that and time, which was quickly running out.

I reached the upper gun-deck and found the weather growing foul. Dark clouds engulfed our ship. They rolled menacingly over the choppy water. Both waters and clouds roiled with the darkness heralding a coming tempest.

But, our mighty ship still plied forward with little change in her demeanor, except a slightly exaggerated slant as her bow dipped and the moving sea could be viewed ahead of her prow, rising and lowering as it came to meet us.

The captain was on deck, though he took little interest in the actions of the watch, relegated to the authoritative command of one of our lieutenants. He stood transfixed, forward of the wheel, watching the last bare spaces of planking dabbed and slopped with the red paint, now coating all our fighting decks.

The clothing of the tars, going about the painting detail, was tugged and pulled by the growing wind. One cursed, forgetting himself in the outburst, as his hat was ripped off his head and it careened about, the fresh scarlet paint, before being lifted by the strong gust and driven overboard.

Had another officer been present, the lack of self-control, especially in the presence of the ship's captain, would have earned the seaman the lash. But, our captain's belly was full of death and violence as was our crew's.

There can be no worse dread left in a tar's gullet, than to have witnessed the expiration of a ship, even if it was not his own.

The Spanish brig, its two masts shattered and sinking beneath the waves, could easily be a foreshadowing premonition of our own fate to come.

Soon, we'd be joining Nelson's Squadron.

Our Lord Nelson was as tenacious as a bulldog. For eighteen months, he had blockaded the French fleet in Toulon, then chased it to the West Indies and home, only to have it escape his grasp and seek the protection and relief offered by the Spanish Port of Cadiz.

Now, his French counterpart, Admiral Pierre de Villeneuve, sat in port, his mighty vessels anchored and docked about as if their war was over. But, Nelson waited, content to keep his Squadron lingering about for the opportune chance, that the combined French and Spanish fleet might sortie, sailing for some new safe harbor or to support the efforts of Napoleon's Grand Armée.

I approached the captain as was the junior officer's custom, seeking to see what new duties I might engage in to free him of his burden.

As always, despite his calm and detached presence, he had more tasks awaiting.

The ship's new colors had been directed at the order of our second officer, though under the strict approval of our captain. It was only one of the many undertakings in the final preparations, we made for war.

"Since, you've already been chosen to aid our good doctor, attending to the sick, I think it best you attend to this small detail," he offered.

"I want the gun-deck's cleared of all unnecessary clutter. Supplies, extra rope, crates, sacks, and the whole of it are to be moved to the two lowest decks and stored as best they can.

"I want the gun-decks Spartan and unencumbered, ready for battle. I find, that like that Spanish brig, we encountered, we ourselves have become to lax."

"Aye, sir!" I snapped.

"Take what hands you need from among the crew and chose the bullies among them, the strongest backs and dullest heads should do. I favor you'll relish getting another chance to move that gawdawful iron box about," he remarked.

I began to protest any concerns for the monstrosity, but he waved me to silence, dismissing my offense.

"I mean nothing of it. But, I too, viewed that heavy crate. Once, we have time in our duties, I'll be as curious as you to open it up. But, there are more important matters at hand. For now, just move it aside and out of sight . . . I dare say, we'll be lucky, if it can even be moved the way the sea is churning about," he fell silent, looking off to starboard.

"Damn strange thing, your box," he relegated it and its riddle to me, "I examined it for lock or hinge and found neither."

"Perhaps, there is some hidden catch or latch spirited away on its surface," I suggested.

"Damn good craftsmanship, if that is the case. I've seen no way into that metal coffer. And, I've half a mind to threw it over the side. It's emitting a foul stink," he returned.

"But, no time for oddities. You best get started, before darkness finds us," he said, as the ship rolled with the tumult of the churning sea. "You won't have much time, the storm's already come . . . make sure everything is lashed down securely, especially that heavy box. Dismissed, Ensign!" he released me, to my duties.

"Aye, sir!"

The men moved in slow resignation, burdened by their heavy loads. A steady stream of barrels and sacks continued to be passed along the line, I had ordered formed. A chain of flesh starting from the second gun-deck led to the three lower decks beneath.

Burlap sacks were gripped by calloused hands and passed from man-to-man along the unbroken chain. The smallest items were redistributed in this manner. Unsteady legs halted and braced as our warship tilted about, threatening to drop man, sack, or crate to the deck.

I had chosen only the strongest among the tars, though a few unfortunate mice stood among the men. It was one of these smaller colleagues, who spilled from his place in the line, nearly plummeting through the gaping opening of the hold separating the decks.

With booming humor, several hands broke into a thunderous laughter as a ready giant, standing near his small companion, grasped the smaller man, preventing his disastrous plunge.

The sacks and crates continued downward, passing to the lowest decks, where they were set about as best they could be dispersed. Behind their progress, the voices and muted curses of laboring men met our ears.

I looked up to the steps leading to the lower gun-deck to find a group of men encircling our iron box. Their backs and legs strained under the enormity of its weight. They fought to keep hold of its smooth surface, devoid of handhold or handles, while they fought the rocking of our ship.

One man tripped over a mate's leg and fell to the floor. The iron crate dipped, pointing down towards the hold.

A shout went out, but it was too late. The ship rolled, changing its attitude and taking on a dangerous slope. One set of hands released its hold, followed by one more pair, then another.

The weight was too much for those still clinging to the iron surface to wrest control of the ungainly box. It slipped from the grip of ten or more men.

Two tried to fall upon its rear in an attempt to pin its enormous weight to the deck above. But, their own weight was too little and their grasp too faint.

The giant monstrosity slid over the edge of the hold above. For a moment, I swore it was frozen there. My eyes locked onto it and my tongue fell silent. I watched it slip over the rim above, edged on by the movements of our ship.

I opened my mouth, trying to cry out a word of warning to the men below. But, I found a dry mouth and a dead tongue, mirroring the inaction of my horrified eyes.

The horrid box teetered over the edge, suspended in space, before its weight tore through the air. It happened so fast the eye could almost not detect the path of its fall. It was unreal, like some demented dream.

A tremendous thud resonated off the wooden deck below. It was followed by a scornful plea as a man's last breath was exhaled.

All froze upon hearing that ghastly emanation. All heard the agony harbored in that final breath. All felt the resigned helplessness of an expiring life.

I forced my eyes ahead. Two tars were pinned beneath that massive cursed box. One was still, his limbs sprawled about, under a heavy corner of the iron monstrosity, pressed into his collapsed chest.

The other tar wept like a child, sobbing silently as he tried to accept the pain of the length of the iron box that had sought out his leg. It was pinned beneath the oppressive weight. His leg was distorted in an abnormal angle to the rest of his body.

Men rushed about with no command from me. They tried to find a hold on the pitted iron surface. Others, who had lost their hold above, dropped to the lower deck, seeking to atone for their failure.

As one, a straining body of tars slowly lifted the offensive container.

The chest of the unmoving tar lifted partially with the rising box embedded in it, until the body's weight dropped the tar free.

The dead tar's blouse and trousers were bloody. A red sticky ooze gelled about them. His mates dropped to him and pulled him clear, while others wrested the second tar's pinned leg to safety and freedom.

I slowly walked up to the sight of our disaster. There was no doubt, that one of the men was dead. But, I knelt to him and studied his lifeless form for a pulse and breath, much as, I had observed our doctor do.

There was no life, I did not expect to find any. But, respect demanded, that I examine our comrade. I did so as reverently and compassionately as I could, surrounded in the presence of the gathered crew.

The voice of the second injured tar ended my inquiry. I rose and moved to him.

His leg was crushed, though how badly was for the determination of our surgeon and his good expertise. There was nothing I could do, but order the men to gently lift the man and carry him to the lowest deck, where our surgeon had set up his newest infirmary, forsaking the ship's tiny sickbay and his earlier quarantine area.

I think the order caused as much consternation, among those present, as the man's injury. None favored the thought of being sent to reside among the quarantined section of the ship, where sickness and dampness now lingered.

The injured tar's face looked up to me pleadingly as if I had evoked some sentence upon him worse than the lash. But, there was nothing else to do. Our good doctor's stamina and skill were already being tested. One could not expect him to travel about our rolling ship, just to make rounds to appease the sensibilities of the crew.

Any injured or ill man would be directed below. It was the sensible and appropriate thing to do.

He cried out as his leg twisted of its own accord, moved by the dangling weight of his broken limb. The shrill din of his voice echoed through our narrow passage way, finding the dread in every man.

I ordered the damned iron manifestation to be placed down, clear of the men and in no danger of falling through another hold or hatchway. I moved to it and studied its surface.

It was still locked as tight as a jar of preserves, taken from a pot of boiling water. The fall had jarred nothing loose. Its lid was intact and locked. My hands dropped to its porous surface. I looked and felt for some novel device or trapping, that might release the box's lid.

There was none. My fingertips traced over the coarse crude metal, expecting to feel the unevenness of a recessed latch. There was none. What trickery was this, that mocked me.

I was an intelligent man, educated by formal schooling and versed in the practicalities of the construction of items, so simple as furnishings to the grand designs of shipbuilding from the books, that I had read.

Yet, this ungainly object puzzled me and any attempt to reason the key to its entrance. It was as if the damn thing was locked from the inside. A preposterous thought.

I relented.

"Get this below!" I blurted out, more angered at my own failure to demise the secret of the container's locked contents, than by the tragic incident, that had befallen us.

The men gathered about the iron box again. Knees bending and backs straining, they sought to free it from the deck.

I watched as they carefully snaked their arms beneath it, other willing hands and arms pressed in to share their burden, lest another mishap befall us.

I watched the horrid iron box moved to the next deck below. I followed the grunting tars, ensuring it was stowed properly.

I surmised, that it would be best to leave the iron container laying flat along the deck, once we had it delivered to the lowest level of the Vanguard. I feared stowing it upright and lashed. Its weight and the rolling of the ship in heavy seas might snap its restraints and send it banging about.

I ordered the sacks of potatoes and lemons to be piled atop it, relegating the offensive thing to use as a shelf.

Twelve or twenty sacks were piled atop its flat lid, others upon the deck before it, burying the damning thing from sight. A line was tied about the sacks, reaching from one beam to another, anchoring the burlap bags in place.

I tugged on the line, assuring it was taunt enough to hold the sacks fast. That done, I returned to the entrance of the hold and checked on the progress of the men.

The last few items were being passed along. Coils of rope and spare parts along with extra pulleys and every other loose item, which had cluttered the gun-decks above, was moved into the bowels of the Vanguard.

Within the hour, their tasks were done and all was secured.

CHAPTER 18

Peg Leg

HMS Vanguard
Sailing off the Coast of Portugal
Day 5-Afternoon

I made my way forward along the lowest deck, searching out our doctor.

I found the injured tar in an anteroom. I was slightly alarmed upon seeing a thin wisp of smoke about the room. But, I ceased worrying, when I saw our doctor standing about some crude small black kettle, set atop a small burner. He stirred its brewing contents, ignorant of my presence.

The doctor's patient laid atop a makeshift wooden table, several boards set atop two carpenter's horses. His left trouser leg was split open, cut in half and draped up high beyond his knee.

The limb was a grizzly sight.

I lost my appetite for the supper, I would be obliged to take within the next couple of hours, joining the company of our captain and officers. I averted my eyes from our injured tar and sought out any distraction from the sight of his crushed leg.

My eyes returned to the pot and its strange boiling contents, black as pitch or tar. Its surface lifted slightly, before a trapped bubble grew and burst. More followed, erupting about its surface. Their presence seemed to satisfy the doctor's stirring and tending. He left it and busied himself about his makeshift infirmary.

The two tars, who had brought our injured seaman, stood to the rear. They watched his examination continue under the flickering candles, set in the lanterns swaying from the ceiling above.

His fingers probed and tested the flesh.

I learned from one of the tars as I took my place beside them, that this was the doctor's third such examination. He was procrastinating about the final cure.

The doctor's face was sternly set. It spoke of the severity of the leg's injuries without the surgeon uttering a word. The tar being examined panted like a wounded animal, despite the generous allotment our doctor had provided from among his infirmary's rum ration.

A half-full bottle resided in the hands of one of the tars, standing beside me.

"Let him have another," the surgeon instructed the tar, cradling the bottle of dark golden brown libation.

The seaman stepped forward to the table.

"Here you go, Harris. You're a lucky bastard . . . I think you did this just to get an extra week's ration of rum and that in nearly three gulps," he said, through a broken and forced smile, trying to hide his own nervousness and fears.

The dull-minded tar, reclining on the table, grasped the dark green bottle's neck and tugged it towards his lips. His rasping breath halted as he tilted the bottle in his mate's hands and greedily partook of the warm throat-burning liquid.

He drank as if the measure was water, stopping only to breathe. He coughed, before dropping back to the table. Pain wracked his body. His hands clenched into fists as he fought the throbbing misery of his leg, still stabbing through his rum-dulled mind.

The doctor came beside us, motioning the mate with the bottle to him.

He grasped the heavy green bottle and wiped its mouth, before raising it to his lips. He swallowed profusely in one large practiced gulp, the sort taken without thought by a man, who was used to heavy drinking.

He halted, bowing his head to the floor and allowing the warmth of the rum to ease his conscious and calm him for what was to come.

In a guarded whisper, he told the three of us, "the leg's got to come off."

His voice was almost indifferent. It was as if he was offering a prescription, he had tendered many times before.

"You can't do that to Harris," the man's shipmate hissed.

"You think I want to this?" the doctor snapped back, his words incoherent to the seaman succumbing to the relieving numbness and induced stupor of the rum.

The seaman fell silent.

"His leg is crushed, including the knee. If it was a clean break, I could set it, he'd probably limp for the rest of his life, but he'd be none the worse for it."

"As it is, the knee and limb's been shattered. Some of the bone's poking through the skin," he pointed, to the broken shards of bone set amongst pools of red and pierced flesh.

"If I let it be, he'll never be able to walk on it again. Worse, I can't promise to keep it free of infection. I've seen this before. Gangrene will set in. If I don't take the leg, we'll loose the man . . . there's nothing left there to save," the doctor stated.

"What do you need of us?" I asked, ending any procrastination by the man's mates.

"I'll need two of you to hold him fast. But, not yet. We'll ply him with more rum. Even drunk, the body knows to fight, when its threatened."

"Fight?" the silent seaman, beside the other's mate, asked.

"I've taken limbs before," the surgeon returned. "It's a horrid business and it's made worse, when under the broadside of a foe. Fear and panic are powerful motivators. I've seen wounded men, near death, lash out trying to halt bone-saw and scalpel, once they got an inkling of what's to come."

"I'll hold him," relented the seaman, who claimed to be the man's friend.

"Aye, me too," the other seaman offered.

"And, me?" I asked the doctor.

"A nasty business for you, I'm afraid. You best take off your tunic and roll up your sleeves. You'll assist me, Ensign," he replied.

"Besides, it will be good practice for what's to come," he added morbidly.

"Practice?" I questioned.

"You don't think you're going to be topside sharing the battle with admirals and captains do you?"

"My God, you do?" the doctor said in amazement, not withholding our conversation from the two tars in our midst.

"Boy, you'll be lucky to see a gun-deck, if anything more. The glory is for the ranks, lad. If you can call it that."

"As a junior officer, you're likely to be used as a runner between the decks, taking our captain's commands to one or more of our batteries. Or more likely, since you've already been predisposed by events to show your worth to me, you'll assist me in the bowels of our ship as the battle rages above. You know, I can't handle the casualties, that are to come alone. And, with your Mr. Higgins taken ill, you are the lowest ranking officer, the one most likely to be afforded me, because of your lack of experience."

I was about to protest, but the doctor moved behind me and began pulling off my coat. He ushered me to a wash basin and filled it from a pitcher of fresh water. He bid me to use a large bar of soap, while I rolled up the sleeves of my white blouse.

As I washed, he instructed the two tars on what would be required of them. His words were simple, suiting their aptitude and leaving nothing to chance. When done, he had described the gruesome task awaiting us and ensured all would do their part.

He joined me at the basin as I wiped my hands in a towel, that laid beside it on the countertop.

Finished, he reached into his medical bag and withdrew a large brown medical bottle and a velvet cloth, tied about itself with a string.

These, he placed atop the counter, carefully undoing the cloth's tie and unrolling it. There, I spied the cruel implements of our doctor's trade.

There were several kinds of scalpels, their tiny blades of different shapes and curvatures, but all were thin and razor sharp by the looks of them. Tweezers were pocketed inside the folds of the cloth. There were three sets of these. They were of long, medium, and short lengths.

And, there were several implements I could not identify, nor did I wish to. All glistened, even from the dim light of the lanterns overhead. I guessed them to be of the finest polished steel, akin to an Admirals sword or cavalry officer's biting sabre.

But, I was wrong on several accounts. Some of them were crafted from pure silver, delicate and precision instruments of the surgeon's trade and craft.

I watched as the doctor removed a cloth covered implement from inside one of the recessed openings in the larger cloth's folds. The instrument was wrapped securely inside a measure of dark blue velvet, a string holding its cover fast.

The surgeon's fingers struggled to undo the delicate string, finding it knotted and tight from last use. The knot, unknown to us, had dried and caked with blood from its tool's last traumatic use.

The cover came undone.

The doctor's hand clasped the short handle of the implement, withdrawing it with a reverence and respect, that seemed coupled with a strange resignation and revulsion.

The bone-saw gleamed beneath the light, its ripping teeth set along the bottom of its short strong length.

I saw the doctor swallow hard, his Adams apple rising in his throat.

My eyes fell to the deck, not envying him, his profession or the cruelty his ministrations often demanded.

"Give our mate another round," the doctor commanded, to the tar about the table as he kept the saw hidden with his body.

"Blimey, he's nearly dead drunk now. If I fill his gullet any more, he'll be heaving his guts," the seaman with the bottle, returned.

"Do it!" the doctor ordered. "I'll tell you, when he's ready."

The doctor removed a cork from the brown bottle and held it above the saw and the scalpel, he'd selected for the operation. He poured a liberal amount of the fluid over the broad flat surface of the bone-saw, liberally dousing its teeth and the front of its used handle. The excess dripped to the floor. He placed it down on the counter and repeated the disinfecting process for the scalpel.

Alcohol was used to cleanse the long forgotten and stored tools. There was little else to be used. In battle, the saw and scalpel would not be cleaned. The tools would go about their gruesome work, serving one man to the next with barely more than a wiping, between use.

The scalpel would be used to make the first incision and a ringed cut above the knee, freeing the flesh from the grasp of the bone, much like a butcher preparing meat.

He doused his hands, rubbing the alcohol about them and between his fingers, before passing the bottle to me to do the same.

He returned to the table, his patient awake, but unaware of his surroundings or the event unfolding around him.

"Enough," the surgeon ordered the tar, still lifting the bottle to the injured seaman's lips. "Give me the bottle."

The tar turned it over to the doctor. To the concern of all, our surgeon lifted it to his lips and drank a short slug, before pointing it down over the tar's left leg and pouring it around the wounded limb, just above the knee.

Some of the alcohol found broken skin and open flesh, but its burning sting raised only a moan from our inebriated patient.

The doctor cupped his hand and swabbed the rum about the leg, its sides and back, seeking to purify the limb of any dirt or germ.

Then, he claimed the awaiting scalpel and nodded for the two tars to hold the man down. Each sailor pressed upon a shoulder, pinning their protesting and ignorant charge under their own weight, while each grabbed a wrist to keep the man from flailing about. They did as the doctor had instructed.

The surgeon bid me, to hold the man's lower left thigh, much like a human clamp, anchoring it to the tabletop and to control a tourniquet, placed high above the thigh to stem the flow of blood.

And so, it began.

The thin blade of the scalpel drew no response from our patient. Thus, was the skill and deftness of our good doctor's handiwork. I watched in awe as the thin blade broke epidermis, than pressed further, reaching along the sides. Nary a line of blood was drawn, so light and precise was our surgeon's touch.

The surgeon's cutting blade did not even disturb our patient, who had now fallen into a drunken slumber. His face wore the stupid stupor of a man, who was ignorant of his surroundings or the events unfolding about him.

It was a blessing of sorts, that the man had fallen unconscious. Awake, there would have been the need to gag him, stuffing a piece of rope into his mouth and between his teeth, not only to quiet his screams, but to keep him from biting off his tongue.

The doctor instructed me to lift the limb, so that he could sever the skin along the back of the thigh, finishing the circumference of the outer ring of his amputation.

Already, the doctor's hands were covered in blood, it shined in the light of the lanterns. But still, he encircled the limb again, his scalpel biting deeper.

Now, blood flowed freely from his incisions, despite the tourniquet, that I kept tight, while still managing to control the limb.

Some nerve or vein was struck that brought our tar to reality, ripping him from the ignorant comfort of his drunken stupor. He screamed, the cry cutting through each man. His right leg thrashed about. The doctor leaned over it and trapped it under his body's weight.

In response, arms and hands pressed tighter, pinning our patient to the table.

We had to work quickly. The longer the open flesh of amputation was exposed, the greater was the chance of infection. The success to any amputation was to do the job quick and seal off the exposed end of the limb.

The tar pleaded to know what was transpiring, but found only silent compassionate stares returned to his wide eyes. His breath panted like some frightened cornered animal. He fell upon begging. He pleaded, that no harm come to him. He sought only release and freedom.

None came.

One of the tars, about the man's head, released his hold. His partner shoved his weight down upon both our patient's shoulders, allowing a free set of hands to relive the doctor, dually-tasked with operating and keeping the tar's right leg from flinging about.

Rum and fear, soon overwhelmed our patient and he, once again, slipped away, fainting into unconsciousness.

The scalpel finished its work and was placed aside.

The skin was pulled back, like one would skin an animal, clearing the way for the saw to come.

He found the arteries of the leg and set about tying them off in a grizzly affair to stem the loss of blood. It was some new technique, gained from experimentation and trial and error upon the victims of the battlefields and set about in the medical journals, intoning the success of the latest advances of our military surgeons

It was a sight, I did not think possible. But, the Napoleonic Wars had seen many advances in surgery and elevated the status and influence of the military surgeon to the forefront and acclaim of the doctor's medical profession.

There were surgeon's on both sides, heralded for their advances. James Syme had become renown for his ingenuity in creating new methods of amputation, the only course left open to a surgeon, when faced with a limb, suffering catastrophic devastation.

France's Dominique Jean Larrey was perhaps his country's greatest military surgeon and was the first to amputate successfully, at the hip joint in 1803. He was bestowed with lavish praise and fortune by the French Emperor himself, after being idolized by the French army. He was bestowed with honors and elevated to baron of the empire.

As brutal as amputation appeared, it was the sole source of survival for many a soldier or sailor. The wars we now fought saw many advances. Foremost, was the goal of surgeons and attendants to remove the injured from the field of battle and tend to them, as quickly as possible.

Prompt removal from an engagement and speed of amputation were viewed as the keys to saving the lives of the wounded.

Our patient's struggling increased as the doctor continued methodically sealing off sources of seepage. The flow of blood still continued, its loss could kill our patient as readily as the trauma of the operation.

The sight of the doctor's administrations was barbaric. Yet, he did all he could to aid the survival of our patient.

He had little choice.

The final act was at hand. The surgeon picked up the bone-saw, in his right hand. He tried to shield its sight from our patient by laying his left hand aside it.

But, the tar craned his neck up, despite the pushing palms of the tar, trying to force him flat across the table.

He screamed incoherently. His eyes and drunken mind fathoming, what was to come. This time, he did not fall back into the ignorant fog, induced by the rum.

"Hold him!" the doctor ordered me as I struggled to hold the broken limb, while the tar thrashed about, trying to move from the path of the saw.

His yells filtered out into the hallway, leading up to the next deck. It echoed mournfully, telling all above, what horrid business we were up to within the darkness of the bowels of the ship.

I marked the howls so frightful, that the men above must

have covered their ears. I know I would have done so, had I been able to reclaim the use of my occupied hands.

"Gag him!" the surgeon demanded of one of the tars, assisting in our gruesome work.

The tar looked about helplessly, before finally claiming the towel, we had dried our hands in. He stuffed it into the patient's mouth and biting teeth.

I pressed the limb to the table with one hand, while using my free hand to douse the surgeon's cut profusely with rum, at his order. The partly filled bottle of rum was knocked from my hand. It tipped over and spilled onto the table, before rolling off onto the floor. The table slopped of blood and rum as the limb moved and the loose flesh tore about.

I pressed the limb flat with both hands as the doctor joined me on the same side of the table and began.

He pushed a loose piece of skin aside as if filleting a fish and drove the saw one length through the exposed ivory bone. There was no sound, the teeth so sharp, they raced through the hardness of the bone.

But, I swear I felt their ripping teeth vibrating in my hands, that held the limb and shook the table. The saw moved back, then pressed forward again. Hard and sharp, is how I remember those ripping forward cuts, chewing through bone and marrow.

And then, it was done.

I felt the leg yield in my hands. It was a sickly feeling. The sight of the severed limb, freed from its owner and free in my hands was a ghastly sight. I had never felt such revulsion.

"In the bucket! Get it out of his sight! Damn you!" the doctor barked at my lack of compassion and ignorance. I spun around as the tar thrashed about the table like a wounded fish, landed aboard a fishing boat.

I spied the bucket in a corner of the room and placed it as reverently as I could inside its round confines. But, it kept slipping about, until finally, bucket and leg toppled to the floor with the uneasy movements of the ship.

My gut wrenched and I felt the warmth of my bile heave forward. It splattered about the deck.

"Come, Mr. Lewis. We can't have that. Stiffen up! This is nothing. Nothing of the likes, you'll witness, when we reach Cadiz," he taunted like a school bully.

But, I understood the truth, he had been trying in his own tactless way to alert me to. This was what was to come. This was a sample of the price of the glory and prize-money, I sought out.

He taught me this, without a shot being fired.

Joined with the cruel lesson, learned of our attack on the Spanish brig, I no longer felt as assured or invincible as my youth had betrayed me to believe. I was of the same flesh as this tar. And, if not for my good fortune at having not stood beneath the crash of our iron coffer, it could just as easily have been me, laying upon the table.

The tar finished writhing. He halted almost as suddenly as he had started. Perhaps, his body had absorbed all the pain, it could accept. Perhaps, he had simply fainted, his mind and body too abused to stay with us. Whatever the reason, the pain or rum, he fell silent and collapsed into himself.

The surgeon left the table, placing his scalpel and bone-saw atop the countertop and claiming the small kettle. He brought it to the table and our unconscious tar.

"Be thankful, he's asleep for this. Now help me and hurry, before he wakes," the good doctor intoned.

I had no understanding of what the doctor was about to do. Yet, I assisted him, moving upon his direction and aiding him. We moved our tar to the edge of the table, where his amputated limb dangled off the side of its edge.

In horror, I could not believe, what I had become a gruesome part to. The doctor held the boiling kettle beneath the amputated limb and raised it, holding its thick metal handle, wrapped in cloth to protect his hands from its heat.

The stump touched the boiling pitch as the doctor continued lifting the pot up to it, submerging the open end of the wound inside its brackish syrup.

My breath escaped me and my mouth and lungs choked.

The wound coated and sealed with the boiling tar. The doctor allowed the kettle to drop away, holding it beneath the dripping wound to catch some of the melted tar. As the tar began to cool and dry, he returned the pot to the table and the small burner, that had warmed it.

I watched as his eyes seemed far distant and removed, viewing the victims and human refuse of another battle or another time.

Now, I understood our doctor's vice and penchant for strong drink. I do not think, I could have held his fortitude and have dealt repeatedly with the horror we inflicted, at this moment. Yet, he quitely and patiently went about his trade, cleaning his instruments and returning them into the security of their soft velvet pockets.

My mouth and throat burned.

All I could do was watch. It was done, but for the memory, that would never leave me.

I heard a throat clear at the doorway to our small room.

It was the captain, come to inspect, what had transpired and to offer some condolence for our injured comrade.

I struggled to stand upright and was only now aware of the glistening gel of the blood caking my hands, the same as the doctor's.

The captain waved off my pretense at formality. The look, he shared with me, spoke volumes. I was no longer his novice and inexperienced junior officer. I was learning the true nature of our business and the costs, any of us could be called upon to bear.

He moved over to the table and studied the limb.

"Will he live?"

"Aye, Captain. If I can keep infection away. And, if he has something to live for," the surgeon answered.

"And, our good Ensign?" he cast a glance my way.

"He did fine, Captain. I'd say, with this morning and our first encounter with the Spaniards, he's stepping into his duties nicely. And, he's done well here. He kept away from the bucket, until the operation was done. For his first time, its quite acceptable . . . commendable, really."

"Good. Very good. If the battle to come is as I expect, you'll be needing an assistant. I'll charge you with our young ensign. Perhaps, before we reach Cadiz and Nelson's Squadron, you might instruct him in the basics of your healing crafts," the captain decided.

"Aye, that would be wise. Perhaps, you might free our ensign from some of his more menial duties. We have officers enough, to ensure the decks are painted and the watches stood."

"It is agreed, then," the captain sealed my fate. "You understand, Ensign Lewis?"

"Aye, sir. I am to be the doctor's new assistant," I replied half-heartedly, in disappointment.

"And, learn as much as he can teach you. I'll expect some dissertation or recital of your new found knowledge at our customary dinners. It will be a splendid change from the familiar complaints and politics, now ringing our table. And, the others might learn some lifesaving aid or ministration in the process."

"Yes, an excellent idea, just in case our good doctor is incapacitated," he added.

"I also came to check on Ensign Higgins," the captain moved to the doctor and went on to the next business at hand.

I returned to the wash basin and rid myself of the blood caking my hands. With that done and the tars cleaning up the foul mess, I left the corner with its vile bucket and the discarded limb.

The bucket's contents and limb were destined to be thrown over the side of our ship. The sea would claim all evidence of our foul work, leaving only its memory atop the waters.

I left, seeking to return to my shared cabin.

I had said nothing of our Ensign Higgns and his horrid marks or my sighting of the shadowy specter the night before. Grim realty and the workings of the bone-saw had pushed foolishness from my mind.

I left the doctor to attend to our patients as he best saw fit.

CHAPTER 19

Our Prisoner

HMS Vanguard
Sailing off the Coast of Portugal
Day 6-Early Morning

I awoke in ignorance of the hour. To find a tar respectfully, yet fearfully rapping upon our quarters' door. He hung onto the door jab as our vessel rolled about.

I had been in a deep slumber, the trials of the surgery I'd witnessed and the sinking of the Spanish brig all raced through my mind, until the events were dulled and cluttered, one merging into the other and sleep had finally claimed me.

Now, the thoughts and images grew in my mind anew as I tried to fathom, what new business required my attention.

The other junior officers awoke to the knocking, before I. Senior to me, they damned my failure to rise, one throwing a pillow at my reposed head.

I lay unmoving, my lungs trying to gulp air as the realities, I had witnessed the day before, continued flooding my mind. The fingers of my right hand stabbed beneath my pillow, finding the cool silver-plated metal of the cross, I had secreted there.

Only now, had I come to realize the trials our good doctor must have come to know. I wondered how he dealt with them, having harbored a legion of travails far greater, than I had witnessed or should hope to in the future.

True, he did drink his measure of pain away. But, even strong drink could not remove a damning memory of which, he had many.

I recalled yesterday's evening supper, less formal and held in haste in the captain's cabin. There was much to do for all as we set about masticating the remains of a roast beef without our usual discussions.

Every man seated at our shared table knew the duties, he must attend to. All had thoughts filling their heads and troubles and shortfalls enough to correct.

A few eyes glanced at me disapprovingly as uncharacteristic to my nature at the table, I partook of one extra measure of wine after the other. I found its sweet taste and relief barely enough to soothe away the brutality, I had witnessed.

Only the captain offered no silent reproach. He doted on me, akin to our surgeon, allowing me a measure of leniency.

He seemed to silently acknowledge the morbid duties, he had assigned to me and their gruesome initiation and rites of passage. I had proven by trial, that I had the wits to be a worthy companion to our doctor. My love of knowledge and books would be put to use, learning the ministrations and techniques of the surgeon's profession.

Though not schooled by university or hospital, I would learn enough of our surgeon's trade to assist him in the trials and butchery to come.

The captain allowed me a measure of excess, letting me take my time and find my own way to step into my new role. Yesterday had been an appalling baptism, a taste of what would be expected of me.

I detested it, but I did not turn away.

I rose from bed, seeking out shirt and pants as the tar entered. He came beside me and reported as he had been requested.

Our good doctor had need of me.

At first, I dreaded the call. I harbored the fear, that our amputee had suffered a turn for the worse and was now in need of some other horrid cure.

Then, I remembered our Ensign Higgins, now resided to the bowels of the ship and quarantined with thirteen other afflicted members of our crew. In dread, I feared Higgins had taken a turn for the worse.

I dressed quickly, fighting the chill, plaguing our damp cabin. The stern rose and set, telling all awake, we were in heavy seas. My stomach protested the hollow fall the stern claimed upon it, setting my stomach's beef and wine to churning.

My light head and sour stomach threatened to be my undoing. I felt the best thing was to move and occupy myself.

Before moving on, I examined my timepiece. It was one-thirty in the morning, an ungodly hour by which to break the deep slumber of our cabin.

Both I and the tar exited my quarters to the relief of those left behind and returning to the warmth of their berths.

I closed the door behind us silently, in a belated measure of respect. But, I held onto its handle, suddenly finding need of the crutch it presented as the ship's bow dipped down and our deck slanted forward.

Carefully, the two of us made for the ladders and steps leading below. There was little need for silence in our passage. Most of the sailors, we passed in their strung hammocks, were awake.

Even the most seasoned veterans among them showed they were ill of the ship's untamed movements. Though our bow was steered forward, it felt, as if the hull moved about all the points of the compass.

My feet nearly fell away beneath me as an unguarded movement of the ship dropped the deck. I searched for my next footing.

The tar ahead of me merely bounced about the length of the hull. His hands and arms sought this hold or that along the beams and braces, set in his path.

Together, we stumbled about, seeking the lower sections of the Vanguard. There, the effects of our vessel's rolling and yawing would prove less exaggerated, merely by leaving behind the Vanguard's towering heights.

I found the doctor seated upon a chair in the anteroom, where we had performed the operation. He looked befuddled and at a loss.

I was about to inquire on the cause of his depression, when a raving howl broke loose. The words were almost inaudible. The voice forcing them from exhausted lungs rasped and panted.

"Our Spaniard," the surgeon enlightened me.

Before, I could reply, the man broke out again.

"He's been ranting and going on like that for a good part of an hour. I don't speak a damn word of that chatter he's spewing from his lips. He's like a mad dog," the doctor protested, expecting nothing to be done, but feeling the better for the release.

The Spaniard's voice broke forth again. The shrill in it was gone. It had fallen to weeping and sobbing, the plight of a broken man.

"Have you attended to him? Is he injured . . . his back?" I began questioning.

"Damn, it's not his back. I checked on his wounds before retiring. They're fine enough, burns no worse, than having been laid out in the sun too long, much too long. But, he'll survive them. Damn, if I can fathom, what gibberish these Catholics speak . . . of my profession, I know some Latin, but nothing of the Spanish tongue."

"I know a few words of Spanish," I admitted.

"I hoped as much," that's why I sent for you. "I've no more patience for this disruption. See what you can do to calm him. Otherwise, I'll ask the captain to throw his lot over the side," he added vehemently.

I turned and was about to move to the brig, down the length of the narrow aisle, when the doctor bid me one more thing.

"I know some Latin . . . strangely, his ramblings sounded like they were mixed with some prayer or incantation . . ." he offered with a shrug, wanting to have nothing more to do with the outbursts of our prisoner.

"I'll see to him," I returned confidently, though irritated at having my sound sleep broken.

I found the brig's heavy wooden door, built of planks and iron. It was locked with a heavy padlock, which I had no key to.

But, there were two openings. One was set low in the door. It was a small metal hatch by which, to pass bread and water through or whatever ration the cell's penitent occupant was deemed fit to receive, under the good graces of our captain's judgment.

A second opening was set head high. It was guarded by bars and an iron frame, leaving no doubt to the cell's denizen of his incarcerated state. The prisoner could only glimpse the cast light of a lantern, set about the opposite wall. The flickering light cast the long shadows of his oppressive bars across the length of his cell.

I edged up to the door cautiously, the cell having gone strangely silent.

Peering through the bars, I saw nothing.

But, I heard the low sobbing and the guttural moans and pleas of a desperate man. I heard moving lips dartingly about, spewing an almost unheard prayer repeatedly, over and over.

The doctor was right, the words were a strange conglomeration, an odd mix of the captive's native tongue and Latin. He prayed. But, his prayer was no austere and reverent incantation of worship, spoken slowly with each word intoning some gentle petition to God and Heaven above.

Rapidly, the Spaniard repeated and renewed the incantation from the start. I heard trembling and fear in his voice as he spat out sacred words from a dry mouth with a frightened tongue.

The few words of Latin and Spanish, I could detect, made little sense, except to lead me to discern, he was seeking protection.

I wondered if some English tar had sought to visit our captive friend to perhaps, bully or torment him.

I asked the tar, who had followed me, tending duty for our surgeon, if this was the case.

He answered, it was not.

So, I leaned forward.

My shadow cast into the cell of the brig in elongated streaks of darkness, that set the Spaniard to scurrying for the other side of the wall, away from the door. He clasped the tiny crucifix, about his neck, holding it tightly in his trembling fingers and pointing it up at the opening, framing my head outside.

He began furiously chanting, lifting an arm as if to protect himself and turning his eyes away, lest he look into mine.

"What's the matter, here?" I barked, finding his conduct disgraceful.

There was no answer, save for the continued incoherent mumbling of some Spanish prayer or chant.

"Answer me!" I ordered. "What manner of folly is this?"

The Spaniard stopped his gibberish. His head turned my way and his eyes rose to find me waiting for an answer.

It was for the first time, that I realized, how much he trembled. The sight was deplorable and disgraceful, that a veteran sailor could show such a lack of fortitude and mettle.

Yet, there was a real fear in his eyes and demeanor.

He shook like a child, after being subjected to the horrible imps and demons, likely to plague the dreams of their youthful sleep.

His fingers clasped the small crucifix, pressing it so tightly, that his knuckles grew white.

"What is the matter?" I asked again, lowering my voice, less it threaten him.

He mentioned some string of words, between panting breaths. He swallowed and choked, upon breath and word, as if in a disoriented and drunken stupor.

But, I knew he had been given no rum, save for a measure to warm him and a blanket, after being plucked from the sea. And, to a seaman, such a drop was not even a taste to savor the distilled liquid or enjoy its warmth.

Such a ration was merely a potion or elixir, a medication to stave off chill and illness or restore the body's warmth.

I listened as he repeated his words, trying each time to produce a clarity, I might understand. He spoke slower as an adult might speak to a child, unfamiliar with the spoken word.

I only understood three words.

He kept repeating "muerte," which means "death." And, he blasphemed "armar un alborto," in English "to raise the devil."

I wondered what trickery these Catholics were about. Perhaps, our captive seaman dabbled in the black arts or witchery. I found his words filled with superstitious rot and falsehoods and was ready to depart his presence.

But, the last word, I fathomed, held my attention. I leaned closer to the locked doorway as he repeated his words, again and again. It was nonsense. It made no sense.

He spoke of a woman as best, I could translate. But, there were no women among our crew. The Spaniard must be mad.

Perhaps, the loss of his ship and crew had finally overwhelmed him. The mind is a fragile thing and sometimes slow to respond to the reality of the moment.

Now, safe, the recent past had beset our captive and had found him mad.

The third word, he did speak to me, was "vampiresa." It was Spanish for "a woman, who preys on men."

There were plenty of women, who occupied both the Spaniard's home ports and our own, who sought to earn their daily bread and the fleeting bobbles and luxuries of life by clasping their harpie-like claws into the purses and flesh of seamen.

Not only did our Spanish captive suffer the loss of ship and mates, it seemed, he was unlucky with women. Of all his concerns, women should be among the least of them.

But, the Spaniards, like the French, often held misplaced priorities.

I turned and left our Spanish sailor. Almost at once, in the absence of my presence, he began sobbing and whimpering like some dismal dejected creature.

I assumed events had simply overwhelmed him. Should I have survived in his stead, having lost all of my crew and the vessel, that had become so much a part of my life, I too would have had trouble bearing the loss.

But, our Spaniard seemed to have no shame. He wept openly. The sight was repugnant and obscene. If anything, he should have had more backbone, being the sole representative of his ship's compliment.

But, the Spanish were an emotional people, bearing their grief openly.

I relished the fact, that at least, I had some measure of reserve.

I had even given a good account of myself in the infirmary during the amputation, when one considers, that was my first exposure to that butchery.

I promised myself to tow the line and give a good account of myself and my actions in our future battle. I would not let the shameless behavior, exhibited by our Spaniard, befall myself.

I promised myself this.

I had a reputation to uphold and my family would accept no shame.

I made my way back to our good doctor and dismissed the Spaniard's yells and rantings. I suggested, they were those of a man for whom loss had become too much to bear. But, I did not make excuses for our captive's behavior.

I found it deplorable and said as much to our surgeon.

The strangeness of tongue and custom are a bothersome thing. I was roused from a much needed and deep slumber, just to bid a man fare tidings and assurances, like a mother would bid a child.

Preposterous, that is what it was. And, it was an insult, to my rank and the uniform I wore. If the Spaniard were not a prisoner, I would have assigned him the lash.

But alas, he had troubles enough.

As I prepared, to return to the upper decks, I spied the spiteful iron box and the sacks of provisions, that had been stowed atop it. The line, that had been tied about the sacks lay askew, its thick cord broken.

The sacks had tumbled about, some of them opening and their contents spilled about the floor. The iron box was resting diagonally about the aisle.

But, despite the ship's rolling yaw, it remained firmly in place in its new position. My mind thought to order some tar or boatswain to form a detail and stack and secure the spilled cargo of lemons, rolling about the deck.

But, it was late and there would be plenty of time to undertake the task in the morning. The iron monstrosity was going nowhere and its bulk threatened nothing.

Our tars might dislike their rations rolling about the floor. But, they had hardy enough constitutions.

I had seen them eat the hard biscuits, a staple of their meals, that substituted for what normal men would call bread. I'd even seen them pick or cut away the small hard rolls, when maggots had infested them.

True to their toughness, when barrels of the biscuits had become infested with the writhing maggots, I'd seen a tar toss a fish inside the barrel, providing a new and more desirable home for the infestation, that abandoned the hard rolls and claimed residence in the smelly stink of a foul rotting fish.

After allowing for their transit, fish and maggots were pulled from the barrel and thrown over the side. And then, the tars once again set upon their hard biscuits.

I was tired and meant to return to the comfort of my berth.

I left our iron box for the morrow.

CHAPTER 20

Onward

HMS Vanguard
Sailing off the Coast of Faro, Portugal
Day 6-Late Morning

Our ship had lowered some sail, coming to, in an attempt to allow another vessel to trail alongside and come about our port side. We moved at a crawl. The waves assaulted our bow, threatening to halt our forward progress completely.

Alongside, a nimble schooner raced below our towering hull. The craft was nimble and quick, compared to the massive bulk of our warship. It had easily caught up to us, before matching our speed and setting about the precarious station-keeping, that paralleled our course.

Her sails glowed with the captured light of the late morning sun, just two hours away from reaching its noon zenith. All, who watched her, admired her sleek hull and lines. She glided across the water, in spite, of the slight chop of its foaming green waves. The Union Jack unfurled proudly off the staff atop her stern.

Unlike, our own warship, the craft approaching us was light and fast. She was unburdened by the massive tiers of cannon of our own floating fortress. Her slanted masts were thinner and more graceful, than those of our own craft. In comparison, we were like the heavy and encumbered elephant to her gazelle-like quickness and spry movements.

She had appeared in short order, after the watchers, set about the towers and heights of the cliffs of Faro, had spied our approach along the port's coast.

Faro's harbor had become a contested coast, much like Portugal itself. The Portuguese now sided with us against the Spanish and the French, who would seek to rob the Portuguese monarchy of its sovereignty and power and steal away Portugal's long established and rich colonies.

British soldiers and ships now found the welcome use of Portugal's harbors and shores in their own fight against the invading Spaniards and French.

We watched as the small craft streamed closer, gliding atop the troubled waters. An alert British detachment seemed intent on reaching us, while we were still far from Faro's harbor.

Those gathered about wondered, if the approaching craft simply had designs on greeting us or if there was some more purposeful reason for its hasty progression.

Many of the off-duty sailors had come topside to greet her appearance and the sight of the coastline. Like me, they anticipated that she was some pilot ship, set forth to aid our entrance into the harbor.

We assumed, we had slowed in preparation to accepting some guide or experienced hand off the smaller vessel, who would aid our helmsmen to steer a safe passage into the shelter of Faro's harbor.

We were wrong.

Below, the schooner's signalman waved his arms about, flashing the semaphore message held within the movements of his flags. Our captain and second officer translated their cryptic message. Our own signalman stood by to relay a response.

Our captain halted beside the rail, lowering his head in thought, while our second officer stiffened upright, staring out across the water at the nearly empty harbor. Faro was forlornly nestled in the surrounding heights of the bare barren hills bordering it.

The elation and anticipation, that had laced the gossip and hopes of our crew, slowly fell to silence. Eyes turned away from the schooner, paralleling our course and fell upon the captain. His hands rested along the rail. He appeared burdened with some heavy decision or deep regret.

He turned around, giving no attention to the crew and issued instructions to our own signalman. The man stepped forward and claimed a precarious perch atop the thin netted walkway, set atop the rail.

In combat, it offered a perch or platform from which our marines might repel boarders or conduct their deadly sharpshooting skills.

In full view of the officers and signalman of the schooner below, our signalman flashed the flagged reply containing our captain's message.

The red and white flags were whipped about their small staffs, held tightly in his hands. They moved with the crisp sharp movements and stiff animated actions of soldiers on parade.

But, the flags moved quickly, their motions deliberately exaggerated to allow no mistake in the clarity of their intended message. The wind ripped at the tar's uniform, threatening to blow him from his perch.

But, he remained stiffly upright, clasping the flags in his clenched hands, perfectly executing one, then another part of the message. Our yeoman of signals went about his task expertly, relaying our captain's reply. Then, he ended the signal, one flag cutting across his chest, before both arms and flags dropped to his sides and he stood as if at attention.

His message concluded, there was a moment of silence on our deck and that of the schooner below.

The captain of the smaller vessel took off his hat and held it high, before waving it about in a gentlemanly and supportive gesture. The act was answered by a lax salute and the grim acceptance of our captain.

And then, the order was issued from our captain's lips. It escaped our ears, made in low resignation for the sole attention of the second officer.

Instead, of barking the command aloud, the second officer moved to the wheel and the two helmsmen and boatswain on-duty beside it. He leaned forward and relayed the captain's desires.

Both helmsmen wrestled the large dual-wheel, laboring to turn it to starboard. Slowly, the bow turned away from the comforting shelter of the harbor to port. We watched as the bowsprint pointed like the needle of some cursed compass and pointed northeasterly.

To a man, we knew what was afoot.

Having some knowledge and ability to read some of the signals, I knew more, than those expectant tars about me of the message's contents. Lord Nelson's demands were greater, than our own.

If I had read the transmitted signal of the officers on the schooner correctly, they signaled of Napoleon's dissatisfaction with his fleet commander, now likely cowering in Cadiz. The French and Spanish fleet were said to be making preparations to sail.

Such information was easily enough obtained by our spies within Spain, observing the docks of Cadiz and the wagons of supplies, most likely bringing provisions and armaments to the Franco-Spanish ships.

This part of the message surprised me little. Like us, the French also had spies about, which had accounted for our entire ship's crew being led to believe our voyage was destined to patrol the English Channel, when in truth, our captain knew we were to join our English ships off the coast of Spain.

But, there was nothing new in either this deception or the existence of spies in each opponent's ports. But, one part of the signal, meant only for our captain and second officer did perplex me.

In truth, it awed me. The signalman below had flashed the intercepted words, from the pen or mouth of the French despot, himself. The flags flashed out Boneparte's order to his fleet, "His Majesty counts for nothing the loss of his ships . . . provided they are lost with glory."

The signal ended, thusly. It caused me to speculate upon how well placed, indeed, our English or sympathetic Portuguese agents had been positioned. If these were indeed the words of Napoleon, it meant, he was no longer content to allow Admiral Pierre de Villeneuve the luxury of avoiding our English fleet.

If the Franco-Spanish fleet was departing Cadiz, Lord Nelson's squadron would need every ship at hand. There was no time to lose. There would be no indulgence of our sick and ill. They would remain with us.

Hearts dropped and eyes bowed in silent resignation, falling to the deck. We would not be allowed the reprieve of the harbor, even if only temporarily, before joining Nelson's Squadron.

Our vessel pointed ahead towards Spain, its coast merely a line above the surface of the water in the distance. A few tars mouthed some utterance among themselves, but guarded their anger and disappointment, less their disenchantment earn them the rebuke of the lash.

But, most held the silent disappointment and resignation of men, who knew not to expect much from their lot in life. They amounted to barely nothing in the scheme of things and they knew it. In the games, played by kings and queens, beset by the entreaties of the admirals and generals, seeking the greater glory of their country and themselves, they were the lessor of pawns.

Three squares a day, a rum ration, and a dry hammock were the best, they could hope to earn for their troubles along with the few shillings, accepted in trade for their enlistment and a small token of the prize-money their ship might come by, should they find themselves in the service of a generous captain.

And, even the latter trinket of wealth was fleeting. It was spent on food or ale along with the distractions of women. The whores, who plied the sea towns of Portsmouth and the world's ports could be counted on to part the tars from their few earthly riches.

Those hard women were crueler, than any sharks or watery predators. They'd leave the men with empty pockets and broken hearts. They'd leave them only with the sea and the ship they served to return to.

The sea was all the tars had. And, most would eventually find themselves claimed by it. If not in battle, than claimed by sickness aboard ship, the greatest killer of any naval vessel's compliment.

And although, the sick men below were the only members of our compliment, which I was aware of, that were in the grips of the ailment, plaguing our vessel, I had heard several labored coughs and seen a few pale and squalid faces to believe others were experiencing the early stages of the affliction.

I feared, they did not search out the hands and talents of our doctor, fearing they'd be removed from the realms of the upper decks and sequestered to the damp darkness of the two lowest decks, destined to become the doctor's infirmary.

I had tried to spy the slightly ill among our ranks, that might exhibit the tell-tale marks, I had witnessed on the men isolated below. But, to a man, upon my approach, the suspect of my inquiry turned about and raced away on some pressing duty, evading my closer inspection.

I could have ordered them about. But, there was no point in it. The doctor had shown, he could do nothing for those succumbing to the illness. And, as for controlling its spread, that was a fanciful illusion.

I'd seen men on the upper, middle, and lower gun-decks, all displaying a slight touch of the sickness. It had a freedom about the ship, that could not be contained. The failure of our ship to make for Faro's harbor had likely only spared the port from the affliction by refusing its haven to our vessel's crew.

Perhaps, that is why the mood on deck fell into brooding and dissatisfaction. We had thirteen men aboard afflicted with the illness, that had already killed two, though one was coupled to the trauma of a flogging.

Of the ill, I fretted the most for our Ensign Higgins and even though, he was not infected, our doctor. The latter was forced by his profession to attend to the sick in the continued presence of the affliction.

Then, there was the tar, who had suffered the unfortunate loss of limb. The doctor had administered to him properly and to all extents, he should recover of his own volition.

But, his recovery would be better assured and certain, if he could be placed ashore. As would our afflicted patients. It was not to be.

More than any other disappointment or setback, this was the greatest blow to our ship's morale. It was bad enough to be sailing into the unknown and violent fate of combat. It was far more damning and distressful to do so harboring illness or plague about our ship.

The second officer ordered other tars up into the masts. Soon, more sailcloth had been dropped to their lengths from their secured spars or booms. Lines were drawn tight and secured as the wind reclaimed a full set of our sails.

The schooner ran off to port, running in a rushing sprint. Its bow crashed through the waves that sought to impede its return to the Portuguese harbor set among the rocky coastline.

Its sails billowed full as its slender hull's bottom slid along, defying the choppy surface and sliding gracefully across it. And, with it went our dashed hopes of one last taste of shore, before the coming battle.

Opposing fleets form up.

CHAPTER 21

Line of Battle

October 21, 1805

HMS Vanguard
Sailing off the Coast of Trafalgar, Spain
Day 8-Noon

The sight defied my attempts to set it to words. Even the greatest poets or bards, that had created the sonnets and plays heralded as the masterpieces of our time, would have been speechless to describe the power and magnificence laid out before my eyes.

Our warships seemed to stretch on without end as they steadily sailed forward. Massive hulls and towering masts vied with the horizon and sky to tame the vastness of the green sea.

They sailed in twin rows as if each ship was garnered a partner for the deadly business to come. Our banners flew proudly from the tops of our masts. A steady wind furled and unfurled them as full sails kept us moving in pursuit of our foe.

Our sails gleemed yellow or light tan in the sunlight gracing the swells our ships plied through. A strange calm had enveloped the waters, before the coming storm of combat. It offered all, a moment of reflection, fathoming the choices one had made in life and searching for the favor of God in the trial, soon to befall us.

But, such thoughts were fleeting as final preparations took place on each ship and no doubt upon the vessels of our foe. One could not look upon our gathered fleets and not be in awe of them. I felt only pride in our gathered squadron

And what a fleet we were. Well forward, sailed the Royal Sovereign. She was an aging man-of-war. Yet, she was as resplendent and powerful as any other vessel in our double columns. Her gilded ornamentation heralded back to a past era, when naval design sought not only to launch powerful multi-deck gun platforms, but strived to embellish within them the ornamentation and sculpture-like grace of palaces.

The goal was not only aesthetic and artistic, it was to engender a floating replica of the power and might of the Empire and our English Monarchy. The Royal Sovereign was a fighting ship-of-the-line and a floating testimony to the greatness our nation and its people.

The sculpted figures adorning her and the ornate trim from bow to stern were a traveling display of English ingenuity, craftsmanship, and the power of our realm.

Other vessels, like Lord Nelson's flagship, HMS Victory or our own vessel, the Vanguard, were more modern and functional. They were designed, for the sole task of breaking other vessels.

Their splendid hulls were meant to travel the seas delivering the power of their broadsides to our foes. Three massive and powerful yellow-striped tiers sported the gun-decks, whose fire would be unleashed at nearly point blank range.

I watched as our vessels sailed eastward, straight and true, the wind favoring our sails.

The combined French and Spanish fleet had set sail from Cadiz, only days ago on the 19th of October, though we had not sighted them, until the next day. Colorful bunting broke out along our English ships as each in turn, passed along the sighting to those in our Squadron.

Apparently, Napoleon had his fill of Admiral Pierre de Villeneuve's intent of sitting out the war in the safety of one harbor or another.

We were well aware of the poor morale besetting the French fleet. Many of its most accomplished and professional officers had fled France to escape the horrors of the French Revolution, that saw aristocrats and seasoned officers led to the sharp blade of the guillotine, their careers ended with the severing fall of its blade and the drop of a head for the appeasement of the mob.

Those inexperienced sailors and revolutionaries, that filled their places, lacked the experience and daring of our own officers. Unfamiliar, with their vessels or the conduct of battle, they had fallen to accepting the defensive in their fighting tactics and attempts to avoid combat.

The Franco-Spanish fleet had set sail for the Mediterranean, knowing full well, Nelson's Squadron awaited its sortie. Again, they ran and we pursued.

For two days, our daring squadron shadowed the combined French and Spanish ships. We finally closed upon our foe along the southwest coast of Spain, near a point identified by our navigator as Trafalgar.

Slowly, as we had been communicated to earlier, we took up Lord Nelson's battle plan. Our ships formed the two parallel columns, our commanding admiral sought to engage the enemy with, lest they spirit themselves away to another protected port.

Lord Nelson envisioned an aggressive action, not content to engage in the traditional and almost gentlemanly conduct of previous naval battles.

For in that game of attrition, two opposing fleets, such as ours, would turn to meet each other along two opposing parallel lines or tacks. The ships in those lines would amble onward, until their broadsides came abreast of an opposing ship and a broadside was released.

Their guns emptied in the exchange, they would clean away the debris and wounded, inflicted by the opposing ship's broadside and prepare to load their cannon to meet the next ship sailing towards them along the opposing line.

The two opposing lines would turn and circle, repeating the deadly game. Sometimes, the opponents became frustrated by the wind and their own maneuvering and both chose to sail on the same tack, running bow to bow,

But, the result was the same, each ship or group of ships matched its opponent, while the crews fed the cannon powder and shot, until a result was awarded or the ships' captains tired of the fight and retired without victory.

But, our Lord Nelson would have his results. Officers had been called to the Victory, summoned to be instructed in our Squadron Commander's strategy. There would be none of the gentlemanly and aristocratic chivalries of the past.

We would bring war to the French.

Lord Nelson had decided to break with tradition. Our fleet was broken into two groups. One would attack the enemy on the line, much as tradition dictated and our foe expected.

They were tasked with raising as much destruction and havoc upon our foe as they could, until other ships could aid them.

The second group was to break the line, attacking the French and Spanish at angles to break through their outnumbering lines. The goal was to inflict as much damage as possible and block the enemy's attempt to break and flee, cutting off their retreat.

It was an aggressive strategy, heralding our commander's own touch and tenacious spirit.

I watched as in the distance, off our port side, the Franco-Spanish fleet loomed larger. Most men were already at their stations, despite no call for it or the accompanying beat of the drums.

Like me, anticipation proved too great a mistress to allow us any comfort and solace in these last few moments. I'm sure each man's thoughts were as labored as my own.

But, I cannot say, that I found dread among the hearts of our tars. True, there was fear. Who could not say, with the battle so close to commencing and the sight of our foe so near, that one was not afraid.

But, it was not as all embracing as I thought it would have been. In fact, I marvelled at the sight of those Spanish and French men-of-war as much as of our own ships. Before my eyes were massed thirty-three enemy ships, armed with over two-thousand and six-hundred cannon. At least, that is what the more expert among our watch dared to speculate.

Framed by sky and cloud, they were a sight only those at this moment and this place would etch into their thoughts and memories for the rest of time. My life, before this moment, had been nothing. My youthful past was merely a dull collection of events as I wandered aimlessly about, seeking the path, that had led me here upon the deck of the HMS Vanguard.

The command "clear for action" was barked about the upper gun-deck. The drums began rolling "beat to quarters."

I turned around and spied our captain and his second officer near the stern. The ship ahead had raised a flag in signal, after itself being alerted to the order from Nelson's flagship, passed from one ship in our two columns to the next.

It was beginning.

I pushed away from the railing, where I had been enthralled, watching the parade of assembled ships in all their regal splendor. I was to assist our doctor below decks and as he saw fit. It was my new station.

No fighting deck or gun crews were to be at my command. I had come for a fight and all the rewards, that my youth and eagerness might reap for me. But, by a twist of fate, no, by my own penchant to do my duty, my enterprise and diligence in assisting our good doctor had earned me his favor. And, with a word to the captain, he had wrested me free of the path, I would have chosen for myself.

At least, I would not be alone in missing the one moment of

history, that I could have been a party to. Our Ensign Higgins rested below in the infirmary.

He was in the grip of the haunted stupor of the others, afflicted with our mystery ailment. It was likely, he was not even aware of the two great fleets, that had gathered for the opposing battle about to commence.

I could not accept the folly of it all. My proud chest dropped as I moved below. Above men prepared for war and I was not a part of it.

I made my way through the tars, that had not yet found their way topside.

Already, sand from wooden buckets was being thrown about our scarlet decks. Its gritty surface ground beneath the soles of my shoes. The sand would help prevent fires and keep our lads from slipping about the blood, that would be strewn in payment for the fight to come.

As I passed to the middle gun-deck, a small cooking fire was extinguished. Its steam wisped upward towards the open hold above. Our captain had sought to provide our crew with a hot meal, fortifying their bellies and perseverance with a hearty soup and a foul beverage masquerading as coffee, made from burnt breadcrumbs and sugar.

I wondered how many of our tars found the ration a suitable last meal? It did not matter. They were fed and rested. They were more, than up to the tasks confronting them.

Already, most of the men had made to their stations and our guns were being serviced. A good crew, practiced and trained in the art of war, could man all of a vessel's fighting positions in ten minutes.

As I descended down into the bowels of our ship, I fretted for those, I'd left behind on the upper deck. The captain and the second officer might rightly claim the glory of the battle to come. But, at what cost?

They and the hands topside were nearly naked and exposed to the withering fires of an enemy's broadside. There were no heavy beams or planks, to protect them from the ravages of shot or shell.

Worse, they were exposed to the descending fire of the French and Spanish sharpshooters, firing from the masts or ratlings. These deadly marksmen had only one goal, to claim the prize of an officer, killing and slaying the ship's commander and cutting off the commanding head of the opposing vessel.

Without a captain or senior officer a vessel soon fell into inaction. Without leadership, crews broke from their stations and abandoned the fight, even when marines, standing behind them, brandished weapons to prevent such cowardice.

And, what of our marines? Like unholy angels, they stood atop the platforms or ratlings of our masts, mirroring their French counterparts. They were open to musket and cannon fire like those on deck. But, they faced the added damning hazard of a treacherous fall to the deck or sea, if either claimed them.

Even now, out of my sight, they were scaling the rope rungs leading to their precarious stations.

As I descended to the lower deck, several tars began tossing the wooden crates, that had earlier held rations, before becoming a table or stool, out the open double doors of the entranceway along the middle gun-deck.

Other useless objects were discarded, freeing the gun-decks for their grizzly business. Orders were barked and loaded guns were rolled forward through open gunports. All was done to the accompaniment of the drums atop deck.

I leaned aside and let two runners pass me as I continued my descent. They were likely heading topside to report their decks ready to our second officer.

I halted on the lower gun-deck and studied the massive 32 pounders. A few late contenders were still being hauled forward on their lines and pushed into place by straining backs.

The crews manning the large guns knelt beside them. A few held their hands atop the barrels unthinkingly. It seemed, they were almost caressing them. It was as if the inanimate objects were worthy of some fellowship or even camaraderie regard.

But, they were the iron mistresses, who would either damn or save their crews. It was hard to part the man. whose life depended upon them, from the ungodly weapons. Yet, the men who serviced them, the cartridge powder, and cast shot fed to the cannon were every bit as one.

If either failed, all were lost. And, for that matter even our ship. Only in operating skillfully and in unison would both survive, the man to live and the cannon to fight another day.

Twelve-man gun crews serviced the mighty weapons. One of them acted as the gun's captain. It was his duty to prime, aim, and fire the deadly weapon. Other members of the gun crew moved the weapon about, feeding its barrel with powder and cannon balls or canister shot.

The remainder of the gun crew formed a human chain, bringing forward more powder or cannon balls serving the iron gun. A trained crew could reload the cannon within ninety seconds. And, a veteran crew showed no mercy or remorse in bringing hell's fury to their opponent's decks.

I left them to the business to come with some regret as I descended towards the infirmary, two decks below the remaining gun-deck.

My days since, had been spent working with the doctor. But, not in attending to our afflicted seamen. They were the least of our worries.

The doctor instructed me in the lessons of his trade. He'd provided me with several of his books, marked to those sections or passages, he deemed relevant to our upcoming battle.

I'd read and fathomed the gruesome mechanics of amputation, gaining understanding of the procedure and the need for haste to keep infection from claiming a foothold in the wound.

I was surprised and sickened by the butchery of our doctor's profession. In truth, I was taken back by how truly basic and primitive his procedures were.

But, I took to his assigned studies, relishing at least the knowledge, he allowed me to share. He quizzed me at nearly each of our meetings, regardless of how short or informal.

And, true to his word, our good captain brought up my studies at our dinners, which had now become more infrequent.

Each officer was, more or less, left to his own devices and tastes. He acquired his supper as he wished, through the fetching of our cabinboys or assigned crew.

I cannot say, that on those few occasions, where we shared a common meal, that the captain was impressed with me. But, I provided enough information and answered his insightful questions clearly enough to show I was an ardent and conscientious student, worth my measure and up to the task, assigned me.

But, I had to admit, at least to myself, that my heart was not in the matter. I still harbored the fanciful dreams of taking part in the battle topside. Had the matter been of my own choosing, I would have preferred captaining a section of our guns or even being placed in charge of a detachment of our marines. I relished the chance to be a part of the fight, failing to be heedful of our doctor's almost defeatist warnings of what combat could entail.

But, my duty was to assist the surgeon.

I took no comfort in the signal, that Lord Nelson had sent to our fleet. It read, "England expects, that every man will do his duty." I found the order, mocked me, though no scorn was intended or directed towards my person.

But, such was the whimsical dictates and pride of youth.

I found the doctor going about his preparations in his infirmary. Preparations, the word mocked me. Above, the crew of our vessel were making preparations, preparations to do battle.

In the infirmary, I found the doctor and his well-meaning tars going about the business of waiting, waiting for death and casualties. They seemed like vultures, lingering about for the misfortune of others. Several more hastily erected tables occupied this space or that.

Our iron box, in the narrow hallway outside, was covered with a large flat board, converting the monstrosity into an awaiting table for a wounded casualty. Water boiled along with several kettles of tar, whose black pitch bubbled and roiled, awaiting a new host of amputees to have their limbs severed cleanly in rapid and quick succession.

This was the duty our captain had assigned to me, when battle and valor laid topside, four decks within my grasp.

I heard the muffled din as did the others gathered about. It was the sound of cannon fire from a ship far distant from our own. Our hull muffled the sound, dulling its retort as it traveled clearly through the water.

Again, the thunder of guns echoed against the hull and our submerged confines. It had begun. I pulled my timepiece, a unique instrument affordable only to officers, from its pocket and opened its cover. I noted the hour. The first shot, we had heard had taken place close to noon. I wondered who had fired first?

I tried to image the sight of one behemoth, its sails unfurled, engaging another such ship. I wondered what damage the deadly broadside would inflict? But, I could only speculate on the shattered hulls and broken bodies, that had likely befallen our French and Spanish foes.

I failed to believe any answering fire could be placed well enough to inflict the same damage upon one of our own ships. Surely, our captains were more experienced seamen and combatants and would turn our ships away from the deadly return fire seeking out our own hulls.

"It's about time you found your station," the doctor barked to me, noting my arrival and the distraction, I found in the distant gunfire.

I merely nodded, affirming my presence.

"You've no time for that lot topside. Besides, its none of your business now! I'm setting up an aid station in the cockpit on the middle deck. I'll want you to be a part of it."

"Aid station?" I asked perplexed.

"You don't think all our casualties are going to fit about down here. Look around!" he intoned.

"No, the wounded will likely be too numerous and not all will be fit to save. I'll need your youth and strength to search about them and tender those, that might have a chance for life, down here to me."

"I'm no surgeon!" I protested.

"Neither are these tars, that will assist you," he returned, pointing to several awaiting seamen, holding the wooden stretchers by which to ferry our wounded, between the decks to the infirmary.

"How am I to decide, who is to survive and who is to die?" I returned.

"You're an educated man, you've your wits about you. You'll know death when you see it. Besides, you've seen my talents first hand. You've witnessed what can be done by surgery."

"An amputation . . ." I began, before being cut short.

"And, that is the whole of it. There will be little time for anything else. We'll remove what little is left of a ruined limb. We'll seal the cleanly cut off stump and move on to the next man. That's it, lad. That's all, that's to be done."

"Later, when the battle's ended, I'll make my rounds and distribute what cures I have in my bag or apply a salve or balm to attend to infection. But, that's all. That's the full measure of it," he said, without emotion.

"I know nothing of medicine. I might cause the death of a man, who could be saved . . ."

He waved my protest aside. "You'll learn, as I told you, you'll learn. And, you'll see the truth of things. Now stiffen up and set a good example for these tars here. They'll be you litter-bearers."

"Every casualty from the lower gun-deck down will be brought here to the infirmary. Every injury on the upper and middle gun-decks will be your charge. Move them away from the fighting to the cockpit. Its slightly protected beneath the wheel and helmsmen topside, offering a second source of steerage should the controls or crew above be shot away."

"Are there any priorities?" I asked.

"Priorities? What do you mean?" the surgeon asked, as another muffled retort traveled through the water.

"How shall I decide, between officer and men?"

"You won't and you won't have to. It's been my experience, that no officer worth his mettle will surrender his post, unless fatally wounded. And, if by chance, you should come upon one, treat him with the same discretion. If he has a chance to live, send him to me for ministration. If not, don't waste my time or the time of your litter-bearers. Save someone, we can keep alive," he returned coldly.

"Now take some supplies with you," he pointed to several satchels, filled with rolls of cloth, twine for tourniquets, and a few primitive tools that might aid the litter-bearers and myself.

The doctor added one more thing, "I've assigned Phillips, here, as your chief litter-bearer. He has experience. Use him and learn from him. And, maybe you'll get through this. And remember, you work for me. No heroics. If you stop to help man a gun or whatever ungodly craft, you feel compelled to undertake, remember you'll be costing some tar his life."

"There are plenty of other hands to take the place of those lost to the enemy's guns and their deadly attrition. You and these tars are all that's been assigned to me. And, believe me, if this falls to the hell, I think it will, none of us will be enough to meet the task. Understood?"

"Aye, Doctor. I'll do my duty," I responded, recalling the signal sent by our Squadron's Commander.

"Now off with you. And, steel yourself. For I've no doubt, I'll be needing you to assist me in this butchery, once we become overwhelmed," he added.

I merely nodded and exited the infirmary with the stretcher-bearers and their unwieldy boards in tow.

32 pounders on the lower gun-deck.

CHAPTER 22

The Cockpit

HMS Vanguard
Sailing off the Coast of Trafalgar, Spain
Day 8-Mid-afternoon

We reached the cockpit spirited away in the middle-gun deck. The thunder of guns from the ships ahead of ours beckoned me to leave the safety of our aid station and sneak topside. But, I remained in place.

I ordered the tars to lower their heavy boards about the empty confines as two more helmsmen stood about the sheltered wheel, mirroring that being manned topside.

The cockpit offered a safe refuge from which to steer our giant vessel, during the raging storm of a sea or battle.

I fear the sight of the stretcher-bearers did little to bolster morale. If anything the bearers and stretchers only resurfaced the dreadful truth of each man's own mortality.

I occupied myself by taking an inventory of what few supplies, the doctor had seen fit, to grace among the contents of our satchels. I placed bandages and twine about, all within easy reach of those tars attending me as litter-bearers. All along I heard the distant gunfire of the ships, further up our twin lines.

I removed a small book, loaned to me by our doctor, from the pocket of my jacket. It advised the novice surgeon of the basics lessons of our doctor's trade. It illustrated and defined the location and purpose of this or that vein or artery. It detailed the body's immense circulatory system and the pressure points by which to cut off the flow of blood, by tourniquet or hand, to a wound about the arm, leg, or other point of the body.

I listened as the distant thunder commenced, once more. Hours were passing and my curiosity grew impatient. More, our own ship had yet to enter the fray. I knew not, what happened, even about my own ship.

My attempts to distract myself, with the doctor's advised medical studies, no longer offered me any refuge. A boatswain arrived at our shared cockpit, ordered below as we closed upon our foe. He was placed in charge of the two secondary helmsmen. He looked every measure the brute, one would find lingering about the docks and taverns of our English sea towns.

No doubt, he had been summoned to our sheltered cockpit to ensure control of our steerage remained in our hands, should the threat of boarders befall our ship.

He sported a club tucked into the front of his wide belt on one side and a flintlock naval pistol, that had seen better days, on the other side. His face bore the stubble of a thick afternoon beard and his presence was joined by the stench of his body in our windowless cockpit.

Only the opening above, through which the ropes joining the wheel on the upper deck to our own, offered any reprieve from his odorous presence. But, I would have had no other mate present. He looked as if he could defend our small quarter of the ship from any challenger or threat.

Even, if he was not of the same ilk as our spit and polish marines, this old salt was every bit the heralded British Jack Tar, looking for a fight and welcoming it gladly.

His arrival offered me the chance to learn of the battle, I so eagerly thirsted knowledge of. He could tell us of the fight our eyes could not spy, through the thick planks and beams of the cockpit, secreted in the stern of the middle gun-deck.

"Any word of what's happening about us?" I finally relented and asked the boatswain, now standing about the awaiting helmsmen.

"It's a fight, I've never seen the likes of," he said, with the elation of a tavern brawler, ready to jump into the thick of it.

Then, he saw my young untested face. And, as if describing some dueling match or sporting contest, he related, "The battle began with the Royal Sovereign, sir. I saw it, only an hour or two ago, before being ordered below to this station. In truth, time escapes me. But, it was the Sovereign. She was well forward of us, but she's the one, that's borne the first blows. She's in the thick of it."

"And the outcome?" I questioned.

"She was fired on by the Spaniards. They fired the first iron. Rumor says, the Spaniard is the Santa Anna, a three-decker. At least, that's what signal the flags have spoken," he recalled.

"The Sovereign took the Spaniard's fire in silence without releasing her own broadside, until her captain and crew drew astern and could rake the Santa Anna's decks. Its a bad day for those Spaniards."

"And, the other ships in our Squadron?"

"I don't know, not the whole of it. I thought, I saw the flags and banners of Nelson's flagship, most likely, searching out the French admiral's own flagship, the Bucentaure. Victory nearly disappeared in a cloud of smoke as seven or eight of our foe's ships opened fire on her. She was leading one of our two columns. She was still afloat, when I last saw her masts. But, I swear she never returned fire."

News of the plight of Nelson's flagship alarmed me. And yet, no word had trickled below. No doubt, closed lips sought to allay the fears, that harm had befallen our adventurous Squadron Commander.

With everything in place and readied, I stowed the two slung satchels, I had inventoried about the deck of the cockpit. All was as ready as it would be.

Ignoring our doctor's warnings and wisdom, I made for the upper gun-deck.

Our ship had yet to partake of the battle. I was intent to glimpse the fighting, if only for several seconds, perchance minutes. Once here, so close to the upper gun-deck, I could not bury my head below decks like an ostrich, ignorant of the history unfolding about me.

I strode out of the cockpit, extoling the tars and Phillips, that I would soon return. Phillips, more experienced, than I, began to protest. But, he relented, taking charge of our stretcher-bearers.

I think, he actually fretted having to report any injury or death of my person to the doctor, should I fail to return from my brash sojourn topside.

I ignored everything and rushed up a nearby ladder.

I froze near the main mast.

Topside, nearly every empty space of our ship, was crammed with man or gun. Even, those perches atop the masts and ratlings the marines hung about, balanced like the small monkey's and primates, I had seen aboard several of our vessels that had returned home from expeditions to Africa or exotic shores, were crammed.

I marvelled at my own insignificance, when faced with the might about me.

Cannon boomed forward of our own ship and several in the line ahead.

I saw a broadside unleashed from a black and yellow striped ship, one of ours. It devastated a Spanish four-decker, her own banners flying in defiance, despite the deadly fire splintering her decks and killing her crew.

A shout rose from our own deck.

Listening to the cheers, I learned the British ship, ahead, was our Lord Nelson's prized Victory. She'd taken her measure from the Spanish and French, maneuvering to close on the Spaniard and deliver her own hellish fire.

Our foe's earlier assumed victory was short-lived. Nelson's ship collided with a French vessel, we would later learn it was the Redoubtable. The two ships were locked in a hated death embrace as the smoke of cannon engulfed the waters surrounding them.

Nelson's Victory, which had led one of our two columns, became entangled in the rigging of the French ship as it became ensnared in hers. But, the frontal attack had begun and Nelson had led the way, showing others the success of the maneuver.

Our fleet began their attacks at right angles, breaking through the mixed lines of Spanish and French ships. It cut off any organized retreat, while allowing the British ships the advantage of maneuverer and the employment of both broadsides.

A British vessel, sailing through the gaps in the enemy's line, could fire at the vessel in the front of the line with one broadside, before sailing to unleash her opposite broadside upon the next ship in the line to its rear. Instead, of one ship paired and matched to another, the British took on two, utilizing their full compliment of guns along both sides of their hull.

As in the case of HMS Victory, other ships could maneuver to a comrade's aid, adding their broadside into an already crippled vessel. Much as the British man-of-war HMS Temeraire closed on the other side of the Redoubtable, locked in mortal combat with the HMS Victory.

While the Frenchmen blasted away at the heights of the Victory's masts, seeking to drop her sails and spars, HMS Victory's gunners continued a withering fire, nearly point blank, into the Frenchman's hull. In the confusion and the added assault on her opposite side by the HMS Temeraire, the Redoubtable found herself sandwiched in between two foes with no escape and only one choice, to try to fight her way free.

I watched for a moment longer. The three great ships fell away beneath clouds of smoke from their continuing broadsides. I could only see the ghostly outlines of the tops of their hulls and their masts towering high above their upper decks. A few spars and mastheads had shattered and lay hanging askew, dangling like broken tree limbs, held only by the ropes of their rigging.

I felt our own vessel turn to port.

I had failed to hear any order or command given for the action. Instead, our bow and its extending bowsprint pointed outwards from the our own line. Our captain skillfully guided the helmsmen's timing and judgment through the turn as we maneuvered for the gap, between two of our own ships in the second line to port.

With sails full, we moved through the space, several ship-lengths long.

Our bow cleared the gap in the line of our own ships and pointed towards the enemy's line. I saw the blazing red stripes painted across the hull of a French man-of-war, whose lines and size were similar to our own ship.

From atop her masts, banners bore the blue, white, and red of the French tricolor. A large oversized French flag flew from a staff about her stern.

Our Captain Shefferd mirrored the attack of our tenacious Horatio Viscount Nelson, seeking to aim our ship between the gap of two French men-of-war. The deck fell into an eerie silence, despite the din surrounding us.

I swore no man breathed or moved. As one, we were locked in fate, all sharing the same brotherhood, our Lord Nelson extoled of us, commending us to be of one body, one navy, one mind.

I wondered what fate befell the men on Nelson's Victory or even Nelson himself?

We pledged our loyalty to a small one-armed man. Nelson was an unsightly commander. He was blind in one eye, but could see the opportunities and advantages of battle, few others could have envisioned. He understood our own strengths and the weaknesses of our foes.

And, despite the threat of sharpshooters, rumor had it, that he was dressed resplendently in his full uniform. He showed bravely to our own men and our foes alike, his rank and fearless resolution and resolve.

But even, his admiral's uniform was a unique accouterment in its own right. In contrast to the more elite and aristocratic among our officers, Nelson's threadbare frock was shabby and worn. It was stained from the salt of the sea. And, its gold lace was worn and tarnished, hardly befitting his status.

Yet, somehow his humble disposition endeared him, not only to his own crew, but the rest of us. He was unassuming, with a true concern for his men and our effort. He could ask anything of us and it would be done.

The Frenchman, we closed upon, became eager and unsteady. We were still far away from the lethal sweep of his starboard broadside. We ran for the gap in the Franco-Spanish line, before his bow. Few of his guns could bear upon us.

But, that truth did not override his good judgment. The Frenchman's cannon fired. A few of the guns, nearest the bow, had tried to angle their barrels and gain the advantage of an early shot.

Like their colleagues, already engaged, they sought to halt us in the water, firing at our masts and seeking to rob us of sail and wind.

One of their "angels" whistled past. Its two chained together cannonballs sailed through the air, far forward of our bow. They splashed into the water, plunging to the depths as another "angel" was lobbed too high and fell short, crashing several lengths off from our hull.

But, one, of the French cannon crews showed themselves

experienced gunners. Their "angel" sped towards the heights of our masts. At first, we thought the deadly projectile would clear us, snaking between the fore and main masts.

We were wrong. The chain linking the two cannonballs, screaming through the air, snagged our rigging. One line snapped, unable to bear the lethal force and weight cutting it.

The chain linking the two balls tangled about one line, then another. They pulled and sagged, before yielding to the joined projectiles, that continued changing their path, deflected by the rigging.

A spar was found first. Its light pine wood offered no contest to the wicked energy of the chained projectiles. Selected for its lightness and to be manipulated easily by the hands aloft, the wooden spar cracked and splintered.

A jagged end tore free of the sailcloth it held outstretched, driving down towards the open deck along with a shower of splinters and debris.

I watched from the hatchway, my chest protruding slightly above its opening. Men cowered, hunching their bodies and sheltering their heads as the deadly shower rained down upon them. In horror, I saw the red and white tunics of two marines falling among the debris.

Having smashed the spar, the projectile twisted about and struck the edge of the fighting platform, midway up the fore mast. Those, that could, clung to their muskets and rifles as they grasped for a handhold about the ratlings or rigging. A corner of the platform was crushed and fell away.

It took two marines with it, their hands left clutching the air as unbalanced, they dropped away to the hard deck below.

And, still we held our fire.

Despite, the competency of our gun crews and their swift ability to reload, our captain was not one to waste the full measure of our broadsides without being assured of their lethal results.

The French guns thundered again. More of their eager gunners judged, we were falling within their sight and range. These next cannon were heavier, rivalling our own 24 and 32 pounders.

Their shots sent plumes of water skyward, missing our hull by the length of a man at their shortest reach. And then, our luck failed us. Or perhaps, it was the maneuvering of the French ship as she slowly began to turn to port, trying to face her starboard broadside to us. Already wise of the new tactics, devised and executed along the line ahead of us, she meant to counter them.

For seeing her sister-ships fall to Lord Nelson's tactics, she seemed to have no intention of obliging us and ignorantly awaiting her turn. I watched, as the red stripes gracing the French three-decker grew closer. Her oversized tricolor waved defiantly from the flagstaff, raised above her stern.

I still remember the deafening sound. It was not the retort of a single cannon or two or three, for that matter. A hellish chorus broke across the water, that was quickly covered in the man-made fog of ignited powder.

I never saw what happened next.

My eyes grew blank and darkness clouded my mind. My ears were deafened by the howling broadside, that erupted from the starboard side of the French man-of-war.

I dropped to the deck below, only aware of some imposing force, that had knocked my feet from their perch on the ladder. There was only silence.

I laid there, knowing not, for how long. It was as if in a dream. I was aware of actions going on about me, but the details of the events escaped me. I heard voices. But, they were muted. Their words held no meaning or understanding.

I felt the presence of others about me, if only their passing feet. The planking of the deck seemed to be covered in a flurry of activity as feet moved about. My side throbbed as a panicked foot struck out at it, quite undeliberately, before passing on.

I tried to wake myself, to fight the blackness, that was besetting me, but found the fog gripping my mind too thick to cut through.

I felt my lips part and my tongue move about, trying to force out a yell. But, my lungs had already expended the breath, that would have projected my scream or words. My throat rasped as I tried to swallow and refill my lungs, gulping at the air.

Slowly, I felt myself returning, fighting away the darkness, that had sought me out. I opened my eyes, only to find my eyelids caked with sand and small pieces of wood. I held them almost closed as my right hand reached up gently, trying to brush aside the debris covering my face.

I opened my eyes and stared up at the open hatchway atop my head. It was wider and larger, then when I had entered it. The squared sides of its large opening were jagged and shattered. Pieces of the upper deck's planking, in which the opening was seated, were blown away.

And yet, I was whole or at least I felt, I was of one piece. Fearfully, I raised my hands before my eyes. I found my limbs numb and sore with the effort. But, they were there. There were two arms and two hands with all their digits intact.

My back and legs felt as if I had been pinned under a pressing weight. What had destroyed the thick planking of the deck above could have easily removed a limb or more from me.

I gasped in fear of what could be, straining my shoulders to lift my head free of the planking of the middle gun-deck, I laid upon. Mercifully, I found shoes and trouser legs still where they should be.

My groggy mind willed me upright, struggling to become seated atop the deck, I had fallen to. I blinked my eyes as I turned my head about slowly. Havoc. All was havoc.

Our guns had still not fired, but several guns along our port side were out of action. Their low gun carriages rested on their sides, bowled over by the impact of the Frenchman's broadside. The crews of the silenced guns slumped or clung in dead silence about their weapons.

Already, other tars, who had been detailed to form the human lines to advance powder cartridge or cannonball forward to the gun crews manning our weapons, had abandoned their own stations.

Their hands grasped leg or arm of their slain or wounded comrades and pulled them brusquely out of the way. A group of tars fell upon one overturned gun, now found laying upon its side. With grunts like beasts and animals of burden, their straining arms and legs sought to wrest the heavy iron barrels upright.

One jammed a rammer under the side of the spilled carriage, trying to add the strength of a lever to their task. The hickory wooden handle snapped, beneath the gun's enormous weight. Curses rose from those grasping the weapon with their hands as they struggled to keep it raised.

Other tars dropped beside the carriage, one dropping his shoulder and another his back under the weapon, locking the gain others had lifted. Their straining arms and backs tilted the weapon enough, so that its own weight now moved and righted the weapon.

Feet moved clear as the cannon tilted and dropped upright to the deck.

Eager hands reached for the lines, that would haul the massive barrel back up to its open gunport. Those not needed to service the cannon, moved on to the next, obeying the barking commands of a wounded boatswain. His blue jacket was torn open and a bloodstained palm of an open right hand clutched a red stain, growing about his white and blue striped blouse.

His curses reached my ears. I had never heard a mouth as foul. Yet, I was glad to have him present. He commanded and the tars obeyed. Even over the din of the French guns, his voice could be heard and understood, even through my own deafened ears.

The turmoil of our decks and the confusion of battle offered him no distraction. Even his own wound was ignored. He was of a single-purpose, he sought to make all his guns ready for action again.

He ignored the presence of the marines, who served the same purpose as file-closers in the ranks of the army. They were to guard against cowards fleeing their stations. He pushed one marine aside, so brusquely, it was as if he was apt to strike him for encumbering his business.

I returned my eyes to my legs, moving one and then, the

other. The knee of my right trouser, was ripped. Blood ran along the knee's exposed flesh. But, it was nothing more, than a horrid scrape, earned through the misfortune of my fall.

I tried to move. Movement came slow from my stiff and sore legs. But, they worked. I was none the worse for my fall, that had likely saved me from death as the wicked French shot had found the rail, near the open hatchway.

I rose slowly, using my right arm to brace my stand. My head craned about as my eyes searched for the litter-bearers, I had been placed in charge of. I had the intention of calling out to the senior bearer, Phillips.

I opened my mouth, beginning to form his name upon my tongue. It was then, I saw him and the other litter-bearers. I fell into shame.

They had no time to waste on the likes of me. I spied two of them making for the cockpit to the stern. A wounded tar was carried about the stretcher, that for all manner of description, might have been better described as a cruel butcher board.

My silent mouth hung open at the dreadful sight of a shattered leg, dangling over the side of the stiff wooden stretcher. In horror, I followed the carried body, grotesquely noting, the absence of a left arm. I looked away.

Phillips stood near the large hatchway of the hold and the steps and ladders leading between the gun-decks. He waved his hands about, directing the traffic flowing down to our deck towards the cockpit.

Two marines carried a wounded comrade between them, despite their own wounds. Their bright red and white uniforms were torn and shabby. Only one still wore his tall leather headgear.

One stumbled and fell under his comrade's weight, leaving the other marine to support their more seriously wounded mate. Phillips dropped to the deck and lent his shoulder to the fallen marine, whose hand finally released its grip upon his rifle and clawed for a hold on Phillips' shoulder.

As the two marines made for the aid station, Phillips followed behind, his shoulder offering a crutch to marine atop his shoulder.

I rose.

I passed behind the guns and crews still awaiting the order to fire. There was the welcome reprieve of silence as the French gunners went about the frantic labor of trying to reload their own cannon.

Our gun captains knelt beside our own weapons, short match or flint in their hands. They bore grim determination and hatred upon their faces, willing the officers above deck to release them to discharge their cannon.

Despite, the anger and loss surrounding them, each man held his temper. Resolve and strength tempered their own passions. They awaited the command of our captain.

I made my way to the cockpit, only several more steps to the rear.

I reached its doorway and the slim protection offered by the sheltered steerage section. God, how I wished I had never entered.

The room was filled with human debris. It was as if all the broken and severed bodies of some hellish triumph or celebration had been gathered as trophies to man's inhumanity to his brother.

I could not bear to look upon the squalor and plight of men who still lived, despite their gruesome wounds. I could not believe the body could have suffered such trauma and abuse, yet still allow a man to seek the next painful breath prolonging his life.

And, as if mocking me, my hearing slowly began returning. Though, still deadened by a painful ringing, I could make out the pleas and cries of those about me. I do not think even the devil would have relished the hellish concert, that those pained voices emitted.

Shrill shrieks and madness were rasped from burning or expiring lungs. And yet, among the hardened faces, I saw laying about, there came the tender petition to leave a message for some loved one or an entreaty for forgiveness as if the wounded could have transgressed some sin, that would not be atoned by the horror now being suffered.

I leaned against one of the massive upright bulwarks. I tried to steady myself, swallowing to keep my stomach down. The closed spaces of our ship were rancid and foul enough, without the stench of spilled blood and gaping wounds. With no fresh water to wash or soap for the tars, the odor mixed with the dampness befouling our ship would offend those with weak constitutions or reserved sensibilities.

Now, with blood and limbs set about the decks, the foul stench of life at sea had surrendered to the sickening fragrance of death.

Phillips deposited the marine, he shouldered, to a small empty space between two prone tars. He turned and faced me, after searching among the gathered faces about the cockpit.

In that moment, I felt helpless and impotent. Yet, his look, rather than, shaming me, drove me to action. I walked forward, slowly and uncertainly.

I forced myself to look about our casualties. All looked in need of our good doctor's attention. I could not judge one man more deserving of our surgeon's administrations and the chance for life, than another.

Phillips rose and moved to me.

"We've no more room in the cockpit. And, we can't place the casualties, in the way of the guns. You've got to decide, who stays here and who goes below," he reminded me of my duty.

My eyes were locked on the bodies, laying or seated along the deck. One man was growing pale from loss of blood. A jagged piece of flesh hung from his right shoulder. He was quiet and unaware of the world about him.

"Forget him! He'll never make it. He's lost too much blood," Phillips advised me.

"That man there!" he said, pointing to the wounded tar with a shattered leg and missing arm, now tied off with a tourniquet. "If we can get him down to the surgeon, before he looses any more blood, he might make it."

I spotted a man with a head wound, a vicious gash ran down the side of his forehead and clear to where his right ear had been.

"What about him? His wound could be sewn . . ."

"Forget him, our doctor has no time to play the part of a

tailor. A bandage for that man, when there's time. For now, only worry about those with missing or shattered limbs. Send them to the doctor for a clean cut and the sealing heat and patch of a kettle of tar. That's all we've time for," Phillips exclaimed, seeing another pair of litter-bearers arrive, their blood-soaked board fouled with another casualty.

"We need the room now! These men can't wait!" he bellowed, as the French warship boomed outside our hull.

We heard the sharp crack of a shot striking among our masts. Shouts rang out, muffled by the thick planks of the deck above us. But, all heard the dreadful din of the mast or spar, that struck the deck above our heads.

"Take him!" I ordered, pointing to the tar with the shattered leg and missing limb.

I walked about the cluttered cockpit and thrust my hand out, pointing to another tar.

"Him!" I yelled, above the unexpected din of our own cannon.

Our captain had finally released our guns. Their gun captains lit match or struck flint above the powder holes, igniting the fury of the loaded barrels, almost at the same instant.

It felt as if our own vessel was pushed aside, moved away from our foe from the force of our own guns. That was how close our broadside had been unleashed upon the French man-of-war.

Already, the men outside the protection of the cockpit labored to clear the barrels of our guns. The smoldering remains of the spent powder cartridges freed, they splashed and sponged water into the heated barrels, dampening any spark or remaining flame.

Eager hands rushed forth, reloading cartridges as rammers pushed them into the depths of the barrels. Lines of men moved the heavy shot forward. They lifted and strained to feed the unholy mouths of our iron weapons.

Phillips halted one set of litter-bearers from returning topside, likely saving their lives as a new volley of French cannon returned our fire, raking the upper gun-deck and searching out our vulnerable masts and sails.

He directed the tars to pick up the first man, I had selected.

They placed their board on the deck beside him and lifted him
unto it. They strained to lift the cumbersome wooden stretcher
and their load.

Our hull resounded with the thunderous and shattering clap
of shot searching out the port side of our ship. The Frenchmen
returned nearly the same measure as we had meted out to them.

CHAPTER 23

The Infirmary

HMS Vanguard
Sailing off the Coast of Trafalgar, Spain
Day 8-Late Afternoon

I labored to carry the wooden stretcher with the tar bearing its front. We had lost three stretcher-bearers in the horrible pounding the HMS Vanguard was forced to endure.

But, the losses, of our good surgeon's meager compliment of aides, were nothing compared to the frightful loss of man and limb, being claimed by the French three-decker and a Spaniard, that had sought to engage us. At least, this is what I had learned from our casualties, relating the heated confusion and trials of our combat.

Captain's Shefferd's attempt to thrust through the Franco-Spanish line, mimicking the attacks of Nelson's flagship and others of our fleet, had proved disastrous. The Frenchman, we had sought to run before, saw as we, the results of our fleet's aggressive tactics.

Though not in a position to help their comrades, well forward of their own line, the French man-of-war had no intention of falling to the same ruse. Our maneuver was contested.

We were forced to engage in a duel with our French adversary from the rear of the Franco-Spanish line. And, a second ship from ahead of the gap, we had sought to run, turned and fell upon us.

Already engaged with a Frenchman, matching us equally in size, cannon, and maneuvering, we were set upon by a Spanish man-of-war. We battled with two opponents, each the equal of our own ship.

My thoughts returned fleetingly to the unmatched Spanish brig, we had engaged days before. Perhaps, in heaven's wisdom and justice, this was some divine retribution for the bullying of our smaller foe.

But, to a man I protested the unfair exchange, we had fallen to. I knew in every man's heart, aboard this ship, none had desired the destruction of that hapless brig. Not like that.

Her foul destruction had cheated and robbed us of a victory and prize-money. Her death had left our hands empty with nothing to show for the expenditure of cannon, except for the half-drowned Spaniard, we'd plucked out of the sea.

I cursed the cruel God, that would make our tars and officers suffer the bombardment now splintering our hull and decks.

The wooden stretcher, we carried, was like a heavy baker's board, used to move dozen's of loaves about a small bakery as they were removed from oven to shelf.

I could not believe how ungainly the board was to maneuver up and down the steep passageways of our ship. More than once, I felt certain, our wounded patient was about to roll off its sides as we continued past rushing men and firing guns.

Upon, our arrival below, we found the lower decks much like the cockpit above. They were teeming with broken bodies and the pleas of the dying. Bodies were strewn about as if so much devilish debris.

The lowest deck of our ship was like a tomb for men awaiting death and its reprieve. It was lit in the half-light of the lanterns strung about. They dangled and swayed with the movements of our ship as our own broadsides rocked the walls of our hull or the enemy's cannon found it.

It was a dismal sight, made all the more distressing by the fact, that our infirmary was sequestered beneath the waterline. Despite, the safety of the thick beams and braces, I think every man present, would have preferred to trade the illusive safety below decks for the comfort of being topside or at least closer to our boats.

But, many of those present had abandoned all concern for themselves. For them, severe or ghastly wounds had claimed all future hopes and dreams from them. They only waited for death.

Like, the men I had left on the middle gun-deck in the shelter of the cockpit, some would never recover from their wounds. Many had already fallen into silent resignation. They knew, they had not been selected to be attended by our surgeon, because their wounds were too great or fatal, beyond any cure or ministration our surgeon might be able to provide.

They watched silently as they were joined by others. And, those in turn, were either deemed fit for our surgeon's scalpel and bone-saw or left to be claimed by death, when she was ready to find them.

Our ship shook. We wondered if it was from the thunder of our own guns or from absorbing the hated fire of our foes. So close, had our combatants drawn near, that one could no longer discern the impact of their projectiles from the point blank blast of our own cannon, unless he was present on the fighting gun-decks.

Moans broke out with the shudder of our hull as if man and ship were one, lamenting the damage to both. The tar carrying the board, ahead of me, moved to the hallway and the iron box set up as a table.

The board atop it had recently been cleared of a wounded seaman, who'd awaited his turn before our surgeon's blade. Now empty, we sought the space for the patient burdening the heavy board of our own stretcher.

An able tar joined me, seeing my officer's jacket and rank and claimed the two dry and splintered wooden handles, that cut at my hands. As the two tars stood holding our charge, I moved to clear the iron box of the empty board, atop it, making it clear for the stretcher.

I lifted the heavy wooden platform, spilling the running blood lingering about it along its diagonal width and onto the top of our ugly iron monstrosity.

The blood pooled about the porous pitted surface of the iron container as I dropped the board to the deck and moved aside, allowing the two tars to place our stretcher down.

Before the tars could snake through the assembled wounded and dying, my eyes fell upon, that cruel metal box. I spied the pooling blood, that had found itself seated in the pitted surface of its cast iron.

I watched in amazement and bewilderment as the small pools and pockets, that had formed, quickly evaporated. In an instant, the gelling blood strained through, what I thought was solid metal. It was sucked away as if poured cleanly, through a sieve. Yet, I saw no holes or openings, no matter how tiny.

The stretcher plopped down atop the unholy surface of the iron box, hiding its elongated surface. The two tars looked up questioningly to me, not understanding the source of my bewilderment.

But, what was there to say? And, what reason could explain, how the blood had seemingly vanished and so cleanly? I saw not a trace of the crimson fluid that my own hand had run off the board, when I removed it from the surface of that elongated monstrosity.

There was no longer any trace of the blood at all.

"Ensign Lewis!" the surgeon barked my name, spying me from about the open doorway of the infirmary.

"Aye," I offered, in a voice humbled by what I had witnessed in the last few hours.

"Get in here! I need your assistance!" he barked, his back turning to me as he attended to a one-armed tar, struggling against one of the seaman, impressed into the doctor's service.

I stood in the doorway. My eyes fell to the wounded sailor seated on the surgeon's table. His blue jacket was missing its left sleeve as well as the arm, that would have been sheltered inside.

The sailor fought against the doctor's assistant, trying to force him to the table. At first thought, I assumed the doctor only wanted my services to quieten the tar, intent on resisting any efforts to severe what little limb was left and dangling out of the torn sleeve.

"You saw how this is done. There's a bottle of alcohol on the counter. Clean yourself off. I need someone to help me cut and saw," he commanded.

I began to do as he bid, though I did so mindlessly and reluctantly as if in some horrible dream.

Only when he saw me attempt to come to join him at his table, did I understand the full import of the task awaiting me.

"Not with me!" the doctor blurted. "Work on your own, over there at that table," he exclaimed, with a nod of his head gesturing to a second board, set atop two carpenter's horses.

"You want me to . . ."

"Damn it! There are too many casualties. You've seen how it is done. You've read the texts, I've loaned you. Now do it, take off your jacket and take up scalpel to flesh and saw to bone and be quick. Men are dying for the wait, they endure."

I stood there, frozen in silence and disbelief.

"Do it!" the doctor commanded.

I moved a small measure, my head turning and my eyes searching the surgeon out.

He ignored me, thrusting his open palms into the chest of the resisting tar and forcing him backwards upon the table. The tar made to protest, forgetting all civility and rank.

In response, the seaman behind him jammed the neck of a bottle of rum between the wounded tar's lips, nearly knocking out the man's crooked yellow teeth. He swallowed to keep from choking on the rich warm fluid.

His fearful eyes fell away into abdication. There was nothing for him to do, except surrender to the administrations of our doctor. His body fell back, no longer tense or resisting.

The doctor turned back towards me as he searched for the scalpel, cleansed only moments before with a wipe of a bloody rag and a pouring douse of alcohol.

"You're the only one, that has even an understanding of what's required. If you don't mend these men with me, I'll have to ask one of these tars to do it. You know how little knowledge, they possess of books and learning, let alone of the use of the scalpel," he offered, as if pleading.

"Put your lessons to the test. All you have to do is cut and saw as you've seen me do. The seaman will apply the tar, others will remove the patient and bring you the next. We have no time . . . do your duty," he mocked and challenged me with his last words and damning eyes.

I stepped forward to the second table, set about the tight confines of our narrow temporary infirmary. Several of the doctor's instruments lay atop the table's crude wooden surface. I removed my jacket.

In the doorway, a brutally wounded seaman was being carried in atop the shoulder of a bulking mate. The large tar lifted his wounded colleague up atop the table with an ease, that defined the measure of his strength.

My patient's eyes were closed. But, he was fully alert and awake. Remorsefully, I was aware of the streaming tears drenching his cheeks and running along his neck. His lips quivered as he fought back the pain of his wracked body.

To my disgust and revulsion, I saw the truth, in how my assistant had been able to lift the tar, so easily to the table. His trouser legs were nearly empty. What was left of his limbs was shattered and shredded.

The sight made my stomach wrench. I turned away unable to halt the bile and vomit running up my throat. It splattered to the deck as I bent in half, choking upon its acid warmth.

I coughed and spat. The seaman assisting my table came to my aid. But, I waved him off. I placed both hands atop the table, more butcher's cutting board, than hospital table.

And so, it began.

I saw to it, that my patient was well plied with rum. I prescribed a more liberal measure, than our more experienced doctor would have done. But, I did it, not to console our patient, but to insure the man would offer no resistance or plague my own doubts with any protestations or movements.

My assistant must have had some experience at attending to our wounded. Without any command on my part, he removed the bottle from our patient's lips and jammed a short length of rope between the man's teeth.

My patient's eyes looked up at me, then as easily closed, awaiting what was to befall him. I saw his jaw set about biting the coarse hemp, that others had closed their mouths upon before him.

And thus, with his jaws set about the bit of the rope, he placed himself into my hands.

I remembered my lessons well. "Work with speed and haste to remove the remains of a shattered limb," that was the key to amputation. I found the first incision of the scalpel the hardest part of it.

But, mercifully my patient offered no protestation. Nor, was there any movement or cry. I did not know, whether the man was that brave or if the rum had run its course. Perhaps, the fatigue of battle and his wounds along with the loss of blood had seduced him to succumb to silence.

I did not know, but was glad for it.

I choose to work on the right leg, first or what little remained of it. My blade cut without the skill of our doctor, at least, for the first thin incision, meant to mark the circumference of the cut. The gory work was in the second deeper cut, removing the loose meat of the man's right leg.

My mouth burned with the taste of my own bile, still receded in the back of my mouth and the corners of my gums. I tried to swallow, but lacked the spit for it.

The cutting done, I placed the scalpel down and groped for the saw. It was not the glimmering tool, I had seen the doctor caress from within the folds of his velvet cover.

The bone-saw, in my hands, was an older implement. Its handle looked as if it was caked with the dried blood or grit, that had accumulated from hundreds of such foul operations. It looked as if the attempts of boiling and steam had failed to remove the evidence, claimed upon it by its user.

And yet, its tiny teeth were sharp and angular. Despite, the implement's age, bone would offer it no obstacle.

I tightened my grip on the horrid instrument and found the bone beneath my cuts. Down and forward, that was the biting motion of the saw as I pushed through, cutting the remainder of the limb.

I pulled through. Then, I pushed forward again, feeling the teeth rip and the saw vibrate in my hand. In horror, I wanted to look away. I could not believe what I was doing. I felt as if I had been swallowed up in the madness claiming our ship.

Thoughts of our proud banners and flags were forsaken. The splendid lines of our hull and the yellow-striped tiers of our three-decker man-of-war no longer held any glamor or majesty. Thoughts of valor or even duty, the brave duty that had entreated me and others, had escaped me.

I sought only the silence of those still awaiting in the halls surrounding our infirmary. Their moans and pleas were for naught. There was little I could do, except offer them a clean cut and a dip in a kettle of tar by my assisting seaman.

The bone-saw cut through. It was nearly done.

I presented the remains of the limb to the seaman, now holding the boiling kettle of tar. Its hot handle was wrapped in a worn dirty cloth, splattered with caking tar.

The limb was dipped and yet, our charge did not scream or cry out as I thought, he would have. I was amazed at his strength and resilience.

It was only after, the kettle was removed and I started about his left leg, that I realized how damp my own face was. I licked the corners of my mouth and swallowed, tasting the bitter salt of my own tears.

Without blinking, I ran my scalpel around the remains of the leg, shot away just above the left knee. I lifted the thigh with a renewed sense of confidence, that came from knowledge and the doing of this hideous work.

I proceeded with the full measure of the compassion, I had learned within only a few hours time.

The vampiresa that confronts Ensign Lewis.

CHAPTER 24

The Risen

HMS Vanguard
Sailing off the Coast of Trafalgar, Spain
Day 8-Late Afternoon

I do not know how many hours had gone by in the hellish kitchen of our infirmary. I remember noticing only one thing, the silence. The wonderful silence of the guns.

The infirmary and the rooms about it had fallen into a strange forgiving quiet. The silence could not mend the broken bodies of the men laying about. But, at least, it offered them some measure of hope.

Our doctor attended to the last patient. There were others,

that needed tending for other slighter wounds. But, the horrible gashes or cuts, requiring thread or bandage, were no longer as pressing as attending to our limbless colleagues. Finally, there were no more of the crew requiring the severing of crushed or shattered limbs.

Of those, they had either been given some chance of survival at the doctor's table or my own. Or, they had passed away, their wounds and loss of blood claiming them, before they could be brought to our tables. It was done, for the moment.

Doctor Radford finished at his table.

He had exhibited nothing, but strength and an inner fortitude, I could not have imagined, he possessed. His hands dropped flat atop the counter, where his instruments and a bottle of alcohol resided. He bowed his head in exhaustion as the sailors assisting him administered the boiling tar, sealing the stump of our last patient's left arm.

It was at that moment, that everything caught up to him. His legs seemed weak and unsteady and his resolve appeared to slowly erode.

Radford raised his head and cast his glance my way. His stern mouth formed a grin or the best his parted lips could muster.

"You did well, Ensign Lewis," he offered, quite sincerely.

His words and eyes harbored the satisfaction of a mentor. He had taught me my lessons well. More, he had shown me the truth of things. He'd shown me the cost of battle and the true price of wars waged at the lift of a finger pointing to a map or chart by a sovereign or despot.

Radford had been right in everything, he had said. At least, he had been right about the cost, the horrible cost of it all. But, I had yet find the truth of what this combat had profited us. We were still afloat. Our guns were silent. We had not been boarded, nor were we taking on water.

Those of us, that had survived, bore the loss of our comrades. We lived, while others did not. There was no fame or glory, there was only the cold emptiness or being spared. I had learned the true cost, our surgeon had spoken of.

But, he did not admonish me of the lesson learned. His smile faded and he turned to one of the operating tables, claiming a bottle of rum left there. It was nearly two-thirds empty. He drained nearly half of its remains in one swift gulp.

His swallow would have robbed an ordinary man, even a practiced seaman, of his breath. But, it troubled him not. He swallowed, washing away the foul taste and smell lingering about our confinement.

He found a seat atop an upturned barrel and sat in resolute silence. The horrors of another battle had come to pass. His bloody hands clung tightly to the neck of the dark brown bottle.

His eyes stared at the floor. He had left us for now, seeking a moment for himself.

I too, felt as if my own legs would collapse beneath me. A dry mouth and burning throat still bedeviled me. My stomach churned from the vomit released hours earlier. My mouth and gut felt unsteady and vile.

But, so much had happened. And, we knew so little of what had transpired, except for the steady flood of casualties, that had streamed down into the bowels of the ship.

Still deep within the hollows of the lower decks, one question occupied all our minds. Were we the victors? And, what prize or profit had been purchased for us at the cost paid by our crew?

Word came soon enough. Runners sent by the captain sought out the status of each deck. They were the slowest, making their way to us, secreted away below the waterline.

They traveled through the debris and havoc, littering each of the gun-decks. But, they came.

And, what glorious news we learned. Spirits rose, even among the most seriously wounded, who had paid the price of an arm or leg, sometimes both. But, their sacrifice had purchased us victory. Their loss was not for nothing.

The runners were descended upon as they fought their way towards the doctor and myself, seeking some report to return to the captain. They told of our fleet's victory. We had won, defeating both the French and Spanish ships.

But, at what cost?

The rejoicing ended sharply as one of the runners told us Lord Nelson had been fatally wounded.

Many among our lot disbelieved him. They cursed the runner and his vile gossip. But, he stood fast and claimed, he'd been on the deck, when the signal was flashed by flags from ship to ship. It was true, he swore it.

A French sharpshooter had claimed our Admiral Nelson's life. A rifle's deadly ball striking him in the shoulder and passing through to a lung, before shattering his spine. He had been taken below to Victory's own cockpit, dying at four and a half hours past the noon hour.

Even now, Lord Nelson's body was placed within the confines of a barrel of brandy, seeking to preserve his remains for the hero's burial, awaiting him in England. Our ferocity and his leadership had won the day, but at what cost.

The runners also informed us of our own ship's losses. I did not know many of the seaman's names. But, all present listened in reverent silence, giving each man's name, that could be recalled, a measure of respect.

The runners mentioned only those, they knew from about the bodies being cleaned from the ruins of our gun-decks.

The mention of one name drew all to an eerie silence. Their breaths ceased upon hearing its mention.

"Lieutenant Loydd caught one," one of the runners said, halting all speech and noise about our deck. A few whispers asked in disbelief for a mate or attending tar to repeat the runner's words.

But, the truth was there. Lieutenant Loydd was dead. Like our Admiral Nelson, he'd fallen to the well-placed shot of a French sharpshooter. The shot had been true and straight, finding the officer's forehead almost perfectly in the middle, symmetrically framing itself in the center of his head.

No sign of joy or pleasure showed among the faces of our tars. But, I knew in their hearts, they felt a measure of justice had been served.

"And, our captain? How fares our captain?" a tar spoke up.

"Well. Alive and well with nothing more, than scratches for the worst those Frenchies could throw at us. He's still in command of the deck. He now orders repairs be started and directs our steerage, bringing us back in line with our own ships.

Voices broke out in rejoicing, as best, as a few of our surviving hands could. Others fell upon silent reflection. While others moved their lips in prayer, thanking the Creator for sparing them from their first battle.

Others stared steely ahead, ignoring all. They'd paid the price once before. Veterans of other battles, they found themselves survivors, spared once again. But, somehow they expressed none of the elation of their first time companions. It was as if they knew or feared, they had only been saved to face the struggle again.

I left the infirmary, seeking some measure of isolation to reflect on what had transpired and to find a private moment of reprieve. So much had happened. And yet, none of it had been, what my expectations were led to believe.

The truth was harder to accept, after facing its realities. Now, after everything, my mind and heart felt dead. I lacked the clearness of thought, that had always been mine. An emptiness and void replaced the world, I had always been so sure of.

I climbed a ladder leading to the next deck, intent on reaching the gun-decks above.

I found the deck above and was shocked to find it had become a macabre morgue. It was littered about with human remains. It was as unorganized and disheveled as the cutting floor of a butcher's shop. Some bodies were covered with pieces of torn sailcloth or the heavy canvas of a hammock.

I did not know if the shrouded bodies were covered in some small measure of respect for the victim beneath or to cover some horrid or ghastly mutilation of the body. I did not want to know.

Despite, all that had happened, it made me halt and choke upon my breath. With night besetting us, it was crisscrossed in the flickering shadows of the guarded candles, set about the lanterns, hung along the sides of the hull.

There was an eerie silence to it. It was part reverent in respect to those tars, that had given their all for our struggle. And, it was in part a strangeness, I could not fathom. It sent a shiver along my back, much like a child experiencing the fear of the darkness or his imaginary manifestations, lingering in its blackness.

I laughed silently to myself, musing at the strange feeling and the childish thought, that had arisen from the depths of my past. How could I harbor such a feeling, especially now, after all I had witnessed and participated in.

The darkness no longer held any fear for me. No, it was the light and the deeds or better said, the misdeeds of men, that had rightfully earned my fear.

Even, with our cause heralded as just, it was not the proud and momentous undertaking, I and my countrymen had been misguided into believing it to be. We were victorious, but it was not enough.

The doctor had been right. The price we paid, the cost demanded, was too much and placed the burden only upon a few. And, it fell upon those, who would least likely reap the rewards of our success.

No, the senior officers and lords would return home to find themselves eagerly awaited among the courts of our well-wishers. But, our simple tars and to an extent, even our junior officers, would reap little benefit of our actions, except to say with pride, that they had been at Trafalgar and had fought among the ships accompanying Lord Nelson.

It was a fleeting moment of fame at best. Perhaps, it would be recalled with respect by members of our own generation. But, the moment would be forgotten by the next generations as they were faced with their own travails and tests.

To the simple seamen among us, that was enough. They expected little else. Perhaps, there would be a shilling or two by which to play the hero's part upon whatever sea town's tavern they returned to, when we could be found upon the shores of home again.

And this, for what? The cost of an arm or leg or both. Or

perhaps, the loss of an eye or all sight had been paid, for that matter. I had seen the price. I had reaped its bitter payment, slicing flesh with our surgeon's offered scalpel or cutting free an owner's limb with the teeth of a saw.

Rubbish! It was rot, that I should now even find a shred of ill ease from being alone in the darkness, standing among the corpses littered about.

But then, I was not. I saw a form further away, towards the stern of the deck above our infirmary. Lost in my thoughts, I had ignored its presence.

The figure was likely the cause of my unease. The true extent of the keenness of one's senses was always a surprise. My instinct had acquired the presence of another, even though, my tired mind had not.

To all accounts, I swore I saw the thin lithe form of a tar, standing above one of the bodies. He possessed the demeanor, pallid color, and light build of the seaman, I had seen upon the night, I stood watch at Portsmouth as he aided his drunken companion up our plank.

I remembered, it was the companion of the drunken tar, the one, that had fallen to his death in his lone revelry, dangling among our ratlings or masts. I watched in silence, halting in the quiet of our would-be morgue.

Many of our fallen were laid out upon the floor, but a few rested atop makeshift tables or crates, much akin to the operating tables of the infirmary.

I heard a labored breath. And, to my astonishment, I saw one of our sailors was not dead. His lungs rasped as he struggled to rise to the form, I had identified as a seaman.

But, the uniform and round rimmed hat, I expected to see or thought I had spied, were gone. But, the figure was still there. I halted, after quietly stepping forward, not making a sound.

I watched as our injured tar rose on one elbow, struggling to lift himself from the grip of the morgue, beckoning him to join his comrades.

I saw the supple shape of a woman, standing beside his

deathbed. I swear it was a frail young maid. She was of thin waist and adorned with a long black mane.

I thought my mind had succumbed to the horrors of the day. I believed the trauma and trials, that I had witnessed had forced my mind to seek some illusion or distraction. Perhaps, I was dreaming.

Perhaps, I had fallen asleep, exhausted from our butchery and the horrors of it.

But, I could not wake, for I was awake. What my eyes saw, was before me. It was real.

I watched as this frail pale maid bent down lovingly, her dark eyes cast towards our tar's own. Her dark eyes embraced him in sight, without touching his succumbing flesh.

The wounded man, despite the pain and suffering of his wounds, smiled kindly. He ignored his own agony and pursed his lips, stretching out to the maid, until his body could reach no further.

I watched as the maid bent lower, meeting him. Her face buried in his own, before nestling about his cheek and following along the length of his neck. There was a soft gentleness about her. And, for the first time, I now saw her adorned in the light flowing fabric of a simple white gown. Her form was no longer hidden in the shadows or the pretense and illusion of the seaman, I had thought I'd seen.

The gown's thin gossamer fabric wafted about as if on a light breeze. It was so light, even the slightest of drafts, running through our dank damp vessel, lifted its delicate material.

The maid took up the tar's left hand. Her lips softly pressed against its fingers. She was not at all repulsed by the blood caking them. Her lips kissed the limb's wrist, before lifting and following the inside of the arm.

Beneath her, the tar looked as if her presence alone comforted him. Her touch provided him one last measure of ecstasy of the worldly delights, he was soon to depart from.

His eyes were those of one entranced, submitting himself totally to her beauty and form. He was bewitched, spellbound.

I watched, myself placed under her spell, despite the ludicrous unreality, of it all. It was impossible. There was no woman secreted aboard our ship. We had been at sea for days, it would have been impossible, amongst a crew of over eight-hundred, for her to have spirited herself away out of our sight.

And yet, there she was. I watched enthralled as her slender form hovered over our seaman. Her long dark mane flowed about her shoulders, cascading along her breasts as she again bent closer to her willing supplicant.

And then, I woke from this dream. Her lips parted. Her teeth showed. They were cat-like or vixen. They tore at the flesh of our seaman's arm. Her jaws were vice-like.

Our sailor's mouth opened, but no scream was emitted from his muted mouth. Hexed or under her spell, I did not know. But, he remained silent, even though his eyes widened in fear and he twisted about, trying to free himself from her damning embrace.

And, like him, I was transfixed. I felt unable to move. Feet and legs were heavy and numb as if I had been standing out in a freezing rain or snow. I felt cold. Warmth and feeling were being robbed from my body. I succumbed to fear.

I tried to call out. But, I found my mouth and tongue silent and empty. I could not voice one word. I tried again, finally persisting in raising a guttural cry or groan.

"You . . ." I half-choked on my own word.

It was enough.

The maid dropped the arm. It fell to the table.

Her mouth was smeared with blood. Her cruel teeth showed between parted crimson lips. And yet, her flesh was white as snow. It bore the same pallor of those dead surrounding us. It was a colorless body, devoid of circulation and the warmth of life.

I swear her evil tongue hissed as venomously as any asp or viper, through her snarling lips.

And, her eyes, of those black orbs, what could I say to describe the darkness harbored there.

The two villainous orbs glared at me as if I had intruded upon some liaison, meant only for her and her intended, our helpless tar. In the flickering candlelight of our lanterns, I saw their dark blackness. It was so deep, it seemed her eyes alone could swallow my soul.

Their spell broken, I sought to shout an alarm to gain the aid of those below or above this abandoned deck.

But, before my mouth could break into words the banshee's snarling mouth calmed. Her lips closed, hiding the small sharp hideous teeth and leaving only the soft pouting redness of her full mouth.

The anger in her eyes subsided and her mouth widened in a stretched grin. At that moment, her allure returned. She craned her neck about, twisting it slowly from one side to the next. She stood up, abandoning the seaman, that she had feasted upon.

Her body assumed a poised aloofness, more akin to that of a great lady or a woman of nobility. She studied me, neither alarmed or intimidated by my presence. She knew, before I, that I had no protection against her.

But, she had fed. She wiped her lips and cheeks along the back of her right wrist, all the while, her eyes remained fixed upon me. The stillness in that large communal room, more hallway or hold, than confined chamber, was unnerving.

I felt my heart racing and fell to calling out again.

The words were forming, forced up through my mouth by the fear exhaled from my lungs.

She laughed. Bowing her head down, then lifting it to find me, once more. Her lips parted, amused at my dilemma.

"Doctor!" I called out, but found my words muted as the beautiful, yet ghastly specter glided towards me. I swallowed, nearly choking on the horror closing upon me. I thought, I was about to pass out and drop into the blackness of unconsciousness.

But, it was not to be.

She moved silently as if floating. Not a step, did I see her take. Not a leg or foot moved as the trail of her thin white gossamer gown flowed behind her.

And there upon her succulent lips was the devilish grin, that continued mocking me. I could not break the stare. My eyes were transfixed upon her face. It was pale white. Whiter than, the powdered faces of the ladies of an aristocratic court or ball, where they choose willingly to border themselves upon starvation, merely to achieve the soft pale pallor, fashion and custom dictated befitting a woman of good breeding and class.

My eyes could only stare at her approach.

Her red lips contrasted sharply with her ghastly pallor. They were darkened a foul scarlet red by the warm blood of our unmoving tar. Her lips pressed against each other, followed by the savoring caress of her tongue, claiming the gelling droplets found about the corners of her mouth.

And then, she was before me.

I could not move. With her presence, so near, I could not move. Aware, of the threat she presented and having witnessed her supping upon our seaman, now laying still ahead and likely dead, I could not lift hand or foot to flee. I was transfixed before her.

It was like the dream of a child. Where dominated by a sleeping mind, he was forced to endure the most horrid illusions or hallucinations, his troubled thoughts and fantasies could bring to life. And, in that fitful slumber, he felt himself powerless, powerless to act or flee and powerless to wake.

I stared into the specter's face.

Though she was clad in the body of a woman, her pallor withheld her true age. But, her form was petite and supple, suggesting youth and firmness was harbored by her shadowy form.

Her dark black eyes held some inner being. It was as if the body presented to me was a cloak or shield, hiding some true inner-self.

Did I not see her first as a seaman? Before, this apparition claimed its current form, had I not only momemts ago mistaken her for one of our own tars?

My breath halted as a thin limb lifted from about her side. It was followed by her frail right hand, stretching beyond the dangling cuff of her wisping gown's sleeve.

The back of her hand rose to my face. It found a place beneath my lower jaw. I was unable to act. I stood unresisting and trance-like as the coldness of her own flesh touched me.

The lightness of her touch surprised me. My jaw, now covered in the stubble of a beard, felt like it was brushed against by the light kiss of the fluttering wings of a butterfly. Light and teasing is how I remembered it, despite the gruesome true nature of the creature delivering the touch before me.

I tried to turn away and resist this cruel siren's lure. But, found I could not. A power or hex bedeviled me, she claimed me.

I stood there in silence, hearing only my own frightened breath. My mouth hung open and I tried to gulp the air about me.

My fear seemed to please her. I saw it mirrored by the glowing delight in her eyes. She lowered the back of her hand, its fingers gliding lightly over my neck. She took pleasure in my fear. She laughed.

It was not the laughter of a woman that a man would find treasured upon some early summer, when the young hearts of lovers sought out partners for life's shared journeys.

It was like the cold cruel laughter, mirroring that of the whores, that inhabited the taverns, where our tars congregated for a measure of their own brand of solace upon visting the shore.

No, it was worse, than those cruel vixens, intent of separating a sailor, from what few coins remained in his purse or pocket.

The sound was barely audible, though I heard it clearly above a whisper. It mocked me as if I were her's for the taking. I offered no threat to her.

And then, it was done.

She moved backwards, abandoning me. She glided across the deck. She moved as quickly as a man might run across its cluttered surface. Without turning around, she avoided the maze of men, littered about the deck or atop the makeshift tables. All along, her gaze remained fixed upon me.

Her form halted, before a ladder and the opening awaiting above it. Then, she was gone.

I did not see her feet mount rung or step. I did not see her hands search out the deck above.

I saw only a shadow for the briefest of moments. It was like, that haunted specter, I had seen clinging to the outside of our hull, during my ungodly late hour watch, days before.

It was a shadow, nothing more. The maid had disappeared, though I had not witnessed the transformation before my open eyes. There was only the darkness of her projected shadow, silhouetted along the wall. The shadow was black, bearing a darkness suggesting it had breath and width, physical form.

Yet, she was gone. Like, a shadow exposed to the light, in the blink of an eye, all was gone.

I closed my eyes, relief flooding over me.

I had been spared, though I knew not why. My mind and senses returned, seeking out old superstitions and religious teachings, searching for some answer to what I had witnessed.

Had I seen the reaper of men's lives and souls? Had I blundered upon death as she went about the grim business of gathering up those of our crew, whose hour had come to leave this life?

My legs began to collapse from under me. I felt weakness claim my body as I fought to remain upright. I stepped forward and leaned atop one of the simple board or plank tables.

I leaned upon it, nearly all my weight bearing down against its coarse surface. My eyes looked down at the shrouded occupant, I shared its planks with. Fear still welled inside me, but not for the silent remains before me.

What had I seen? Had I really seen anything at all? I panted like an animal, my lungs still sought to fill themselves. I had called out, but no one had heard me, no one had come.

I raised my head and looked about the deck. Except, for the corpses surrounding me, I was alone. The haunting specter was gone. I was left alone in the flickering light of the lanterns' candles, spaced about the low deck.

Already, my mind struggled to return to some sense of normalcy. I was already making note to report the hazard of the unattended lanterns. There was not a living soul about to account for their lit flames.

The simple act of noting the violation and contemplating some response to it, brought me a measure of comfort. It drove away fear and halted my spinning mind from racing headlong towards insanity. I rose from the table, I leaned on.

With some measure of my wits restored, I rushed forward to the table bearing the tar, who I had seen seduced by the specter. His body was laid flat against the table's coarse planks. His head faced toward the deck above. His eyes were open, but rolled upward. Only their whites showed. There was no sign of breath or life.

I knew what I sought out as I hovered above his now still corpse. But, I feared searching out the truth of my suspicions. But, I had to know.

My hands and trembling fingers dropped to the seaman's left arm. I claimed it, finding the limb cold and clammy in death's embrace.

But, the marks were there. Those dreaded little nicks, that haunted our doctor and defied any explanation or cure. They were not the bites of rodents nor any earthly animal.

I had witnessed the lips that had traced lightly over this tar's flesh, before the vixen's teeth had set about piercing it and claiming the warmth of the fluids within to satisfy her thirst.

I backed away from the corpse before me, backing into another table set about with a shrouded body. I turned around to face the corpse, whose eternal slumber my disrespectful awkwardness had nearly disturbed.

I turned around to find the body was an unknown figure, its identity cloaked beneath a cut section of sailcloth, likely downed on the upper deck by French or Spanish guns. The cloth was marred by burnt powder and a tattered end, shredded by the violence of battle.

Calmer now, though still ill at ease, I stared at the covered victim. Some strangeness or morbid curiosity bid me to cast my eyes about its cloaked form, covered from head to toe. And yet, there was something about it, some quirk or oddity, that vied for my attention.

My eyes detected some slight movement from the table beneath me. I turned my eyes down to the shroud and noticed the length of cut sailcloth about the body. It moved.

I stood still. Perhaps, in the haste of battle, one of our attending tars had mistaken, whether a fellow seaman was wounded or dead. In dread, I realized a wounded seaman might have been left among the dead. He could have wrongly been presumed to have shared their fate, because of the severity of his wounds or unconsciousness.

With all, that had happened, I stepped back. I was horrified by the prospect of the gruesome wounds, I might find, once I lifted the shroud from the man atop the table. Slowly, my right hand extended the full length of my outstretched arm.

I had to know. I had to offer any assistance, that I could render.

But, before I touched that torn white cover, it rose of its own accord. Like Lazarus, the body rose struggling to sit up upon the table.

I withdrew my hand and stepped back. My voice was robbed from me, once more, as fear swelled up inside me.

In horror, I recognized the man atop the table as the length of canvas fell away. It was Lieutenant Samuel Isaiah Loydd. But, all knew him to be dead, fallen in battle, the victim of a French sharpshooter.

But, there he sat. The sailcloth fell about his shoulders and dropped askew to the ground. Reflex urged me to respond. Compassion bid me to step forward to aid our second officer.

But, fixed in the center of his forehead was the gaping hole the runners had told us of below deck. It was a hole big enough to stab one's thumb in, amidst the shattered bone of the front of his skull.

The long hair about the back of his head was caked in dried blood. His neck bore the dried streaks of blood, that had streamed down from the missing piece of skull at the rear of his head. It had been blown away by the conical hollow round, that had pierced his head.

Loydd's eyes opened suddenly, startled and as if returning from a fitful slumber.

They mirrored the creature, I had seen only moments before. Dark and black orbs, devoid spirit or life, stared into mine. Emptiness and a vile darkness lay within the man, even more, than when he was alive. That is what I saw.

Our second officer rose as did others about the deck, that had become our morgue.

From the floor or table, men surrendered from life now sought to reclaim it. They sat upright, before me upon the tables. One or two bolted up off the deck's floor, their bodies were as stiff as rails, sallying forth as one would step upon the prongs of a rake laying about the ground.

I called out to them. A foolish thing, but at the time, it seemed quite natural. But, their ears did not hear or heed me. In turn, each opened his eyes now replaced with the dark black orbs, I had witnessed about the face of the specter.

They blocked my way back to the ladders and steps leading up to the lower gun-deck or down to our infirmary. I called out, But, it was to no avail. Of those about me, none heeded my words.

And, those members of the crew, below or above this hated deck, failed to hear my shouts. They were muffled by our ship's thick planking and the work of our salvage crews.

Beside me, Loydd's gruesome head bent forward, studying his own limbs and body as if disbelieving his own eyes. His movements were stiff and unnatural as if his own body was now a foreign form to him.

Perhaps, it was the severity of his wound, that had robbed him of some mental faculty. But, the delay was short-lived. Soon, instinct or whatever was harbored within Lieutenant Loydd's body took command. His head turned towards me.

The eyes, that in life held hatred and detachment for all those about him, now magnified and revelled in the newfound animosity harbored within them. He rose off the table, stiff joints cracking and bending with the effort. It was a ghastly sound and sight.

Behind him, three more tars rose, blocking my last exit of retreat from this unholy morgue.

I ran, sidestepping our second officer as his arms stretched out. His fingers were like crooked claws, abruptly thrusting out for me, but missing my bloodstained tunic.

I halted only when I was clear, my eyes anxiously searched the passage, that ran between the decks. Its way was blocked. Several more tars rose up. Their presence defied reason and sanity.

Three were missing limbs, two were one-armed with vicious wounds about their faces and torsos, creating gruesome imitations of what had been a living body.

But, all had the deep black eyes, that seemed to swallow their souls and command their forms, mirroring the specter and our Lieutenant Loydd.

The ladder and hatchway, the specter had retreated by, was surrounded by more of the rising dead. It was as if Loydd, once an officer in life, was now a commander in death.

I watched as his mouth opened and his right hand thrust up and forward, pointing damningly to me. No words came from his parted lips, only a vile reptile-like hiss.

But, to a man, those risen slowly began to turn towards me, coming from before me or behind as others awoke and blocked any avenue of escape.

I backed up with my back against an inner wall, several lengths away from our hull. I wanted none of these foul spirits or creatures to come up behind me, unaware. My hands groped the planks of the wall behind, feeling its surface to guide me.

I moved, while my eyes darted about, searching for the nearing creatures.

I spied the thick doors of the small storerooms set around the deck. But, they offered no escape to the decks above or the one remaining below. They were merely extra stowage areas for rope, pulley, or sailcloth crammed within their overloaded confines.

But, there was nowhere else to go. Escape eluded me. I could not go forward or backward, nor up or down. I moved to the first doorway and stole a desperate glance through its barred window. Folded sailcloth was stacked from the floor to ceiling among its crowded shelves.

There was nothing within sight, that offered its use as a weapon or shield to halt the advance of these fiends surrounding me. I moved to the next door only several footfalls short of four approaching living corpses.

I flung myself inside, pulling the heavy plank door behind me.

But, safety eluded me. The door bore no lock. It had only a simple handle on either side. For who would be want to steal a length of rope from among the coils stored there.

But, with no lock, there was no way to make it fast and ensure my own safety.

I dropped to one of the coiled lengths laying upon the floor, quickly undoing one of its ends and snaking it about the door's handle. I ran it to the brace of a strong shelf and tied it fast.

No sooner done, the door protecting me pulled, drawing taut the rope. The door budged slightly, a crack, but no more. The line held, even as other hands grabbed upon the short handle outside.

The door held a small opening nearly eye-level from which one could gaze about the contents inside the room without entering. It was blocked off, as was the custom and design of the door's of our ship, with several iron bars.

I snaked another length of rope through these, surprising the creatures outside with my quickness. Too late, their own stiff limbs creaked and cracked trying to snare my hands, threading the line through the bars.

Like the line to the door's handle, I made this rope fast, but to a metal ring, lining the inside of the hull, that I had not spied before.

Hands clawed at the bars and tightly drawn rope. But, the door held.

Fists pounded against the door's heavy planking.

In fear and resignation I dropped to the floor. I drew my legs and knees up to me, cradling them in my arms. It was madness. I saw, yet still I could not believe. I did not want to believe.

I still held onto the delusion, that this was all a dream. That soon, I would awake. Yes, that had to be the truth of it.

I had been burdened and overtaxed by my duties with the doctor and the horrors of battle. Certainly, I had fallen asleep after leaving the butchery of the infirmary and now my mind deceived me with this gory nightmare, creating some illusion to block away the truth of the day; the loss of limbs, or the cut of scalpel and bone-saw.

It had to be this and nothing more.

All else was madness.

The door tugged. The two fastened ropes grew taut, their thick weaved cord threatening to break.

The door slammed closed with a deafening bang and suddenness.

The ropes sagged slightly, their tied lengths tested, but holding.

There was silence.

CHAPTER 25

The Awakening

HMS Vanguard
Sailing off the
Spanish Coastline
Day 11-Mid-Morning

"We found him locked away in the spare rigging locker. Locked, that's not the word for it. He tied the door shut from the inside. It took the tars nearly twenty minutes to get him out of there and he was unconscious, at that," I heard Radford's voice drone hollowly through a daze.

"That means, he was in there for two days . . . alone." the surgeon added

He took it badly, then?" I heard Captain Shefferd's voice, behind my closed eyes.

"Nay. I cannot say that, at all. In fact, he did quite well or so I thought, at the time. It was a gruesome sight down in the infirmary. The worst I have seen in years. But, he took it well. He did all I asked of him," our surgeon returned.

"Then what could have transpired from the time he left you?" the captain asked.

"God, how am I to know? Perhaps, it was because it stopped.

The damn battle ended. With his hands no longer busy and his mind not distracted by the horrors inflicted on our casualties, I am afraid our young ensign had the time to reflect on what had happened. It must have been like seeing it clearly for the first time. He had to face all the horrors at once. He had to try to rationalize them or find some way to cope with the madness, we were surrounded amid."

"He was with you the entire time?" the Captain inquired.

"No. And, I fear, that may be the problem. I sent him to attend to the casualties topside, the ones delivered to the shelter of the cockpit. I've no idea, what he saw up there," Radford answered.

"It was bad enough. I hope never to see the likes of the fighting witnessed that day again."

"As do I," the surgeon replied.

"He's stirring," the captain pointed out.

"Its about time. I was beginning to fear I administered too powerful a potion," Radford added.

"Potion? I thought young Lewis was unconscious, when he was discovered by the tars, bringing our dead up from the infirmary."

"He was, sir. But, I felt it best to sedate him to offer his mind and body the relief of undisturbed sleep and rest. Both measures and time are the only sure cures for witnessing the likes, he's seen," the surgeon spoke.

"Has a cure ever worked for you?" Captain Sheffered asked, his voice comradely, sharing the burden of bane and guilt, both veterans had come to know and shoulder silently.

"A drink from the bottle, that's enough to see me through and push my memories behind me," Radford answered.

"And, our ensign?"

"I've administered an opiate. Its strong and a measure I only reserve for the most seriously wounded or the afflicted among our officers. The potion is distilled of a seed cultivated in the Far East and India. Its true measure and purpose are still unknown and untried among our medical community. But it is the best I can do. There are no antiseptics or anaesthetics for the crew, save for our barrels of rum."

"The opiate is a strong potion. It's just as apt to claim a man's soul and body as relieve it from its agony. But, I felt it might help Ensign Lewis swallow his first bitter lesson of combat more palatably. At least, this once," Radford reasoned.

"Well, he's earned the rest. God, I only thought you'd have him assist you, not pick up the damn saw himself," the captain returned.

"There was no choice. The infirmary was overwhelmed. Besides, you knew what was coming, the same as I. He was the only other officer with any training. And of that, only the little, I could teach him, before we reached the coast of Trafalgar," the surgeon advised.

"He's coming around," the captain pointed.

"A good morning to our hero," the doctor said.

I blinked. My eyes were dry and crusted as if I'd been asleep for days and now fought to awake.

Even the act of opening my eyes seemed beyond the strength of my exhausted and fatigued body. I was aware of laying atop a table or board, staring up at the bottom of the planks of the next deck above.

The room was in the semi-darkness of the lanterns.

I remembered.

I bolted up, alarming Surgeon Radford with the quickness of the act. His hands stretched out, trying to restrain my movements.

The open palm of his left hand caught the center of my chest. I must have been weak for his aging hand and arm halted me, while his right hand pinned my shoulder, keeping me forced down, seated atop the table.

"Easy lad," the doctor admonished me. "You've been out for nearly two days. We found you in the rigging storeroom. But, everything's fine now. All is well."

"No, no, no! You don't understand!" I blurted out, the insanity of my nocturnal encounter flooding my mind.

"Hold him!" the doctor ordered, a nearby tar.

The large seaman left his place to the rear of the captain and claimed a vise-like hold upon me. Except, for being able to writhe about beneath his huge hands and pinning weight, I could do nothing.

"You don't understand!" I shouted, recalling the danger we were in the midst of.

My panicked eyes darted about the deck. I was still in the level of our ship, that had become our temporary morgue.

Bodies surrounded us, lit only in the dimness of the candlelight, searching to free itself from the confines of the guarded metal frames of the lit lanterns.

The lanterns cast about the same shadows, I had witnessed the night before. Haunting and fearsome is the way I would describe the pallor and trappings of the deck, where I had seen the dead return to life.

"No . . . listen. We're in danger. We're all in danger!" I blurted out as the seaman tried to recline my body with an approving nod from our surgeon.

"Danger? What danger is this, Ensign?" Captain Shefferd asked, in the fatherly voice of a mentor.

I fell silent, realizing the insanity of what I was about to speak. I choked on my own words and thoughts, not knowing how to express them without being judged mad or worse.

"I saw . . ." again, my words halted.

"You saw what, Ensign?" the captain inquired calmly.

His face was masked in the shadows of the darkened deck. We were fathomed below the ship's waterline. In the bowels of the ship all was hidden in darkness, blocked from the light of day and the gun-decks above.

"I saw the dead . . ."

"Yes, Lewis . . . unfortunately, we've all seen the loss. It's a grim thing . . ."

"No, Captain. I saw . . . I saw the dead, alive!" I forced the words out of my mouth.

The captain shot a concerned look to Surgeon Radford."

"I know it sounds insane, Captain. But, it's true. I saw the dead rise up among our ship's slain crew. I even saw our second officer awake," I offered in testimony.

"Our second officer?" the captain's face grew disgruntled and serious.

"Ensign, Lieutenant Loydd is dead. I saw him fall myself, struck by the round of a French sharpshooter," he informed me.

"Captain, I speak the truth. I saw him dead down here. A hole about the center of his forehead. But, he awoke," I turned under the holding hands of the tar above me and pointed to the table, where Lieutenant Loydd's body lay.

I halted. The air in my lungs was claimed from me. All about the deck the tables and floors were lined with the draped bodies of our fallen. Bloody sailcloth or hammocks were wrapped or pulled about our slain crew.

There, where I had seen Loydd's body the night before, rested a covered corpse, sailcloth interring the form beneath it.

The captain left me and slowly walked over to the corpse.

My eyes spied the cuff of Lieutenant Loydd's gold braided uniform jacket, dangling out from beneath the cover.

The captain halted before the still body. His right hand stretched out to the thick sailcloth. He picked up a corner of its material, near the corpse's head and slowly lifted it aside.

The tar, holding me down, allowed me to rise with the approving nod of our good surgeon. I rose slowly, not wishing to alarm either man and studied the captain's progress.

The sailcloth dropped aside, a length of it touching the deck. Before, our captain lay the slain remains of Lieutenant Loydd.

Our captain's face grew stern, though no color marked his ire against the pale pallor of his face. I did not know if the anger found there was for the French bastard, that had claimed his second officer or for my own entreaties, that now forced him to view the disfiguring and hideous wound, besetting the front of Lieutenant Loydd's skull.

The captain turned around slowly, coming to face me.

I sat atop the makeshift table, reserved for our dead, but attending me in my moment of need.

"I can assure you, our second officer is quite dead. I don't know what you saw or imagined. But, our second officer, as obstinate and tenacious as he was, most assuredly did not rise, nor will he.

I saw the disapproving, yet concerned glance, he gave our good doctor.

"I think our doctor should allow you some measure of time to recover within the privacy of the junior officer's cabin. There are still enough officers and men to attend to the duties and repairs being made underway, that I can spare your services," the captain decided.

"And, it's only fitting. You've done your duty, more than, I could have asked of you. Take some time to rest and grow strong of body and mind. Peace and tranquillity, that is what's needed now . . . wouldn't you agree, Doctor?"

"Aye, sir! That's the ticket for sure. Some hot food and rest should do Ensign Lewis fine. And, I can even prescribe some potions to aid his sleep.

I was about to protest and tell them of the other bodies and the spiteful maiden, I had seen consorting with our dead. But, I could not.

I would be deemed mad. In truth, even I could not believe the sights, I had seen. In the presence of the morning with stillness claiming the morgue and its corpses, I wondered how I could have seen that, which could not have been.

Perhaps, it was some sense of madness, that had found me. The mind is a fragile thing. The horrors, I had witnessed and my own participation in them, could have caused me to imagine . . . no. No!

I had seen what had transpired before my eyes. There was a cruel vixen, half woman, half specter, about our ship. It was she, who had afflicted our tars of illness. The scarring marks about their limbs were not the work of rats.

They had come from her cat-like teeth, finding flesh beyond

the lips of her cruel mouth. I had seen it. I would not deny it to myself. But, how to tell others without being judged mad? The captain returned to our surgeon's side. Their words were guarded, though they tried not to offer any alarm or offense to myself.

But, I knew what they said, even without hearing their conversation. Still within earshot of my youthful hearing, I heard several of their comments.

They believed me mad, at least temporarily. Both believed I suffered some loss of my mental faculties from fatigue or stress.

Had either of them told me a similar tale, even partly as much as I had now discharged, I would not have believed them. It was impossible, save for our Christian savior, for a man to return to life.

And, what of the horrid wounds of the corpses I had witnessed coming after me? A man missing a leg or arm would bleed to death, not walk about the ship, let alone pursue another.

And, had not the blind searched me out as well? How could the sightless follow in pursuit? For that matter, how could the dead pull upon the door, I had secured behind me or pound on it with cold lifeless fists?

"Let him be of his own accord. Try to allow him some measure of recovery without strong opiate or potions. I fear our young hero needs no more encouragement of his imagination. Hallucinations or delusions can not help him now."

"I agree," returned the surgeon. Seclusion, rest, and food . . . and perhaps, time and a stiff drink or two," Radford added.

"Your own prescription?" Captain Shefferd commented.

"It's served me well, though it has its own price," the surgeon offered in self-judgment.

"As you see fit. I release him from duty and into your hands. And, see to it, that no one speaks to him," Shefferd added.

"Is it to be isolation or imprisonment?" the doctor questioned.

"I'll give our young ensign his due. But, I'll not have rantings or madness jeopardize the morale and good health of the Vanguard. We'll continue to mete out extra rations and regain the strength and minds of our tars. But, let nothing disturb the tranquility of this ship. Especially not the loose rantings of a mindless or mad tongue. Understood?"

"Aye, Captain! We'll return Lewis to you in good measure." The captain left.

My eyes followed him as he claimed a ladder to the next deck. It was not until he passed close to one of the lantern's, hanging near the hull, that I noticed the pale pallor of his own complexion.

He moved slowly as if weak or emaciated. But, he moved. He was not dead. Yet, he seemed as if some part of life had left him. He lived and he headed for the light, away from the accursed damp semi-darkness of our secreted morgue.

As I watched his retreating form, I recalled the sickly pallor of those early tars, afflicted with the haunting disease, defying a cure at the hands of our doctor.

"Well, you've earned yourself a rest," Radford barked to me, feinting the confinement to my cabin as a reward and not a penance.

"Doctor, I have to talk to you," I said in a whisper.

I halted my words as I spied our attending tar, "privately!" I added.

"In good time, Mr. Lewis. First, I want to take you down to the infirmary."

"The infirmary?" I questioned.

"No need to be alarmed. I just think you'd prefer to be rid of this place," Radford pointed about the morgue.

I can't see staying here among the dead, no matter how honored, to give you an examination. Besides, you can see the results of your handiwork from two days past. You can see how many men still live, because you took up scalpel and saw. And, you can visit our Ensign Higgins."

"Higgins, I'd forgotten of him completely. How is he?" I asked.

"None the better. But, I dare say, his lot is more enviable to those now sharing our overcrowded infirmary. The whole ship might as well be a sickbay for all the wounded or afflicted, we're harboring," the surgeon exclaimed.

"But, more important, than admiring your handicraft or cheering up Ensign Higgins, I want to see what harm has come to you. You were topside," the doctor admonished, "don't deny it. I learned the truth from Phillips, your senior stretcher-bearer. You sought out the excitement of the battle and nearly forfeited your life in the bargain," the doctor informed me of his own knowledge of my selfish sojourn topside.

"That's true . . ."

"You fell a deck. You're lucky to be alive as I've heard the tale told. It seems a cannonball struck the rail, not far from where you rose to watch our ships forming for battle."

"There was no harm. I was not hurt . . ."

"No harm? Do you think, that if I were of the same persuasion and temperament as our slain second officer, you'd not find yourself before the mast, for leaving your post . . . and that, in a time of peril and battle," Radford added.

I fell silent.

"I thought as much! And, what did you gain. You spied a few French and Spanish ships cut loose their broadsides. They're no different, than our own. It's all the same. We both reap death. And, your life was nearly claimed, though I'm not so sure of your mind."

"When we get below, I'll examine you for some unseen wound. Perhaps, there's a knot along the side or top of your head. That's probably the true cause of these mad hallucinations, you've seen," he added in disgust.

"But, I wish I had an answer for that mad Spaniard down in the brig below," he mentioned as an afterthought.

"The Spaniard?" I asked, puzzled.

"The blighter's mad as a hare. He's gone off claiming, he's seen some unholy vision or some such rot. We should have never picked him up," the surgeon remarked, picking up his black leather bag from off the floor.

The bag's presence and the small vile, he returned inside it, had escaped my vision earlier.

"Help him rise. But, be slow about it. I think his head will be spinning, once the blood rushes to his feet."

"You're damn lucky, lad. And, doubly so. If you hadn't pulled your weight with scalpel and saw, I would have insisted to the captain, that you go up before the mast for punishment. As it is, you've a talent for the surgeon's craft. Even, if you don't wish to pursue it, you're a value to this ship."

"We'd have lost a lot more tars, if I couldn't have relied on the addition and skill of your hands. As it was only twelve men died of their wounds last night and six the night before."

"Recovery is never certain and infection is want to set in even among those we attend to. It would have been more, had you not aided me in the amputations. You've done well, but don't let it go to your head. Now, let's be off and get you looked at," Radford turned and headed for the deck below, motioning for the tar aiding me to follow.

"You can witness the value of your work and then its off to your berth and the seclusion of the junior officer's cabin," Radford's voice trailed off as he descended the steps to the deck below.

CHAPTER 26

Casualties of War

HMS Vanguard
Sailing off the
Spanish Coastline
Day 11-Mid-Morning

The tar beside me lent his shoulder. I found my body drained and my legs unsteady. The ship's rocking motions would have sent me tumbling, had it not been for the solid bulk of the large tar aiding me.

The steps and ladders leading to the deck below took on the form a hazardous obstacle, mocking the youth and strength, I had possessed only days before.

But, youth and strength were not the only casualties, that had been claimed of me. My own spirit and convictions had dulled. No, dulled was not a descriptive enough word to describe the loss of heart, our battle had inflicted upon me.

The eagerness and excitement, even the sheer awe, I had felt moments before the first cannon pummeled our hull had left me. I had fallen soul-less and now resided in some empty limbo. The things I had cherished in the past, even the promise of future wealth and fame, or the prize-money to be gained meant nothing.

All too suddenly, hammered into me by the swift violence and suffering our ship and crew had endured, I now found meaning in the doctor's earlier words. The knowledge, he had openly sought to pass on to me, had eluded me, until I had learned on my own, the true cost paid for victory.

His words were no longer the defeatist ramblings and rantings of a drunkard. Radford had spoken the truth. I understood only now, too late.

I ambled down the steps, the seaman beside me claiming my waist, lest I plummet to the deck below. Together, we found the deck of our make-shift infirmary. It was the heart of an ever expanding sickbay and morgue, besetting the Vanguard.

We walked among the tars seated or laying about the hallway, leading to the rooms housing the most seriously wounded and the ghastly operating room, I had attended the day before. There were few sounds, not even the anguished moans, I had remembered leaving two nights before.

Everything had settled down. The infirmary's earlier disorganized fury, when the doctor and I had operated, was gone. The earlier continuous flow of wounded, arriving from topside and being crammed about among the already crowded deck, had halted.

There was a heavy silence as if all below held their breath, not wishing to relive or renew the horrors of the days before. It was the silence of another reprieve, another chance at life, despite the loss of a limb or eye.

As we reached the doorway, I noticed the elongated iron box was no longer present. Instantly, my mind flashed with the sight of the blood, that had pooled atop it and been sucked down through its porous surface.

My body slackened as the repressed realty of two nights before beset me. I saw clearly the spectral vixen, that had roved among the dead of our morgue. I remembered Lieutenant Loydd rising from death.

I recalled the horror of others, dead men all, trying to claim me as I sought out the safety of the rigging storeroom.

"Doctor!" the seaman beside me blurted out as my legs collapsed beneath me and I began to drop from his firm grasp.

The horrible visions of an evening past flooded my mind.

"Damn! Get him on the table. He's not fit to walk," I heard the surgeon's voice bellow as my eyes closed and sought the refuge of the beckoning darkness of unconsciousness.

I awoke atop one of the boards, that had been an operating table. It had long ago been scrubbed clean. But, the wood of its planks was still stained with the blood and remains of the tars, that had taken their turn upon it.

My eyes blinked, finding the dimness of the lanterns hung from the beams above. A shadow began to block out their faded light, the surgeon's face coming into my blurred viewed.

"You took a turn for the worse," Radford informed me. "You scared our bulking seaman, gentle giant that he is."

I felt the doctor's fingers touching about my head, probing beneath my hair.

"I was right about you though," he remarked, his fingers halting upon a growing knot along the back of the right side of my head. I felt a sharp stabbing pain, despite the lightness of his touch.

"You see. As I said, you suffered a wicked bump, most likely in your fall between decks. A concussion is the likely culprit for those mad dreams, that beset you. Such foolishness and rot you spouted. Seeing our Lieutenant Loydd up and about, him with a hole in the middle of his head, no less," Radford continued, checking the expansion of the growing bump.

"And you, an officer, no less. If I didn't know you better, I'd have thought you were attempting to incite a mutiny among our crew . . . them having already grown so acceptingly accustomed to the loss of our second officer. Still, officers like Loydd serve a purpose."

"Every ship needs its disciplinarian. But, Loydd enjoyed the role too much. I doubt, if there'll be a wet eye among the crew over his passing. But neither, will any admit the pleasure of our second officer's release from life. I'll say this for our tars, they understand their place and tender respect, even without the motivation of the lash," the surgeon said, finishing my examination.

"The iron box . . . it's gone?" I blurted out.

"Blast, after all that's happened, you're still concerned over that metal monstrosity. I'll say this for you, you're single-minded and stubborn-headed, at that," the surgeon answered, taking a step away from the table.

"Your iron box has been moved. Taken to the captain's own quarters," Radford interjected, before I could ask where.

"It seems its peaked his curiosity too. Though I doubt, it will offer him enough of a distraction, trying to solve its riddle and unlock its secrets."

"Did you see our captain's sickly pallor?" the surgeon went on. "I think, he's taking on too much of a burden, blaming himself for the great losses we've suffered. He's fallen into the grips of a stifling malaise, taking to his cabin and sequestering himself in almost total seclusion. Except at night, when I'm told the watch about deck sees him come topside to stare at the stars or sea," the doctor continued.

"Our watch, now there's an unhappy lot. Its seems our captain has picked a small group of men to attend to the navigation and security of our ship topside. Two trusted helmsmen and a boatswain steer us, under the captain's direct supervision. At least, in the evenings.

And, a detachment of marines has been posted topside, guarding us from Lord knows what, now with the Franco-Spanish fleet laying on the bottom of the sea."

"Our captain's acting queerly. Isolating himself, eating little of what his cabinboy brings to him, and avoiding nearly all. It's just not like him," the surgeon went on.

"I deemed it part of the loneliness of command. But, its quite unlike his character. Still, there are other things about him, that show me part of the man that was, is still with us. He's become openly generous with the rations, even the beer, I might add."

Anyway, if you're still interested in that damn iron box, you'll have to contest the captain for it. He'll have time enough to solve some way of opening it and fathom its hidden riddle on our journey home."

"Home?" I asked.

"Yes, home. By the good grace of God, we're headed back for Portsmouth. Our casualties and the damage to our ship have earned us that. But, I lament the cost of it. We've paid too high a price, much too high a price. We've over three hundred men dead. As I've said, I believe the captain blames himself."

"Three hundred or more of our fellows lost. At least, that's our estimate. No one's taken a count or struck the names of those claimed off the muster list. It is a cost that will all too quickly be forgotten by those, that were not here."

"They'll know nothing of our sacrifice, except to remember the name Trafalgar and that our Lord Nelson died there."

The doctor moved to his medical bag and withdrew a small brown bottle. He pulled out its cork stopper and returned to me. He took my right hand, holding it palm open and shook a measure of the crushed powdered contents into it.

"You know what this is?" he quizzed, knowing I had seen the powder, before.

"Willow bark," I answered.

"Good. I see you haven't lost all of your faculties. That's a start to mending your knot as well as your mind. Take it to your mouth and wash it down," he ordered, raising a tin cup of water up from a nearby counter.

I took the dry bitter powder, gladly washing it down my throat with the water.

"I'd keep your nocturnal visions to yourself for now," the surgeon advised me. "Otherwise, everyone will thing you've gone mad like our Spaniard."

"What of our Spanish prisoner?" I asked, seeking out some witness or companion to the nightmare, I had witnessed along the deck being used as our morgue.

"What of him? The man's daft. He's been bellowing in his

cell, worse than the night I had you roused from your bed. He's claiming to see demons or spirits, according to one of the tars, who knows a few words of Spanish from visits to the Spanish colonies."

"How did he describe them, his exact words?" I asked.

The doctor halted and studied me with uncertain eyes.

"Oh, what's the harm in it. You know better now, that your affliction comes from a knot on your head. So, mind your tongue and your imagination. I'll tell you what was told to me," Radford began.

"He speaks of crosses and crucifixes," according to our tar. "He's ranting about salvation and not losing his soul. Madness and rot, likely coming from the fear of nearly having joined the rest of his crew at the bottom of the sea."

"Does he say anything, specifically? Does he describe these phantoms or spirits that come to torment him?" I asked.

"The tar, I questioned, said something about it looking like a woman, but not. Something about the spirit changing its form and then, even claiming, it had no form at all. He speaks of shadows and the darkness, seeing things, where there is nothing to be found. He's mad, lad," the surgeon offered, staring down at me with a concerned fatherly gaze.

"I've told you what's caused your own affliction. Now mind my words and prescription. Rest, until your head and mind are mended. Nothing good can come from the rubbish, that Spaniard spews about. Your own eyes saw for themselves, our Lieutenant Loydd is dead."

I remained silent, acknowledging the truth in the doctor's words.

"I'll grant anyone, Loydd was a perfect bastard. But, he's not the likes of the Lord and he has no power to rise from the dead. You had a dream, a bad one, at that. But, don't make it to be anything more. I'd hate to see you end up as miserable as our Spaniard. It'd be too great a waste of the talent in your hands."

"In fact, I've a mind to instruct you further. Why you might even take my place one day," the doctor mused.

"Besides, any similarities between his ranting and your inflicted visions are coincidence and nothing more. Do you understand, Lewis?" he turned to stare down at me, affirming that any further speculations or fantasies, on my part, would prove damning.

"And, what of the tars among the infirmary, the ones you mentioned passed during the night?" I asked

"What about them?"

"Did any have the marks we saw afflicting the tars earlier, the ones we mistook for rat bites?"

"Rat bites? What is this nonsense? You go from searching out specters and ghouls to ferreting out rodents."

"Did the men that died during the night have the marks?" I blurted out.

"Aye, some did . . . of others, I did not look. But, do not raise your voice about me or these sick men. Bite or no bite, it is of no matter. Rodents did not claim their lives, but the traumatic wounds of cannon-fire, amputation, and their accompanying loss of blood did. I will ask you to cease this nonsense, it does no one any good."

"And, our captain has far more important matters to attend to, than giving any credence to your imaginary emanations. Get your wits back and swallow any unsavory memories away. You're an ensign in the Royal Navy . . . you've much to account for. And, after our day at Trafalgar, you've much to be proud of."

"You two!" he commanded the attention of two nearby healthy tars. "Make ready a stretcher and take this officer back to his quarters. I won't risk having him fall down, just to get him tucked away in his berth."

The surgeon held up a hand against my protestations and desire to walk on my own. "You'll do as I say. I'm the doctor. And, as for a tour of the men you've saved or a visit to Ensign Higgins, we'll leave that for another time, when you're stronger."

He turned to one of the approaching seamen, bearing the litter and said, "After you've seen him to his quarters make for the galley and fetch him something hot. Likely, our ensign hasn't had anything to eat, since before the battle. Why, he probably fainted earlier, from lack of food. Two days with an empty belly, he should have known better and him an officer."

"You'll be glad to know, the captain has lifted the restrictions on fire for the galley, now that our battle has concluded. There's soup and cooked meat a plenty. Every day has become a feast for our simple tars. Our fires are lit and the cook is whistling," the doctor mused.

Ships rules permitted only two men to whistle, besides the boatswains calling men about or to order. Of these, one was the ship's cook.

It was reasoned if he was whistling in the presence of the galley, it assured all, he was not spitting in the food.

The other was the mess cook, who prepared the forenoon meal. He also prepared a "duff," a simple mixture of dried fruit and flour. If he was whistling, it meant he was not eating all the dried fruit.

The amusing lore was trivial, but it meant the ship had returned to some measure of normalcy. I soon learned the captain had chosen to offer up our provisions in a plentiful feast for the surviving crew.

Contrary to their normal rations of a pound of beef or flour or a pound of biscuit-bread, the crew were treated to the unending stores, which would last well beyond our journey home to Portsmouth and only rot in the belly of the ship, when docked, unless removed.

And, contrary to naval discipline and good judgment, the crew's ration of a gallon of beer a day was raised . . . if only for these last evenings, but not to excess. Two additional pints were to be provided each man not on watch and topside.

A standard measure of alcohol was traditionally distributed twice, once at the noon hour and later at dinner. When the measure was rum or other strong drink, many men saved their noon libation to enjoy it in the late hours of the evening and by combining it with that issued at dinner, bolster the alcohol's effect.

Others, used their extra ration of rum or beer as our ship's legal tender, paying off debts or favors as if the fluid were coinage, shilling or pound.

And others, youthful boys attending cabins or officers in the manner of servants, found their efforts rewarded with only a half measure of their adult counterpart's ration.

But these days regulations and measures were nearly forgotten. Of food, all partook, until their bellies burst. There was food for all, according to our doctor, with only our cook and his assistants the worse for it, sentenced to labor in the galley, while others frolicked.

Besides, we had lost enough men to make up for the difference in the food stores, now being squandered. Our ship's compliment was left with more rations and fewer men. So, why not allow the men full bellies.

The effort imparted two things.

It rewarded the survivors, though some might find it ghoulish to be the recipient of a feast, earned by the loss of their fellows. And second, the extra measure of alcohol helped ease the burden of the loss of friends and comrades, taxing their minds. In the past, none would seek to abuse the extra ration or its offered generosity, lest the captain end the feast.

But, the rules of our ship had changed by our captain's own hand. Leniency ruled. In the past, any man slow to rise to his duties or lax in their conduct from overindulgence could rightfully find himself the recipient of the lash. But, not now. Under this new relaxation of the rules, charity and clemency were granted by our captain.

Our captain had lowered the ship's standards, where Lieutenant Loydd would have not. Our ship and men had almost been broken. The crew still suffered the ravages of being hammered by the French and Spanish cannon.

As one, we needed to mend.

With no threat about us, we were one of the first ships to depart the squadron early. Because, of the serious nature of our casualties, we sailed for home.

Our men were content to enjoy the generosity provided by

our captain below decks. And, once full and their thirst satiated, they relished finding the warmth and comfort of their hammocks.

I rolled onto the hard wooden board surface of the stretcher as the two tars leaned it atop the table.

"Take care now, Ensign Lewis. We sail for home. Time to put all this behind you and prepare to claim a hero's welcome," Radford smiled, before leaving to attend to his other charges.

I stretched out in my berth, pulling my blanket about me. Fatigued, I had claimed my bed fully clothed, except for my jacket and shoes.

The seamen, who had attended to me, had long since left. One had returned shortly after our arrival with a pint of beer, a bowl of soup, and a generous measure of bread and cheese.

Except, for a remaining crumb of bread and a bite of cheese, I had eaten all. The soup had been heartier, than I had ever remembered. The cook had apparently ignored any weighted or measured portions.

I had found nearly a full pound of beef in the rich gravy-like broth, garnered with a healthy portion of fresh vegetables, mostly onions and carrots, simmered in the flavorful stock. The doctor was right, with a full stomach a man easily became content.

The pint of warm beer seemed to add to my comfort and ease more, than the soup or cheese, It was a fair start to my recovery.

Staring out the windows to the stern of our quarters, I wondered how the nightmarish madness of the morgue could have ever been. Tying fast the door of the rigging storeroom now seemed like insanity.

The doctor was right, he had to be. All was madness. There was no way I could have seen the things, I had claimed.

I reconsidered his words and those of the captain as I rested. And, rested, I took several moments to update my journal.

Journal, one would probably proscribe another word for the small leather-bound book in which, I kept a miniscule record of our journey at sea. It had fallen into a small collection of notes and observations of the ships we had sighted and the places we had sailed to.

It was little more, than an ambitious and youthful attempt to keep some record of my young career. So that in the years ahead, I might look back longingly at my youthful past and where my career had started.

I had even been ambitious enough, to crudely sketch several of the vessels we encountered, noting precisely their number of masts and sails.

In any event, it was a way to pass the long evening hours, when left to my own preoccupations and not subject to the demands of a posted watch.

What a tale or better said, a youthful fantasy, it was. The small pages were crammed with tiny words, scribed by my own hand, within their narrow sheets. I scrupulously wrote a description of the young maiden, I had thought, I had witnessed.

Somehow, writing of the incident seemed to make it less real. How could such a wondrous and horrid creature exist, simultaneously projecting the illusion of beauty and femininity, yet existing underneath as a vile dark beast?

Perhaps, the captain and Radford were correct. It was a dream or the fatigue of my mind, after being faced with the brutal horrors of our battle. I had to admit, that even now, fed and rested, I still felt drained. The strain and exhaustion, coupled with the shock of observing such a cruel loss of life and limb had taken their toll upon me.

Perhaps, it had been a dream.

And yet, had not the Spaniard, even with the barrier of language, only affirmed my nocturnal observations by his own rantings.

The knot at the back of my head throbbed. Surely, that was the reason for my hallucinations and the deception my own mind played upon me. Reality and science bid, that no man, save the Savior, could rise from the dead. Everything, I had imagined, was just that, a figment of my dreams or stress, a symptom of my concussion and nothing more.

I picked up the small journal and thumbed open its leather-bound cover. I leafed through it, until I found the most recent entry, accompanied by the charcoal sketch of the young valiant, I had observed.

I was not a professional artist, but those sharing our cabin found my depictions rendered by a skillful and talented hand. It was a hobby and distraction, I had honed from childhood on, though I had never the ambition to pursue it for any other reward, than to please my own eye.

Drawing my illusive specter had proved an easier task, than I had thought, at least, the rendering of her general features. Her image was haunting.

No man, having seen her face, could have forgotten it. I could still recall the softness of that almond-shaped face. It mirrored those of the young cultured and well-bred ladies of fortune and grace, who were heirs to the Ladies and Lords of Britain's wealthiest families and noblest courts.

My eyes stared at the long dark hair, I had drawn and shaded in. It framed the whiteness of the page and the bewitching face, drawn from memory. The lightness of my thinly traced lines suggested the ghostly pallor and softness of her form.

But, almost as ghastly as her own damning eyes was my attempt to draw them. I had rendered a discomforting recreation. But, the charcoal's darkness could not make those piercing orbs black enough. Though, I pressed the small piece of charcoal hard to the page's paper, I could not create the blackness, reproducing the depth and emptiness held within those eyes.

Perhaps, my attempt to duplicate her image reinforced the reality, that she had not existed. But, the image I had drawn was captivating, except for the mouth.

I thought, I had ruined the drawing trying to render the frail features of that exquisite, yet horrid face by trying to fashion the crimson red lips, I had viewed or thought I had seen. No attempt to reproduce that foul mouth and its seductive lure seemed accurate.

I tried four times, lightly tracing a thin suggestion of the mouth, but no effort, I aspired to, could duplicate its allure or vulgarity.

Yet, my attempt to rub away my efforts created by accident the mere suggestion of the lips, I had witnessed. The smeared charcoal shadow smudged about the corners of the image's mouth mirrored the bloodstained corners of the cruel orifice, that had feasted upon our wounded tar.

And yet, the drawing proved too ridiculous to believe. The more I looked at it, the more I began to believe the cruel vixen in her white ghostly gown was only a trick of my imagination and my own naive innocence, succumbing to the distress and trials of battle.

I closed the small book and returned it to the small watertight metal box, I kept it treasured inside. It nestled inside the container along with two small pieces of thin charcoal as I closed the container's lid.

My legs and arms relaxed beneath the comforting warmth of the dark blue blanket tucked about me. I bent my right arm and snaked its hand beneath the pillow behind me.

Luxury, that was the best I could describe the simple pleasure of relaxing in my berth with my stomach full and body warm.

I contemplated returning my journal to its secret hiding place, spirited away from the possessions of our shared junior officers quarters. But, I had no wish to leave the warmth of my berth.

One of my predecessors had an opening made by the ship's carpenter. Its secreted vault resided in a beam alongside the doorway's entrance.

The carpenter had been a skilled artisan, even making a cover, which defied detection of the small wooden pocket, large enough to secret away my journal in its close-fitting metal box. The unusual and nonstandard carpentry was engaged in secretly and for the woodwright's profit during a lengthy overhaul, when the HMS Vanguard was devoid of her normal compliment.

Unlike I, its former owner spirited away a flask, whose contents were used to take the chill off the long ungodly and cold lonely midnight watches topside. His advancement and a posting to a new warship transferred the dry and safe repository to me. His generosity, in informing me of its existence, gave me a means to remove my journal's words and thoughts from prying eyes.

I placed the metal box beside me, comfortably out of the way. I stretched my arms under the pillow beneath my head. My hands snaked underneath the feather-filled cushion as I lingered there in simple comfort and detachment.

And then, I touched it. The fingers of my right hand felt the pointed corner of the object I had secreted beneath the folds of the pillow earlier. It was the silver cross, given to me by my mother.

I claimed it, my fingertips gently searching out its cool polished surface. I pulled it away, cherishing it inside my grasping hand. I held it before my eyes.

The words our doctor had claimed the Spaniard ranted returned to me. The Spaniard claimed the cross or crucifix was the some aid to salvation. Surely, he spoke in theological terms. In his own way, he must have been describing the emulation of the Savior and a righteous life as the true path to heaven, nothing more.

The doctor was probably correct in assuming, that with the loss of his brig and the dreadful claim upon its crew, our Spanish prisoner had become overwrought. If like all the rest of his Catholic brethren, he was devoutly religious, it was right to assume he had fallen back upon his religious teachings, seeking an answer for the frightful loss of his ship and his own remarkable survival. He was simply overwhelmed and searching for answers. He was likely trying to understand why he alone, had been graced with God's goodness and allowed to live, when so many others had perished.

I had been alone on the deck serving as our morgue. The Spaniard could not have witnessed the things I had seen. Yet, he had seen something. But, what?

I held the silver cross between my thumb and fingers. I caressed its smooth comforting form. The light from the windows behind me glittered on its surface.

Within moments, my hand had fallen aside and my eyelids had restfully closed. I was asleep in seconds, entreated to slumber by the rhythmic lapping of the waves following in our wake to stern.

CHAPTER 27

The Price of Revelry

HMS Vanguard
Sailing off the
Spanish Coastline
Day 11-Midnight

I awoke with a start.

I had forgotten where I was. The comfort and warmth of my berth was deceptive. I heard the lapping of the waves. My mind and body became aware of the motions of the ship.

The Vanguard rolled softly to starboard, before halting and beginning a returning roll to port. There was a stillness to things both inside the cabin and outside.

I do not ever think, I had heard our vessel so quiet. With over five hundred survivors aboard, surely, there should have been some sound. If not, from the well fed and inebriated crew just beyond the cabin's door, then from the watch topside.

But, there was nothing.

There were no shouts of revelry or frolicking. There were no barked commands guiding our passage through the night. All was silent.

I opened my eyes. For the moment, I was content to remain

reclined atop my berth. The air inside the cabin, shared with the other junior officers, was laced with a damp chill like so many nights before, when the coolness of the sea permeated our ship.

I looked about. I was alone. None, of the other junior officers were in their berths. I had not expected to find Ensign Higgins about. He would still be confined to the bowels of our ship, quarantined.

I pulled my blanket about me, fighting the urge to empty my bowels and bladder of the soup and beer with a visit to one of the heads. The head, what we at sea called toilets aboard our ship, was well forward in the bow.

In foul weather, the heads sat in the discomforting cold and wash of our plunging and rising bow, just behind the bowsprint and forecastle. Even in calm waters, a visit to them was want to induce seasickness in those with weak constitutions.

They were left to the cabinboys or those men, who had earned punishment before the mast to clean. Either way, they were an uncomfortable and foul perch, better visited and vacated as quickly as possible.

I did not desire to leave the comfort of my berth, even though the officer's heads were fully enclosed, offering tall and narrow box-like rooms to provide us a measure of privacy, attending to our bodily functions.

The officer heads contrasted in comparison to the crews open heads. Their toilets consisted of two triangular shaped boards. One stood to port, the other to starboard. Both boards had rounded edges, if that could be of any comfort and holes, dumping their human waste along either side of the bow.

Either way, the journey and discomfort of abandoning the warmth of one's berth or hammock was disagreeable, though unavoidable to officers and tars alike. The only alternative was the use of a bucket. But, ship's etiquette and the offended nostrils of one's mates demanded that it be lugged topside and cleaned of its foul contents.

The act of carrying the container topside was filled with the hazard of a spill, especially in heavy seas. And, the unfortunate clumsy oaf that befouled our decks was faced with punishment for his untidiness, coupled with the unhappy prospect of cleaning up his squalid refuse.

I rose, casting my blanket and its sheltering warmth aside. In the act, the silver cross my sleeping hands had released clanked against the wooden sides and frame of my berth. My hands searched about for it in the darkness of the cabin. The unlit lanterns mocked my search.

Its silver surface gleamed with the soft moonlight cast through the windows of the cabin's stern. I retrieved the religious symbol.

Next, I claimed my blue jacket, buttoning its ornamental fasteners and tugging its sleeves about by their thick cuffs.

I found a place for the silver cross inside one of the jacket's pockets, spiriting it away without a thought. I considered it more of a precious keepsake, than a religious icon.

As an afterthought, I pocketed the small metal box and my journal, having no desire to leave it laying openly about.

My watch was secreted away in the opposite pocket. Being curious of the hour, I withdrew the timepiece and opened its cover, seeking out the whiteness of its face. Despite the thin delicateness of the watch's hands, I easily read the hour.

It was nearly ten minutes past midnight.

I returned to dressing, donning my shoes mindlessly. I halted, turning towards the stern of the cabin. To the rear of our ship our wake glistened in the moonlight. The waters were as black and rich as fine velvet. The night sky was a deep soft blue, beset with the tiny orbs of light from the stars scattered above.

All was tranquil as the HMS Vanguard plied the waters silently for home. Despite the chill running about the deck, I began to relish the trip topside, if only for the distraction the stars and moon would provide.

For the first moment, since the battle had ended and I had succumbed to the horrors, that had beset my mind, I felt a sense of peace and relief. Perhaps, the doctor had been correct and none of the horrors, I had presumed to have witnessed the previous night, had ever occurred.

In the peacefulness surrounding me, I had to agree, that the delusions and madness, I thought I had fallen to, might well be the manifestations of the concussion I had suffered. Even now, the knot on the back of my head still throbbed dully. It shot a sharp stabbing pain just beneath the bruised surface of my skin at irregular intervals.

I moved to the shared cabin's two doors and opened the one closest to my berth.

I stepped out into the gun-deck. It was lined tightly with strung hammocks.

All was quiet.

I must have been daft, to even have mentioned what I thought, I had envisioned nights before. Everything was as it should be. Tars were slumped in their sagging hammocks, finding the restful peace of slumber and the contentment of full bellies and relieved minds.

And, the extra rations of beer had found a few content to drop off to sleep sitting upon the deck or stretched out where they had taken to singing or accompanying the few seaman, talented enough to be able to play the fife or concertina, treasured in their possession by all.

But, any music or distractions had fallen by the wayside.

Our tars had fought hard. Now, with their meager reward bestowed by the grace and generosity of our captain, they sought the refreshing slumber, that would find them ready to take on the days ahead and put the horrors of the past behind them.

I snaked through the strewn out hammocks and the lads resting along the deck.

My own slumber must have been very deep indeed. I had not heard the crew piped to their hammocks. I had heard nothing after eating my own meal and dousing it down with warm beer.

Here and there came the restless creak or groan of our ship's mismatched timbers. Built of aged wood and green timber for those parts of our ship, the woodwrights found lacking, our vessel now fought against itself.

The dry porous surfaces of the aged wood easily absorbed and retained the dampness and moisture of the waters the

Vanguard found herself amid. But, they quickly dried out with the coming of the morning sun. Their timbers moved against the green wood, still laden with its own natural moisture and that soaked up from the sea

Even cut, the wood making up our beams, braces, and planks was a living thing. In the almost total silence, the timbers of our vessel spoke to one, though a man could not understand their language or meaning.

The ship rolled gently, sending the hammocks swaying about. They swung softly as if the sea was the invisible hand of some shared mother, rocking our tars to slumber.

I claimed the steps leading topside. With my legs still unsteady, I had no wish to ascend by ladder. I stretched out my left arm and braced my climb along the side of an adjoining brace.

My face was greeted to the brisk breeze of the ocean, dancing along the upper gun-deck. My first instinct was to turn my head skyward. I considered myself blessed to be able to witness another night and the magnificent splendor of the stars and heavens above.

It was a simple luxury many of our crew would never experience again.

I noted the sails above or more rightfully, the lack of them. We ran with only six large canvases unfurled, despite the steady wind. I wondered, if the lack, of sailcloth was an oversight.

But, I ignored it. There was a watch on duty. It was their charge to carry out the captain's orders. It was not my place to question our master.

Perhaps, he only wanted to ensure the crew a measure of calm. Certainly, with many enjoying the extra ration of beer, our captain probably saw it fitting not to have too much canvas aloft, lest an unseasonable wind or sudden storm require too many dull-minded men aloft among the masts and spars.

Aloft in the rigging was no coward's work. And, it was certainly not work befitting a drunkard. But, though many had drank an extra measure, I doubted it would have robbed them of the nimble fleetness their feet and hands demonstrated about the heights of our masts.

Still, there was no reason to chance endangering the lives of men, who had already proved their bravery. Courage was one thing, but folly and recklessness were quite another.

I fully understood, the lack of sail and our captain's wisdom, despite my eagerness to reach home and Portsmouth Harbor. But, there was time.

I estimated, we moved at little over four knots, if that. The wind seemed light, though steady. A dark cloud, its shadow cast beside our ship by the moon, quickly outraced us. I grinned in the knowledge, that the wind was off our stern, pushing us along on our homeward path.

About the wheel, two helmsmen guided our ship under the watchful gaze of a boatswain. Near the rail, not far from them, stood Captain Shefferd.

Our captain looked only a portion of the commanding form, he had appeared before the battle. And, even in the moonlight his face had a pale pallor about it. But, more than any other man aboard, I think our captain bore the burden of our loss the greatest.

I remembered having learned from the doctor, that our captain had sequestered himself inside the confines of his cabin during the day. I wondered if he bore some shame for the horrendous loss of life, claimed aboard the HMS Vanguard.

It was not his fault. But, his self-imposed exile showed he held himself accountable. As I was told, he now lingered above deck at night, hidden by the darkness. In spite of our victory, there was loss.

His frame was thin, swallowed up by the dark blue jacket and its hanging tails blowing in the breeze, running across the deck. Though, he allowed all to feast with extra rations for a second day, it looked as if he had partook of little or nothing for himself.

I wanted to offer some kind word to alleviate his burden. But, there was nothing I could say.

And, I feared the spoken word, lest my own tongue betray the madness possessing me. I saw things, that others would not believe were there. In truth, with the diagnosis of our surgeon, I wondered if I had seen anything at all.

A bump was the cause of my demons and specters. That was what the scientific and trained mind would diagnose. But, though I feared to say it, I believed otherwise.

But, topside with the wind blowing against my face, it was even hard for me to now believe, I had seen what I had observed, let alone, that I had even imagined it. It was unreal. It defied belief. But, I swore it had happened.

I moved forward. I found the upper gun-deck occupied by several of our marine guards. They patrolled their rounds lackadaisically, probably moping like unwanted children, that they had not been allowed to participate in the generous rations being lavished upon the rest of our crew by being forced to stand watch.

I assumed wrongly, that they would inherit their just reward and a belated, but fair portion, after their watch had been completed. There was no smoke about the exhaust from our galley.

The kitchen fires had been extinguished. If it was a hot meal our marines relished, it had escaped them.

The feast looked to be a liberty, their commanders would not allow the seafaring soldiers.

But, more likely, our good Captain Shefferd had not interfered in the way the marine contingent was disciplined or guided by their immediate commanders. For some reason the marine contingent was not party to our meager reward, their commander deciding thusly.

I thought it a terrible thing, that they might not be allowed to partake in the same generous bounty and reward as our tars. It seemed an abusive wrong, especially after they had faced the peril of the open masts and decks, during our battle.

As I grew closer to the head, I spied several more marines. They were gathered near the bow, standing stiffly in perfect unison. One of their sergeants stood nearby, noting my approach.

All stood still in silence like those of our crew on watch. They were like the bastard unloved children of a great household. They were present and nothing more. But, they failed to enjoy in the inheritance and joy, reserved for the rightful heirs of the manor, though they were no less deserving.

So, here they stood, going silently about their business along the upper gun-deck. Several more small groups of marines tread about the deck, relegated to the servitude of their posts, while our tars and others feasted and slept.

I passed them silently, though respectful of their presence. There was no need to excuse myself or add insult to their disappointing lot by offering salutation or greeting, followed by the closing of the door to one of the officer's heads.

The door closed and I heard them go about their drill. It was an ungodly hour to be conducting a parade practice. But, that is what I heard.

The commands were called out lowly and not barked out as was the regular penchant of the non-commissioned officers. Apparently, they were encouraged to show some amount of respect for the slumber of our tars below.

I heard rifle butts slap the deck and feet move and space about the planking, before the assembled men were broken up and ordered to roam about the upper gun-deck. Most likely, our captain, upon recalling our encounter with the Spanish brig, wanted no similar fate to befall us in our own lax state.

I doubted there was a French or Spanish ship about, that would dare to sail towards any ship, no matter what her size or displacement, should she be flying the Union Jack.

But, authority came with its own responsibility and dread. Undoubtedly, our captain was aware of the fickleness of fate and sought to prevent any harm befalling our ship and crew through overconfidence or laxness. The lesson of the Spanish brig was still fresh in all our minds.

And so, our marine contingent or more rightly a detachment of its surviving force patrolled our upper gun-deck. They added their eyes and ears to those of the small group of sailors, forming a skeletal watch.

The small watch was the reason, I had spied so many other seaman asleep about the deck below. Normally, of our entire compliment, half the men were on watch or employed in useful duties, while the rest took meals or slept.

But, not now. Normal duties and tasks had been suspended.

I returned outside, glad to be out of the foul stench of the head. The tall narrow stall was partially lit inside by the splintered holes, that punctured its roof, remnants and cruel souvenirs of our battle.

Outside, our marines continued about. They patrolled their posts. But, none walked with the stiffness of a parade or drill. They merely roamed about the decks, their eyes lost to the darkness of the sea on either side of our ship.

Unlike, our earlier journey to Cadiz, we no longer bordered the coastline, even distantly. The comforting reassurance of land, no matter how far away, was gone. No shore was in sight.

We sailed amid a dark sea of emptiness and quiet.

I leaned beside the rail as two marines passed behind me, slowly descending the steps to the next deck below. Both were guided along their path by a lantern with a shrouded light, forcing the candle's light down about the deck, lest its faint glow reveal our presence at sea.

In short order, two more marines, carrying a similar masked lantern, descended near the bow. The pairs would be making their rounds about the decks, ensuring all was well.

It seemed like a waste of their time and efforts. It was certain, that all they would glimpse would be the snoring and well-fed forms of our seamen. But, discipline and purpose drove them.

Our marines were intent on doing their duty, whether it was necessary or not. I watched, as the long barrels of their slung weapons disappeared beneath the tops of the hatchways.

A cool breeze woke me from my thoughts and brought me back to reality.

I was still troubled by the awful vision, I had seen or thought I had witnessed. But, it was folly to even give it further thought or credence. The dead do not rise. It is a physical fact, bolstered by the laws of nature and science.

But, it had seemed so real. And, so had the ghastly apparition, that had taken the form of a seaman and then, a maiden. The haunting memory mocked me. For how could anybody so readily change forms or image. I had thought I'd seen a sailor scavenging about the morgue. Then, I had lost sight of the tar, only to find a beautiful and alluring maiden.

She, in turn, had changed into a ghastly specter. The foul lips and teeth of her vixen-like mouth had struck terror in my heart before she left my sight. And, in her leaving, I had witnessed another transformation. Her form had become lost, receding into a shadow, a ghostly apparition, until it too had vanished.

Madness! All had been madness, caused by a blow to the back of my head. It had to be. It must be! Shouldn't it be so? Except for the loss of our tars, the Vanguard had returned to normalcy.

But, what was normal?

Normal, the word raised visions of a past world, that I and others had taken for granted. Its comforting routine and simple toils, now escaped us all. The mundane tasks, such as washing clothes or drilling on our cannon on Mondays or cleaning out the hammocks and airing their bedding on Tuesdays, seemed lost in a forgotten and distant, though more tranquil past.

Normalcy was the scrubbing of sails. Normalcy was taking part in the exercise of furling the sails on Wednesday, after they had been cleaned. It was the inspection of the men's uniforms on Thursday, keeping an eye keen to call attention to any defect for later mending with needle and thread.

Normalcy meant the routine of the washing and scrubbing the decks with the heavy and hated holystones and water from the fire pump. This was normalcy. It had disappeared from our daily routine.

How comforting was the illusion of routine, when Sunday would see clean hammocks drawn. And, there was respect to the Lord as services were held and our captain read the chosen prayers or bible verses, the years had deemed pertinent to him and our life at sea.

Now, things appeared strange and odd. Our ship's reassuring

routine had given way to laxity and reprieve, strangely instigated and approved by our captain. Order seemed forgotten or misplaced.

But, this was my first true combat, less the bullying encounter with the Spanish brig. Perhaps, nothing was amiss or abnormal. Perhaps, this was the way of a warship, which had survived a life or death struggle. Like, a wild animal bearing its pain and injuries, we sought out an isolated corner of the sea and sat about licking our wounds . . . recovering.

I forced the matter from my thoughts and tried to think about what awaited us at Portsmouth. My mind filled with the images of awaiting crowds lining the docks. There would be young women and sweethearts eagerly anticipating our arrival.

I lent my imagination to the embraces, that would befall each man, not only from loved ones, but from perfect strangers caught up in the euphoria of the moment.

I had seen it before as a child, when other victors had returned home from the sea. Now, it was to be my turn and that of the rest of our ship's surviving compliment.

Because of the great loss of men among our crew, we had been detached from the squadron before all others. We had hoped to be the first home. But, our journey progressed slowly without the full benefit of a complete set of unfurled sails.

But, I suspected a full set of sails would be unfurled with the coming of daylight and hands as eager as I to get home. I could not imagine, we would forfeit being the first to reach the shores of Portsmouth, given our early start.

We could claim the first laurels of victory and savor the fame, due all of Nelson's ships. I could only dream of what great financial reward would find my purse, when prize-money made its way down among the ranks, after admirals and captains claimed their share first.

I wondered what wealth might have been captured from among the defeated French and Spanish ships. Suddenly, my elation left me with the realization, that I knew of none in tow.

But, because I had not witnessed any captured vessels, did

not mean there were no prize-ships. Yet, the combat was fierce. What if none had been claimed. I feared, with the fighting so bitter and contested, the only enemy ship desired might have been a sunken one.

If that was the case, what had it profited us? We'd earned a moment of fame and little else. A hearty meal and a well done, was that all we could expect?

Again, the doctor's earlier words haunted me. The truth was now open and bare to me. The lies of valor and battle had been exposed. The true burden was the cost borne.

I awoke from my thoughts, finding myself staring down at the darkness of the moving water. It swept by our hull gently, offering my mind the distraction and solace of its rhythmic movement.

The marine sergeant, on deck barked his dissatisfaction, unwittingly claiming my attention.

"If they've taken one liberty, either a bite of bread or a drink laying about, I'll see to it they receive a hundred lashes. And, no whip for them . . . the cat-o-nine-tails!" he fumed to a subordinate, he was intent on sending below decks.

The man was tasked with finding out why the two pairs of marines were delayed in returning topside.

"Aye, sir!" the private returned, tugging about the sling of the long rifle slung over his right shoulder and hampering his attempts to keep up with his sergeant, pacing angrily about the deck.

"Well, off with you! Find the bastards!" the sergeant bellowed, his voice loud enough to break the sleep of even the deepest slumbering soul below decks.

The younger marine took off, shuffling his feet hurriedly across the deck, before disappearing after the other four marines.

The sergeant turned around, spying my still presence. In his anger, he was unaware of my nearness.

"Begging your pardon, sir. I didn't mean to disturb you with the color of my language . . ."

"No offense, Sergeant," I offered.

"I'm not exactly on duty myself. I'm supposed to be in my cabin . . . ship surgeon's orders," I mused.

The sergeant seemed to recognize me. "You're the one, that was in the cockpit and later the infirmary . . . , sir." he added crisply, leaning his rifle upright against the rail.

"Yes," I answered uncomfortably, having it noted, that I was not topside during our battle.

"I saw you down below," he added. "Not, that you would have noted my passing or that of some of my men. We carried some of the wounded below, after the surgeon's stretcher-bearers took the worst of it topside. "I saw you cutting bone, sir," he explained.

"Gawd, I'd want no part of that. I've the stomach for battle, but not the blood of my mates. A gruesome business, you attended to," he offered, in a low guttural growl, mirroring the closest thing to compassion for a sergeant of marines.

"It wasn't exactly of my choosing," I returned.

"I know what you mean, sir. Every man must do as he's called on. Like our Lord Nelson commanded, every man to do his duty . . . that's our lot."

The sergeant halted and looked towards the hatchways leading to the lower decks. His impatience showed on his worn leathered face, despite the darkness.

"Perhaps, there's damage below detouring or delaying your men," I offered.

"No, sir. I've been below. The steps and ladders are fine enough. It's my men's bellies and thirst, I suspect has led them astray."

"Surely, the captain will allow your own men a measure of the extra rations, once their watch is over," I suggested.

"I'd have thought it likely. But, I've learned as they, the galley's closed and its fires put out. Any beer ration is locked away. This is the second day my lads have missed sharing in their measure of the ship's feast."

"But, my lads are quite an enterprising lot, damn thieves, actually," he added. "If there are any loose rations or spirits about, they'll be tempted to help themselves. Off-duty pilfering is one thing. But, if they do it on watch, my watch, there'll be the piper to pay and the boatswain's lash," anger rose in his voice.

"I can't understand it. There are more, than enough men still left aboard to offer my lot a chance to claim their share of the rations and a comfortable stay down below. But, they've kept us relegated topside. The captain doesn't even allow us to the hammocks below deck. We string hammocks inside the weather deck, behind the wheel, taking turns at a nap. And, even that's partly open to the wind and sea."

I listened to the sergeant's lament. The permanent posting of these marines made no sense to me. I wondered what the captain was guarding our upper decks from. Did he fear French or Spanish pursuit or that, we might be boarded, in our broken state?

If that was the case, why allow the men extra rations and drink? Why allow them to seek out and claim the comfort of their hammocks, if danger was about?

The sergeant's eyes searched the accompanying hatches and found the alternate routes of entry and exit vacant.

"Sir, if you'll excuse me, I best see what's wrought this delay," the sergeant interrupted in excuse, claiming up his own rifle.

"Sergeant, I'm headed below anyway. I'll accompany you," I returned.

"Suit yourself, sir. But, mind your ears when we find them. I'll not be taken advantage of . . . even, if my marines rightfully deserve a reward or medal for what they've been through. I will have order."

CHAPTER 28

Missing

**HMS Vanguard
Sailing off the
Spanish Coastline
Day 12-After Midnight**

I regretted my decision to accompany our sergeant of marines below decks. Already, we had passed beneath the upper and middle gun-decks with no sign of his wayward marines.

I held a lantern high, searching for the steps, that moved beneath each step I took with the gentle roll of our ship. Ahead, the sergeant lowered his own lantern, searching the last few steps, that descended down into the improvised morgue.

All was cloaked in a dark heavy silence.

"A nasty business this," the sergeant offered, without turning around to face me.

"Sergeant?" I questioned, not fully understanding his comment.

"These tars assembled about," he returned, stretching out the lantern in his right hand and waving it about the gathered corpses. Its not right. I've never seen the likes of this before."

I remained silent, slowly succumbing to my own fears and

the memories of the manifestations of the dream from two nights before, if it was a dream.

"I've served on other warships. And never did we so morbidly cling to our dead. A shroud and chain or rock from among our ballast, then, a quick burial ceremony would have dispatched these men to the bottom. But, this? It's got a bad feeling to it. It's unnatural," he added, moving to the next set of steps and the adjoining ladders.

I halted. I was in disbelief, that I had returned to this hated deck. I expected to see the dreadful images, that had plagued my mind and had nearly driven me to madness. Madness and fear had driven me to close myself off in the rigging storeroom.

My eyes studied the deck and tables. It was with the workings of a perplexed mind, that I tried to recall the images I had last seen there. Something was amiss. But, it escaped me.

Our sergeant continued his journey without turning rearward to check on my own halted progress. In fear of being left alone in the confines of the morgue, I followed.

His lantern's light dropped below the morgue's deck, casting a glowing uplight about the ceiling of the morgue, directly above the hatchway. The steps creaked from his weight and bulk, their worn and dried out wood protesting his passage.

I cast my eyes about, taking one last look around the morgue. It was like a child's fearful search as he walked about a darkened woods or a street cloaked in the night's fearful blackness.

I half expected some spiteful horror to spring up at me. My breath was shallow, almost halted in dreadful anticipation. But, nothing appeared before me.

The horrid apparition I awaited, did not show. There was only the lingering silence of our dead and their shrouds.

Realization suddenly dawned upon me. I knew what I found amiss, the shrouds!

There were lengths of sailcloth laying atop the tables or deck. They laid flat with no lifeless corpses beneath them.

My mind spun as I tried to remember, which table bore the body of a tar and which did not. The morgue was still overwhelmed with covered bodies, save for these few empty shrouds of an askew hammock or piece of sailcloth, that had been left from our cloaked dead.

The glow of the sergeant's lantern disappeared as he made his way along the lowest deck of our ship. I abandoned the morgue, seeking out the safety and comfort of the sergeant's light and presence, despite the lantern in my own hand.

Here and there, I spied several tables or shrouds without their attendant bodies. But, there could be reason enough for their absence.

I turned back towards the morgue as I reached the edge of the steps leading below. Again, the silence of our brave tar's bodies mocked my childish fears.

Except, for the slow rolling movement of the ship and the creak and moan of her timbers, there was nothing to justify my fears. There was nothing here, but our hallowed dead.

I followed the sergeant's path.

He had forged ahead, apparently anger pushing aside any unease or apprehension of entering the darkness of the lowest deck.

A few lanterns were lit. They were suspended from the ceiling or hung on the walls of the narrow hallway, running between the many smaller cramped anterooms of the lowest deck.

I spied the far end of the hallway and the door beside it, that led to the infirmary. A moving glow about the doorway's frame, showed me where our sergeant had gotten to.

The thought of entering that grizzly room, even though, it had long since been scrubbed down, after my own gory work there, slowed my progress. My head and mind, that had cleared and reveled in the simple relief of the cleanliness and freshness of the night air only moments before, was once again flooded and clouded by the recent past.

But, any thoughts or fears fled me as a shrill scream filled the narrow haunts of this unsavory deck, secreted so far beneath the waterline.

I recognized the pained voice, that blurted out. I heard the metallic clink and rattle of keys. There was the sound of feet stomping about and the creaking of rusted hinges opening as a heavy lock was removed.

The yelling began anew.

Several nearby tars, laying on the floor or in strung hammocks, stared up in the semi-darkness lining the infirmary, when I entered. Their eyes glared with hatred for the Spaniard, who had once again disturbed their slumber with his wild ranting.

I moved through the infirmary, finding the small space behind it, similarly cluttered with more of our injured tars. Having lost a limb or eye to the Franco-Spanish fleet, they had no compassion for our mad prisoner.

I moved past them, ignoring their upturned faces and their relief at seeing an officer, finally arrived to deal with the problem of our restless and distraught prisoner.

I halted in the flickering light of several moving lanterns as the sergeant and his missing marines united to deal with the Spaniard. The delay of the four marines, meant to patrol about the bowels of the ship, had been at the order of our surgeon.

I extinguished my lantern's candle and placed it atop a cluttered counter. I thought to assist the marines and our doctor, but the area was too confined for the group of men already gathered about.

Our doctor meant, once and for all, to quiet our captive. He held some potion tightly in his right hand as he followed behind one of the marine privates, forcing his way into the tiny wooden and iron cell, harboring our prisoner.

The Spaniard screamed out as if a blow had been delivered to his body or a cutlass or bayonet had pierced his flesh. In truth, only his hands and arms had been grasped by two of our marines. Their hands were free, their weapons left safely outside the confines of the brig with a trusted companion.

They pushed him hard against the wall of the hull behind him, before wrestling him to the cell's deck.

His head darted about from side to side. It seemed as if he would snap his neck. The violent movements tossed his coveted crucifix about. It bounced along his chest, now exposed by a torn loaned shirt.

One of the marines dropped a hand to the prisoner's chest to

steady him. It ripped the small religious icon free as its chain
tangled among the marine's forceful fingers and broke.

The Spaniard yelled, his words calling upon Heaven's angels,
to intercede in his defense. His darting tongue recited some prayer
of protection in a maddening rush, spewing between his parted
lips and panting breaths.

A third marine, still holding his rifle, pummeled the Spaniard,
delivering the brass buttplate of his rifle into the prisoner's
abdomen.

The Spaniard dropped. Another marine dropped to the deck
and claimed the Spaniard's legs about the ankles. Thus pinned,
the doctor moved forward and pressed a small brown bottle against
the prisoner's mouth.

The Spaniard fought. The bottle's thick brown glass mashed
against his clenched teeth. But, the contest was a losing battle for
our prisoner. The prisoner exhibited a strength, that defied his
thin small body. But, pinned and squirming, he succumbed as
the doctor skillfully pinched a nerve near the prisoner's neck.

In an involuntary response to the stabbing pain, his clenched
teeth parted. The fluids inside the bottle passed into his mouth,
gagging the Spaniard, until he choked. A skillfully applied hand
along the bottom of the prisoner's jaw prevented him from
discharging the precious contents.

Our doctor's hand guarded, that the prisoner had no choice,
but to swallow, if he wanted to claim another breath. In
resignation, the prisoner fell still. His body slumped in the hands
of the cradling marines. It was done.

The doctor waved for the marines to release their hold on
the prisoner. They did so with apprehension, expecting him to
rise in reprisal and strike out at them. It did not happen. The
Spaniard's fight was gone.

The doctor stepped out of the cell, followed by the three
marines. A fourth marine pressed the heavy plank door closed,
its hinges protesting the door's movement, while he guarded the
two leaning rifles of his comrades.

A hinged bar was closed over a metal yoke, awaiting a heavy

padlock. In moments, the brig's door was closed and locked. The Spaniard inside was silent.

The four marines stepped away, seeking the privacy of the hallway beyond the infirmary, away from the injured seamen scattered about. They were followed by their sergeant, whose booming voice demanded an accounting of their temporary disappearance.

Their frightful inquisition was interrupted by the merciful intercession of our surgeon. Radford explained his commandeering of the enlisted marines as they arrived, making their rounds. He had needed them to aid in quelling another disturbed and fitful night by our Spanish prisoner. The sergeant had readily witnessed as much.

I poked my head outside the infirmary, watching silently as our surgeon calmed the non-commissioned officer, still intent on unleashing his wrath.

I spied the crude metal crucifix, still clutched about the clenched fist of one of the marines. Its broken chain swayed about, just beneath the man's tightly clasped fingers.

The marine skillfully pocketed the coveted icon with the dexterity of a London pickpocket. He did so, while looking straight ahead into his sergeant's stern face. His own face was set gauntly, showing no emotion and offering no betrayal of the act of petty larceny.

In the blink of an eye, the religious icon was gone, having a new owner. The marine did not look the religious sort, despite our hellish battle, that would have made believers in the Almighty out of even the coldest heart. Yet, the thief before me, seemed devoid of redemption.

Likely, he would pawn the religious jewelry off in a tavern or small shop back in Portsmouth. He'd likely embellish the trinket with an outlandish story, claiming the chain and crucifix were ripped off the neck of a Spanish boarder, repelled off our own ship at Trafalgar . . . though the tale would be a lie.

But, such was the life and deceit found among the docks and piers of Portsmouth or the hard living ports or harbors of any sea town.

A scandalous lot easily pried the money from the pockets and purses of the naive and innocent. Those ignorant of the sharks on land, both male and female, proved ready morsels to be easily devoured.

I ignored witnessing the theft. I had no desire, after all that had transpired, to be the one to put a tar's or marine's back to the lash. Besides, the Spaniard had brought it upon himself.

Perhaps, without his precious jewelry, he'd finally fall silent. I took a measure of comfort, that whatever potion or concoction the doctor had administered was quickly taking some effect.

The brig was silent, to the relief of all.

The doctor returned to my side, leaving the four marines to their sergeant. We conversed as the sergeant still managed to find some slight or defect, allowing him to dress the four men down.

"If you had a problem, even brought to you by the surgeon, one of you should have returned topside to report it to me!" his firm voice chastised the four.

"It seems our marines can do nothing without the watchful approval of their keepers. I did not mean to get the young lads in trouble," the doctor lamented.

"You've done no such thing. You did as was required to halt the lunatic rantings of that damn Spaniard," I returned, supportively.

The doctor cast a worried glance towards the doorway leading to the marines in the aisle, before raising his head in my direction.

"And, you? How is our young ensign?"

I kept my tongue for a moment. My eyes fell to the deck.

"Surely, you're not having delusions . . . God, you still have doubts about what you thought you saw?" Radford blurted out, shaking his head in disappointment.

"Doctor, I still feel the knot on the back of my head and its shooting pain. And though, reason bids me to see the folly of seeking out truth in delusion . . ."

"But, you still have doubts of what you've seen?" the doctor empathized.

"It was so real," I returned. "And, there's the matter of our Spaniard. If I alone saw phantoms or specters, it would be enough for me to affirm the fault or madness was mine and mine alone. But, our prisoner is plagued by unholy visions . . ."

"So, you think to share his madness or does he share yours?" the doctor shot back.

"What if it is not madness? What if what was seen was real?"

Radford shook his head, before saying, "Look, no one else has seen these specters or the dead, you say have risen to life. You've been unconscious for the better part of two full days and you've faced stress and dread few men witness . . ."

"I do not subscribe to the fatigue or the weariness of battle for my malaise. When I left your infirmary, I was wide awake and of my senses."

"Yes, of course. That is why, you claim to have seen our second officer rise, even though he resided, but several tables away from you, dead as a stone, when you awoke. You saw the captain examine Loydd's body. The wound to his head was fatal. No man rises from an injury like that."

"But, think back further, to the marks afflicting our tars," I beseeched.

"So, its back to rat bites and the bane of rodents," Radford returned with a shrug of his shoulders.

"You, yourself, could not explain the affliction some of our tars and even Ensign Higgins still harbor within their bodies. It was you, who diagnosed the affliction as some infection from the rodents."

"True enough, I did think rodents were the cause of the illness. Rodents, not some ghostly specter or shadow."

"I saw something . . . I did not relate it to you or the captain, when I awoke in the morgue. I saw a woman, but she was not. She was feeding upon the flesh of our fallen about the morgue . . ."

The surgeon raised his hand halting my words.

I lowered my voice as he strode forward.

"Keep your words low, there are others about. It is the captain's desire, that you keep your delusions to yourself, less you create rumor and disruption among the men," the doctor warned, casting his eyes to the men, crowded behind us in the rear of the infirmary.

A few stirred in a restless slumber. But, none spoke or gave any sign, that they had listened to my words.

The surgeon ushered me aside, claiming a storeroom wide enough to stand in, but too small for the injured tars to stretch out in. In a guarded voice, he informed me of the captain's desire to exile me to my quarters, until my good senses and sanity had been returned.

Thus warned, he allowed me to relate the vision, I had seen as if in talking, I might relieve my mind of some burden it still clung to.

"And, you've not seen this woman again, have you?" he asked.

"No. No, I have not," I answered.

"So, what's that tell you? If she was as evil a specter as you claimed, why wouldn't she still be feeding upon our men or you for that matter? If she knows you've seen her and have witnessed her presence, why hasn't she sought you out, if for no other reason, than to silence your tongue? Wouldn't she fear you'd warn others?"

I was silent. Again, the doctor's analytical approach and reason had rendered my testimony nil. It even plagued me with doubts, that what I had seen, was so.

"Ensign, take both the captain's and my own advice. Sleep it away. Take advantage of the rest afforded you in your cabin. There are few aboard, who would not envy your lot. You may do as you wish within your cabin or even nothing at all. If that is what suits you."

"Stare out at the sea through your cabin's windows. Have the cabinboys or a seaman wait on you as if you were the lord of a manor. Enjoy our captain's generosity," Radford intoned.

"But, do not test his temperament or patience. A ship is a strange world unto itself. It is like a town or city afloat. But, it offers none of the luxuries or conveniences of land. In truth, it is more prison, than sea town."

"A man can botch up his life in a town, yet have the reprieve and choice to abandon his lot there and move on to the next town or city to start anew. But, aboard a ship, especially a warship, there is no such escape."

"Earn the ire of the ship's master and there is nowhere to run or flee to. Pity our tars with only a hammock, fourteen inches in width, to call their own and that for only their turn as they sleep in shifts."

"I warn you to keep your mind and words to yourself. The captain can not have the crew stirred up with figments and fantasy from you hallucinations. He has a ship to pilot and the lives of many to account for."

"May I speak to the Spaniard?" I interrupted, trying to find a way to confirm anything I had seen, no matter how small, I pleaded.

"No. I cannot allow it. Besides, it will do you no good. I gave the Spaniard a powerful potion, an opiate of the same type I gave you a small measure of."

"The potion will silence his tongue for hours or days. It will occupy his mind or rather, rob it of any will and those ghastly delusions plaguing it," the doctor mused.

"But, what could you have hoped to learn from a madman?" Radford added.

"He spoke of a "vampiresa," I offered. "It's Spanish for "a woman, who preys on men."

The doctor stared at me. His judgmental eyes made my words seem ridiculous.

"I thought, he was speaking of the whores, that feed on the pockets and purses of men among the sea towns. I assumed, he spoke of some lover or sweetheart . . . troubles with women. At the time, I did not know what to make of his words," I lamented.

"And, you do now?"

"Vampiresa, it would describe exactly what I . . . what I thought I saw. A woman feeding upon . . ."

"The flesh of our dead tars . . . madness," the surgeon hissed, stepping forward in the confines of the small storeroom and grabbing my arm.

"Lewis, you've done well. For your first time in battle, your character and integrity have proved outstanding. I beg you, cease this rambling and do not mar the pride and bravery, you have earned. No good will come from it," Radford's face flushed in the dim light, filtering into the room from the lanterns hung outside the storeroom.

"You've nothing, but comrades and friends aboard our ship. No one, let alone a nocturnal specter is coming for you . . . or your soul, if you still have one after Trafalgar.

The marines outside began to move, following the dismissive order of their sergeant.

"Come," the surgeon ordered me.

We exited the small storeroom and pushed on through the infirmary's entrance. The marines were making for the steps and ladders to the next deck.

"Sergeant!" Radford's low voice called after them in a hushed tone as he tried to capture their attention without disturbing our injured.

"Sir!" the sergeant answered, halting behind his men, already mounting the steps.

"Would you do me the favor of escorting this young officer back to his quarters. It is the captain's desire, that Ensign Lewis remain in his quarters. His confinement is necessary for the proper healing of a head injury."

"No problem, sir, we're headed topside now," the sergeant returned.

"I fear our young ensign might need some assistance as he's on unsteady legs. He's suffered a terrible blow to the head during our battle."

"We'll care for him properly, Doctor," the sergeant ensured.

"You, ahead," the sergeant called to the two marines about to mount the steps and follow their two comrades. "Let the officer ahead of you . . . two men ahead of him, two men behind. That's it, lads. And, see that he doesn't fall," the sergeant instructed, ushering me between the staggered ascending column of four men.

I looked back forlornly at the surgeon, feeling more prisoner, than patient.

He barely returned my gaze. His retreating eyes offered no compassion or understanding. They only affirmed the desire to uphold the wishes of our captain.

His words had been clear enough. Keep my mouth shut and keep the peace. I could appreciate the simple-mindedness of his intent. Rumor and dissatisfaction could easily stir up trouble upon a ship, especially amid the simple and superstitious minds of our sailors.

The cause of a disruption to the ship's well-being and peace could easily find himself suffering the wrath of the captain, forced to endure the instigator of such insolence. A man could easily earn himself the lash or even be chastised and abandoned at a passing seaport or harbor.

And, discipline knew no friends or favoritism. An officer could be as easily punished as the lowly tar. Though, it was unlikely he would be lashed before the ship's compliment, lest the spectacle lower the status of all officers in the eyes of the crew. There were other ways to discipline infractions or insubordination among the officers, though rarely, was such behavior to be found or exhibited.

A far greater penalty was disgrace. Being dismissed from the ranks suffered not only the officer, but followed him home to his family. The stigma and shame were borne, not only by the offender, but by his loved ones.

The captain wanted nothing of the folly, I spoke of. Neither, had the doctor, a brave soul and already outspoken in his own right, shown any desire for the foolishness, I was entrapped in.

I placed a foot, atop the first step up. The thick worn board creaked with my weight. Heavily, I treaded the stairs to the next deck above, following two red-coated marines, while two more followed me.

At that moment, I felt more prisoner, than officer. Worse, I felt myself a prisoner to my own mind and thoughts or madness as our doctor would have deemed it. The reality of my position was clear. It was never clearer as I took my place among my escort.

I had seen . . . but, no one would believe me, except for a Spaniard, similarly afflicted with my madness and now succumbed to a strong potion, that stole him away from any discussion of it, as the silence of slumber claimed him.

The weather deck.

CHAPTER 29

Found

HMS Vanguard
Sailing off the
Spanish Coastline
Day 12-After Midnight

One of the two marines ahead of me opened the louvers, shielding the shrouded candle of his lantern. Below decks, there was no danger of the insignificant light of one candle being seen by another ship or from the out of sight coastline.

The flame of the candle inside flickered as the lantern swayed about, the open air disturbing its unshrouded flame and threatening to extinguish it.

The dim light cast an eerie pallor about the deck being used as our morgue. Its sight reminded me, that I had forgotten to question the doctor of the empty shrouds and tables about the morgue.

I was unaware of any burials or ceremonies honoring our dead. But, space was a prized commodity aboard any warship. It was likely as not, that even the dead felt their rest intruded upon, due to the needs of space aboard the Vanguard. Morbid as the thought was, some of the corpses had most likely been moved to economize on the little space available on our damaged ship.

I was about to place the thought of the empty shrouds to the back of my mind. But, curiosity or instinct beckoned me to look about.

I saw the tables in the semi-darkness of the lantern ahead of me and the two lanterns to my rear. I cursed my own absentmindedness and the failure, to bring the lantern, I had descended with.

But, there was no harm, its flame was extinguished. But oh, how I now would have gladly welcomed its light, held in the length of my outstretched hand.

I peered out, searching the moving glow of the lanterns held by the others. I had not taken a count of the empty tables and shrouds as I'd descended with the sergeant earlier.

I halted, causing those behind me to stop in suit. One raised his lantern higher, a natural response to the delay in our progress.

"What's wrong, Ensign?" the sergeant's voice rasped.

I did not answer, seeing more tables empty, their shrouds of torn sailcloth or discarded hammocks littering the deck or tabletops.

I grabbed the ringed metal loop atop the lantern of the marine behind me, snatching it from his protesting fingers. I pushed away from my escort, holding the lantern high.

I remembered the morgue as I had seen it last, when the sergeant and I had passed through it to the lower deck. There were more empty shrouds about. There was no mistake of it.

"Sergeant!" I demanded his attention.

"Sir!"

"Look about. What do you see amiss?" I questioned.

He remained silent, not answering. Then offered, "Amiss, sir?"

I held the lantern high, reaching the first empty table. There was no doubt in my mind. I had pointedly searched over the tables and covers as we passed through the morgue earlier, fighting my own fears to do so.

Now, there were more empty tables with their sailcolths and hammocks, used as covers, dropped to the deck or left askew atop their flat surfaces.

"Aye, I see it now," the sergeant's memory returned.

He had almost blindly descended into the depths of our ship, his eyes seeing, but not noticing the changes among the morgue, until now.

"There were more bodies about before. What's the meaning of this?" he said, exasperation filling his perplexed voice.

"Look about," I commanded.

"Blimey, for what?" one of the enlisted marines, muttered.

"Do as you're told, Collins!" the sergeant ordered.

"Yes, Sergeant. But, what are we looking for?"

"Show some respect for the dead," the sergeant bellowed to the private.

"It's obvious, that with the bodies set stiff, they must have rolled off their tables. We'll find them and set them right. Isn't that so, sir?" the sergeant questioned me.

I could not speak the truth, lest the sergeant and his gathered men think me mad. "They didn't leave by their own accord," I said, fighting the fearful doubt, rising in my voice.

The lanterns moved about our makeshift morgue as one and then, another of the marines snaked through the rows of tables and chests or crates, set up to lay our dead upon.

They tugged and pulled at one shroud after the other, clearing the table or floor beneath. But, the corpse, that should have been near, was nowhere in sight.

"What's all this about, sir?" one of the privates asked, after several frustrating attempts to seek a body, where none was to be found.

"They were here. I remember," said another, unease gathering noticeably in his voice.

"Aye, there were a few empty tables and spaces among the floor, when we came down. But, not this emptiness surrounding us now!" another exclaimed.

"Besides, the ship's not rolling bad enough and the sea is to calm to send a man, even stiff in death, rolling off a table," the sergeant reasoned as stumped as the others and myself.

Shadows were cast about the beams and planks as the lanterns continued swaying over one table to the next. Their dim glow searched for the missing bodies. A few shrouds were lifted and a gruesome pale stiff corpse was found, resting in eternal slumber beneath the coarse thick cover of a length of sailcloth or a hammock.

The sight of a broken body sent one's stomach churning, raising a foul bile in the back of a dry throat and mouth. The elongated shadows of our upright bodies danced among the dirty white sailcloth and canvas, or the hammocks used as shrouds.

There was silence, except for our own harried footsteps and our anxious breaths.

"Enough!" I ordered.

I had seen enough to confirm there had been a change among the bodies, that had laid in rest amid this deck. But, who had moved the bodies? I refused to acknowledge the truth, harbored in my deepest thoughts. They had moved of their own will and accord.

The lantern's light flickered and dimmed as the marines began to return to the steps and ladders leading to the gun-deck above.

My legs felt weak. But, not from the concussion, the surgeon blamed as the cause of my supposed delusions. Fear welled up in me. I envisioned the ghastly specter of the young maiden in my mind. The image was as keen and clear as I had seen her, two nights before.

It was real. Everything I had seen was real. It had to be. There was no other explanation.

But, fear of being proved wrong, once more bid me to remain

silent. I feared, I had succumbed to some madness, that might yet, prove my undoing. Who was to say, there was not a logical and justified reason for the disappearance of the bodies from our morgue.

"Sergeant, let us continue topside," I suggested.

"Aye, sir," the non-commissioned officer acknowledged my weakly issued instruction.

He was content to stride forward, somehow eager himself to be out of the depressing gloom of our morgue. Despite, his rugged stature and aged brawn, the sergeant placed the lantern in his left hand and took up his rifle in his stronger and favored right hand.

He clenched the weapon tightly, his knuckles showing white even in the dimness surrounding us.

He mounted the steps leading to the next deck above. One, then another creaked noisily as they accepted the weight of his large form. He was followed by two privates, eager to leave the uneasy haunt of the morgue behind them.

I followed quickly enough, having no desire to remain within the bowels of the ship, where I had come so close to the hated specter, that reveled in the death of our men.

I held the lantern, I had taken from the marine private, who I now found close beside me. His own flintlock rifle was held up across his chest in tight clasping hands as if ready to block away any attacker, that might appear on the steps or deck above us.

The fourth enlisted marine followed closely behind. Without the benefit of lantern and candle, his form was cloaked in the trailing darkness behind us and the sullenness of the morgue.

I saw the glowing orb of the sergeant's lantern disappear on the deck above, blocked out by its heavy planks and his own body. His footsteps moved forward slowly.

He exercised a caution not befitting his rank, falling into the unnatural superstition and lore, I had thought his bulking form and rough demeanor would have long ago abandoned. Yet, in the darkness and quiet of the Vanguard, I could not blame him for his ill ease.

It mirrored my own.

I stepped onto the lower gun-deck.

The marine sergeant had boldly strode several lengths ahead. He was among the strung hammocks and our sleeping tars. All was calm and nothing was amiss as our sailors rested in slumber.

The sergeant awkwardly sought to manipulate lantern and rifle, moving both to one hand. His motions showed, that among the living, he had fallen at ease. His lowered head shook as he silently admonished himself for succumbing to the childish and foolhardy fears, arising from the darkness of the morgue and old superstitions, he still harbored.

The two marines, that had followed him, had halted. They shared the warm glow of the lantern, one of them possessed, while they awaited my arrival on the next deck.

I strolled forward, somehow similarly relieved at being among the living, once again. I passed by the two marines.

The sergeant froze several paces ahead of me. I swear his giant form halted in fear. He was frozen to inaction by the sight ahead of us.

I halted, just short of his large form. The sight, he saw was framed ahead of me, over the right shoulder of his red-coated uniform with its wide white sash.

"God!" is all I heard him exclaim, the sound barely a whisper above his expelled breath.

I saw it. We all witnessed it.

A tar was bent over one of the crews' hammocks. Of itself, the sight would not have proved alarming, save for the nature of the tar.

The sailor bore the same horrid pallor of the sailors resting in the morgue. Worse, his form was a mangled representation of its former self.

I was not alone in what I witnessed. Surely, the tar hovering over the slumbering seaman in the hammock was dead. He could not be otherwise.

His uniform was shredded, likely man and uniform had been struck by the blast of a canister round. Such rounds were a thin tin can filled with tiny round balls, turning our ship's giant cannons and those of the enemy's into giant blunderbusses, that spewed a deadly and expanding hail of the small projectiles about in a widening pattern of death and destruction.

Canister rounds were favored for firing upon the open upper decks of an opposing warship. They easily mowed down the unprotected officers and gun crews of the exposed upper gundecks. With no protection topside, except the rail, their deadly fire was devastating.

The tar we observed and his disfigured flesh, or what was left of it, was bleached white. It had no color or hue to it. His blouse was riddled and his flesh pocked or torn away.

His wounds were evidence of the violent ripping blast and speeding balls, he had the unfortunate fate to have caught about his right side.

It was a wonder, that the tar or the corpse, before our eyes, could stand at all.

I heard the sergeant's mouth exhale, the last disbelieving breath of his lungs.

The marines closed ranks behind me. Our group bunched up amongst itself. All stared in disbelief.

Ahead, the pale tar seemed ignorant of our presence, despite the dim glow of our lanterns. He was single-minded in his efforts. Seemingly detached from all around him, his mouth opened and his parted lips caressed an exposed limb, an arm of the sailor resting in the hammock.

We watched as one. The tar's foul lips parted and his teeth searched out flesh. His victim did not stir, somehow immune or indifferent to the tearing bite inflicted upon him.

Behind me, one of the marines took a horrified step to the rear. In fear and dread, his balance escaped him as the ship rolled, ever so slightly. It was enough.

He dropped in an awkward fall. His rifle casting about and striking the floor as he tried to use the weapon as a crutch to break his fall. He slammed into the hard surface of the splintered and worn deck planks, a sliver of wood pierced the open palm of his right hand.

The din was enough.

The creature, that had been one of our tars, halted. Its mouth lifted, still open from feeding upon the seaman, who would be its feast. The tar's lips were caked with blood, that now trickled from the corners of its mouth. The blood stained the tar's uniform and deck alike.

As if to affirm his disbelief, the sergeant raised his lantern high, casting its meager light several lengths forward.

The tar ahead squinted his eyes. But, not quickly enough to hide his dark black empty orbs. They were the same evil eyes, I had witnessed of the others, two nights before.

I was not alone in witnessing the vile act of feeding upon the flesh and blood of the living. This time, others saw as I did. I was not mad!

The gruesome tar's parted lips hissed and his tongue moved as if he was trying to form words to speak. But, a foul madness or evil claimed his body and spirit. No words came forth.

There was only the guttural emanation of a vile beast or animal. The sounds made no sense. They had no language about them. At least, not to our ears.

And, then our eyes saw what the darkness of the sleeping deck hid from us. The foul tar ahead was not the only one of his kind about the deck.

In the dim semi-darkness lit by our few lanterns, slowly one, then another of the similarly disfigured and grotesquely wounded tars appeared.

I turned to the right, stretching out my extended arm and the lantern it held. Three nearby hammocks were coated in blood, several arms dangled lifelessly over their sides, attesting to the nocturnal visitation, that had robbed their seamen of life.

And, near those hammocks lingered other ghouls.

Like the sergeant ahead of me, my feet were wed to the deck. I could not move. Awe and amazement, disbelief and madness, all flooded my mind. Madness and insanity had come to me again.

The marine, that had fallen, struggled to pick himself up off the deck. But, the sight of our troubling specters seemed too much for our haphazard companion, strewn about the deck.

He was the furthest to our rear, nearest the hatchway to the morgue. Mirroring our own inaction. He froze, half-sitting atop the deck's planks as he grasped his rifle by its forestock. Its barrel pointed to the next deck above.

The creatures, who had been men, sailors among our crew, slowly began walking forward. Their heads turned towards us, but I wondered if their dark black eyes actually saw.

Their movements were stiff and unnatural as if fighting the rigidity of their limbs, claimed by death. I heard an ungodly snap and crack of a limb beset with rigor mortis. It echoed hollowly about the deck as the ghastly apparitions, that had once been our crewmates, neared.

It was enough for our sergeant ahead. He placed his lantern on the deck and dropped his free hand to his thick black leather belt, withdrawing his bayonet, a vicious spike, from it sheath.

He affixed it to the barrel of his rifle and barked, "fix your bayonets!" to the three marines, standing about in dumbfounded silence and their awkward footed comrade on the floor.

Two of the marines, those closest to us, obeyed immediately, shrugging off the damning stupor of disbelief and awe.

A third, fumbled about in the darkness, searching awkwardly for his bayonet. It escaped the grasp of his trembling fingers.

Behind him, his companion on the deck rose to his feet, leaning on his rifle with the effort.

But, no sooner had he stood, than the deck resounded with the dull thud of his collapse. I turned around to find his legs entrapped in the clawing hands of two foul fiends, mirroring those moving upon us.

One of the hands was devoid of flesh. Its wounded limb and bony digits sunk into the marine's uniform and flesh. He cried out in alarm, his companion reeling and raising his own rifle, preparing to strike at those claiming his comrade.

The marine's brass buttplate lashed out in a panicked swing.

JOHN CONRAD

It missed, smashing into the planks of the deck and nearly sending the man, delivering the blow, to the floor.

He retreated a step, drawing back, before delivering a second blow. Unable to fix his bayonet in the darkness out of fear or confusion, he sought to club the other's attackers.

His buttplate struck the head of one of the pale specters, breaking bone and splitting the side of the creature's skull open. But, his effort gained him little.

Neither ghoul released their hold upon the marine in their grasp. Instead, the struck monster merely raised his head and lifted his eyes, seeking out the eyes of his attacker. When their eyes met, our marine stood mesmerized. Halting the defense of his comrade.

"Don't look into their eyes!" I warned, remembering the black eyes of the young maiden, that swallowed my will and left me defenseless in her presence.

It was too late. The marine had succumbed, falling into an inactive stupor. The marine at his feet was dragged over the edge of the hatchway with a swiftness, that defied our eyes and belief. He was gone, pulled into the darkness of the morgue below. His haunting scream trailed away as we heard his body pummeled and beaten.

Ahead, the sergeant thrust his rifle's barrel and spike forward in a predetermined and practiced step.

His spike plunged into the riddled chest of the ghastly tar, that had fallen the fatal victim of a canister round. The bayonet made a sloshing entry, followed by the stench of the corpse's trapped bodily gases, accumulated in death and now released in our midst.

The sergeant withdrew the pointed weapon. His rifle like those of the other marines was unloaded, lest the sea and moisture dampen their powder. There would have been plenty of time to load the weapons topside, upon sighting the masts or hull of an approaching ship.

But, here among the sudden onslaught of these creatures, despite their animated movements, there was no time to load the long barreled weapons.

He thrust the rifle forward again, stepping into the thrust and jabbing both arms forward.

Again, the spike found its mark expertly. Again, the sergeant withdrew the bayonet, leaving behind a gaping wound as he pushed downward with the release of the spike and tore a horrid gash.

But, still the creature came forward.

"Damn, damn all!" the sergeant spat out in disbelief, taking a step backward and finding a new footing.

This time, he thrust for the head. The spike stabbed just beneath the lower jaw and found the tar's neck.

The sergeant twisted the forestock of his rifle about in his large hands, drilling the spike home and gashing it from side to side. He twisted it right and left, until the tissues and muscle of the neck released the skull above.

The creature's head dropped to the floor. It's mouth opened and closed agape, the likes of a beheaded fish being butchered in the marketplace. The creature's eyelids remained open, its black orbs reflecting the light of the lantern on the floor.

I moved forward and claimed the lantern, freeing our sergeant's hands to defend us. Several more ghouls approached in slow stiff steps. There was the ungodly snap and creak of their stiff joints fighting their own movements. The sound was repulsive and sickly. It made their presence all the more unbelievable and ghastly.

A few seemed to have grown accustomed to their new movements. Though retarded, in the beginning, by their stiff motions, they seemed to leap or plunge ahead, finding a bizarre new strength in their former limbs.

The marine sergeant stepped backwards, making his way to the steps and ladders leading to the next deck above. Two of our three remaining privates claimed a perch upon the ladders leading upward, while the third hastily loaded his rifle.

His weapon was no sooner loaded, when another foul creature appeared at the hatchway leading up from the temporary infirmary's deck. An arm swung out, stiff and animated. Its movements were slower and inhuman. It jerked about in an unnatural spasm, unlike when the arm's owner could be called alive.

Clawing fingers searched the air in a powerful sweeping arc, trying to claim the marine's leg or foot.

The marine lowered his rifle, its length nearly preventing him from tucking its stock under his shoulder as its barrel and fixed bayonet nearly touched the floor.

The trigger pulled.

The cocked flintlock resounded metallically among the closing footfalls of our attackers and our panicked breaths. The barrel remained silent. The marine in his fear, had forgotten to place the small piece of flint beside the powder hole of the rifle's striker.

Plugged with powder and ball, the rifle pointed impotently at his attacker. Only the marine's swift and sudden movement, prevented the ghoul from capturing his left leg.

The private stepped backwards, clearing the reach of the phantom, whose dull mind and dark blank eyes had finally realized, he had missed his mark.

As the creature retraced the arc of its arm and its other hand snaked out over the edge of the hatchway, that lead to the morgue, our marine struck.

He abandoned searching out the small pieces of flint, residing in the stiff black leather rectangular box, attached to his uniform's belt. Instead he raised the rifle and brought its bayonet down sharply, plunging the spike into the presented head of his attacker.

The marine's two mates scurried up the ladder, abandoning his plight.

I reached the private's side and found the creature withering about the bayonet. The deadly spike was jammed diagonally through the top of the fiend's head on the left side and exited through the bottom of its right jaw, before reentering the body below at the right collarbone.

The creature squirmed, impaled on the long murderous spike. Despite, the grotesqueness and fatality of the wound, it still lived. Its skull's contents oozed forth from its broken bone. But, it showed no pain, merely the anger and fret of being locked in place, halted in its attack.

Its gyrating movements were self-defeating, ripping and tearing itself asunder as it struggled to free itself. Yet, it continued and so violently, that it threatened to rip away the rifle from our struggling marine's grasp.

I stepped up to the opening and the fiend below. With a quick stomp of my left foot, I kicked down. I delivered a blow to the top of the entrapped fiend's head. Skull and body fell free of the private's spike, dropping to the bottom of the ladder.

I motioned the young marine to move up the next set of ladders, while the sergeant delivered a final thrust to the closest of his own attacker's. His bayonet plunged into the ghoul's chest with such force, that it sent it backwards into its approaching companion.

A swift forceful kick freed the ghoul of his bayonet's sharp spike and sent both creatures dropping to the floor. They struggled awkwardly, the use of their limbs evading or escaping them.

Our sergeant made for the ladders, following the start of my own ascent.

My climb was awkward, my left hand bearing both ungainly lanterns in its single grasp. I feared the dark. I dare not let a light behind. But, I feared what the dim light of the lanterns' candles would reveal next. I climbed.

Behind us, the first of the two displaced ghouls rose from the deck. To their rear, more of their demonic companions had gathered, seeking to search us out.

My hands clung onto the rungs of the ladder as my weary and unsure feet pushed upward.

I heard the labored breaths of the marine privates up above, the last of their feet leaving the ladder and seeking out the firm support of the middle gun-deck.

"God, they're here to! Damn, what are they . . . what's happening!" cried out an unseen voice.

"Load your rifles! Damn, you!" the sergeant's baritone voice bellowed as his hands reached the rung of the ladder, my right foot rested on.

"Move it, sir!. Move!" he blared beneath me.

Shaken by his outburst and the spurred by the panic intertwined in his voice, my feet and hands moved. My left hand was burdened by the two lanterns, held by their wobbling metal rings.

I climbed through the hatchway, placing the lanterns on the deck above as I used my arms to quickly extricate myself from the large opening. I saw the white trousers and leggings of our marines. They were grouped in some semblance of a line, standing abreast of each other. Their small line was not even a quarter of the width of our great ship's beam.

They were in various stages of loading their weapons in the dim glow of a single lantern, now resting upon the floor in front of them.

Ahead, a host of creatures, who had been our tars and comrades, moved on them. These moved quicker, than the fiends we had encountered below. They moved with the familiarity and confidence of their rigid bones and muscles, having likely awakened from their eternal slumber well ahead of those below.

In the darkness, to the right of the marines, I caught sight of a blackness, a dark shadow. It thrust itself out, diving head first for the floor. But, in its stiffness, the lunge took on the likeness of a dead fall.

It was enough. The fiend's outstretched arms and hands found its mark. The lantern before the marines was sent flying and in the act, its candle knocked from within it and sent tumbling to the floor. The quick movement was enough to extinguish the candle's tiny flame.

The deck before us fell black.

There was a spark and flash from one of the marines' rifles as the seafaring soldier fired blindly ahead. I heard the sickening thud of an almost point blank strike. But, there was no following sound of a body falling to the floor.

I heard only footsteps.

I rose to my feet, trying to raise one of my own lanterns as quickly as possible. I saw only the marines' feet and their white trousers and leggings, until the lantern rose.

The ghouls were upon them. They bore the same black orbs, I had witnessed before. Their parted mouths were filled with the pointed teeth, I had seen in the foul mouth of the maiden. The creatures were bestial and hungry. They were men turned into animals. No, they were worse, than beasts.

Beasts fed to survive, to live. The creatures before us seemed to relish inflicting pain more, than feasting upon us.

A second shot rang out. Smoke rose to the planking of the deck above, that formed our ceiling.

A third marine had no time to finish loading his rifle. I watched, frozen in fear, as a ghoul descended upon him. Its hands grasped the man's weapon.

Both struggled, pulling on the weapon and trying to wrest it free of the other or pushing it into the other combatant, using its bulk as a weapon to displace the other's footing.

The contest was mismatched and the marine fell backwards under the dead weight of a creature, whose bulk and body, even in death, were larger and greater, than his own.

Another marine clubbed his rifle into the center of the creature's back. The blow had no result, except to evoke a puzzled look about the ghoul's blank face.

But the creature's attack continued. He pinned the marine beneath him and his hellish mouth opened, exposing a vile breath and fangs a face-length away from the beleaguered marine.

The sergeant rushed past me.

Again, his spike dove towards the deck as he ran. The pointed bayonet barely missed his own man's face, before lunging into the neck of the fiend, pinning one of his men.

The sergeant's bulk and run spun the fiend backwards, collapsing him on his back, before the non-commissioned officer placed a foot atop the fiend's chest and withdrew his spike.

But, before he could take a step backward, more of the hated creatures appeared before him.

"God!" the sergeant's voice rose in disbelief. His yell was part plea and part blasphemy as he took the Lord's name in vain.

He had little time to say anything else. Two more ghouls pushed towards him.

With no room to deliver another thrust of his bayonet, he jerked the butt of his rifled outward, delivering a blow into the hip of the nearest creature. The brass buttplate shattered bone and the fiend collapsed to the floor.

Before, the second creature could move against him, the sergeant reversed the sweeping arc of his rifle, pulling its butt in and casting out its barrel and bayonet in a wide wild and indiscriminate arc.

As he knew it would, the honed edges of the spike found the second creature's face, slashing at the black orbs, hidden in the sunken hollows of its brow.

The creature emitted an unholy scream. Its stiff hands and digits rose to its lacerated eyes. A sickly gel rolled down upon its cheeks and sheltering hands. It dropped to its knees, humbled by the savage butchery of our sergeant's rifle and spike.

"Topside! Everyone topside!" the sergeant barked.

I stood beside the hatchway. An officer, I impotently had no commands to give. I could only flee to the upper gun-deck as instinct and the marine sergeant beckoned.

I left one lantern upon the deck, claiming the other and the nearest rungs of the ladder beside the steps leading upward. I nearly choked as fear took my breath away.

I gulped and swallowed, trying to fill my lungs and push away the fear claiming me. I heard the feet of our marines reach the edge of the deck several rungs behind me.

A shot rang out. Our sergeant, a skilled and professional marksman, managed to load his weapon in short order and fire a departing shot, before claiming the crowded ladder.

I looked up to find faces atop the hatchway, staring down at me.

I halted to the consternation and curses of the marines behind me. I did not know whether the faces ahead were friend or fiend. Silhouetted in the darkness, framed by stars and moonlight, I did not know if death or allies awaited me.

I climbed.

"That's it, keep coming, sir!" a boatswain encouraged, claiming the underside of my right arm and pulling me upwards.

I cleared the hatchway, followed by the first of the marines. He scurried over the lip of the open hatch and rolled atop the deck. His movements were frantic and panicked. He rose and fumbled for a new powder cartridge and ball.

Trembling fingers freed the ramrod along the underside of his rifle's barrel as his companions cleared the opening and mimicked his own movements, seeking to arm themselves.

I spied a cutlass in the boatswain's right hand. Along the deck, slightly to our rear, were the severed heads of two corpses, corpses mirroring those, that had died and risen.

Our marine sergeant shoved his way through the open hatch. He released his grip upon his rifle, dropping it atop the deck as his hands sought out the heavy wooden grate cover to block the exit's opening.

One of the privates rushed beside the sergeant and they lifted the hinged cover, before dropping it. The heavy wooden and iron grate smashed down upon the heads and hands of the living corpses, seeking to grasp a handhold on the upper gun-deck.

Their shadowy forms disappeared, propelled in a downward fall by the heavy cover colliding with them. They dropped below.

Our eyes searched about the upper deck, looking rearward to the weather deck and the sheltered captain's quarters, sequestered further to the rear in the shelter of our high stern.

Several more corpses were littered about. Here and there, a remnant of our marine contingent, that had been mercifully posted topside, stood among the remains.

A rifle and its fixed bayonet pointed down at one of the offending corpses. Its spike cautiously probed the pale rotting flesh, that had been dead for days, but still had managed to walk in life, once more.

"You've seen them too," I blurted, no longer afraid to speak the truth, that I had hidden, believing myself succumbing to some madness. "The captain, how is the captain?"

"I've no word. He refuses to answer from his cabin," the boatswain, in charge of the helmsmen, returned. "I sent a runner, when we first saw one of these . . . phantoms," the boatswain fell into a mixed silence of awe and disbelief.

"We've got to check on the captain's safety," I blurted out to anyone, that would hear.

Ahead of me, the marine sergeant jammed the hatch locked. But, there were others. Our greatest threat lay in the large open hold, devoid of covers beneath the launch, small boats, and captain's barge.

My eyes spied the sergeant, sharing my same thought. As one, we cast our heads in its direction, only to find the creatures, that had once been our tars and mates emerging from its steps and ladders. Still, others appeared in the empty center of the hold, devoid of ladder or steps, they seemed to scale or rise in the air among the cavernous spaces of the hold, bounding up from the deck below.

Their numbers grew as they claimed the hold, encircling it and the lashed down small boats, that offered us an escape from our mother ship and the nightmare engulfing it. They held their place, neither coming forward or engaging the few marines, further forward near the bow.

Quietly, the few marines forward along with the tars assigned to the our topside watch, weaved about the deck, cautiously clearing the intruders. They made for us and safety, taking as wide a path about the ghouls as the deck would afford them.

I heard the hated hissing and guttural growls of beasts without mind or reason as the creatures threatened to attack, but stood their ground. As if commanded by some unseen force, more joined them and encircled our boats, at least those lashed to the upper deck.

There were still two boats hanging from the davits about the stern. Those two cutters would offer more, than enough room to hold our meager compliment of survivors topside, if we could reach and launch them.

In dread and shame, my thoughts filled with the images of our surgeon and the tars still below decks. The infirmary and its residents were entombed in a living hell as these creatures blocked any hope of escape from the bowels of our ship, beneath the Vanguard's waterline.

"To the stern!" I ordered, disbelieving the words parting from my mouth.

The sergeant turned around and faced me, halting at my attempt to take over the command, he had instinctively assumed, delivering us from the hell inside our lower decks.

His face showed the scorn, he rightfully held for my exerting my rightful command, after it was he, who saved us from peril. Yet, it showed he had no other answers, save for his brute strength and stubbornness not to relent or surrender to our unholy foe.

Almost in resignation, he silently assumed his place within our disorganized ranks.

"You men!" his voice bellowed, "join on me . . . form a line!"

His voice broke the paralyzed stupor of those standing about in horror. Drill and training replaced loathing and awe. As one, though from different points about the deck, they moved abreast of the sergeant, adding their forms to his and forming a line. It ran nearly two rows deep and stretched the width of the ship's beam.

Yet, as formidable as their human wall of thrust forward spikes appeared, they seemed almost defenseless against the horde of specters, that continued to gather about the deck.

The hatchway, our sergeant had jammed shut, was beset by bare flesh and bones, that pounded upon it.

Clenched fists missed or grazed the wood and iron reinforced bars, poking through their grids. Pale rotting flesh tore from the limbs and hands, assaulting the cover.

It shuddered as the last measure of the cover's hardwood frame and grid surrendered to the unholy onslaught. The wood shattered and iron bent as the hatch's cover yielded to the creatures forcing it skyward.

Slowly, one, then another of the ghouls emerged. Some rose stiffly upon the ladder, leading upward. Still, others seemed to rise, lifted by the supernatural power of some unholy hand, their arms and legs hanging motionless from their bodies.

All stared upon us with the blackness of their empty eyes.

"Lash the wheel on our course!" I bellowed, realizing we could not stay out in the open against such numbers forming to combat us.

I looked around, seeking to claim some sense of who was still about the ship. I sought to find what forms among us were still men, still of the living. The helmsmen hurriedly looped and tied the ropes about the wheel, locking us on our westerly course.

Our bowsprint pointed out towards the Atlantic, well south of Portugal and the starboard turn, we'd yet to make to place us on course for England and Portsmouth Harbor. All, now seemed impossibly far away.

I looked skyward as if to check our sails and the winds. I found only darkness and the black moving clouds, that threatened to block out the light of the moon and stars above.

In shock, I saw several lookouts, still manning their posts above.

"Lookouts to the deck!" I ordered.

I watched as the first of them made for the nearest ratling. His movements were slow, pained by fear. But, his fear was not of the heights, he routinely scaled to and called home.

His actions, normally agile and nimble, had escaped him. His hands grasped each rope rung slowly and tightly. He was more fearful of the creatures beneath him, than the heights, he must descend from.

His eyes were fixed on our deck, watching our thin line form to confront the gathering horde of hell's children. He likely saw himself surrendering the safety of his loft, only to join our own imperiled fate.

And, then it happened.

As if they were birds or winged demons, several of the ghastly tars, who had encircled our boats rose. They leapt in bounds greater than, the swiftest deer or other graceful and fleet-footed animal.

They beset the ratlings, moving with a swiftness, that saw them nearly float along their rising lengths. In moments, they were upon the lookout, hesitating in his descent of the fore mast.

They tore into the lookout's flesh with tooth and claw. In his screams, he released his grip upon the ratlings. He began to fall, in danger of plunging outward with the gentle roll of our ship and being lost in the darkness of the sea.

But, just before he escaped the horror of his attackers for the peril of being set adrift, a strong stiff hand grasped him. He was yanked back into the ghouls straddling the lines and ratlings of the mast, that had been his perch.

His lungs exhaled in agony, expelling a final cry, before succumbing to death.

I looked to the remaining lookout still perched along the main mast.

In horror, he stood frozen as more of the demons, who had once been our crew, scaled the ratlings without effort. One of the demonic creatures clasped his arms and legs about the thickness of the main mast.

In unbelievable haste, he scaled the layered mast, releasing his partial encirclement around it and nimbly running up its length with only his fingertips and the toes of his shoes, searching out the slight handholds and footholds, offered by the mast's encircling iron bands.

The ghoul raced ahead of those about the ratlings.

In horror, I watched as our lookout appeared to chose the death of a fall over that, which had befallen his companion.

But, in the last seconds of his fall the tar claimed the rope, he had lurched for in the air. His hands wrapped hold around it. His legs snaked and wrapped about its coarse cord.

While still plummeting down its length, he tightened his grip with encircling hands and legs, beginning to break his plunge, just feet above the deck. He released his hold, falling the last few feet.

He landed hard, his right foot striking the deck first, before folding painfully beneath him. He collapsed to the deck, his left leg unable to find a footing and keep him upright.

He rose and began limping towards our line, circling the ghouls guarding our boats. He was almost to us, when those creatures still aloft descended. Descended, the word had no meaning to describe their plunge or what befell our lookout.

One, two, three, and more of the ghouls dropped from above. They plunged downward without any regard to their own bodies. One slammed the deck so hard, I heard its limbs shatter and break.

I did not expect to see it or its ghastly cohorts rise. I knew more of the body, since my studies and tutoring by the doctor. The bones were broken.

I had heard them break. I had seen their flesh and limbs go crooked at unnatural angles, the sight was extreme enough to make anyone witnessing it sicken. Yet, the fiends rose off the deck.

Bones snapping and grinding, they straightened their limbs and set about walking stiffly again without concern. There was no halting their progress towards our limping lookout, whose eyes, that had reflected relief from his narrow and daring escape, now filled with alarm and fright.

He had not escaped. He had merely prolonged his capture and death.

Our marines yelled at him to rush towards our line. A few daring and brave souls among them broke their formation's width and edged forward, willingly extending our shield and seeking to shorten his path.

It was not to be.

In a single leap, one of the specters was upon the lookout. The ghoul jumped in a cat-like lurch, its creaking bones announcing its flight across the deck. Its flailing arms and hands were like the claws of a demented beast.

As a lion leaps upon its prey, the creature claimed the back of our lookout, dragging him down to the deck. Other members of this gruesome pride joined in.

An arm was ripped from the lookout's socket and held up to the night sky in grim celebration as a prize. The victory was made sweeter to the demons feasting upon the still living lookout by his anguished scream for pity.

There was none to be found among the vile and heartless fiends.

It was too much.

"Sergeant, fire into them!" I ordered. There was no point in trying to save our fallen comrade. Our bullets would only offer him the relief of a quick death, if they missed their intended marks.

"First line, take aim!" the marine sergeant's baritone voice boomed.

He was relieved to have something to do, instead of just witnessing the unholy carnage.

"First line, volley fire, commence!" he bellowed.

The retort of our rifles broke the damning conspiratorial silence of the night, wrapping itself about us. The men, in our forward ranks were covered in the haze of the smoke from the barrels of their expended rifles.

"Second line forward!" the sergeant barked.

As one, the red-coated marines to the rear of the first line moved forward, brushing past those, who had fired and were now feverishly attempting to reload their weapons.

"Second line, claim your targets!" the non-commissioned officer directed.

He looked about, seeing the new line was sparse by eight men, compared to those, that had retired to reload.

"Volley fire, now!" he blurted, seeing some of the specters release the lookout and join others, that advanced on the new threat, we presented them.

All was horror.

Our sharpshooters were accurate enough. Their rounds struck

the chests or heads of their intended targets. Had these been any normal men, it would have been enough. Their wounds would have been judged fatal, offering no chance to mend or recover.

And true enough, their targets dropped. They fell to the deck.

But, they did not stay there.

Slowly, as if labored by some great weight or chain about them, one, then another rose. The sight was unexplainable. It was beyond reason or sense. But, the hated specters rose.

"Retire to the stern! To the safety of the weather deck!" I shouted.

Our marine sergeant amended my order, coaxing and cursing his lads into an orderly withdrawal. As one, they moved towards the stern, walking backwards with their rifles and the spikes of their bayonets thrust forward ahead of them, presenting a wall of pointed steel.

"God, what are they?" a marine's voice haltingly questioned our sergeant as fear swelled up in his throat and his feet treaded rearward.

"Vampires," I heard myself call out, before our sergeant had a chance to reply.

I could not believe, I had voiced the madness, proclaimed by the Spaniard, aloud. But, that is what he had called them, more specifically "vampiresa," a female vampire.

It had to be. The ungodly spirit, cloaked in the form of a young woman, a delicate, yet foul maiden dressed in a virginal white gown was the cause of this. My fear of being claimed mad had abandoned me. The truth stood before our eyes.

"How do we kill them?" the young marine returned.

"You shoot them or stick them with your spike!" bellowed the sergeant. "Now keep your eyes forward and your mouth shut. "Do as I tell you!"

It was madness.

I turned and moved to the starboard side of the stern. I peered over its side.

I was relieved to find the comforting sight of a cutter, dangling from its davits and tethered to our ship's side by several lines, keeping it from being torn free. The boat offered escape and salvation from this nightmare, if we could free it and ourselves of the Vanguard and the ghoulish horde overwhelming it.

It had its own oars and sail along with provisions and barrels of fresh water for the contingency, that we might have to utilize its small haven.

But, elation soon escaped me as I spied the dark shadows of several forms, clinging to the side of our towering vertical hull. Unnatural tars moved about, its steep planking with the agility and certainty of flies or spiders.

They released their grasp from the hull and flung themselves towards the small boat, that would be our salvation. Their haunting faces and grizzly wounds, suffered before death, confronted my eyes as they clung to the swaying side of the boat to starboard.

Slowly, they raised themselves into it. Their daring climb was followed by others, scaling along the side of our hull. They emerged from the gunports about the decks below and through the hatchway, used to service our ship at dock, running along the middle gun-deck.

"Sergeant, send me a group of men!" I ordered, detouring to the weather deck and claiming a cutlass from about an arms rack.

I had no sooner finished arming myself, when five marines joined me. I had to do nothing, except extend the blade of the cutlass outward towards the boat, pointing out the newest threat.

One marine hefted his rifle to his shoulder and tucked it in tightly. Its long barrel swayed about, before he fired.

The blast of his muzzle lit the night. His bullet struck a fiend, standing upright in the center of the boat. The force of the round kicked the hellish tar backwards, knocking him off balance and dropping him out of the boat.

There was a moment of silence, followed by the rewarding splash of his body hitting the sea, adrift and free of our ship.

The irony fell upon me, that the only way to rid ourselves of these hellish creatures was to drive them overboard. We would let the sea swallow them up as it had claimed the rats that had plagued the Vanguard.

Another shot rang out. Smoke from another nearby barrel wafted over the stern. A second specter dropped away, but almost barely.

Its groping hand struggled to claim a perch along the rim of the boat, he was crawling onto before the bullet struck. But, the rigid bones of his hands lost their grip. The force of the bullet's impact cast him adrift on the dark waters, he fell to below.

By now, others had joined those, who had originally claimed the boat, a small cutter. There were too many for the five marines joining me to repel. There were too many for the rest of the marines and their sergeant. We were being overwhelmed.

A ghoul flung himself over the boat's side, flying through the air for our rail. A quick thinking, but frightened marine held his ground. Thrusting his fired rifle outward, he impaled the flying demon upon the spike of his bayonet.

The demon's hands grasped the front of the barrel in a death-lock grip. His falling weight pulled the rifle downward with him, nearly taking our marine along on his frightful plunge.

The marine released his grip, after nearly being pulled over the edge of the rail. Rifle and fiend disappeared into the darkness of sea, their entry masked by the continued horde of ghouls, appearing along the side of the hull and climbing to the boat.

"Back! Back to the weather deck," I ordered.

The marines fired one last shot or thrust out at the boat beside us with their bayonets. I moved to the rearmost davit and swung my cutlass's short blade with all the might I could muster.

The honed blade sliced at the thick cord, holding the boat above the sea. It cut nearly halfway through the rope's thickness.

I swung again. The blade cut the rope's weaved cord, but still did not sever it cleanly. I struck thrice.

The cord parted. Its length ran through the davit, releasing the stern of the boat. It dangled haphazardly, dropping down towards the sea, but snagged along its other securing lines.

They twisted the upright craft askew, dumping the creatures harbored inside into the sea, except for one or two, that managed to cling to its seats or rim.

I moved to the next davit, but abandoned any attempt to cut its rope.

Beneath me, the creatures scaled the hull vertically, seeking the top of the rail, I leaned against. I pushed away and ran to the port side of the ship.

I reached the port side of the stern. There, I found more of the creatures mirroring the attack on the starboard boat.

They'd already claimed the port boat, our third cutter. I hoped to dump them all into the sea, mirroring my action to starboard.

I raised the cutlass above my shoulder and drove it in a fierce downward arc. The blade found the thick cord of the forward davit. Dulled by cutting the other rope and slicing into the wood of the rail, it cleaved only a third or less of the thick cord.

I freed the blade and tried again.

But, before I could swing the cutlass, a creature lurched out. He lunged into the night sky, leaping from the tethered boat suspended to port. He nearly cleared the rail, his open right hand stretched out, trying to grasp the blade in my hand.

I stepped aside, changing the sweep of the cutlass's arc and sliced away the threatening limb. The fiend's right arm dropped away into the darkness.

But still, the ghoul continued after me. His left hand caught the rail, only long enough to claim a footing for his feet. Then, he thrust out at me.

His unstoppable gait forced me backwards with such force, I tumbled to the deck. I rolled onto my back and stared up in fear, that any moment, the demon would be upon me.

In that momentary glimpse, I saw him jump off the rail with the forceful movement of a powerful beast's hindquarters.

My breath left me. There was no escape.

I heard the sharp crack of a rifle. The fiend was halted in midair, dropping aside towards the stern with the impact of the conical bullet, that had struck him nearly point blank.

I craned my head about and found our marine sergeant,

standing nearby. He proved to be my stalwart guardian. He did not hesitate.

He rushed forward, driving the spike of his bayonet hard into the corpse. The thrust was so forceful, that it stuck into the hard wood of our deck, driving clear through the demon's body. With a foot atop the corpse's chest, the sergeant withdrew the spike. The act was accompanied to a sickening slosh.

Showing no mercy, he thrust it into the specter's neck and ripped it about in a foul ballet of violence, separating the head from its owner. He withdrew the spike again, plucking the head with its point through a damning eye socket, before thrusting the skull and its gaping jaws over the rail.

As I stood up, our sergeant claimed my shoulder and ushered me to the rest of our survivors, sheltering in the semi-open protection of the weather deck.

I was nearly frozen in fear, escaping death or a worse fate by the slimmest of threads and the good graces and diligence of our marine sergeant.

"Hurry about you, sir! We've no time to view our efforts," he added matter-of-factly.

We moved.

Captain's barge, pinnace, launch, & cutter lashed topside.

CHAPTER 30

Boats

HMS Vanguard
Sailing off the
Spanish Coastline
Day 12-Early Morning

Time escaped us.

Our breaths were labored, breathing in the cold early morning chill, that burned our throats and lungs. The topside crew, that had survived the initial onslaught of these monstrous creatures, huddled in fear and silence under the protective shelter of the weather deck.

With the wheel lashed, we moved as far back into the deck's recesses as we could. The weather deck's sides and its open front forced our ghastly foe into the funnel of its restraining walls, while its roof, the deck of our raised stern, prevented the ungodly demons from dropping down upon us.

The weather deck's open front forced our foe to attack us head-on, if he dared. The confining funnel ahead of us left them only one route of attack, lest they pour through the two doors to our rear, which led to the captain and second officer's cabins.

To our dismay, both doors were locked. Worse, the captain, said to have retired to his quarters hours earlier, failed to heed our rapping pleas to wake him.

I feared the worse as did those, who watched my frustrated attempts to illicit an answer from him.

Even the damning din of our marine sergeant's rifle butt, banging against the thick oak door, did little to raise him from his slumber or indifference. Or perhaps, our captain had succumbed to something far worse.

No one had seen the master of our ship leave his quarters. He had to be inside.

But, could not these unearthly demons have claimed him, entering his cabin from seaward, much as they clung to the sides of our hull to wrest control of the two boats, strung about the sides of our stern.

Beyond the weather deck all had fallen silent. The ghouls, that had encircled the launch, cutter, pinnace, and captain's barge loitered about the hold's thick timbers and braces or hovered about the small boats they guarded.

They reminded me a mindless swarm of insects, often content, to gather about and land in one place. They stood about silently, eerily guarding any approach to our small boats, the last venue of escape.

Barely audible, above the sound of one's own breath, we could discern a low guttural hiss from each horrid groups' combined breathing. They sounded like some angry body of insects, warning us of their presence or the advent of a coming strike.

I could not describe the sound any further. It was like that of the small insect world of nature, yet it was not. The creatures had a life of their own. Yet, they were not alive. A hum or buzz did not properly describe their sound.

It was distorted and abnormal. Lungs, once halted in death, labored to breath and rasp again.

Their ghastly heads and dark eyes stared ahead at us, judging the strength and determination of our line.

Our marines had doubled up. Their weapons awaited, pointed forward with their hated spikes and long barrels offering the only buffer, between us and the ghouls. Their loaded rifles and spike bayonets were our only defense, except for the few cutlasses or the occasional axe, that had been gathered up in haste.

I had inquired of the sergeant, how many rounds each marine had in his possession. I disappointedly learned, each man had started his watch with twenty cartridges of powder and twenty bullets.

Of the latter, ten were the hollow conical projectiles, favored over the obsolete balls, used in earlier firearms. Regrettably, the other ten rounds in their possession were the less favored, but still deadly balls.

I had seen the handiwork of the conical projectiles. These grim rounds entered a man cleanly, but upon penetrating flesh and muscle, their hollow interior allowed the piercing point in the front of the bullet to misshapen and flatten.

Thus deformed, the round's remaining energy became a grizzly destroyer of men, ripping away flesh and muscle and shattering bone. And, its exit was just as traumatic, ripping out a larger hole, than that through which it had entered. Loss of blood and shock were enough to kill its found target. The resulting wounds were horrid disfigurements, leaving little for a surgeon to attend to, unless the victim had the good fortune to only be grazed by the round.

More likely, where the deadly hollow conical projectile had found its mark and the man lived, there was little to be done for an injured limb, except amputation.

But, these undead tars' bodies swallowed our deadly rounds,

taking little toll from them, except to knock the demons down and slow their advance.

I looked ahead and tried to count our foe's number in the darkness.

As I did, more of their number appeared. I wondered, how many of our crew had become so afflicted and how many more had joined the ranks of these demons set against us?

"Vampiresa," that was the warning our Spaniard had spoke of. He warned of a woman, who fed upon the flesh and blood of men. I had ignored it.

I had ignored the visions of my own eyes, the shadow clinging about the side of the ship, the young maiden besetting our morgue, . . . I had ignored all.

And, now our ship was nearly wrested from our control. Our captain did not answer our summons. A handful of the ship's company and myself were all, that survived the madness enveloping us.

Several of the creatures stirred.

"Keep awake, lads!" our marine sergeant chided his men and the few surviving tars of the watch.

I raised my head, noting the movement beyond our line.

A few nervous marines cocked the flintlocks of their rifles, searching out the gathered demons for any sign of a threat.

Despite, their stiff joints, rigid muscles, and limbs, the specters ahead of us had exhibited an uncanny ability to leap and bound unnatural distances. Their skill and agility at climbing the heights of our masts had defied any human counterpart's abilities.

They had strength, beyond that of men. They could cling to the side of a vertical hull with the grasp of a fly or spider. And, they seemed almost impervious to pain.

Our eyes had witnessed them drop from the masts, shattering bone and limb, yet rise and continue on as if no harm had been done.

And, even the vicious attacks of our sergeant, a trained and professional killer, did little to halt their advance. His plunging spike and accurate fire had only slowed our foes, save for the slicing removal of their heads.

Parting their minds from their bodies had halted a few of our attackers or so, we thought. We did not seen them rise again or renew their attack. But, none of us had lingered about to bear witness to their final demise.

"Try the captain's cabin!" I ordered two marines, standing before its thick oak door.

"Sir, there is no answer," came a dejected reply from the nearest.

"Keep pounding on the door. Use the butts of your rifles, but wake him. If he doesn't answer, break the door down!" I blurted out in frustration.

The two marines renewed their efforts to rouse our captain.

Their rapping and pounding, on the thick panels set in the ornate door, found no answer from the other side. One drew up his rifle, pointing its barrel rearward as he aimed its brass buttplate towards the center of the door.

He swung the weapon forward, carefully aiming its strike.

It cracked the wooden frame in the door's center.

I ignored the door's strength yielding.

Ahead, I had counted over eighty ghouls, before their forms were hidden from my sight by their own masses.

Nervously, my right hand groped in the pocket of my jacket, feeling the reassuring shape of my timepiece. And, there with it, almost forgotten in the folds of the pocket, were the sharp corners of the silver cross, given to me by my mother.

Despite, the horrors facing us, my thoughts fled away to home. I tried to recall the faces of my parents and the simple shop and dwelling, that had been my home. Remarkably, even the tiniest detail flooded my mind, returning the simple pleasures and past, that I had so readily forsaken for the lure of adventure and fortune.

The Spaniard called the cross or crucifix his salvation. At

least, that is what, the doctor had told me. I fell to praying, moving my lips silently. I searched for some angel or miracle, that might deliver us from this ungodly plague, seeking us out.

The ghouls ahead stirred.

Several moved about in supplication as another form appeared in their midst. The dark specter strode up arrogantly, causing dismay and loathing in even the gathered demons. Yet, they obeyed him.

Over eighty of the fiends stood ahead of us. We numbered barely thirty men, among the illusive safety of the weather deck. The demons were clad in the darkness of the shadows from the clouds overhead.

Fearfully, I noted the clouds blocked out the little light of the moon, leaving our eyes to strain in the dim candlelight of the lanterns, trying to keep our foes in sight.

I wondered if there were any other pockets of survivors trapped on the lower decks, now making their stand against the demons, intent on claiming our ship?

And, what would happen to those survivors? Would they be claimed and join the demons' ranks to confront us in our devilish battle? Or, would we fall and become demons like our fellow seamen before us, searching out any of the living, who had secreted themselves in isolation aboard our ship?

The figure halted beside the main mast. His form was tall and thin. In the darkness, I could not recognize him. But, there was something about him. It was an evil presence, even greater, than that of the creatures about us. But, there was a familiarity about its evil.

The clouds moved. Perhaps, their motion was in answer to my silent prayers and those of the other survivors, standing about in fear.

The moonlight filtered through the clouds, slowly casting its beams about our deck. Its light walked slowly towards the main mast and the haunting figure, set there like stone.

The white light of the moon fell upon the figure's shoes and stockinged legs, rising along the blue uniform trousers and the jacket of an officer. The jacket's gold embroidered cuffs hung down over clenched fists.

The light continued rolling along the standing figure.

I choked, my breath escaping me.

It was our second officer. It was Lieutenant Samuel Isaiah Loydd.

"Damn! It's the Second Officer," a marine private gasped in dismay.

"Hold your tongue and keep your wits about you," our marine sergeant demanded.

"I won't mind taking a shot at that bastard," another uttered in curse, barely above his breath.

"Enough of that. You'll shoot, who you're told, when you're told . . . hold your fire, until you're ordered," the sergeant snapped sharply.

I ignored their banter.

Ahead, Loydd removed his officer's hat. Its rich blue material and gold trim were splattered with the blood of his original fatal wound. But, he held it cupped perfectly in the fold of his right arm as if preparing to be announced to some aristocratic court or formal gathering.

His stance mirrored affluence and breeding. Even in death, he showed a contempt for others.

He bore the same black lifeless eyes as the others, set against the pale pallor of his dead flesh. In the moonlight, his thin vile lips were hued blue.

He stood silently, the the tails of his jacket blown about by the light breeze, running over the deck.

He said nothing, merely content to view us. His lips parted. He grinned. He was finding amusement in our suffering and dread. I stood there in disbelief, watching his head lift to the night sky. His mouth parted and exhaled a hollow laugh from his lungs.

But, the sound was not filled with the rejoicing or the gaiety of frolic. Even our second officer's voice had left him. The laughter turned to the rasping expulsions of his breath. His voice was devoid of life or any semblance of it.

I think the sound of his own laughter tore at any last shred of a soul our second officer still had. His head lowered, his own eyes seemed horrified at the realization of what he had become.

I glimpsed the damning mark in Loydd's forehead, where the French sharpshooter's round had struck. It defied reason and reality. Loydd was dead. Yet, there he was.

He was intent on claiming a new unearthly crew. He was intent on taking command of the Vanguard.

His mouth closed as his black eyes darted about, pained by what he had become, yet relishing it. The deepest evil harbored inside him came forth. It was freed. It ruled him.

His lips parted and he exerted several guttural commands. They were senseless to us. They sounded more like rasping moans or rantings, not words.

But, his new crewmen understood and that was all that mattered. He had commanded and they obeyed. In death, they obeyed.

We watched in horror as the ghouls gathered about the stowed boats began smashing at their wooden sides with whatever implement was at hand. Some of the ghouls used their bare hands, smashing bone through wood.

The sight was unreal. A madness seemed to set upon the fiends. They exhorted their own fearful melody as rasping voices joined as one, exerting a hellish chorus, that drove them on.

They beset the four boats about our deck, the launch, barge, pinnace, and one of our three cutters, the other two out of sight, hanging off the sides of our hull. All were amazed, at how quickly they wrecked the launch.

It was the biggest boat on board, nearly thirty-four feet long, larger than, even the thirty-two foot length of the captain's barge. The launch saw sixteen oarsmen seated side by side, row her large form and seated officers and men. But, despite her size the demons crushed it with ease.

The bulking launch was relegated to the heaviest tasks of all our smaller boats, such as raising the anchor for which it was equipped with a windlass of its own, a davit, and a small wooden crane. And, like the captain's barge, it was provided with a sail.

Our boats had many other uses, besides offering our crew the salvation, being robbed from before our eyes. Besides, escape from our ship. They were used to move men and provisions from ship-to-ship, shore-to-ship, or vice versa in the role of amphibious assault.

The boats even aided our docking, when used as "tugs." And, during the absence of a wind, the boats were used to tow the mother ship, linked in a single line, connected to the lowest point of the bowsprint of the Vanguard.

But, their usefulness and salvation escaped the foul hearts and thoughts of the ghouls, seeking only to deny them to us. Now, they were destined to be wrecked and smashed. We watched dumbfounded as they were destroyed before our eyes.

Wood splintered and cracked as the creatures attacked our boats with a vengeance and hatred, I had never witnessed before. They were possessed by madness. They sought to render us unable of fleeing the ship, fiend and man now shared alike.

Hands tugged and pulled at the planks of the broken boats, pulling them apart and casting their wood over the side to the sea below. In its turn, one boat after the another was beset upon.

They attacked the craft as if they were living things, hated and reviled for some transgression or offense.

Several of their bare hands shattered against the firm wood and construction of the larger launch and our captain's barge. But, nothing halted the assault. The devilish horde continued about the task, ignorant of any injury inflicted to their own bodies.

They were joined by others brandishing axes and boat pikes. The boats became the center of their hatred. The fiends swung the sharp blades of their axes or thrust the points of the boat hooks against the frameworks and caulked panels of our boats. Within minutes, one boat was stripped bare of the planks. Its hull became a naked skeleton, stripped down to the thick lumber of its keel.

In horror, we watched as the meager provisions, stored upon each boat, were hefted skyward, only to be thrown into the darkness and the sea below.

And, all along, Lieutenant Samuel Isaiah Loydd stood facing us.

He damned us with his stare. His glare welcomed and challenged us to join the ranks of his new command.

Behind me, the banging of our marines upon the captain's door barely rose above the devilish din ahead. A wooden door panel split and broke, pushed inward by the weight of our marine's body, pressing against the buttplate of his rifle, after the preceding blow.

He was joined by his comrade, who thrust the stock of his own rifle at the heavy oak door. His own targeted panel was cracked in several places, yet it still held.

Two more blows were delivered. The panel split cleanly, one piece falling inside the entrance of the cabin.

CHAPTER 31

Captain

HMS Vanguard
Sailing off the
Spanish Coastline
Day 12-Early Morning

The marines pressed against the broken door, trying to force it inward. It was to no avail. The shipwrights and carpenters had seen to it, that not only was our captain's door a masterpiece of craftsmanship and art with its ornate bevels and hand-carved designs, but it was also a formidable barrier.

It offered the captain and those retreating to its seclusion a last bastion, should boarders successfully overwhelm the upper gun-deck. In spite, of the two marines brawn and zeal only two of the door's upper panels had been splintered and pushed inward. It was enough.

The two ceased pushing against the door. There was still enough strength in the door's frame and remaining panels to block their passage. But, there was enough of a gap to reach inside the door.

One of the marines stretched his arm through the broken panels, his hand and fingers searched in the darkness on the other side of the door for the lock, holding it fast.

The captain's cabin was crisscrossed with the shadows of the stern's windows and framework along with the moon outside. Little of the room could be seen in the darkness, lingering about the cabin and engulfing the captain's writing desk and bookcase along with his berth and closets.

The marine's fingers found the door's handle and the keyhole below. But, it was devoid of a key.

"There's no key in the lock!" the marine blurted out, snaking his sleeve and hand back out of the jagged opening.

"Shoot away the lock!" I ordered. "Get into that cabin."

I was intent on learning what had happened to our captain. But, I feared we were too late. If the creatures could scale the steep surface of our hull, climbing the tiered ornate surface of the stern to the officer's cabins would present them no obstacle.

The marine placed his rifle's buttplate on the floor of the weather deck and removed its ramrod. His right hand fumbled with the small box-like black leather carrying case, mounted to his belt. He withdrew a paper cartridge, filled with a measure of powder.

He bit off its end and poured the contents of the paper wad down his rifle's barrel. He tapped the butt of his weapon sharply atop the deck, seating the powder, before fingering one of the round balls from his case to the rim of the barrel and dropping it inside.

He feverishly worked the thin ramrod down the barrel's length, pressing the powder and ball projectile home. With the bullet and powder seated, he cocked the flintlock and inserted a small piece of flint in its holder, pressing it beside the powder-hole for the striker.

He motioned his partner aside as he stepped back and withdrew the length of a rifle and a good pace added, aiming the weapon at the lock.

He squeezed the trigger slowly, trying to steady the long swaying barrel against the gentle motion of the ship.

The rifle fired a spark beside the flintlock as a plume of fire and smoke erupted from its barrel. The metal lock smashed.

The second marine pushed against the door, grabbing its handle as I and the sergeant retired to the rear of the weather deck to join them. I moved swiftly, holding a lantern in my left hand and the cutlass in my right.

I saw the marine was still pushing against the door. The damaged lock and door frame jammed from the discharged round.

"Stand aside!" the sergeant bellowed, wanting to waste no time.

He took one last look to the main mast and the ghouls smashing the remains of our boats. Satisfied, no attention or interest was being directed against our double line of marines and tars, he rushed at the door.

His right leg rose as he reached his final step. His outstretched stride was aimed at the door. He traveled at it at full gait. His shoe slammed into the door's resisting wood.

The blow was delivered just below the broken panels and almost directly beside the smashed lock. The door broke free of its jammed grasp in the door frame.

It was flung aside wildly, striking the wall inside.

Despite the din and fury of our sergeant's attack, the inside of the cabin was silent. I heard the rustling of our uniforms and our own footsteps as we joined the non-commissioned officer, now raising his rifle up at the doorway.

The spike of his weapon entered the darkness before us. My lantern lit our way.

The dim glow of the lantern's candle gave little light or life to the foreboding confines ahead. The captain's berth lay empty. Opposite it, the bookshelves were filled with the leather covered logs, charts, and guides, favored by our captain along with a few cherished and well-read tomes.

I stepped past our sergeant as he favored the right side of the room. I chose the left. There, before the small writing desk, I saw a darkened form slumped atop a pulled out chair. The form moved not.

It was bent over, its head resting in folded arms, laying atop the narrow desktop. The head was partially buried by the adjoining shelves and nestled drawers, framing the top of the ornate mahogany desk.

As I neared, my light left no doubt as to the identity of the form seated at the desk. It was Captain Shefferd, clad in his blue jacket, trimmed about the cuffs and lapel with the gold ornamental braid of an officer.

His uniform hat, mirrored that of the second officer, save for its golden thread. It rested atop the small desk's letterbox. He looked as if he was deep in sleep or perhaps, in contemplative thought, save for his stillness.

I raised the lantern. The light drew no response from him and I continued nearing slowly, expecting to find the worse.

I halted, just short of his back. My eyes stared in dread, fearing I would find, he had turned into one of the black-eyed specters, claiming our ship. My fingers searched out the center of his back.

He moved.

His movements startled me. My breath halted as I withdrew my hand, almost jumping back. My own movements alarmed our sergeant, who quickly spun about, swinging the rifle in his hands in both the captain's and my own direction.

He halted with both spike and barrel centered upon our captain, only six paces away. The room fell heavy with the tension of uncertainty.

Even though, we knew our captain's identity, we feared some ghoulish deception. We did not know whether he was one of us or had joined the haunted vile ranks of the likes of Lieutenant Samuel Isaiah Loydd.

His head rose and lifted from the caress of his arms. His eyes blinked, before he turned around and faced me, squinting at the light of the candle and raising an arm to block its meager glare.

I lowered the lantern in respect, but still kept it between us, so that I could study our captain's face.

He wore the same ghastly pallor as I had witnessed earlier. His paleness could have been from sequestering himself below decks in the isolation of his cabin. The doctor had told me, he had appeared wrought with guilt and grief, blaming himself for the large number of our fallen tars.

But though, his face was sickly and ill, his eyes were not those of the half dead and half alive tars and other lost souls, beyond the front of the weather deck. He lacked the black depraved orbs of Lieutenant Loydd and the others.

Instead, of the vile darkness, harbored in their orbs and filled with malice and hate, our captain's eyes were blank and sorrowful. They mirrored the loss plaguing our ship. They held some measure of life, but seemed to be without sense or purpose.

Yet, they were strangely not alive. It was as if our captain was in some induced stupor. I wondered if he had taken to drink. His cabin was amply stocked as our earlier dinners would attest.

Yet, there were no glasses or empty bottles about. But, any evidence of such weakness could have easily been ejected through the windows to the rear of his cabin and now be found floating in the flotsam of our wake or plunging to the depths of the sea.

"What do you want, Ensign?" Shefferd's lips parted in a mumble.

"Sir, our ship is . . . is being assaulted," I could think of no other way to explain the madness inundating our ship, . . . his ship.

"Assaulted?" he answered without emotion or alarm.

The sergeant stole a glance at me as puzzled as I.

I did not know what to do.

It was while I returned his questioning look, that I saw the dreaded iron box laying to the rear of the cabin. It was open.

I strode towards it.

"What is this business of an assault?" the captain raised his voice, coming alive and standing up. His stupor and indifference fell aside as I neared the oblong iron monstrosity.

"Ensign!" he barked.

I halted. I wanted to turn and answer him, explaining everything.

But, there was that evil box. And, now it lay wide open, its secrets revealed to any, who would look upon it. I stepped forward, ignoring our captain. The act meeting with the consternation of our proper and disciplined marine sergeant.

The iron box beckoned me. I moved closer to it, but was still too far away to see inside its confines.

"Ensign, halt!" the captain ordered.

I stopped. His words were those of a man, our ship's master. Yet, they did not seem like his own. I turned around and faced him, taking several steps forward as I prepared to explain everything.

His uniform was wrinkled and disheveled. It looked as if he had been living in it for days. He made no attempt to straighten it or assume his characteristic model of primness or respectable dress.

He stood ramrod straight. In the lantern's light, I could see his neck muscles tense and his eyes fix on me in anger, that I would hesitate in obeying his commands. The collar of his wrinkled jacket was unbuttoned. The jacket's lapels were adorned with golden thread. They were rumpled and hung along the sides of the jacket's open front.

But, it was his neck, that drew my attention.

There, along its left side, next to his stretched jugular were the hated marks the doctor and I had witnessed on our afflicted tars. There was no doubt, not even in the flickering dimness of the lantern's candle.

The marks explained our captain's sickly pallor and fatigued form. Yet, he was still among us. He was of the living. He was not of the dead, like our Lieutenant Loydd or those members of the crew, who had joined him.

But, something was amiss. His character and manner were not his own.

It was as if the master of our ship now served another, his soul and mind were possessed. His eyes harbored anger, but not for my failure to quickly answer him. It was our intrusion into the solitude of his cabin and our nearness to the elongated iron box, that stirred his ire.

Despite, our rapping pleas, he had chosen to ignore the

pounding on his cabin's door. He had even disregarded our
marines' attempts to smash through the heavy oak door.

He did not want us here. And, I doubted, he wanted to hear
anything, we had to report. But, his words continued.

"You spoke of an assault . . . the French or Spanish, what?"
the captain questioned, his voice pointed and sharp.

"Sir, . . ." I did not know where to begin. "We are in the
midst of some dreadful horror . . . a mutiny."

It was the only way I could appease his anger and give some
focus to the madness engulfing us. "A group of our men are
mutinying. Lieutenant Loydd is among them. They are smashing
our boats as we speak."

The sergeant looked on in disbelief. His mouth opened as if
he was about to tell all, to warn the captain of the ghastly fiends
outside his cabin's walls. But, he fell silent, like I.

How could one explain what had transpired without having
seen it. And, even having seen it, how could one believe one's
own eyes.

"Lieutenant Loydd instigating mutiny?" the captain returned,
his eyes blank as if lost from us.

"Aye, sir. The second officer and others have sought to destroy
our boats, the launch, pinnace, cutters, and your own barge.
They've killed several members of our crew . . ."

"Enough!" the captain barked.

The sergeant edged closer to the iron box, while I engaged
the captain.

"Sir," I began to protest.

"I am not to be disturbed! Ensign, you were to be restricted
to your quarters, until fit to assume your duties, once more. Has
the surgeon made such pronouncement?"

"Nay, Captain, But, there are . . ."

"Enough. Enough, I have said. Do not make me repeat myself.
I will stand for no more of your madness. You are ordered to return
to your quarters and follow the proscriptions of our doctor."

"Sergeant!" he spied the non-commissioned officer closing
on the iron box.

"You will escort Ensign Lewis to his quarters and place a guard on him to assure he remains there as I have ordered. Then, attend about your duties," the captain intoned.

"Sir," the sergeant began, "I fear you do not understand . . . our ship is beset . . ."

"Enough. Sergeant, you will do as you are told. You've not stripes enough to save you from the lash or my wrath," the captain barked disapprovingly at the senior marine.

In doing so, he spied the two young marines still huddled about his doorway.

"What is this? Who has done this to my door?" he exclaimed, seeing the shattered and splintered panels of the oak door to his cabin as if for the first time.

"Who did this?" he bellowed, his eyes taking on an assumed anger, that had not been present earlier. His stupor had fallen away, replaced by irrational madness and anger.

"I did, sir. I was following orders," the private spoke up timidly, perplexed by the absurdity filling the cabin.

"You'll pay for this, marine. From your purse and by your back, you will pay for this insolence," the captain returned spitefully.

"Sir, it was I who ordered the door broken," I interrupted.

"Enough. Enough of you, Ensign!"

"Now all of you, out of my cabin. I am not to be disturbed. Out!" the captain rasped.

"Aye, sir!" the two privates answered in unison, before withdrawing from the dimly lit cabin, leaving only the sergeant and myself.

"Sir, you do not understand the import of what is transpiring . . ."

"Ensign, you have your orders. Carry them out . . . Sergeant, see to it!"

"Aye, sir," the sergeant returned, in the crisp manner honed by the tradition of his profession.

We exited, pulling the door closed behind us.

As we did so, I ordered the marines outside to block off the captain's cabin, using two nearby benches within the haunts of the weather deck. We moved away from the door, leaving our captain.

He was not one of us. But, he was not yet fully one of the ghouls, facing our line of marines ahead.

"What did you see?" I asked the sergeant.

"Sir?"

"The iron box. What did you see in it?" I questioned, my voice irritated.

The sergeant grew quiet. The madness was too much. I was now asking him to place into words more of the madness, he had witnessed.

It did not sit well with a man used to only black and white and the cold stark realities of life and death. He was trained and used to dealing with things, as they were.

Everything we witnessed tonight and during the onset of the early morning defied reason and reality.

"What did you see?" I asked as a comrade and friend.

"The box was empty," he began. "Except . . . except, for a small silk covered pillow and sheet. It was the damnedest thing. Satin white, they were and each adorned with lace."

"But, neither were the trappings of a brothel. They bore the fine embroidery, one would find upon the wedding vessels and trappings of a bride. The lace was like that of a wedding gown and there was a sheer fabric about the sides of the box, thin and light, like that of a bridal veil," he added in a low voice, puzzled and disbelieving.

"This is madness," he added. "Worse, our captain lends it no merit. He ousts us, when only we would protect our ship," he said, raising his eyes to meet mine.

I was silent. I shared his apprehension and dread. We were alone among our shipmates and crew. I wondered how many other members of our crew were at this moment fighting to remain from the grasps of these fiends enveloping us.

"What do we do?" the sergeant asked, bewildered and having no answers.

"We fight. We fight, as best we can," I returned.

But, I knew I had to get to the doctor. I had to get to our Spanish prisoner. Perhaps, that superstitious Spaniard knew of what he spoke. Perhaps, he knew some way of freeing ourselves and the Vanguard from the creatures encroaching upon our ship.

He had said prayers. I had heard their frantic words or at least, those I knew the meaning of. His lips could not utter the chanting words quickly enough. There had to be some magic or charm, some divine intervention in those words.

With most of our crew having succumbed to the evil engulfing us, he had remained unscathed. He must have knowledge of some protection or cure for this evil.

Yet, the doctor had put him asleep, rendering his mind incoherent with a powerful potion. The potion was so strong and rare, that the surgeon reserved it only for the officers. It was rumored the opiate came from the reaches of the Far East. It was a rare and treasured mixture.

I hoped it would not separate the Spaniard from us. I hoped I would be able to find him and illicit his aid in defeating the menace about us.

I searched for the words and argument, I would need to gain the support of the sergeant. I would bid him and the others to join me in descending down into the bowels of the ship and the hell locked away beneath our decks.

I needed the wisdom of our doctor and the knowledge, religious or lore, of our Spanish captive. We needed their knowledge to survive.

CHAPTER 32

Holding On

HMS Vanguard
Sailing off the
Spanish Coastline
Day 12-Early Morning

The marines held our line at the open front of the weather deck.

The ghouls ahead had gathered in a solid wall. It ran across the deck ahead and stretched from one railing to the next, running the width of our upper gun-deck's beam.

Among them were the skeletal remains of our boats. Their smashed and broken remains crushed any hope of escape, that their small hulls offered. The boats' broken hulls robbed us of flight. I wondered if the two boats, now dangling haphazardly along both sides of the stern, had also been targeted by the fiends.

It was likely. They seemed intent on holding us aboard the Vanguard, either to sup on as their last living hosts, until we reached land or to join their unholy ranks.

It had only been within the last hour, that the ghouls had begun to stir.

The deck was filled with the horrid creak and snap of their limbs moving about. It reminded one of the chirping sounds of crickets on a summer evening, save for their magnified melody and its grotesque source.

They moved without speaking out in words. Their earlier indiscernible sounds emanated from their guttural mouths. Their rasps and moans directed their unified actions. They moved with purpose.

And, all was overseen by their master, Lieutenant Samuel Isaiah Loydd. His pale face and black eyes twisted about as he silently intoned obedience from his horrid crew.

A wave of his hand or a pointing limb saw new fiends move forth or take positions beyond our view. They were massing. Our foe was preparing.

In horror, the horde ahead of us rose as one. They flung themselves at us with a speed, that defied their creaking limbs and stiff bones. I swear one or more of the demons flew at us as if lifted upon the breeze running across the deck.

"Make ready. Present bayonets!" our sergeant bellowed.

The order seemed unreal. But, the marine sergeant's voice was obeyed. It gave our small band of survivors hope, a fleeting reassurance, that we might yet, survive this hellish darkness besetting our ship. If they obeyed his commands the men might survive.

The lengths of our marines barrels were thrust forward. They slanted upwards and presented the vicious spikes of a double line of bayonets.

The deck was tormented with the horrid din of the closing creatures.

"First row, down!" the sergeant barked.

Nearly fifteen men dropped to one knee, bracing their rifles and their spikes ahead at our charging foe. They used their bodies and bayonets to form an impenetrable shield for the second group of marines and tars behind them.

The ghouls were only paces away, when the sergeant bellowed, "Second row present weapons and take aim. Second row . . . fire!"

Their weapons' clamor was tumultuous. Smoke and flame spat from the marines' lengthy barrels and those of several displaced tars, that had sought out the rifle or musket of a fallen comrade.

The front line of the charging ghoulish horde staggered. Several fiends were kicked backwards as the impact from conical and ball rounds slammed into their bodies.

One or two fell, but more continued on.

"Second row, reload!" the sergeant instructed calmly as if conducting a drill.

He led by example, believing that if shown the proper behavior and mettle in the face of opposition, his men would mimic it.

A ramrod fell from a pair nervous and frightened hands as a sailor, unpracticed in the art of marksmanship, lost his hold on it.

The sergeant halted as if there was all the time in the world left to us.

I watched, moving to the forefront of our lines and raising my cutlass to confront our attackers, as he bent and retrieved the sailor's ramrod, rolling on the gently rocking deck.

He handed it back to the young sailor with a short comment, more encouragement, than damnation.

He turned, to see the nearest fiends upon our lines.

"First row, fire!" he blurted.

Again, the din of our rifles broke the stillness of the darkness.

Many in the assaulting horde folded over or were thrust backwards. Those, who did not, found themselves eagerly impaled on the swift thrusts of the spikes, held by the men kneeling in the first row.

Many in the forefront of our own line stood. They sought a firmer footing for thrusting or lashing out with their deadly spikes. The wounds they inflicted were horrid. But, their grizzly work failed to bear the intended results of their strikes.

They momentarily halted our attackers, even forcing some to retreat or succumb to dropping to the deck. But, they killed none of the horrid creatures . . . creatures already without life. It was a madness and derangement our minds could not fathom.

"Reload and fire at will!" the sergeant shouted, raising his own loaded rifle to his shoulder and releasing its round into a lunging specter.

The creature was in midair, when the round struck him. His head jerked backwards as his flying form was halted abruptly and dropped hard to the deck.

But, others followed.

I entered the fray.

I found a gap in our line, created as two marines stepped rearward, distracted with loading their weapons.

I swung my cutlass's short blade down in a slashing arc. Its blade found a fiend's extended arm and claw-like fingers rushing at a weary marine. The ghoul's grayish flesh cut cleanly, the arm severing and dropping to the planks of the deck.

I stood back a step. My eyes were filled with horror. The ghoul turned around and faced me. The brow above his black eyes furrowed. He cast a maddening glare at me.

He was not troubled the least by his limb's loss. Instead, he turned his attention, mindless as his mind was, upon me. Devoid of a right arm, his stiff left arm popped up rigidly.

Unbending fingers and knuckles now moved. They snapped and cracked as the intractable limb stretched out towards me.

I raised my cutlass.

I was knocked to my feet. My first instinct was to hold onto the cutlass, my only weapon and defense.

Above me, the foul face of one of our former crewmen appeared. His leathered skin framed the horrid dark eyes mirroring those of the rest of the horde, assaulting us.

His mouth parted. I could not bare the foul breath. It was as if a grave had been opened and the rotting body, interred inside, released.

I tried to swing the short blade out into the face of my attacker.

His left hand clamped down upon my right wrist. The grip was vice-like, firm and unbreakable. I tried to press forward my attack. Its bony grasp stabbed into my flesh.

Each movement I made to free myself was blocked. The fiend's lips parted in a demonic grin. Instead of laughter, hissing exhaled from his vile smile.

I moved my left arm to strike my opponent. But again, he was quicker and stronger, than I. His left hand grasped it, capturing it in a lock about my wrist. I struggled as a child would wrench and twist against the strength of an adult. it was pointless.

The nauseating mouth drew nearer, closing to my own face. The small animal-like teeth of his incisors filled my eyes.

I heard the roar of a shot, so close, that it deafened my ears.

The ghoul rolled to his right, driven by the impact of the shot.

I raised my eyes to find the young marine, upon whose behalf I had interceded, standing above me.

I began to smile in gratitude . . .

The marine was bowled to the deck as another ghoul butted headlong into him. Both rolled about the deck, mixing within our thin lines.

As I stood, I saw the fiend's face burrow into the young seafaring soldier's face, then run its head down along the length of the marine's neck. His mouth was out of sight. But, I knew what was to come.

I heard the anguished cry of the young marine. There was nothing I could do. As I stood helpless, cutlass in hand, more of the creatures descended upon us.

I swung out wildly, not bothering to mark my target. It did not matter. They were all about us. Others screamed and yelled. I thought, I heard my own voice cry out aloud in some dreadful curse, so vile its words and utterances escaped me.

Several more shots cracked out. Then, our firing stopped. We had descended to fighting hand-to-hand. The ghouls would not make the mistake of allowing us the luxury to reload.

It did not matter. We had not bullets enough to stop them.

I found myself standing with my back to one of the walls of the weather deck. Three ghouls stood before me.

Their attack halted as they seemed to linger about me,

relishing my captive presence and eventual destruction. They tormented me with hellish hisses and snarls from their foul mouths.

My right hand tired of cutting and slashing about with all its force. I traded the weapon to my left hand. I swung the blade with all my remaining might. But, the fiends merely stepped back out of its deadly arc.

I only kept them at bay, forestalling the inevitable.

Their faces feinted amusement as I reversed the blade and retraced its swing in the opposite direction. I found no target.

In the weather deck's haunts, I heard another of our men claimed by the ghouls. He screamed, preparing to gasp his last breath and accept death at the hands of one of the fiends.

It was not to be.

In horror, we watched helplessly as he was dragged across the deck by his legs. His hands flailed at the air, before he disappeared into a gathered group of the horde ahead.

The screams stopped.

I jabbed my right hand into my jacket pocket. My fingers ignored the timepiece there and searched out the cross, our Spaniard's foretold path to salvation and a keepsake from my mother.

I wanted to touch it one last time. It was a fleeting grasp to touch one last small measure of comfort from my past.

My trembling fingers clutched it.

I held it in my grip, even as the first of the three ghouls made his attack. His claw-like hand slapped against my right arm with such force, that it knocked my limb from its pocket, tearing the jacket's fine material.

I dropped the arm to my side, clearing a path for another arcing sweep of my cutlass. As I did so, the cross was exposed in the dim lantern lights of the weather deck.

A howl went up from the three creatures surrounding me. One raised an uplifted arm to shield his eyes. Another cast his head aside, averting his sight, while a third stepped backwards. Their black eyes could not look upon the silver-plated cross.

I swung the cutlass.

Its short blade found the neck of the nearest distracted ghoul. It severed its head off. I kicked at the rolling skull and gaping mouth as I turned the path of the blade around and slashed out to the left.

The cutlass found the side of the ghoul with the uplifted arm shielding his eyes. He shrieked from the blow, but did not collapse.

He retreated.

I held the cross out before me. Its polished silver caught the light of the candles and what little moonlight filtered into the weather deck from above.

One, than another of the fiends halted their attacks on our survivors. I pressed forward, closing upon them, trying to free those marines and tars in peril from the creatures falling upon them.

Our combat ceased as foul snarls and an ungodly hissing, like that of a nest of vipers, rose to fill our ears. Slowly, without a word from me, the creatures began to withdraw.

I came as near as I could to our survivors. My presence invited them to join me, to stand with me behind the protective shelter of the cross, reflecting its insignificant, yet compelling light and image into the faces of the ghouls.

The attack halted.

I kept my gaze forward, searching the slowly retreating horde at the mouth of our weather deck. They mulled about, low grumblings and growls emanating from their dead throats and mouths.

Silence, once again claimed the upper gun-deck of our vessel. It was broken, only by the creatures staring back at us with guarded glares and hissing in anger and revulsion at the small cross, I held up in my outstretched hand.

I felt the shoulders of the others press in beside me as our sergeant formed up a new line, keeping me in the center of our survivors.

Those laying dead about us, though they'd been comrades

only minutes ago, were unceremoniously dragged and rolled out from the safety of the weather deck, thrust into the no-man's land between ghouls and men.

The marines and tars beside me pushed closer as if somehow, just the press of our bodies, joined against the fiends, offered us some relief and bolstered our courage.

I kept my eyes fixed straight ahead, waiting for one of the fiends to lunge at us. I suspected one or more might try to wrest the religious icon free of my grasp.

But, none seemed able to move against its simple austere form, a symbol of goodness and righteousness.

I saw the black eyes filled with hatred cast down upon the deck. Shame replaced the frightening and contorted evil grins or the bloodcurdling looks about their faces. It was as if they were forced to look upon themselves and realize, what they had become.

But, of all those creatures ahead, our fearsome Lieutenant Loydd seemed the least perturbed by the religious symbol, that bid him and the others to keep their distance.

Despite, the cross's newfound protection, the second officer looked past its silver shape. I swore his eyes pierced into mine. His mouth gnarled, emitting a throaty snarl, carried across our deck by the winds, that had now turned against us.

Without a crew to tack our ship or maneuver it about to catch the wind, our large vessel's progress halted. We lay dead in the water, our sailcloth above dropping to hang straight and limp, powerless and devoid of wind.

I took comfort in the sight of our line and its rifle barrels and spikes pointed forward. Some among those in our line took advantage of the lull in our hellish battle to reload their rifles.

Hands nervously fumbled about for wads of cartridges, filled with the small measure of black powder, that would propel their deadly bullets or balls. Others were content to savor the quiet of temporary reprieve.

I heard their noisy breaths, mirroring those of my own lungs. Our eyes were open in horror. Our tongues were still silent in disbelief and terror. Even, the veteran marine sergeant had fallen silent.

There was no point to bellowing orders. Each man among us knew what was to be done. We had no choice, but to fight. Failure was too horrible to dwell on.

Several of the tars, who had not pistol or musket, claimed up the remaining rifles of those, who had fallen in our struggle. One made no attempt to load the weapon, the soldierly act escaping his knowledge.

He joined our line, enthralled to exchange the spike at the end of the rifle's long barrel for his former short bladed cutlass. He relished the extra length of his newly acquired weapon, that would keep the ghouls more distant.

Thus, armed and shielded behind the reflective form of the small silver cross, we waited.

I wondered what the hour was. In this ungodly stillness, it seemed as if time might be standing still. I wondered if time too, was horrified and had held back the hands of a watch or clock, frightened into disbelief and holding its forward progress, much as we now held our own breaths.

My heart raced, fueled by fear and the dread of what was to come.

I fought the selfish urge to claim my timepiece from the torn pocket along my jacket's side. I could still feel the heavy watch and chain poking about my side, inside the pocket's ripped thin cloth liner.

I desperately wanted to view the watch's small delicate hands and hear the comforting movements of its clockwork. It was not to be.

I stood frozen, keeping my place at the center of our line. It seemed like an eternity. I was afraid to move. I was afraid, that if I weakened and lowered my outstretched hand or in any way showed a sign of weakness or the lessening of my resolve or belief in the thrust foreword icon the demons would be upon us.

Like Moses with his hands raised to part the waters of the Red Sea, allowing the safe passage of the Israelites in their exodus, I kept my tiring limb thrust forward.

I noticed a movement among our foes.

Several of the ghouls had become agitated. They mulled about as nervous men pacing about the confines, they found themselves boringly trapped within.

Their uncontrolled and pointless wanderings about the crammed deck ahead drew the attention of Lieutenant Loydd.

He turned around abruptly, hissing at his lowly denizens.

But, his authority was not as whole and complete as he would have assumed. As animals or a pack of wolves, several hissed back or snarled, challenging his dominance.

Several retreated as their leader pressed rearward, seeking out the insubordinate threat to his authority. We watched in horror as he focused his hellish attention on one of the offenders.

Both Loydd's and the transgressor's mouth opened. But, no words came forth. Gnarls and rasps, the pants and vile emanations of beasts filled the air, breaking the uneasy silence cloaking us.

The insubordinate tar stood his ground, contesting our second officer or the surviving likeness of him before our eyes.

Loydd's anger seethed. His head cocked back, offering a disapproving sideways glance at the tar. His black eyes, though far away, gleamed with the reflected light of the moon. I saw only anger and hatred.

Loydd's right hand and arm thrust forward in a wide sweeping arc. His blow was aimed for the tar's head, his hand was transformed into a clenched claw with nails like those of a beast.

His claws struck the tar just below his jaw as the transgressor expelled a damning hiss. But, the insubordinate's rebuke was meaningless.

Loydd's claw dug into the soft light gray rotting flesh of the tar's neck. It sliced open a wide black gash. No blood came forth.

It was as if the tar was hollow. The wound emitted no blood or innards. There was only the barely audible sound of some gas or foul air being released from the wound.

The tar was too late in raising his own hands to block the blow. Even in death Lieutenant Loydd's movements were driven by hate. His blow was quick and violent.

Even, as the wounded ghoul raised his hands to the tear in his neck, Loydd was preparing to strike again.

Loydd's hand thrust out, retracing the brutal arc.

The wounded ghoul's eyes, black as they were, widened. His mouth spat out one last condemnation, before Loydd delivered a second blow.

His claws caught the other side of offender's neck, burying and trapping within the ghoul's neck.

A horrid scream pierced our deck. It was not human. It was not animal. My outstretched hand trembled. My flesh chilled.

Loydd's face was overcome with grim delight and satisfaction. He moved his buried hand about, twisting it inside the tar's neck, slowly ripping the seaman's head free of its muscle and bone.

With all the trepidation of ancient warriors, who in their victory lust, severed their foes heads and impaled them atop the ends of pikes to parade before their defeated survivors, Lieutenant Samuel Isaiah Loydd hefted the tar's severed skull and flesh skyward.

He mounted the low height of some crates or stores, twisting about as he lofted his gruesome prize above for all to see. Fiend and man alike gazed at the abominable sight.

It was as if the act was some hellish ritual, confirming his dominance above his fiendish horde. He cast his black eyes about as if seeking another challenger.

He was surrounded by foul seething hisses. Several ghouls screamed in elation, cheering their hellish commander on as he raised the severed head higher.

Along our closed ranks, I could feel the fear of the men pressing in beside me. I wanted to close my eyes and turn my head away.

But, I could not.

I had to know what was happening about me, lest the ghouls push forth in a renewed attack. In fear and sullen curiosity, I watched. I watched the spectacle unfold.

My breath escaped me.

But, Loydd's display changed nothing.

Slowly, the horde before us began retreating down into the bowels of our ship. Slowly, one, then another of the fiends sought a hatchway or the opening of the HMS Vanguard's deck to return to the comforting darkness below.

I wondered how long we had been besieged about the weather deck. It seemed like minutes. It seemed like hours. It seemed longer, it seemed forever. I did not know. Time was meaningless.

Fear dominated all.

Loydd protested the abandonment of the upper gun-deck with the hellish horde's victory so near.

I looked about those standing with me. We numbered twenty or less men. We had numbered thirty or better at the outset. The others had fallen, but would soon rise to join the rabble Lieutenant Loydd commanded.

I looked up at my right hand and the cross it bore. The limb trembled. It felt numb and lifeless from the chill of the air about us. I wanted to retreat. I wanted to run away.

But, there was nowhere to go.

I offered myself the illusion, that perhaps the two cutters, the small boats hung from the davits about the sides of the stern, might still be intact. Perhaps, there was a means of escape. Perhaps, we might yet choose life.

More of the ghouls left the ranks of the mob ahead.

Their absence enraged Loydd. He threw the severed head up into the darkness. It disappeared as its lobbed shape fell to the sea. The ghoulish tar parted from his body would surely be dead.

More of the ghouls left the deck.

Loydd became incensed with their departure. His head lifted skyward as our bow pointed westward. He howled as if a wild dog or other predatory beast.

The sound was an unholy blend of disappointment and rage.

I watched and listened as his bones cracked and creaked. With stiff joints, he dismounted his perch atop the crates and moved towards one of the hatchways.

A few wounded ghouls crawled about the deck. They were devoid of limbs, cut away by our cutlasses or severed by the ripping of our spikes. The hatchways, that could be claimed within paces of a walking gait, eluded them.

Lieutenant Samuel Isaiah Loydd looked down upon their crawling forms, mirroring the disgust he held for the lower class and enlisted ranks during life.

He turned his glance away, their pitiful forms unworthy of anything, but his indifference.

Moments later, except for those crawling forms, barely moving about the surface of our deck, he and his horde were gone.

I could not believe my eyes. They had us, if they wanted us. Their numbers could have easily claimed us. We had not the powder or bullets to halt them. We did not have the strength.

To the west, the sky was still cloaked in darkness and clouds. A few stars hung in the heavens, tiny pinpricks of light among the lifeless night. But, the darkness was receding.

A light, barely noticeable, was rising behind the weather deck.

The sergeant and I looked at each other from our positions in our gathered ranks. Almost thinking the same thought, we strode forward to the fret and consternation of our comrades.

I cleared the weather deck first, turning to face our stern, laying to the east. There I saw the thin golden glow of the dawn breaking across the horizon. The sun, that warming glowing orb, was rising from its celestial slumber.

The waters behind us glistened. The tops of the gentle waves flickered with the darting sheen of the first rays of sunlight, dancing and sparkling atop them, as its light streaked out beside the length of our ship's path.

I returned my gaze forward to our sergeant. The veteran marine pointed his rifle towards the few mangled creatures, crawling slowly towards the hatchways and our hold. Their remaining limbs took on a new desperation as they clawed at the splintered and worn planking of our red painted deck.

I saw one fretful creature turn his gaze towards our stern. His mouth dropped in horror, mimicking the view I had seen among our tars, attacked by the fiends.

His movements hastened.

The sun was just breaking above the horizon behind us. The tip of its orange-yellow orb barely crested the distant waters to our rear. The remaining ghouls withered about the deck. They were like worms, fleeing the drowning grass on a rainy day.

The sun rose.

I watched as one of the ghouls neared an open hatchway. Despite, his wounds, he would not rest or halt. His single arm and grasping hand groped for the raised lip of the hatchway.

With all his might, he pulled his broken and lacerated torso towards the opening. Like, an animal going to ground, dropping into its protective burrow, the creature pulled himself over its rIm and fell through the opening.

He disappeared, seeking the darkness below.

His injured companions were not so lucky.

The sergeant and I strode forward. I wielded the small cross and cutlass, while the sergeant pointed his loaded rifle and deadly spike down at the nearest form.

We halted several spaces short of the squirming corpse. His wounds were ghastly. I could not tell, which had been inflicted during our recent battle about the weather deck and which had been borne at Trafalgar.

He halted, laying facedown and exhausted.

He began to roll over, seeking the comfort of his back, when he spied the silver cross in my hands. He hissed lowly as he lifted his lone arm up to shield his black eyes from its sight.

His face reflected grim resignation. He knew he had no time to reach the hatchways or hold ahead. Still, some of his compatriots struggled to seek the shelter of the sheltering darkness below.

"Stop them!" I ordered.

Our line of marines and tars stood frozen, none were willing to abandon the shelter and protection of the weather deck.

"Its the light! It harms them. Halt them! Don't let them reach the shelter of the decks below!" I bellowed.

Our sergeant led the way, seeing the fear and angst in our

men's faces. He moved to one of the foremost creatures, nearly at a hatchway. He thrust out his arms and his trusted rifle. Its spike skewered the fiend beneath him. Its point drove through the ghoul and into the wood of the deck.

With the sergeant pressing his weight atop the rifle, the ghoul was pinned in place. He screamed for mercy, though only a few of his words or sounds held any meaning for us.

His tongue withered and protested in a foul language of his own. It was bestial and understood only by the hated ears of demons. His pleading was intermixed with a few sorrowful words, seeking to evoke some sense of pity or abandoned camaraderie in us. It failed.

We found him revolting, an abomination.

His shattered and severed limbs, some mere stumps left by the honed blades of a cutlass or bayonet, flailed about helplessly.

His panic was complete. The creature used his last measure of strength to try and break our sergeant's hold. He found no mercy or forgiveness.

Our non-commissioned marine crushed his weight down upon the rifle, holding its spike in place. The ghoul squirmed about.

But, he could not break the deadly vice of our sergeant, holding him to the deck.

The sun rose.

It incited the captive ghoul and those still atop the deck to squirm and twist unnaturally about. Some tried to cloak their clothing about them. One removed his dark blue woolen jacket and draped it about his head and the exposed flesh of his hands.

For a moment, he found some reprieve from the light.

I watched as other fiends mirrored his effort or tried to hasten their journey across the deck.

Soon, some of the sergeant's men mirrored his attack, pinning other fiends to the planks of the Vanguard's deck. The captive ghouls repeated the futile and desperate attempts to break free of their tormentors and the approaching sun.

I stood as an observer, watching the glowing orb to our stern rise slowly above its ornate trim. The shadows of our masts and sails retreated westwards, as the morning light slowly walked across our deck.

Its beams crawled over the weather deck, reaching the planking to the rear of the main mast. Slowly, it continued its unending rise and crawl forward, reaching out from the east.

The first creature it fell upon laid in forlorn silence. Then, as the warming rays touched his form, he began to gyrate and flail about. It was as if he was on fire. He rolled about, casting his head backward in a wretched scream. His mouth was wide and his tongue darted about as if his throat and insides were aflame.

The figure shook, convulsing wildly as he gyrated and squirmed about the deck. Steam, no smoke, rose from beneath his clothing. Soon, both it and his flesh were ablaze. He burned.

It was indescribable. His body combusted into flame. I feared his form might set the deck afire.

"Sand, fetch buckets of sand!" I ordered.

But, no sooner had I issued the command, than the creature, blaze and all, disappeared. It left only a blackened mark upon our red deck.

I raised my head to find other ghouls aflame. Three were caught under the pinning spikes of our heralded marines.

Our sergeant's eyes were steeled to the grim sight beneath him. His leathered face and stern mouth grimaced at the foul sight.

His entrapped fiend twisted about as if a madman possessed. It did him little good. Our sergeant knew no mercy.

Grimly, he kept his spike plunged into the fiend. He watched as the creature burst into flame and rolled about the penetrating spike, still running through him.

In seconds, it was over. His foe was gone, claimed by the sunlight, bathing our upper gun-deck and the other remnants of the dreadful horde, trapped above decks.

With the new day, we had been given a new reprieve, another chance at life.

CHAPTER 33

Loyalties

HMS Vanguard
Sailing off the
Spanish Coastline
Day 12-Dawn

We stood about the deck. A handful of survivors, we loitered about the red-painted deck of the Vanguard in a mindless blur of bewilderment and confusion.

We had witnessed the horrors of our own battle. Yet, there was no evidence about the deck to affirm, it had even happened. The grim corpses, that had come to life were gone. Most had retreated to the bowels of our ship. A few left only the darkened remains of scorched outlines burnt upon our deck.

There was nothing, except the haunting dread, that the sun now continuing the rise to its noon zenith, would eventually fall and just as readily retreat. Darkness would come again. And, with it, we could expect our foes to rise anew.

The wind blew across the deck, scattering the locks about my head. My beard had grown rough with the stubble of several days growth. I had no doubt I looked as fatigued and vexed as those about me. Their faces and eyes held the burden of loss and fear.

Their fear was exacerbated by the hopelessness of our lot. After our attackers had fled, all in turn moved about our stern, seeking out the condition of the two remaining boats, the cutters hanging from the davits.

The boats were still there or better, what was left of them.

Like the four large boats atop our deck, their hulls had been shattered and broken. They were no longer seaworthy craft. Our last chance of escaping the cruel captivity of the HMS Vanguard had been dashed. It had been stolen from us.

I claimed a space at the rail of our strangely empty deck. With the wind from our sails lost, nearly half of the ship's compliment should be atop the deck or in the heights of the masts, moving lines and sail about to regain the blossoming fill of the wind that had changed its path.

The helmsmen and watch should be wresting the wheel about, moving our giant rudder to tack the ship, angling to claim the winds and begin our sideways ballet as sail and ship were manipulated to carry us westwards.

Instead, nothing happened. We stood about the deck in dumbfounded silence.

Even, our veteran marine sergeant was lost to his own thoughts. Like myself and the others, survival seemed enough for the moment. Those present about the deck stood by the rail or held a rope leading upwards to our towering masts.

A few men had nearly collapsed, sitting on the deck or among the smashed remains of its boats.

There was nothing to be said. We had a moment of reprieve. There were only hours left to prepare for the next assault, that night and its unholy darkness would bring.

The men were ruing their own deaths, that would certainly come.

I heard banging.

I turned to face the weather deck behind us. To its rear, the benches and debris, that had been placed to block off the captain's cabin door, dropped aside. The door was still jammed, but partly agape as the captain continued pressing against the door, his form visible through its broken panels.

The din drew the attention of others nearby. Some, still shocked by our encounter only minutes earlier, turned to raise their weapons at the blocked doorway.

Their faces fell blank registering a mixture of apprehension and the fear of some unknown threat and then, shame for having raised their weapons against our commander.

Eyes fell to me and our marine sergeant.

The door burst forth, the last restraining obstacle impeding our captain's progress pushed away with a wide sweeping thrust of both arms. He strode out of his cabin and into the shelter of the weather deck.

Captain Shefferd stood before us.

His eyes squinted in the early morning sun. His face bore the same sickly pallor as those first tars suffering from the affliction, that had found our ship.

His gold braided trimed hat cast a shadow below his brow and shielded his face from the brilliant light, rising in the east to his back. But, he stood out in the sunlight, our deck silent with his presence.

His eyes looked about the deck, before raising to the masts. He saw the lack of sailcloth unfurled above. He sensed our ship laying almost dead in the water. The HMS Vanguard had lost movement.

But, he said nothing. He barked no commands. He stood there in resignation as if the fault was entirely his. He lowered his head and eyes, glimpsing the few of us about the deck.

A sound and reasonable man would have inquired into our predicament. There was an absence of the watch and the crew, that should now be tending our sails and shifting them about to catch the wind. Our helmsmen should be tacking the ship, heading from side to side to capture the wind in our sails and push our behemoth vessel forward.

But, these things escaped our commander.

Shefferd said nothing. He lacked life, at least the vitality and spirit, he had been so willing to depart among the officers and crew, only days earlier. He moved, claiming the helm and releasing the ropes, that had lashed it in place. He wrested the large dual wheel about, despite his frail form.

His experience and expertise slowly pointed the bowsprint to the northwest. The movement of our ship was slow and labored, but aided by the wind beginning to partially fill the few rigged sails aloft.

I moved towards the captain as did the sole surviving helmsman and the boatswain, who oversaw him.

The two sailors seemed regrettably ashamed, that they had forsaken their station and the HMS Vanguard, they had been entrusted to pilot.

They halted, just short of the wheel. They waited for Captain Shefferd to order them to assume the helm. It did not happen.

In silence, our captain continued to maneuver the wheel, which was taller, than his own short stature. The sails flapped and billowed, despite our running almost against the wind. Captain Shefferd skilfully returned movement to the HMS Vanguard, beginning to tack our giant vessel.

He stepped forward and claimed the foremost of the two wheels.

His forward perch allowed him a clear view, away from the obstructing shelter of the weather deck. He turned his head to starboard, searching the distance.

As he did so, the boatswain and helmsman rightfully claimed the wheel. Shefferd noted their guiding hands about the rear wheel and released his own. He moved to the rail and peered over the side.

I could not fathom what he saw or searched for.

"Hard to starboard," his lips mouthed, barely above a whisper from a dry and rasping throat.

The boatswain and helmsman seemed want to reply. Both turned their eyes towards me and our marine sergeant. The actions of the night before had placed us as the saviors of the ship, despite our captain's rank.

In silence, they refused his order. Their eyes and worried faces showed they no longer knew who to trust or believe, save for those, who had stood in our contested line and survived the night and early morning.

I stepped forward and said, "Hard to starboard! Aye, captain," motioning the two hesitating crewmen to obey.

I could see no harm in the maneuver.

I knew to our right, likely laid the coastline of Portugal. We might not have small boats to escape by. But, land was surely within several hours sailing time of our present position. Its nearness would not only provide us the comfort of its sight, but it would gain us a lost avenue of escape.

For now, I was content to obey the captain's command. It could suit our own purpose, escaping the horror burrowed below in the Vanguard's decks.

Ahead, several of our marines had gathered about the hold and our four smashed boats. They pointed their rifles and spikes down into its darkness.

I do not know if it was relief or disappointment, that registered in their faces as they found nothing, but the lower deck's shrouded darkness.

Our sails interrupted my thoughts as they cracked and whipped about with our course change. The wind found our starboard side and the presented sails above. Motion claimed our vessel and the boatswain and helmsman set about bringing back the wheel, steering our rudder straight ahead.

In the distance, I could make out the shadowy fog known to seamen to encircle a distant coast. But, no land was in sight. In truth, land might lay a full day's sailing time away.

"Ensign, Lewis," our captain bellowed, ignoring the presence of the two seamen at the wheel.

"Aye, sir," I offered respectfully, but suspicious of our captain and his loyalties.

I no longer believed he held the well-being and safety of the HMS Vanguard or our crew above all else. True, he was not yet one of the fiends we had contested. But, neither was he one of us, at least not completely, even though he stood among us in the light.

"See to it, that we hold on this course. It will bring us around the tip of Portugal," he instructed, without the aid of chart or plot from the sightings and deductions of a sextant.

I did not know what thread of land might lay ahead or how far off it might be. To me and the others about deck, it could be Portugal or it could be Spain. In the tumultuous confusion of the night and early morning hours, we had lost all sense of our position, knowing only the points of the compass, but little else.

Yet, our captain had no doubt of where we were or even where land would lay. To the rest of us, we could be miles out into the Atlantic.

"Once around the point, continue homeward. I seek to reach Portsmouth at the earliest date possible," Captain Shefferd insisted.

"Aye, captain," I returned, though I had no intention of avoiding land, let alone seeking out the long perilous course home, that would see us at sea for days.

But, land was only part of our salvation. Judging by the bare horizon in the distance, that encircled us about all points of the compass, we were likely a day from the sight of land. And, we were surely too far away to reach its sheltering comfort before night.

The others and I had to seek out any survivors, that might have locked themselves below, in the safety of the storerooms as I had done. More importantly, than our comrades, we needed to retrieve the knowledge our Spanish prisoner held.

My thoughts fell to the doctor and the wounded crewmen abandoned in the depths of the ship below the gun-decks. I wondered if any had survived the hellish onslaught, that had befallen our ship.

"I will be in my cabin, Ensign," the captain spoke, his words trailing off on the wind pushing us forward.

"Aye, Captain," I answered, recalling the foul iron box, sharing the confines of his cabin.

I still had no answers to its presence, though there was no doubt of its link to our distress. Lined with white satin and lace, its interior matched the gossamer delicateness and fineness of the seductive and unearthly gown the young maiden haunting our ship had worn.

Yet, within the cabin earlier, our sergeant had spied it empty.

This "vampiresa" now fed upon our crew. Worse, her foul mouth and actions had enslaved them, transforming them into creatures of her own ilk.

My heart raced with the realization, that we might have one last chance at survival, one final attempt to claim the shores so close, yet so distant.

We could come close enough to swim ashore and set the HMS Vanguard adrift. Releasing her out into the open sea, where devoid of fresh flesh the fiends could fall upon themselves.

My mind spun with the insanity of it. The thought of our heralded warship sailing the oceans without a hand upon the helm, except with the coming of darkness was too much to brood upon.

The thought of sending our warship adrift to ply the waters as a phantom, a ghost-ship, was madness. It was the height of irrationality. We'd be condemning our crew to a life as specters, a living hell.

But, I forgot of our captain, who somehow seemed to be under their control, dominated even through his own dazed and lackadasical stupor. There might be others, such as him. They were not fed on enough to drain them of life or transform them into the foul creatures embattling our ship.

They were left in the limbo existence of our captain. The captain was not dead, but he was not of the living . . . not like men possessing their own wills and minds to choose for themselves. He and likely others lived in servitude, doing in the light of day, what the fiends could not.

Yes, they might have left a few of us in such a state, if only to keep the ship held on course, until darkness allowed them the reprieve of the night's blackness to foray froth and continue their baneful spread of malfeasance and sorrow.

Yet, on a ship devoid of the living hosts, how long would it be, until those few survivors, held in servitude, would soon fall victim to the ghouls fiendish mouths and hunger.

In time, I imagined the HMS Vanguard as a ghost of its former self. Cloaked in the dreadful silence of a plague ship as death claimed her and her crew completely. The Vanguard would only be adrift by day. At night, her hellish crew would once again claim the helm. And, as now they'd set the course for home. They'd make for Portsmouth.

There had to be something, that would allow us, the Vanguard's living survivors, to escape. I prayed there was some way of freeing those, that had succumbed to this living damnation upon earth.

We had to act. We had little time.

The captain retreated to the solitude of his cabin.

He resided inside, showing no interest in what transpired beyond the broken panels of his closed door.

I sought to act, joining our marine sergeant and sharing my plan.

We talked in whispers and guarded tongues, not wishing to alarm our distraught survivors any further.

My course of action shared no favor with our sergeant. But. I persisted. I spoke the truth. I spoke of our distance from land and the inevitable fall of night.

We would soon have to confront the vile demons, that had nearly claimed us, again. This time, they would come anew, fresh and rested. And, as likely, they would be confident and accustomed to their new found movements and strengths, which they had tested in our previous encounter.

We had to act!

CHAPTER 34

Below

HMS Vanguard
Sailing off the
Portuguese Coastline
Day 12-Past Dawn

The sergeant and I were the first down the ladder, nearest the hold. Below, the center of the middle gun-deck was bathed in the bright light filtering down from above. But, fore and aft, the middle gun-deck was cloaked in shadows and darkness.

All the gunports were closed. Closed, they blanketed the deck below in darkness, in spite of the hour of the day.

The lack of light piercing through the joints of the closed gunports attested to the craftsmanship and quality of our English shipbuilders and woodwrights.

My eyes anxiously scanned about the deck bathed in the semi-darkness below. Its dark recesses were broken only by the light seeping in from the openings leading to the upper gun-deck. Save for the rows of 24 pounder cannons, now resting stowed and silent, the deck was empty. But, even with the open hold and hatches above, the deck below was menacingly masked in shadows and a grim darkness about its isolated sections.

Neither light nor water would find a willing opening.

"Get the gunports, surrounding the hold, open! Quickly!" I ordered the sergeant and the men accompanying me.

The sergeant hesitated as did the men gathering about the ladders.

I tucked the pistol in my hand under my belt. It joined a second loaded pistol, already there. I felt for the silver cross now tied about my neck to free my hands.

Assured it was still safely there, I moved about the semi-darkness of the deck. With a cutlass in my hand, I knelt down to one of the gunports and undid the line, holding it fast. I pulled a second line, leading to the top of the gunport and controlling its hinged cover. The cover rose outward.

Inside the gun-deck was bathed in a bright white line of light, streaking across to the other side of the deck.

Seeing my actions, the others understood and mirrored them. Soon, the red painted deck was crisscrossed in the glaring swatches of light as more of the gunports were opened. Their intersecting beams of light offered protection from the ghouls, that might be hidden about in the darkness and shadows.

The sunlight guarded the landing and deck, we dared to descend. We dropped to the lower gun-deck. Again, our intent was to open the nearest gunports and turn them into portals of light, using them against the darkness of the demons' refuge.

I halted along the lower gun-deck as others continued opening the gunports, leaving their cannon withdrawn and allowing nothing to obstruct the light flooding in.

I steeled myself to go further, to descend into the depths of the first of two lowest decks below our waterline. My thoughts were filled with the recent memory of the morgue, still decks below.

I recalled the haunting specter of the young maiden, part beautiful creature and part unholy specter of the shadow world residing in the bowels of our ship.

The sergeant joined me beside the ladders and steps leading below as his marines opened the last of the gunports.

We had descended from the upper gun-deck and through the middle and lower gun-decks, but had not seen one of the fiends.

There was little doubt, they rested below, crammed into the narrow passageways, storerooms, and spaces about the two decks below us.

The sergeant saw the fear in my face, I know it. It was mirrored in his own eyes, though his hardened features did better at hiding his doubts and worries. Unlike myself, armed with two pistols and a cutlass, he seemed confident and reassured, bearing only the lone rifle and its fixed bayonet, grasped in his right hand.

He leaned on its worn, but polished barrel, its brass buttplate resting against the deck. He waited for my order.

I turned around, searching out the men with our lanterns. I found two marines holding eight of the unlit lanterns, freeing up those, opening the last of the gunports.

"Time we lit their candles," I pointed to the two marines, bearing the lanterns.

"You heard the officer. Strike a match to the candles . . . we go below!"

It was all, he needed to say. The men obeyed, though dread and apprehension filled their blank faces. One passed a lit lantern to the sergeant, who in turn, offered it to me.

I held it over the pitch black darkness of the hatchway leading below. It was like a black abyss, a dark void of silence and evil.

No sound came from below. There was not even the dim glow of a lit lantern or the constant dank damp draft, that permeated the lower bowels of the ship. There was only the rank foul stench of rotting flesh, death.

The smell sickened me. It forced its way past my nostrils and deep inside my lungs. I could taste its foulness. Swallowing refused to remove its vile scent.

I looked to our marine sergeant and several of the marines, that had drawn nearer.

Without a word, I threw my feet over the side and mounted the rungs of the ladder leading below. Burdened by my lantern and cutlass, I chose my footing and handholds carefully, before dropping the remaining few feet to the deck below.

My breath escaped me as I found our dead tars and marines packed about the confines of the deck. The sight was revolting. It damningly magnified the eerie reverence and unease one would shiver at, upon seeing the dead of a crypt.

Our sleeping dead rested shoulder to shoulder, atop the deck or tables, left about the morgue. They lingered, dormant and motionless, waiting for the sun's descending passage, so they could once again awake and claim life.

Some had taken to covering themselves, draping sailcloth or unstrung hammocks around their bodies. Some stood in place like porcelain statues, unmoving and stiff.

Those lain bare and unprotected were a ghostly sight. The exposed flesh of their bodies had taken on a grotesque hue. The pale white pallor, they'd exuded earlier, was replaced by a sickly gray tone. It was strange and inhuman as if their flesh was devoid of circulation and concealed from the healthy light of day.

The pale tissue was festered and pocked with sores and decay ravaging their skin. Their skin seemed artificial as if it was the ghastly creation of some artisan, who upon painting or enameling their sculpted forms, had erred in his selection of colors and finish.

Some held their hands folded across their chests, mirroring the images of the famed mummies, excavated from the Egyptian burial tombs or the laid in state forms of high officials or royalty, whose resting bodies were allowed a final viewing by the multitudes of the public, showing respect and reverence for one last time.

Yet, their folded arms showed no discomfort in clasping themselves about their chests. They were like stiff carved wooden figurines, frozen in their poses and unaware of the world about their stiff lifeless existence.

My heart raced as my lungs struggled to fill. The act was made all the more difficult by the stench amid the deck.

I turned slowly in a circle as the sergeant scaled down the ladder to my rear. I found more of the lifeless forms. They were devoid of animation.

They were like insects, who upon winter's arrival, ceased activity and function by instinct and nature's design, choosing to halt their lives by falling dormant, until the thawing spring.

But, I knew full well, that the foul creatures around us would come to life with the setting of the sun. Now, they merely remained in the darkness below the waterline, seeking the depths of our ship for protection from the light of day.

I froze in disbelief as I found several of our former shipmates hanging upside down. They hung from the rafters and beams, supporting the next deck above. Shoulder to shoulder, they mirrored the packed bodies of bats, clinging to the ceiling or walls of a cave or abandoned barn.

I cupped my free left hand over the cross about my neck, lest its presence disturb or raise the demons, lingering about us. I viewed the grotesque forms, that had once been members of our crew.

Despite, the unnatural poses of their bodies, there was no movement or any sign of strain about them or their limbs. Like the others, they were still as if asleep. There was no sound from them. Not a breath was heard.

There was only silence.

It added to our dread.

The others took their turn descending the ladder. All, in turn, were revulsed by the ungodly sight. One man froze, clinging to the rungs of the ladder as if he would not or could not let go.

Our sergeant neared the man, silently reassuring him with a comradely poke to one of his shoulders. A wave of his hand, beckoned him down the final rungs.

I could not count the number of bodies wedged into a space, so small, it seemed impossible to bear them. They were like a catch of herring or other small fish, stuffed into the confines of a basket or wooden crate. The ghoulish tars were crammed into nearly every empty space, that might offer some protection from the threatening intrusion of the light from the upper decks.

We stared in morbid wonder and disbelief. We were no longer among comrades or men.

I knelt to the next set of steps and ladders. Its darkness mirrored that of the deck we stood on. It bleakness held an even worse sense of terror and fearful awe.

Somewhere below were our good doctor and the mad Spanish prisoner. I wondered if they were still among the living or had joined the ranks of the hellish crew, that would claim our ship with the coming of night.

I lowered the lantern over the edge of the deck. The last deck beneath the waterline awaited.

There, in the narrow passageway below, that led to the infirmary and the spaces bearing our worst wounded, more of the ghouls rested. They stood or laid in silence, mirroring those about the morgue's deck, we now stood on.

The silence was broken only by the rushing waters along the sides of the ship and above our heads. The waters' discord heralded the approach of the rough swells as fall beset the waters of the Atlantic Ocean.

Their sound was joined by the uneasy rocking motion of our ship and the slanting of our decks through their axis. We spread our feet apart, searching out sure footing as the Vanguard's hull yawed.

I fought the urge to check my timepiece. The hour did not matter. We had to do as we needed . . . before darkness came.

I prayed only, that we could accomplish our goal and find survivors below. We would rescue who we could. I prayed our doctor and the Spaniard, who might have the key to our dilemma, were still among them.

And, if fortune smiled upon us, I prayed we would reach land, so we could depart this damned ship and the souls claimed aboard her by the haunts of darkness.

I descended the ladder leading below. I was resolute in my beliefs and in the protection provided by the cross, dangling about my neck. I went on.

The lowest deck of the HMS Vanguard was cloaked in blackness. Not a single lantern was hung or lit. I knew every deck held its share of the rounded and iron banded lanterns, hanging from the sturdy framework of our ship's skeleton.

Yet, in the deepest part of our ship, none were lit.

I held onto the rung of the ladder as tightly as I could with my right hand, while my left hand and the extended lantern in its grasp swayed about. In its glow, I searched for some sign of survivors . . . or foes.

The latter were readily present. Like the deck above, the fiends were crowded about, shoulder to shoulder.

Many had no form to them, their flesh rotting or wasting away to skeletons. A few, whose bodies were already claimed by age, devoid of hair atop their heads and taken to walking about in the stooped crouch of the elderly, now looked like the demons of lore and religious myth.

Their bald heads and sunken cheeks framed bony brows and sunken closed eyes. I halted upon the loathsome sight. Their presence recalled the images rendered in religious paintings or adorning the illustrated pages of a bible or missal.

They looked like the defeated angels cast out of Heaven with Lucifer into the depths of hell. Beaten, that was the word, I would use to describe them. Their bodies' vigor and health, their very lives, had been claimed from them. They hid in darkness from the light, much as, Lucifer and his fallen angels could not face the light of God.

But, though their outward appearance was an abomination, there was something awry in the silent aurora, their ghastly forms presented. Despite, their grotesqueness, I found myself saddened by their countenance. Outwardly and in every encounter, they had proved themselves the denizens of evil, reviling in inflicting harm among our crew.

But, in their helpless and vulnerable slumber, they seemed pitiful and pathetic as if they should be the subject our mercy and forgiveness. They had become the damned. They would know no rest.

They would be forever bound to wander upon the earth. A sentence made the less bearable, when one considered the joys of light would be denied them. No more would they find the solace of other human beings or know the simple joys of life.

The pleasure of the human touch, the shared embrace of a lover and spouse, all eluded them. They had become beasts, seemingly taken of one purpose, to feed and spread the cancer enslaving them.

Death was all they would reap as they fed on the living, spreading their vile disease and affliction. There could be no joy or hope for them. They were worse, than dead.

Yet, it seemed there could be no death for them. They were to suffer a continuing existence, denied the escape and comfort of life's inevitable end.

And, their bodies, what would become of them? Even now, their flesh rotted and any substance of their human forms fled them. They were creatures, vile and foul. They were worse, than dead. It was as if they had been vanquished and exiled from the family of man and God's charitable and forgiving grace.

But, their vanquished and defeated lot was only a short-lived retreat. With the coming of darkness, they'd rise again. Unless, we could learn of some way to defeat them.

The sergeant descended, his feet halting several rungs above me and waiting for me to reach the floor.

I carefully stepped down several more rungs. I halted beside the ladder. The sergeant, his rifle and its wicked spike pointed downward, followed.

We remained beside the ladder's frame. Both of us gazed about the ungodly culmination of ghouls, framed in the dim light of our sole lantern.

Above, one of the marines lowered his arm and lantern over the side of the hatchway. His added light revealed the gory host of ghouls lined about the narrow hallway, leading to the infirmary.

"We should kill them all. Kill them in their sleep," the sergeant hissed, his weapon and its dreaded spike pointed towards the nearest group of fiends.

"Yes. But, how? They're dead. You saw it. They rose from about the morgue."

"Part their heads," the sergeant's ire rose as did his voice.

I motioned for silence with a raised hand and cutlass.

I could hear sounds. I would have said breathing, but that could not describe the emanations from the gathered and slumbering horde.

"Quiet, lest they rise. You hear it?" I said

"Breathing?" the sergeant returned as the first of our other marines, began descending to our deck.

"No, it can't be," I said, pointing to one of the nearest creatures. "There's no breath, no heaving or movement of the chest."

We moved forward several paces, halting until the others could descend and join us.

My ear's pricked with the low rhythmic sound, magnified by the large number of creatures harbored in the confines of the HMS Vanguard's lowest deck.

"A heartbeat?" the sergeant offered, his face bewildered and puzzled.

"Not a heartbeat, but many. Beating as one," I returned.

The gathered horde existed as one. It was as if their vile hearts shared the same throb and pulse.

The weapons and gear, of the marines behind us, rattled. Each descended the ladder and bunched up behind us.

"I'm for killing as many as we can, now!" the sergeant exclaimed, agitated by the unnatural melody emanating from the living corpses.

"First, we find the doctor and any survivors. And, take care to retrieve our Spaniard. I think he's the only one, who knows the answer to this godless riddle bedeviling us.

"That damn prisoner. He's probably the cause of this," the sergeant's words bit, though barely above a whisper.

"No, its that damn iron box up in the captain's cabin, that's got something to do with this. I know it. You saw its insides, white lace and fabric. It was done up like a damn coffin," I snapped back.

There was silence as our gathered group gauged the inactivity of our opponents. They seemed unaware and undisturbed by our presence, even though, as our sergeant suggested, we could slay them as they slept. If only we could.

I'd seen enough topside, the night and early morning before, to doubt the truth of our sergeant's angry bravado. We'd wounded many with wounds horrible enough to bring a sailor to the deck, waiting for death to claim him. Yet, they had continued on as if the severed limbs and dastardly gashes about their bodies were nothing.

Only the severing of their abominable heads had gained us a moment of reprieve. But, I had to attest, I'd seen none remain unmoving, despite the loss of a head, save for one corpse, whose body our sergeant seemingly dispatched by tossing the decapitated head over the side.

I did not know what foul punishment our fiends' bodies could absorb and still return to plague us.

Besides, if we went about severing heads from bodies in this enclosed confine, crowded with the ghouls packed so tightly together, there was the threat, that they might rise.

There were hundreds of our crewmen, that had succumbed to this hellish existence. We could not oppose them all in the darkened confines of the lower decks, if they woke. We would be overwhelmed.

No stealth and knowledge were now our best weapons. I was sure, the Spaniard knew something. If he was still alive, I would learn it and use this new found wisdom to rid our ship of this bane or effect our escape.

I stepped forward, leading the way to the infirmary upon silent footsteps, cloaked in the dim glow of the lantern stretched out before me.

A fiend stirred as the light of the lantern passed beside him.

He was without a shirt. His thin body seemed emaciated and malnourished. I could almost see the lines of his bones through his body, most certainly, I could see his ribs pressing against his sickly flesh.

In horror, I froze. The fiend's eyes opened.

They stared blankly up at the ceiling, the underside of the next deck above.

His eyelids did not blink. His face showed no sign of alertness or awareness, save for a slight uncontrolled twitch. Otherwise, there was no movement.

I stared in gruesome amazement at his eyes. Where a man's eyes might be white and his eyes centered amid them, our ghoul's eyes were yellow, speckled by the trailing thin lines of red blood vessels, surrounding the black dark orbs of soulless eyes.

And, those eyes. They were so deep and dark. It was as if by looking into them, one could be swallowed into their empty depths. There was something entreating about that cold wicked gaze, peering up blankly.

I turned my head aside, breaking the hold, this demon's slumbering eyes claimed upon my mind.

I headed for the infirmary, our sergeant pressing beside me as we tried to move two-men wide along the narrow aisle.

We passed the first of several storerooms. They were small anterooms, much like the rigging storeroom, I had sought refuge in, days before. I had deluded myself into thinking it had been a dream, the temporary madness of my mind being overwhelmed, falling victim to the trials of combat and the cruel brutality of scalpel and bone-saw.

I had been wrong. I had lied to myself. What folly, it had all led to this.

I swallowed, trying to find the strength to continue, to suppress my fears. We had to succeed. If we did not, death awaited us or worse, we would join the ranks of Lieutenant Loydd's ghastly command.

The first anteroom was packed with the creatures. They resembled insects, their spiny limbs folded up about them as they pressed against each other. The stench was frightful, trapped about the lifeless lower deck, devoid of the draft of a breeze or fresh air.

We moved on.

We passed several more small storerooms and enclaves. Each

was beset by more of the fiends, jammed and packed tightly against each other, wedged into every dark space. A few, nearest the doorways, stirred at our passing. The dim lights of the candles inside our lanterns seemed to test the solidness of their unnatural slumber.

We reached the infirmary.

The sight was appalling. On the floor lay the remains of what had been our wounded seamen. They had fallen victim to the hated ghouls, providing the creatures a helpless meal, a terrified feast. The temporary infirmary had become a trap, offering our seamen no escape.

But, even though they had been descended upon by the unholy horde, now sheltering about the deck, I knew they would never rise.

There was nothing left of their bodies. There were only pieces, a bone with some flesh, here or a severed leg or limb, there. Our wounded tars had been set on, ripped apart and devoured. The dried pools of blood staining the deck told all.

My stomach churned, its acid rising in my mouth.

Some, of the ghouls still remained in the infirmary, content to reside in slumber among the remains of their feast. They laid atop the floor or rested atop the tables, that had seen the brutal butchery of the doctor's and my own cruel operations.

I swallowed. I could no longer keep my fears and revulsion in check, held in the tormented gut of my stomach or the disdainful and fearsome thoughts of my mind.

I pressed forward with abandonment, nearly brushing against two of the resting ghouls.

Our sergeant followed as I raced towards the brig.

We ignored the slumbering fiends sitting or reclining about the deck or the walls of the lower hull.

I halted, only upon finding the heavy framed door and iron barred window of the Spaniard's prison.

In dismay, I saw the padlock was gone. It lay strewn about the deck with a large metal ring, bearing the keys to the brig and several storerooms nearby. It left no doubt in my mind, that the beasts had descended upon our Spanish prisoner.

But, I had to know. I had to know for certain.

Ignoring the whispered protests of our sergeant, I continued forward, threading my way among the bodies of the ghastly fiends, littering the floor. The boat rolled slowly, threatening to unbalance me or wake the creatures at my feet.

I threw caution away and kept on.

I reached the door.

I peered inside.

My spirits soared. My face could not hide my elation. But, I remained silent, lest I wake our living corpses.

There, inside the small cell of the brig, were the handful of survivors of the infirmary. Our good doctor and tars along with several slightly wounded patients were crammed about the cell's tiny interior. They pressed against the shivering body of our Spaniard.

All bore terror in their eyes. My presence provided them a glimmer of hope, the promise of salvation. I could tell from their apprehensive gazes, that none inside trusted me.

Surviving their hellish confinement below, they could not know if I was ally to the ghoulish usurpers, that had wrested control of the Vanguard or still a man, a human being like them.

I could not fault them.

My eyes spied the ropes, lashing the door fast from the inside. Those inside sheltered behind the heavy door. They had done the same as I had, days ago. Several of the tars held makeshift weapons, a piece of wood or metal to use as a club or spike.

Our doctor held a small scalpel, tightly in his hand. His shirt was covered in a brackish fluid, bearing little resemblance to blood.

All bore fatigued eyes, that had claimed no sleep.

"Ensign Lewis?" the doctor questioned, wanting to see what soul or demon remained in my body's presence.

"Aye, Doctor," I answered allaying his fears. "Now, keep your tongue quiet. We have to get topside. We're making for land and intend to jump ship, when we're close enough."

"The boats?" Radford's face lit up.

"Nay. They've been smashed. These fiends have seen to that. We've got to get off this ship by nightfall . . . . or . . ." I did not need to answer.

The surgeon set about encouraging the tars inside to release the knots and holds of the ropes securing the door. They worked feverishly.

They were now men with hope, a renewed hope, that none had ever expected to have again. One produced a small knife and began slicing, through a resisting knot.

It was our Spaniard, who failed to see the salvation presented to him.

Again, the fool fell into madness.

His eyes popped open as if he was just startled awake, even though, he too had not slept like the others. His hands were free of the restraint of the tars, now freeing themselves from the brig's cell. His limbs flailed about as he took to ranting.

He protested their attempts to free the door. His words started out as guarded, but rasping whispers. But, madness soon claimed his tongue.

His first outburst stirred several nearby demons, laying on the deck.

Our sergeant and another marine pointed their rifles' spikes over the creatures' chests, waiting to plunge the honed steel through, at the slightest attempt of the demons to rise.

A second outburst berated those, releasing the first rope. It slid free of the bars it had been tied to, panicking our captive.

I could not understand the Spaniard's words, they were so fast and fleeting.

Radford questioned a tar, who had dropped to the prisoner, capturing him in his arms as the doctor moved to clam him.

The Spaniard's arms fell to his side, under the forceful grasp of our larger tar. But, the Spaniard's tongue still ranted on.

The tar knew the Spanish tongue better, than I. He set about trying to still the prisoner. His words tried to coax him to silence for all our sakes.

Another tar dropped to his knees, preparing to smash the prisoner in the mouth and silence his mindless words, lest we all become imperiled.

I halted his attempt. Ordering him to cup a hand about the prisoner's mouth and muffle his discord.

"What's he saying?" I asked the tar, trying to quiet the Spaniard, while my eyes searched for signs of a threat from the demons among us.

"He said not to open the door. He's saying they'll rise!" the tar translated.

"It's not nightfall," I returned.

The Spaniard continued, breaking free of the hand over his mouth with biting teeth and a twisting head.

"He's saying, it doesn't matter. They're safe amid the darkness. There's no light here!" the tar advised.

"How do we rid our ship of them? Ask him?" I demanded, keeping my voice low and ignoring the Spaniard's warning.

I allowed the tar to translate my words, instead of trying to form them in the Spaniard's tongue, myself. The tar showed an uncanny ease in conversing in our enemy's language.

He spoke firmly, delivering the seriousness of my inquiry without alarming or distressing our frightened captive.

The Spaniard's eyes showed the understanding import of my query. The fear residing in his eyes slipped away. It was quickly replaced by bewilderment, than a mad and almost eager willingness to reveal the knowledge, he possessed.

He claimed the chance to strike back at our foes. He realized, we no longer thought him mad or deranged. I had asked for his advice and now, he could not impart it quickly enough.

Our tar raised his hands, freeing the Spaniard of his grasp. His open palms and protesting fingers tried to slow the verbal release, spewing from the prisoner's lips.

The Spaniard guarded his voice, he no longer had to seek our attention. He had found us responsive accomplices, eager to learn anything, he knew of the fiends surrounding us.

His words were too fast for myself and the tar, more fluent in the prisoner's native tongue. He spit out this or that warning or proscription. None made any sense.

The tar managed to halt the rambling diatribe. It had been part lore, prayer, and myth. But, it had been too rapid and broken to make any sense.

The tar rested a hand atop the Spaniard's shoulder, physically affirming his presence and coaxing calm, before slowly intoning the Spaniard to repeat himself again.

The Spaniard swallowed, the act nearly choking him.

His head fell to his chest as his lungs filled and he searched for the strength and repose to start again.

His words came through clenched teeth, frustrated from his failure to impart the dire wisdom, he alone held. His tongue and lips moved exaggeratedly as he reformed the words, he'd raced through only a breath before.

About us, the marines stood among the gathered fiends. Their loaded weapons and biting spikes were aimed at the nearest ghouls about them.

The tar beside the Spaniard returned my gaze and thoughts to those inside the brig.

The last rope, holding the thick plank door fast, was released. The tar undoing its enigma, a myriad of knots, dropped the thick rope to the deck.

"He's saying, they're in no danger from the light down here. They can move about as freely as in the night. We have to leave . . ."

"God!" one of the marines, to my rear, exclaimed.

I turned around to find one of the ghouls laying atop the makeshift tables of our temporary infirmary. He sat straight up. The move was unnatural as if some unseen hand had pushed him up abruptly.

His back and head were in line, both stiff as a board.

His eyes opened, just as suddenly as he had sat up.

Our young marine had fallen silent, staring into the fiend's eyes and falling into a stupor of shock and disbelief. He was oblivious to the clawing hands thrusting out and searching for him.

A companion stepped forward, brushing hard against one of the corpses on the deck. In a swift thrust, he planted the length of his spike through the fiend, that threatened his comrade.

The steel skewer plunged through the ghoul's chest, near the right lung. It ripped out ghoul's back, impaling the vampire on its length.

The ghoul's mouth opened in a fearsome cry.

Behind me, the Spaniard continued. He began shouting as my attention was distracted away from him.

The ghoul's scream rose. It was not like the shouts of men. No word was formed by its tongue or imparted by its lips. It was a vaulted shriek, a cry of alarm.

Slowly, devoid of the strength, that darkness seemed to impart upon them, the creatures about us rose. The repugnant snap of joint or knuckle filled our ears, sickening our hearts and minds.

Fear rose in every one of us.

The marine pulled his spike from the hellish sentinel, giving alarm to the others. But, the sound did not halt.

In an attempt to thwart the unholy scream, the marine swept the butt of his rifle across the fiend's head, striking the creature hard in the mouth. Teeth crushed or flew from the open orifice.

But, still the screech pierced the bowels of the HMS Vanguard.

Several of the demons had already risen to their feet. Their open eyes searched us out as if their dulled minds still did not understand the reason for the alarm, emanating from their fiendish comrade.

In desperation, the marine pummeled the ghoul before him, knocking him flat on the table. But, the creature's blank eyes and mouth remained open.

A marine in the aisle, beyond the infirmary, who guarded our path of exit pushed inside.

"They're awake! They're blocking the hatches. There's no way back up!" he exclaimed, his voice breaking in terror.

He had almost reached the marines, standing near the sickbay's temporary infirmary, when a creature standing as stiff and rigid as a plank, beside the wall, thrust his arms out. The movement was as quick and sudden as a steel trap.

Its clawing bony hands entrapped the marine's neck in a deadly vice-like hold. The surprise was complete.

The marine dropped his rifle and hung suspended in the air as the fiend's arms lifted him. His still running feet left he deck. His eyes searched us out in horror and dismay.

They pleaded silently for our aid.

The marine, who had frozen, when the ghoul on the table rose, spun about. He shed his hapless stupor and raised his rifle. He cocked the flintlock weapon and struggled to hold its swaying barrel steady as he aimed it at fiend and friend alike.

The spike at the rifle's end fluctuated wildly about. It seemed as if the young seafaring soldier would not be able to distinguish his comrade from the fiend, holding him so close.

The barrel halted. A sharp retort leapt from the rifle's powderhole and flame and smoke spat from the weapon's long barrel.

Ahead, the trapped marine's chest exploded as the round struck it. His body was thrust backwards as was the demon's, whose body was found by the conical bullet, travelling through both.

The demon released his grip on the young lad's comrade as the failed sharpshooter withdrew his weapon's ramrod and fumbled about his belt and attached leather boxes for a new paper cartridge of powder.

He had lifted the tiny paper wad of powder to his mouth, tearing off an end with his teeth as the demon lurched forward. He dropped the paper, still filled with a precise measure of black powder.

He began hefting his weapon upright in a defensive block, pointing its spike forward. But, it was too late.

The demon was upon him. It brushed aside the rifle as if it never presented any threat. Its fingers and long nails clawed out at the marine's face, before claiming his eyes and then, a hold about his neck.

The creature raised it foul head to the deck above, emitting a shriek of elation at its newly won victory.

A shot echoed about the small anterooms, joining the infirmary and brig.

I turned around to see our marine sergeant and the smoke surrounding the barrel of his discharged weapon.

His shot was well placed. It smashed into the top of the demon's skull. Bone and a foul gray essence from inside the creature's head spattered about. The impact sent the demon backwards, almost tumbling him.

But, he rose. Slowly and deliberately, he mocked our attempts to defend ourselves. The vile demon rose.

Our sergeant was furiously trying to reload.

Again, the demon sought to repeat his attack, this time targeting our veteran sergeant.

I stepped forward. I raised my cutlass high and began a swinging downward arc of its blade. I aimed it towards the demon's path.

The creature ran into my blade as if he had never seen it or feared its severing chop. The honed blade found the stretched gray neck of its foul skin. It cut.

I stood in horror. I was unable to withdraw the blade, wedged nearly half way through the beast's neck.

A black brackish fluid, thick like sap gelled, then ran forth from the wound.

I could not breathe. I could not swallow. The foulness of its escaping odor and its sight brought me to inaction.

"Get back!" the sergeant yelled as the demon lurched forth again as if my blow had never found or harmed him.

The sergeant's shout pulled me from my stupor. I moved aside, freeing my cutlass from the fiend as the creature charged again.

A sharp crack filled the narrow confines, we were trapped within. Again, the demon was kicked back by the forceful impact of a well-aimed round.

Again, the horrid creature began to rise, but this time, its ascension was slow and labored. Its head hung askew. But, it still came and more hellish comrades were joining it. They filled the narrow infirmary.

"Come here!" the surgeon yelled. "Seek the safety of the brig!"

I turned around to spy Radford and several more of our marines cramming themselves into the brig with the tars already there.

A tar was lashing a rope about the door's window bars. He strived to tie the door fast and seal themselves inside, once more. In shock, I saw the one man, who might aid us, standing outside the brig's door. It was the Spaniard.

He turned and ran away from the infirmary and the sanctuary of the brig.

"Sergeant!" I yelled, "Follow me!"

I chased after the Spaniard, darting about the rising corpses littering the floor ahead. My lantern swung wildly about its metal ring as I held it in my grasp. Its light reflected on the silver cross, dangling from my neck.

The icon was in sight of all as it swung within the lantern's light, then it was gone, flung about my neck, only to return into the lantern's glow as it traveled about with my next movement.

Some of the ghouls spied the silver cross, swaying wildly. Arms and hands rose to shield their awaking black eyes from the holy icon.

I tightened my grip on the cutlass. I was frightfully aware, that I and the Spaniard were fleeing away from the protective band of our small group. We left the meager defense of our outnumbered survivors. We ran away from their safety and numbers.

To the rear, I heard our sergeant following. He called out to me. But, in the madness of the chase and amid the shrieks of more rising ghouls, I could not discern his words. I ran on,

swallowed up in the darkness of the bowels of the Vanguard
with only the lantern, in my hands, lighting my path

Our Spaniard moved with an agility, I could not have
imagined, he possessed. His frail form moved out of fear and
desperation.

He passed several anterooms, storage lockers for our ship's
gear and weapons. He had passed three heavy plank doors, before
I closed upon him.

My heart raced with fear and exhaustion. The madness
enveloping us was too much. I began to welcome death, if only
to end the panic and trepidation enfolding us.

The Spaniard stumbled, running headfirst into the wall, beside
a storeroom. His feet failed him as he dropped to the deck.

I ran up upon him and clasped a hand about his left shoulder.

My breath was panting like some wild animal. I looked up
to find the way ahead blocked by a swarm of ghouls, running the
breath of the narrow aisle. There was no way ahead.

I pulled the Spaniard to his feet and pressed into him with
my left shoulder, pinning him to the wall to our left.

I had halted his flight, but to what good? Ahead and behind
us, save for the approaching sergeant, we were surrounded by the
ghouls. I felt a last shred of abandonment as I heard the brig's
door slammed shut. The ropes securing it, drew tight as the last
knots were tied off.

The sergeant, Spaniard, and myself were alone.

My mind recalled the gruesome remains of the tars, that had
been feasted on in the infirmary, Gnarled down to the bone,
their remains were nothing more, than a few ghastly pieces of
limbs and flesh, that had proved too unsavory for the foul mouths
and full bellies of the demons surrounding us.

I switched the cutlass to my left hand and groped for the
smooth slender grip of one of the pistols, tucked in my belt.

I held it forth. For the first time, I saw the fear engulfing me.
My hand and pistol shook. They trembled uncontrollably. My
aim wandered haphazardly about, falling among one, then another
of the approaching ghouls.

I cocked the flintlock and pulled the weapon's trigger.

The pistol fired, sending a plume of white smoke to the ceiling.

One of the ghouls was pushed backwards by the impact. But, he was not knocked off his feet. Instead, his legs moved to absorb the shock of the blow and his stance became defiant.

His eyes looked down at the hole torn in the center of his chest. Its flesh was ripped open, revealing a black liquid, that seemed to hang within the wound. It was black and thick, like syrup or tar against the ghoul's foul gray flesh.

His head and eyes lifted, seemingly surprised, that no damage had been done to him, save for the ball lodged inside his chest. His mouth opened, his lips parting in an evil grin. His foul orifice yielded the appearance of sharp pointed teeth.

They were small and animal-like, reminding me of the hated snarl of a malicious cat or cornered fox. His eyes filled with glee as his attention and that of the others turned on me and the Spaniard.

The sergeant's rifle cracked. The shot sped past our Spaniard and found the head of the enraged and newly confident fiend, renewing his assault.

His skull cracked and nearly a quarter of it flew towards the ceiling or wall behind him. The ghoul halted, but did not fall.

I looked behind us, to find the sergeant rushing forward, after halting to fire the well-aimed shot. Behind him, other creatures had risen.

I twisted my neck to the left and found a storeroom beside us. It would have to do. My fingers reached for the cross around my neck. I clasped it in my shaky hands and pulled it free of the thin leather strand, looped about my neck. The knot broke and I held the cross aloft along with the lantern in my left hand.

The fiends ahead halted. Again, evil hisses like those of threatening vipers or asps, filled the deck's confines.

"Get the Spaniard! Throw him in there, the storeroom," I yelled, as the sergeant's footsteps fell in beside me.

I glimpsed our marine sergeant's hammy hand reaching for

our captive. He encircled one of the Spaniard's thin arms and pulled him abruptly to his feet. He hefted the prisoner up from the place on the deck, where he now lay, collapsed and shaking in fear.

He brushed against me as he muscled the prisoner into the storeroom. Haltingly, I entered its doorway after them, one step at a time, keeping the silver cross held high in the glow of the lantern.

To my right, down along the other anterooms and towards the brig, the aisle had fallen into darkness, except for the glow of the lanterns, confined to the brig's small enclosure.

The wall behind me rang out with a thud. The fiends, in the aisle on either side of the storeroom's entrance, had begun to throw whatever was handy at me.

I saw the dark shadow of another barely seen object sail towards me. I ducked into the storeroom, but not fast enough. My left arm was still outside its sanctuary. The object, thrown with the strength of an unholy angel, struck my left hand.

The blow was so hard it knocked the lantern free of my grasp. The rounded iron banded walls of the lantern rolled about the deck, until the candle inside became unseated and fell from its protective confines.

The candle extinguished in its unguarded roll.

Darkness engulfed us.

The sergeant's hand fell atop my right shoulder, pulling me inside as he shouldered the storeroom's door closed with a slamming bang. In the darkness, I heard him block off the door. Blind and fearful, I did not see what he used to secure it.

Devoid of light and no longer threatened by the image of the silver cross, the demons outside beset upon our door. Hated fists pounded on its heavy plank surface.

We could hear the dreaded hisses and seething of the demons on the other side.

In darkness, I heard our sergeant remove the ramrod of his rifle and with practiced determination reload its long barrel. The door shuddered as the weight of the gathered demons was set upon it.

Its iron hinges creaked and groaned. The demons hammered and pushed against it. My hands searched about my pockets for a match, one of several held in reserve to light the lost lantern.

But, fear had overwhelmed me. In the blackness, I heard the whimpering sobs of our Spanish prisoner. He had given up, ceding to the inevitable. He had no more hope, he only wanted it all to end.

His lips mumbled the beginning of some ritualistic prayer.

"Stop it! Stop it, you bastard!" the sergeant's voice bellowed as the din outside the door rose.

I stepped away from the heavy door, fumbling the silver cross in my hand. It seemed like nothing could save us. We would never reach the upper decks again. I abandoned the search for the loose matches in the folds of my jacket's pocket.

The Spaniard continued his ranting, falling back upon the comfort of some long forgotten and little used prayer. He recited it fervently, gasping breaths to fill his rasping lungs in between each scared line and nearly choking on a dry parched mouth.

I understood a few of the words, such as "muerto," the dead. He was praying for the dead or those soon to be dead. He was praying for himself. He was praying for us.

His madness was infectious. I stood silently in the darkness. I had surrendered. I had given up. I did not want to fight anymore. I wanted the nightmare to end. I wanted to be free of this madness at any cost, even if it meant joining the mindless savage creatures, that had once been our crew.

My stomach soured. It was hollow and bitter with fear.

The clamor about the door continued. It seemed as if the door would soon burst free of its hinges. It shuddered under the ferocious attack as hands clawed and banged against its splintered surface.

I heard the sergeant's rifle cock. His feet moved apart as he stepped forward, pushing into me. He tried to find a new footing for a fighting stance behind the door.

I marvelled at his perseverance. I could not see what he hoped to gain by continuing our nightmarish struggle. Amid madness and the certainty of defeat, he still remained unbowed and unconquered.

Even, in the darkness, I could feel his rising anger and scorn for our foe beyond the door. He would offer them no quarter and would not surrender. I did not need light to know the confident and defiant bearing of the veteran, unwilling to accept defeat.

A combatant to the end, he meant to exit this life in a final brawl, leaving it as belligerently as he had lived his soldiering existence. His tenacity awoke me from my resignation.

I clasped the silver cross in my left hand and searched about my belt for my second loaded pistol. I stretched out my left hand, to find the sergeant's shoulder.

I slapped it, affirming my presence and nearness. The cocking of my pistol's flintlock told him I was ready to fight beside him.

The pounding on the door took on a horrid frenzy. Several of its vertical planks sounded as if they were splintering or loosening. Dust fell from the ceiling above, finding my open eyes, that stared blindly ahead in the darkness at the door. A hinge jumped, becoming loose on its mounts.

The hissing and screeching on the other side of the door raised in a nefarious and rejoicing chorus.

Then, there was silence.

The pounding stopped. The demons fell silent.

The door's strength was no longer tested.

CHAPTER 35

Trapped

HMS Vanguard
Sailing off the
Portuguese Coastline
Day 12-The Hour Unknown

I did not know the hour. I was tempted to strike a match and examine the face of my timepiece. But, I had only four or five of the wooden sticks and their combustible heads scattered loosely inside my jacket's pocket.

In our exiled darkness, using them for such a frivolity as searching out the time seemed a waste of their good resource. I was content to find a place upon the floor, beside the Spaniard and wait.

Since the silence, he had calmed. But, his body still shook. As I had found from lightly pressing my hand atop his arm, searching out his shivering form in the darkness engulfing the storeroom's deck.

I offered words, in his native language, to calm him. I could do little else. Somehow, either my words or nearness offered him some peace. Perhaps, just having another near was enough.

I searched for the words, I needed to speak in his own tongue, to try to solve the gruesome riddle confronting us. I spoke of his religion. It seemed to be the key.

But, again his words fell to rantings of crosses and crucifixes. Somewhere, between his spewing wisdom and labored breaths, he intoned, how they could be used to repel the ghouls, the vampires, who because of their damnation, could not look upon the image of salvation.

Slowly, I made him understand, that I knew of the repelling significance of the religious icon. We had used my cross to fend the demons off in our earlier battle, topside on the weather deck. But, how to kill the creatures? That is what I quested to learn.

Slowly and with difficulty, I tried to translate my inquiry into his tongue. But, our meanings and intent were lost in the hodgepodge of mismatched and translated words.

He rambled on about "madera," wood and "fuego," fire. He spoke of waters, holy ceremonial waters, blessed by a priest. It made no sense to me. I tired to halt his mouth and tongue as they rapidly spewed forth a verbal deluge, I could not readily translate.

He talked too fast. His words besieged me. I could feel his body shuddering. The knowledge, he tried to impart, was gnawing at what little sanity, he still possessed.

Rantings, his words were the rantings of a madman.

I laid down my weapons and I tried to calm him and his restless tongue, placing both hands about him, trying to ease his distress.

I moved back with a start as his own hands clawed at my wrists, grabbing them tightly. I could feel the fear in their trembling grasp.

He halted his words and spoke slowly.

I could feel his breath and nearness about me.

"To the heart," was the best I could translate his words. "Driving wood through the creature's heart would kill them."

"Burning," his mouth hissed as if the thought elated him. "Fire would kill them," his translated words intoned. There was a glee, an infectious satisfaction, rising in his voice with the thought of the demons on the other side of the door sent to the hell they so richly deserved by the flames, lit in the eyes of his imagination.

I allowed him to continue on. The thought, that we might contest the demons, seemed to gratify him. It was an indulgence, that soothed and calmed him.

"What's he going on about?" the marine sergeant, trapped with us, questioned.

"He says, the demons or vampires can be killed," I returned, reluctant to believe or trust in our newly acquired knowledge, that was probably the rot of superstition and lore.

"How?" came the veteran's return.

"Fire. He says, they can be burned," I answered.

"A ruddy lot of good, that does us. Start a fire on board this ship and we burn with it, not to mention the powder stored about. When we sailed, we had thirty-five tons of blackpowder and one-hundred and twenty tons of round shot for our guns."

"And, wood . . . they can be killed, by piercing their hearts with a piece of wood," I relayed.

"More rot and lies from that lunatic," the sergeant bellowed. "If bullets and spikes won't slay them, do you think a sliver of wood will? Rot!"

He cursed the madness of it all. He fell silent in the surrounding darkness as I worked my wrists free of the Spaniard's grasp.

"What else have we?" I challenged. "Do you want to remain here and curse the darkness?"

The sergeant remained silent.

"There's wood about," I remarked, feeling some of the crates stowed about in the storeroom's darkness, "with your bayonet, we can make stakes, even more crosses."

As for our Spaniard's liquid repellant, we had no water or priest to concoct his hallowed mixture, blessing drinking water and transforming it into the holy water, he spoke of. Surrounded by an ocean of water, our Spaniard's potable cure escaped us.

Our position was perilous. We'd no water or food. If we

choose to remain within the blocked off shelter of the storeroom, we'd waste away to nothing and soon find ourselves lacking the strength to do anything.

"He was right about the cross," I offered, as proof of the Spaniard's superstitions and lore. "The demons fear it. You saw it. We all witnessed it, sheltering behind its protection, above on the weather deck."

"Aye," his low guttural voice answered, as I heard him still standing and facing towards the blocked door, acting as our vigilant protector in the darkness.

I stood.

I felt my way towards the door, my left hand extended as I walked blindly. I felt the back of our towering sergeant and made for the heavy planks of the door.

I pressed against it, feeling for the cracks between the door's planks, that had nearly yielded.

"Doctor!" I yelled, pressing my moving lips and mouth to the door's cracks. "Radford!" I bellowed.

"Aye," came back his reply, echoing through the small opening, set into the top of the brig's door.

"The Spaniard says, the creatures can be killed!" I started, before revealing, what little I had learned from our prisoner.

I told him and the others listening of driving stakes of wood into the ghouls' foul hearts. I spoke of using fire to burn their putrid wasting bodies. And, I spoke of our battle on the weather deck above and how the silver cross and the intercession, it had wrought from Heaven, had halted the assault of the demon horde, that had fallen upon us.

I heard other voices engage our surgeon. One sounded as if it was admitting to some transgression or sin, which it sought to unburden from its soul or mind.

Our doctor's voice returned, dominating the outburst of voices, that either sought to believe what I had revealed or to deny it.

"Ensign Lewis, do you still have that cross?" Radford barked.

"Aye," I shouted, my lips brushing against the thick wood of the plank door as they moved.

"We've a crucifix," Radford returned, adding to our meager arsenal. "It seems one of our marines pinched the trinket from our Spaniard's neck," he added, almost laughing at the penchant for larceny among some of our hardened crew.

Beyond the door, there was only silence. Our own voices were all, that disturbed the darkness.

"We can't stay here," I advised. "It's certain death."

"What do you suggest? We can't just open our doors . . . we need a plan of action," Radford's analytical mind returned.

"And, weapons . . . we need to fashion weapons," I added.

"We've none in here, except the rifles and bayonets your marines brought with them. The tars with me have some odd pieces of metal and wood . . ."

"Fashion the wood into stakes . . . use the bayonets to sharpen their ends," I suggested, my words halting as I realized the madness of what I proposed.

"Your Spaniard's sure of this?" Radford returned.

"He says it's so. A piece of wood piercing the heart yields death to these creatures . . ."

My words halted.

There was a presence beyond the doors.

I thought I heard footsteps, but there were none. But, I swore there was movement beyond the closed protection of our door.

The movement was slow and precise. As if a single creature stirred stealthily about.

"Who's out there?" I shouted to the doctor, "we've no window in our door."

There was silence.

"God!" I heard a terrified and repulsed voice exclaim.

"It's Lieutenant Loydd!" Radford exhaled in disbelief.

There was silence, except for the whisper of footsteps as if feet, gliding above the deck, had returned to it. Their movement stopped somewhere between both our doors.

I heard a rasping voice. It barely formed coherent words.

I strained to make out its slurred and almost inaudible speech.

"Doctor . . ." the voice hissed.

It was our second officer's voice, yet it was not.

I heard other feet slowly and heavily treading about the deck outside. I did not need to see the ghouls to know they were gathering about. I could hear the strange insect-like sounds of their clicking jaws and tongues as they formed up, outside our closed doors.

Fear welled up inside me without even seeing the horde, I knew was gathering outside.

Even with fire and stakes, I did not see how we could challenge or defeat, such an evil host. To leave the sanctuary of our shelters meant we'd be overwhelmed. Death or a worse fate seemed inescapable.

My heart dropped as dread replaced the momentary hope, I had begun to cling to. How could I have been so arrogant as to presume to be able to battle, such an ungodly army.

The ship was theirs. The HMS Vanguard belonged to the damned of a floating living hell. I would never wrest her free. I would never escape this nightmare with my life.

Worse, the fiends claiming our vessel now had the means to sail about the world, spreading their disease among the unsuspecting ports and harbors awaiting them. They had become the vanguard of an invading horde, threatening not only our small band of survivors, but the rest of an unsuspecting and oblivious world.

My thoughts returned to Captain Shefferd. The master of our ship had been turned into their willing servant. He willingly ignored the misery, that had befallen his ship and crew.

He was one of them, yet not of them. He was not set aflame by the light of day. He lived in a half-world, not man not creature . . . he was merely a servant to their grim desires.

And, what of that hated iron coffin? I had no idea how it had come to find our ship. But, I had no doubt, that the evil maiden, that I had encountered, our Spaniard's "vampiresa," resided inside its abhorrent confines during the day.

It was she, who had brought this affliction and disease upon our ship and crew. Somehow, she had to know of our destination to join Lord Nelson's fleet and the battle, that had come to pass. She had come to sup and succor upon our wounded in a grizzly demonic feast.

And, in the act, she had contrived an army, creatures created of her own foul image and black heart. And, for what purpose? That, I did not know.

I heard a light scratching outside our door.

"Ensign Lewis," Loydd's haunted voice whispered, his rotting throat rasping with the effort.

"So, the shopkeeper's son has some mettle and wits, too," he hissed.

His voice was hollow and strange, even through the cracks in the storeroom door. It was like that of a dying man faced with choosing between a final breath or departing some last words.

I said nothing.

"We need two," Lieutenant Loydd remarked cryptically, speaking to the darkness in words, we could just barely understand and not the jaded hisses of the demon's barbaric tongue.

I could not understand, why he spoke so unguardedly or had decided to make us privy to his intentions. His next words left no doubt. He wanted to torment us.

In death as in life Loydd was the consummate bastard, reveling in the misfortune and suffering of others.

"From that door!" his breath and words wheezed from a decaying mouth and lungs.

Blind, behind our windowless door, I did not know, which room our second officer had marked.

"They're coming!" I warned the sergeant, who was already stepping back, the same as I, preparing once more to defend the entrance to our temporary haven.

Our hearts raced as we stood amid the room's darkness. We heard everything. We registered every dragging footstep gathering outside. They were muffled, almost muted.

It began. The attack was launched against the solid iron bands and heavy wooden door of the brig.

I hung my head in relief, that it was not us the ghouls sought out. And, just as quickly, I felt shame rising over me for the selfishness of my thoughts. Our comrades, several lengths away, were being besieged.

Unlike, the attack on our own door, where only fists and limbs pounded, upon its planks, I heard the strike of an axe and the stabbing poke of an iron pike.

As they had smashed our boats above, the demons now set upon the brig's door. A vulgar chorus of their voices filled the narrow aisle leading about the storerooms and the infirmary.

Rigid spiny hands tore at the splintering wood. We could hear the door being pulled away, ripped and broken free.

And yet, those seeking sanctuary inside the brig could not fight back. The small window, set high in the door, offered no portal for the marines bearing rifles to fire upon their attackers. It was too high and misplaced to allow them to thrust their deadly spikes at the ghouls. It restricted unleashing an aimed shot.

We listened as the fiends continued their unopposed assault on the heavy plank door. I leaned into our own door, searching for some way to help. But, I was helpless, impotent.

The brig's door creaked on its weakening hinges. The iron bands, locking its planks together, were yielding.

Part of the door must have been torn open enough to allow those inside an opening to view the horrid attack. Their voices yelled out in horror.

My eye peered through the crack of our door's mated planks, searching out the darkness outside. I spied a weak light illuminating the aisle outside our storeroom as the glow of the lanterns, inside the brig, spilled out through the damaged door.

A shot cracked. One of the defenders unleashed his rifle, point blank into one of the demons, besetting the shattered door.

But, as the echoing din of the rifle retreated down the length of the deck, the evil refrain of the incensed demons' voices grew. The shot had done nothing to slow their assault.

Their rasping vile voices rose as they renewed their attack with increased vigor.

"Use the crucifix!" I yelled. "Hold it before you!"

There was no answer to my desperate suggestion.

The sergeant brushed beside me, pressing his mouth close to the door. "Use the Spaniard's crucifix, you thieves!" his voice boomed, trying to jar his men into action.

There was the appalling sound of wood splintering as part of a shattered and cleft door plank was pulled by unholy hands. Its last shred of union with the door, surrendered with a sharp snap.

The fragment was dropped to the floor.

Another rifle barked in a loud retort, likely deafening those inside the cramped brig. With so many men trapped inside, there would be little room to swing a rifle or thrust its lethal spike about.

We heard the panicked voices of those trapped in the brig. Terror had found them.

"Use the crucifix!" I yelled helplessly.

The ghouls shrieks rose. They did not mask their elation, they had penetrated the formidable door of the brig.

Another shot boomed. By the sound of the body thrust backwards, it repelled the attacker, but only momentarily.

Screeching voices pierced the darkness. The demons assailed those inside the brig. Light darted about the wall opposite our door as lanterns thrust and swayed about.

"Give that to me!" I heard the surgeon's voice rise above the ruckus.

Vile hissing and condemnation followed. Radford must have wielded the crucifix. But, it was too late.

I heard the struggling forms of some of the brig's occupants being dragged from the brig's narrow broken doorway.

"Nooo! No!" a tar protested as we heard the rattle of our marines' gear moving about. One of their unseen spikes was thrust forward, but missed. We heard it strike along the brig's wooden wall.

The light glowing against the opposite wall dimmed. A lantern was snatched from one of the brig's occupants. Its light was extinguished and the darkened lantern was thrown to the deck.

Exalted by the welcoming semi-darkness, the demons drove on with their attack.

"Back!" Radford's voice boomed, the remaining lantern's light flickering in the aisle.

Unseen, I imagined him standing before the demons as I had upon the weather deck.

Yet, the demons still pressed their attack. A club's blow was heard shattering bone. And, there was the awful sound of a spike finding its mark within the flesh of one of the ghouls. The release and evacuation of the fiend's rotting bodily gases made a horrid sound.

Even, from our haven's distant spot, I could smell the putrid and pungent discharge. The clamor inside the brig continued, despite the tiny crucifix. The brig had been too full, too crowded, for those inside to muster a true fight.

Its cramped space had left no place for its occupants to shelter away from the abhorrent hands, seeking to grasp two new victims. We heard feet kicking about, smashing into the broken planks, their possessors were dragged through.

Then, it was over.

An uneasy quiet fell upon the semi-darkness outside.

"Radford?" I searched out. "Radford, what happened . . . how are you?"

There was silence, though I heard the survivors stir within the brig.

Radford's voice came slowly. "They've taken two of us," he responded, in a wavering voice, filled with dread and shock.

There was no more to be said. I lowered my head forward, my forehead resting in shame and defeat against the coarse splinters of the door's coarse planks.

We had done nothing to come to the aid of the others.

Outside, I heard a thin scratching. It was the sound of metal being dragged along the sides of the wooden wall outside. It cut along the wall, scratching from the brig towards our storeroom door.

In the silence befalling the deck, it claimed our sole attention. It halted, stopping nearly atop our door.

The thin tip of a captured spike burst through the crack between the planks of the door. It sped alongside the right side of my head, scratching a thin wound along my temple.

Its thin slicing cut burned. I raised my hand to it.

"I smell blood," our second officer's voice rasped in a gruesome taunt.

I backed away from the door, fear welled up inside me.

I heard Lieutenant Loydd sniff the air, the act was deliberate and exaggerated as he continued his diabolical games.

Unseen, his tongue licked his lips, smacking them noticeably as if in preparation to enjoy some treasured delicacy or banquet.

"I could smell your scent, even from atop the main mast," Lieutenant Loydd scoffed, "as can the others. They're like sharks, one drop of blood in an ocean of water is all they need to be alerted to their prey . . . their next meal."

I said nothing. My hands ripped a piece of cloth from my shirt to press against the small wound.

"You'd best remain behind that door and that religious trinket you favor," Loydd's voice hissed.

"What have you done?" I snapped out.

"What your companions?" Loydd returned, not wanting an answer or expecting one from me. "I needed to add to the crew topside to aid our good captain. The sea is turning rough and more hands were needed to navigate the Vanguard in the light of day. They'll not be killed and they'll not become like us. They need to be able to stand in the open sunlight. But, they will serve and willingly."

A shriek echoed about the aisle, coming from the far reaches of the steps and ladders leading topside. It was human, one of our tars.

I said nothing.

"What did you think, I'd allow my men to feed upon them?" Loydd crackled, unable to mirror the amusement of a human laugh. "They've fed enough. Now, it's time for them to earn their keep. We've much to do."

"But, you're right . . . our journey will still take days. We will feed, though sparsely again, until we reach Portsmouth were our appetites can reign unchecked," the second officer pondered aloud, his words slurred and venomous.

His words halted.

The door shuddered about the spike as Loydd's powerful and unnatural hand clasped the bayonet, that had been taken from those about the brig. The wood protested as the honed spike yielded its thickness and reversed its course through the crack between the planks.

He said nothing more.

The aisle, beyond our door, began to fall silent, when a second scream filled the darkness. Our two tars were being enslaved, no doubt, by the bite of the fiends. I recalled the sight of our captain in his cabin and the marks set about his neck.

He was no longer himself. The master of our ship had been reduced to a servant as were the two tars claimed from the brig.

I pressed against the door. My eyes searched the opening, enlarged by the spike. Peering through the hole between the crack, I saw the ghostly shadow of our second officer, nearly out of sight.

He halted, making me fear, he had sensed my presence against the door. My hand pressed tightly against the light wound beside my head. The cloth, I held, was warm with my own gathering blood.

But, I was not the object of Lieutenant Loydd's attention.

There coming into view of the opening, no bigger, than an enlarged keyhole, was the specter, I had seen days ago.

The young woman, I had seen standing beside the sailor's deathbed in the morgue, had returned. It was the same young maid.

She was clad in the delicate white gown, her long black mane flowing about her shoulders. Both her hair and the thin gossamer fabric lifted and wafted about on the slightest of drafts, running through our damp dank vessel.

She moved so lightly, she appeared to float or glide atop the deck. The glow of the lights, coming from inside the brig, highlighted a ghastly aurora about her thin frail shoulders.

One of her thin slender limbs stretched out and claimed our second officer's shoulder. Her hand rested atop it approvingly as Loydd's head bent down in complete submission to her ghastly charms and power.

Yet, there was no love to be found among them. Loydd was the supplicant, the humbled servant and she was the enslaving mistress. In a ghostly pageant, she turned and he humbly and adoringly followed.

To their rear other ghouls joined them, forming a cortege, more appropriate to the etiquette of a royal court, than the demonic haunt the HMS Vanguard had become.

They left. But, I heard the low guttural sounds of other demons about. I did not need to see the fiends to know there was no escape.

We few survivors were trapped, held in the darkness of the bowels of our ship, deep below the Vanguard's waterline. Hundreds of the creatures blocked our return to the light of day.

CHAPTER 36

Waiting

HMS Vanguard
Sailing
Course Unknown
Day 20-The Hour Unknown

My eyes stared at the opening torn into the door of our haven, now turned prison. I rubbed at the thick bristles of the beard covering my face.

By my count and the notches scratched into the wall of the storeroom by our sergeant's spike, we had been held captive for the better part of eight days. We had been relegated to the role of prisoners, held below the Vanguard's waterline.

The door's bottom had been the target of a vicious assault, one day after we had sought the storeroom's refuge. I had thought the attack marked our demise. But, no sooner had it started, then it ended.

The fiends had no intention of harming us. Apparently, we were still useful to them, if only to become slaves and be their surrogates in the daylight, that they shunned.

The opening, torn in the bottom of the door, was not

intended to invade the closed off sanctuary of the storeroom. Instead, it opened a link between captors and captives.

It was a link, meant to ensure our survival for the moment.

Food, water, and even a lantern were passed through the jagged breach within the door.

I stared at the jagged opening, remembering the axes' detestable din as they struck its heavy planks. And then, there had been the horrid grasping of those hated hands, pulling and ripping at the splintered shreds as they enlarged the opening.

Even, a shot from our sergeant's rifle and several thrusts of his bayonet's spike failed to halt the storm besetting our door.

We were certain, we were to meet our end, either claimed by death or united into the unholy clan dominating our ship.

It was to our astonishment, that instead of meeting the demons beyond in one last dire conflict, they pulled away. Instead, of a final desperate combat, nourishment and a lantern had been passed through the gash in our door.

We were fed. We were to be kept alive.

Ample provisions were provided for the three of us. Though, the palatability of our austere fare was less, than desirable. Salted beef and biscuits were the sole and redundant items of our lacking menu.

But, more than the food, we cherished the light provided by the welcomed lantern.

It was enough, that we had light to push away the darkness and somewhat allay our fears. The lantern's glow seemed to offer our Spaniard some comfort. Though in truth, it was only temporary. He lay about the floor, hunched and balled into himself.

With his disheveled hair and unshaven face, he looked the part of a lunatic. I'd have judged him mad, had I not shared in his cursed derangement. But, our Spaniard found no peace even as others now believed his words and shared in his grief.

His anxiety returned with the unnatural movements and noises of the creatures beyond the storeroom's door. They stood guard about us and those trapped in the brig.

From the doctor's voice, several lengths away, I had learned the brig's occupant's were being similarly cared and provided for. All tried to push away the reason for our ghoulish benefactors' generous gifts.

We well knew, we were being kept alive, either as slaves or as food.

Over the last eight days, three more men had been claimed from among those in the brig. I believe only one was claimed for work topside, joining the enslaved ranks of our captain and his accompanying watch.

I feared the other two had been fed upon. Their screams had echoed through our deck and carried to the deck above. I bore the fear, that their flesh and bone had been found by the cruel mouths and gullets of the fiends hungering for human pulp.

We had nothing to do, but wait within our grim quarters, suppressing our apprehension and dread. We were waiting to die. Though, I was certain our sergeant had no intention of going benignly. He would fight to the last as would I, when the time came.

For now, we waited, amid the depressing and frustrating enclosures confining us in the depths of the Vanguard's hull.

Over the days, we had become accustomed to the dank stench and dampness, permeating the bowels of the Vanguard. And, with the passage of time, we'd learned to ignore our own shared mix of body odors, combining with the rotting stink and reek of the decaying corpses, that had cheated death and half-lived about us.

The wait had been anxious and fretful for the better part of three days. Our anxiety was high, expecting a new attack to be mounted at any moment. We assumed it likely as well-fed and sinking into the depths of boredom, we lazily lowered our guard.

But, no attack came.

Instead, there were only additional rations, stark and unsavory as they were. They were delivered almost unseen or unheard at the broken opening along the bottom of the storeroom's door.

I kept the silver cross at the ready, should any demon's skull protrude through the break in the door. But, none challenged us for the small confines, which we sheltered within.

I kept my two pistols close, having reloaded both. My cutlass was only inches away from the anxious fingers, of my hand.

We had all knelt or stood behind the storeroom's door awaiting a further attack, in the beginning. But, after the opening in the door had been breached and the provisions left about its gap, all had fallen silent.

Slowly, we lowered our guard, coming to the realization, that immediate danger had eluded us. We were given a reprieve by our captors, who seemed to have lost all interest in us for now.

But, the terror would not leave our minds.

It was worse for our Spaniard. The silence seemed to overwhelm and drown him in a sea of despair. He had fallen inside himself, no longer finding any solace in the ranting recitation of the prayers, his lips had so agitatedly repeated.

His head lay bowed, clasped into the arms, folded around his drawn up knees as he sat on the storeroom's dank deck. His dark hair and buried head hid his distraught eyes and face. But, I knew and mirrored the hopelessness, I saw there.

The Spaniard was almost silent, except for a low whimpering, more accorded to the sad melancholy of a lost child.

His presence and its lack of fortitude visibly sickened our stolid sergeant. The marine's face could not mask the disdain for the coward, littering the floor. But, such was our sergeant's way.

Our sergeant was no longer the spit and polish icon, a proud manifestation and representative of his vaulted Royal Marines. More than I, his beard was coarse and thick. With his leathered face and foreboding brow, it gave him the look of a ruffian or thug, despite the wrinkled red and white uniform, he wore.

He choose to occupy himself by checking his weapon. He examined the workings of his rifle and the edges of its spike. He produced a small honing stone from about his pocket and began running it in slow caressing strokes along the length of his spike's deadly outline.

The sound of smooth stone, gliding across the metal's surface, seemed to calm him and allay any fears or dread threatening to well up inside his bulking form.

All of us remained quiet. There was nothing to say. It was better to remain silent within our own thoughts and the memories of happier times from the past, rather than to speak of the terror, we now found ourselves amid.

I had chosen to preoccupy my mind by withdrawing the small metal box and its secreted journal from my jacket's pocket. Sleep had eluded all of us, save for our veteran marine sergeant.

With nothing else to do, but keep his weapon ready, he seemed content to rest as best he could. During those few moments, when he was not standing in wait and anticipation of some new threat, he tired to rest along the Spartan discomfort of our deck's hard floor.

But, by his twitching and turning, I wagered his sleep was fitful and discomforting, yielding none of the simple release or escape he sought. The dread surrounding us had surely penetrated his dreams.

He rarely seemed able to sleep or remain unmoving for more than an hour, at best. Then, he sat up stiffly as if startled awake, reclaiming the comforting grasp and feel of his cherished rifle.

At least, it appeared he could sleep, if only momentarily.

I envied him for that.

Since, our captivity I had hardly slept. I had closed my eyes and rested. I had dozed about. Yet, my mind would not stop. It could not rid itself of those terrible images, I had witnessed. My mind would not let me forget the horrors awaiting only a door's length away on the other side of the storeroom.

I took stock of our position, such as it was.

At least, our strength would not escape us. We were to be fed and watered, if like nothing less, than cattle to our foul captors. And, like animals penned away, we were separated from other like souls. Our doctor and those trapped about the brig were removed from us by several rooms and their thick wooden walls.

I halted my writing. The small piece of charcoal, blackening my fingertips, had dulled. I claimed the cutlass laying beside me and lightly ran the thin piece of charcoal against its wide glaring blade. With its tip sharpened, I continued writing the gist of our dilemma and grizzly journey.

I was certain our end was near.

I turned around, hoping to find our stalwart sergeant as confident and belligerent as ever. I found strength in his example and tenacity. I willing attempted to mirror his perseverance. He would not quit, until he was dead. There was something comforting in his brute-like persistence and unwillingness to quit, despite the odds.

I found him sleeping.

Even in sleep, his leathered face attested to his gruffness and the harsh life, he had chosen to live. Yet, he slept soundly as if he had not a care in the world.

In my heart, I believed he was obstinate enough to believe, that the demons outside feared him more, than he feared them. I was glad to see, he was able to find the peace of sleep, if for no other reason, than to regain his strength and refresh himself.

Our days of captivity had allowed me the time to reflect on what had happened, on everything. In some measure, I had seen my own small part in things. In the aftermath of our heralded victory at Trafalgar, everything had taken on a new perspective or better, insignificance.

My own part in the battle had been small and fleeting, save to those, who owed their lives to the skill of my hands and the fortitude of my resignation to wield scalpel and bone-saw. I had been carried along like the other travelers of our ship by a sea of events.

I was there. I did as I had, simply because the tasks were assigned to me, not because of any speech intoning obligation or duty. I had been prepared by our surgeon, studying the ways of his profession, before the battle.

When the need of those skills arose, I was the most able to aid our doctor. The duty had fallen to me.

Now, a new duty was becoming clear to me.

I stopped writing, aware of a movement on the other side of the door.

There was neither footstep or breath, only the light din of a wooden tray and its wooden bowls being placed down, before the opening torn in our doorway. I heard a voice speaking in the demon's bestial tongue, more hiss and snarl, than words.

The ghoulish servant, that had delivered our next daily meal left. But, there was another presence beyond the door.

I thought to wake our sergeant. But, without any of the fiend's trying to breach the safety of the door, I could see no point in alarming him. The tray was delivered as it had been for several days before, while we sailed aimlessly about.

We were unaware of the course the Vanguard followed. We knew only, that the sea had grown slowly worse as the bow dipped and rose with the adjoining and discomforting roll of our ship.

The HMS Vanguard's lurch was worse during the day, when only a few hands remained topside during the daylight. But, at night our course steadied as did the travel of our vessel.

Ghoulish hands likely climbed the masts and set the sails, that drove the Vanguard in the black of night. No doubt, our second officer commanded the deck and its demonic crew, only to return to the darkness of the bowels of the Vanguard with the approach of the morning sun.

"Wake ye, wake ye, rise and shine, the morning's fine, Ensign Lewis," a voice rasped in taunt, mocking the British Navy's traditional wake-up call, though I did not know the hour and thought it well past morning.

But, in the exiled darkness below the waterline, who was to say.

"Eat hearty, Ensign Lewis," the voice entreated further.

I held the silver cross up before me in my left hand as my right hand searched out for one of the loaded pistols.

"We're almost home. The Isle of Wight is in sight and Portsmouth is close at hand . . . we've come home, Ensign," Samuel Isaiah Loydd forced the words from his lungs, barely above a whisper as if a man in the throbs of death.

I said nothing in answer. I'd had my fill of Loydd's taunts and intimidation in both his life and recent death. I cocked the flintlock pistol, after ensuring a piece of flint was inserted for its striker.

"I've brought you home and this is how you repay my generosity," Loydd mused, hearing the act.

I heard his words through the cracks higher up in the door and aimed my pistol's short barrel towards it.

As if he saw my actions his voice trailed off. I was left in silence, hearing only the labored breath of our slumbering sergeant and trembling body of our Spaniard.

Loydd's voice returned, "eat well . . . it's your final meal, lad. When we reach the shores of Portsmouth, there's much to be done, with or without you. We've a new power and force to claim rule over our island and its inhabitants."

I kept quiet. Loydd confirmed the fears, I had suspected. I had deduced, that the affliction and plague, that had befouled our ship, was being brought home to land. The foul maiden, that had haunted the HMS Vanguard, had now raised a ghoulish army and seemed intent on returning home.

She brought home an invading horde, a vanguard of creatures, embodying her own damned form and existence, not dead and not alive. They reflected her own evil, though they had been spawned of it and were like the pawns of a chessboard or the soldiers of a general's battlefield.

She had established herself as a ghastly queen, intent on usurping life and power from those ashore, as readily, as she had claimed power aboard our ship. And, how could those innocents ashore fight her or the vanguard of her conquering army, which would only grow.

Ignorance and superstition along with disbelief and the predisposition of madness for those, who would even speak of her cruel acts, would hide the awful truth of her existence and baneful plans. Hadn't I seen and not believed?

How could I convince others to believe my accusations or warnings and not deem them the rantings of a madman? I had only to look to our Spaniard, seated nearby, to see the folly of thinking I could raise an alarm and have it believed.

I lowered the pistol's upheld barrel, hearing nothing more from the other side, of the door. The lantern's flame flickered as if a draft cut through the opening in the door's bottom. It was as if some specter had passed.

Its flame wavered, threatening to extinguish, until the slight breeze halted. Then, the lantern's flame rose straight and steady, bathing my shaking hands and comrades.

I rose to my knees and cautiously approached the tray, set in the smashed opening. A artful finger of my left hand caught the rim of the wooden tray and pulled it inside our confines.

Again, we had been provided with a meager ration. Its intent was merely to keep us alive. Yet, there was more. Besides the stale biscuits, whose outside was as hard as a stone and the salted beef, there was a bottle.

I studied its thick brown glass, so similar to the bottles of rum residing in the ship's sickbay or like those, that had been so greedily gulped by our wounded in the confines of our temporary infirmary.

I removed its cork.

I was about to raise it to my lips to sample its warm bittersweet taste. But, I thought the better of the act. It was a strange sense of foreboding, that overcame me. I feared poisoning. I feared, that the demons might hope to incapacitate us, so they could claim us unopposed.

I placed the cross in my lap and cupped my left hand, raising the bottle in my right, after distancing myself from the door.

I poured several drops into my open palm. A rich dark liquid poured forth. But, it was thicker, than the rum, I had expected to find. Yet, in the dim light of the lantern, I could not make out the substance.

I bent to the lantern and moved my left hand towards it.

Blood, it was blood. It was the foul dark blood, brackish and black, that I had witnessed spewing from the wounds, we inflicted upon the demons. My gut wrenched as I wiped my open palm about the coarse surface of the deck, ridding myself of the foul liquid.

My stomach heaved, its contents spewing and splattering to the deck.

My movements were enough to wake our sergeant.

Our Spaniard, who I was sure was awake, remained with his head buried in his arms.

"What's wrong?" our sergeant barked, already bringing his rifle up and pointing its sharp spike towards the door.

I ignored him, coughing up the bile, that burned my throat.

He stood over me, spying the tray and food. He saw the uncorked bottle.

I raised my face to his, vomit still running along the side of my mouth. "Don't drink from the bottle. It's blood, it's the ghoul's blood. They mean to poison us!" I coughed out and spat the remains in my mouth.

"Poison us or make us like them?" the sergeant returned.

"Warn the doctor. Warn the others," I said, only now thinking of the threat posed to all.

"Aye!" the sergeant said, moving closer to the door.

"Surgeon!" the sergeant bellowed.

His answer was not forthcoming.

"Doctor Radford!"

"I hear you!" Radford returned.

"The bottle's poisoned, it's blood! The ghoul's blood!" the sergeant alerted them to the new threat.

I returned to the tray as the two yelled between the void, separating our divided havens.

I looked at the biscuits and salted beef. Neither were appetizing, they were meant as a staple to our tars' rations. The biscuits often fell victim to the invasion of maggots as they rested in their wooden barrels. The foul pests could be rid from the biscuits merely by throwing a rotting fish inside the barrel, to which the maggots would migrate, freeing the hard rolls of infestation.

And, the tough strips of dry salted beef were almost inedible.

They were like hard leather strips. Yet, I now held both biscuits and beef suspect.

I grabbed up one of the hard biscuits and tore my fingernails into it, ripping it apart.

Inside, its risen flour was softer, white and . . . I saw it!

The biscuits had been meddled with. The ghouls had tampered with our bread, laced inside was a fine dark stained trail of blood, filling their porous core.

"The foods been tampered with too!" I blurted out.

My warning was instantly relayed to those residing among the shelter of the brig. I dropped the hard roll and studied a dark strip of beef, picking it up in my hands.

The strip of meat had the consistency of a strap of leather. I saw no way to hide the demon's foul solution among its dried and stiff shape. But, the evidence yielded in my hand. My fingers were coated in the vile filth of the blood as I touched the meat.

It could have easily been mistaken for grease or the decaying slime the meat was known to accumulate over time. But, it was a thin application of the vital fluid of life, that was the essence of our demons.

My mouth gaped open in revulsion.

The sergeant standing over the tray saw my discovery and shouted a warning to the others.

We learned too late. Some had already eaten. They'd become too accustomed to the regular meals, provided by our captors. After partaking of the same fare, day after day, for eight days, they had no reason to suspect the deceit now being inflicted upon them.

We heard them trying to rid their mouths and stomachs of the vile and disguised nourishment, they had so greedily feasted upon. We heard the cursing and lamenting of mouths, who could not retract the foul blood, already set to work in their bellies.

The fear and loathing, they had lived with daily, since our imprisonment, descended into cries for mercy.

The fiends had sought to turn us, either into obedient slaves or creatures like themselves. Within reach of home, we were now to meet our demise.

I recanted our second officer's most recent visit to the sergeant and informed him of our nearness to home.

The revelation was met with cold silence, joined by the frustration of being helpless among a host of demons, numbering in the hundreds. What could we do?

"We can't even save ourselves," the sergeant chided at a loss to deal with the crisis confronting us.

Soon, the demons would invade our shores with an unsuspecting onslaught, which no rational mind or fanciful imagination could contemplate. And, nowhere among our landlocked countrymen was there any alarm or warning of the menacing horde about to strike the shores of home.

"We can't save ourselves. But, we can end it! We might allow this horror to pass those ashore," I offered as I pushed aside the tray and its tainted contents.

I sat back up on the floor, closing my eyes. I was no longer afraid, too much had happened. Fear had been surpassed by the need to act, to halt the evil carried by our ship.

I did not raise my head to look at our sergeant as I extended the offer of a grim partnership to him.

His eyes stared blankly at the door he guarded, while I relayed my scheme. It was a mad contrivance, desperate and likely prone to failure. But, it was an attempt, an endeavor to try to do something and not simply leave ourselves to be slaughtered and feasted upon.

My words eluded our Spanish colleague, necessitating my trying to translate my expectations to him, as best, as my limited vocabulary of his native tongue would allow and manage.

To my amazement, my words returned him to us. I first warned him of the tainted food, ensuring he would not be tempted to partake of it by showing him the tampered biscuit and the loathsome putrid blood, laced inside its baked roundness.

I threw both biscuits and beef through the broken opening in the bottom of the storeroom door. They were followed by the bottle, which I swung with such force, that we heard it break along the wall, opposite our haven.

Then, I explained the plot, I had revealed to the sergeant. His eyes and gasping mouth mirrored the realization befalling all of us. We had come to our end.

He was with us, for whatever his allegiance was worth.

I removed my timepiece from my pocket. I had to think, whether the hour its face and hands intoned was of the night or day. In the vault holding us, the hours and days had slipped into a meaningless abstraction. We were already lost to the world above.

It was already night, I recalled. It was early evening by the hands of my watch, nearly eight o'clock. Everything had sided with our foes, who would now be free to roam topside along the Vanguard's deck. They would be at their strongest, not hampered by the light of day or restrained by their nearly dormant sleep, during its brightness.

We would need help. I engaged the sergeant to illicit the obedience of his men, calling out briefly to the survivors of the brig to join us, when the moment arose. But, we did not reveal the details of the plan, lest our ghoulish watchdogs be listening and understand our words

We prepared for our perilous foray. I surrendered one of my loaded pistols to the Spaniard, who had already claimed a metal hook from among the stores and tools gathered about.

We halted for a moment, while I searched his eyes to judge his loyalties. There was no doubt, who his new enemies were. I found his eyes afire with an almost religious zeal to combat the demons engulfing us, contrasting his previous distraught behavior.

Perhaps, it was enough, that all now believed his earlier rantings. But, more likely, he did not relish the thought of being left alone in the depths of our ship.

There was only one more thing I wished to finish.

I returned to my small journal, making note of the threat sailing for shore and our rash hopes of defeating it. My words were few. The tiny piece of charcoal, spirited inside the ornate box housing my journal, would force me to be brief.

The plan was simple. We meant to ignite what remained of the thirty-five tons of gunpowder, still aboard the Vanguard. Stored here in the depths of our ship, beneath the waterline and most at stations along the gun-decks, the black powder would rip the warship asunder, turning her exalted planks and timbers into splinters and debris.

And, in destroying ourselves, I hoped to destroy the cursed metal coffin and its resident, scattering it and its vile maiden to the bottom of the depths. At least, that was the final hope, I harbored.

I even held the whimsical and illusive hope of reaching the upper decks. I entertained the prospect of contesting the foul maiden or befouling the iron coffin, I was now certain was her daily resting place and refuge.

With the demons overwhelming our ship, it seemed like an illusion. But, we had to try. Time had run out. As Lieutenant Loydd had taunted, we were near home. If not stopped, the repugnant horror would spread and multiply.

I continued writing, what would likely be my journal's final passage. Its words were cold and empty. The small piece of charcoal threatened to break, it stained my fingers. The journal had lost the wonder and relish, I once held for life and the promise of the future. It had become an epitaph.

I ended my journal with a final plea. It was more a prayer for absolution, than a petition for understanding of our undertaking.

> *"I and several of the crew have taken it upon ourselves, to see that this evil does not reach our home shores. May God forgive me for the lives, I am about to take and not damn me for claiming my own."*
>
> *Ensign Robert Lewis*
> *HMS Vanguard*
> *November 2,*
> *Year of Our Lord 1805*

I closed the cover of the small book, feeling its worn leather between my fingertips. It seemed pointless to have even written the words, ending its brief record of the fate of our ship.

But, I felt a record must be told. Our ship's log entries had no doubt been neglected. Our story had to be told, though I doubted the tale would ever be recovered, if we proved successful in our endeavors.

I pocketed the small text into the crafted metal box, that thus far, had proved watertight, its carefully crafted metal lips and clever design creating a watertight seal. It would likely perish with me, finding its way to the depths of the dark waters, off the shore of Portsmouth Harbor.

I pressed the lid of the metal box tightly, ensuring it was closed. I marveled at its metal surface for one last time. It was a unique functional creation, constructed of two symmetrical halves, forming a hinged hollow shell.

Its ornamentation and design was an extravagant piece of artwork. It was the skilled rendering of a jeweler and metalsmith. Its lattice grid work face folded in and about the exterior of each half of its shell. A fine delicate clasp secured the tight fighting halves, sealing them without the benefit of a lock.

I pocketed it away in my jacket.

Above me, our sergeant gathered up several shafts of wood, their edges carved and honed to sharpness earlier by his deadly spike. He shoved them inside a burlap bag along with several wooden renditions of my silver cross.

Their crude wooden shapes bore little of the craftsmanship or design of my small original. But, they would bolster the meager defenses of our Spaniard's tiny crucifix and my own icon.

I rose, looking about for any other materials, that might aid us in our final battle.

Fire would be our ally. We had our lantern and those of the others, inside the brig, along with my matches.

The sergeant and I moved some of the stores in the room, about. I halted, finding several stacked small wooden casks. I recognized their shapes.

They were the small wooden containers, holding the oil for some of our ship's lanterns. Some of our warship's lanterns used candles. Others used the highly flammable and hazardous fluid.

The state of the sea sometimes dictated which lanterns were used. In a rough sea, with the sailor's bane of fire an ever present hazard, the oil lanterns were ordered extinguished and stowed. Candles or darkness, then ruled the confines inside our ship.

Now, the fire, whose presence was dreaded aboard ship, would aid us. We took as many of the casks as we could quickly carry. We placed them inside burlap bags, whose contents were dumped out on the deck.

Before, reason and fear halted our purpose and determination, we freed the broken door ahead and moved forth. Burdened by the burlap bags and their contents, we stepped out into the darkness, crosses held outward in the glow of our single lantern.

CHAPTER 37

Sacrifice

HMS Vanguard
Nearing the Coast of Portsmouth, England
Day 20-The Final Hour

We looked like some ragged impersonation of devoutly religious monks or clerics. Our cautious procession inched along the deck. Our hands held crosses of wood and silver and our Spaniard's crucifix high.

Along the walls, our shadows hung suspended in a haunting stretched out phantasm of what our waning lives had become. We were cloaked in silence, our feet treading so lightly, that they left no sound.

But, the demons stirred. They had moved as soon as we'd exited our haven. Their senses were like those of wolves or the beasts. I think their foul senses, their hearing and smell, were keener, than those of any wild animal.

They were nocturnal hunters, who now relied on their ghoulish instinct to survive and hunt their fellow man as prey.

But, they did not move on us, not now.

We were protected among the sheltering shield of our upheld crosses and the lantern's light, that brazenly illuminated their raised images among the demons. We saw a fleeting shadow cling to the darkness of a wall or anteroom.

But, none dared show themselves, nor face the hallowed reverent image of the cross.

Our shadows continued to move about the aisle's narrow walls leading to the steps and ladders, rising above. The dark shapes cast about the ship's planking took on the image of a trailing procession, more akin to that of the good monks and abbots or sisters, living their austere and holy lives in the cloistered and isolated retreats of monasteries or abbes.

Our Spaniard seemed the strongest, both physically and emotionally, since any moment I could recall during his captivity. He held his cherished crucifix aloft in one hand, having traded one of the large wooden crosses, crafted by our sergeant, to our surgeon to regain its cherished form.

The surgeon had freed it, from the pilfering hands of the marine, now clinging devoutly to a wooden cross made from two slats of a broken crate.

Some of us were burdened with the burlap sacks, laden with flasks of oil. Others carried lanterns and weapons. Some clasped wooden stakes made upon the advice of our Spaniard.

I spied the thin skeleton-like form of a demon ahead. The creature seemed only half human as he dared to remain in our nearing path. He was defiant of the crosses, bidding him to yield way.

His black eyes seemed incensed with hatred. And, though they spitefully stared at us, testing our convictions and belief in the religious symbols we thrust high, he could not hold his ground.

Like the others, his grotesque form ceded. I watched as the creature, its hair nearly pulled from the graying rotting flesh of its head, raised an arm up to its eyes. But, removing the icons' sight of salvation and piety was not enough.

Our cadre of moving crosses had a life and power of its own, that could not be blocked out or dimmed, even by removing them from one's sight.

The fiend hissed, before turning around. Its skeletal limbs protruded from beneath the sleeves of a torn blue striped shirt. Our former tar leapt for a nearby ladder, scaling it in almost a single bound.

His rapid movement startled me. It was like the uncoiling thrust of a snake. I halted, studying the path ahead. I was fearful, that as easily as he had fled, he might drop upon us.

My hesitation and fear was all, that was needed.

Our small band of men bunched together, crosses and rifles yielding spikes merged into one body with none having ample room, to thrust his weapon about or fire without concern for the man beside.

The demon's retreat was short-lived.

Their attack came from behind. The cowards, that had fled into the shadows of the anterooms, emerged. Spiny limbs and clawing hands stretched out from the darkness of the adjoining rooms, ignoring the hallowed protection of the crosses we held.

But, we were ready.

One marine discharged his rifle point blank into the fiend, that had thought him within easy grasp. With no time to reload, he swung his handcrafted cross at the ghoul, smacking it into the decaying flesh of its cheek and forehead.

The creature shrieked, more pained, than when the powerful bullet had struck it and raced through its ebbing body. Its flesh seemed to scald as if a hot iron had been pressed into it. It burned.

It was enough, the horrid apparition dropped to the deck. In supplication, it backed away, shamed and humbled by the touch and sight of the cross.

Our procession was halted as it became embattled. Spikes plunged into the lithe forms leaping at us. Another weapon fired. A lantern dropped to the floor as a defender clung to his cross with both hands, while a demon grasped it with hands now burning as if on fire.

Shrieks and howls filled the narrow aisle. And, there were more shouts, including the shout of one of our own.

I glanced rearward, even though my upheld silver cross was

raised to the fiends at bay in front of me. I saw the red uniform of one of our marines being dragged away, disappearing through the doorway of one of the adjacent storerooms.

Foul hands dropped upon him, joining with those, that had wrested him from our protecting enclave. He screamed.

It was too late to aid him. We had no time. We had to move on.

The attack ended as suddenly as it had began.

We were left numb, another horror repeating and driving home the desperation facing us and the threat, soon to reach our shores. I prodded the others to move on, taking the first steps forward to regain the momentum our purposeful procession had lost.

I heard our sergeant's harsh voice, goading our frightened charges to move. I took comfort in his gruff unwavering voice and stalwart resolve.

I raised my cross up, nearly above my head, aiming its flat surfaces towards the hatchway above.

I saw the repugnant eyes of the demon, that had bounded upward, lingering about its rim. They were joined by other orbs. Their gruesome eyes reflected my lantern's light like the eyes of villainous cats. Cloaked in darkness, only their foul orbs showed their presence.

They hissed and seethed at the shape thrust out in my hand. Their mouths offered nothing, but vile contempt and condemnation for its sacred image.

Slowly, they moved away, their eyes and presence unable to stand its closeness.

I climbed the ladder, ignoring the awkwardness of the lantern in my right hand and the pistol and cutlass tucked about my belt. I ignored the deck that had served as our morgue and kept climbing, passing it and seeking out the lower gun-deck above. I left behind the two decks below our waterline.

My goal was the gun-lined deck overhead, harboring the stores of powder that had been set out for our battle at Trafalgar. The others followed my ascent.

I reached the lower gun-deck.

It was like coming amongst a swarm of insects.

Alarmed, by those guarding us below, nearly a hundred of the fiends had gathered about the lower gun-deck with more appearing at the entrance to the hold and the hatches leading above it to the middle and upper gun-decks.

Their ghastly forms lingered near the object of our sojourn. There, towards the center of the lower gun-deck, were the lashed barrels of gunpowder secured from rolling about by ropes and netting bound about their round forms.

The fiends seemed bolder, bolstered by the growing presence of their own numbers. Though, the small silver cross in my hands still repelled them, it only kept them six paces or less away.

Some hissed and snarled like mad dogs. Other foul mouths expelled hideous and distorted emanations, neither animal nor human. They mirrored no animal or viper's warning, it was an evil sound resonating from their breaths.

I moved forward, waiting for the others to join me along the rim of the opening of the lower gun-deck. I silently and thankfully prayed for our captain's laxness in letting our crew enjoy a generous reprieve, after the battle at Trafalgar. The gunpowder was still lingering about on the lower gun-deck with its silent weapons.

Normally, the gunpowder was held in the decks below the waterline, but much of it had been brought nearer to the surface, so that our crews might work our guns with greater speed and haste, not compounding the hazard of moving the unstable blackpowder about in the heat of battle.

We could succeed. We could halt this madness!

The demons closest to us must have seen the infectious rejoicing in my eyes and those of the survivors about me. The gunpowder and our plot were all within reach. Our true intent and purpose dawned upon their ghoulish eyes and dulled minds.

Yet, they seemed without direction. They were like mindless laborers or dim-witted drones of a beehive, waiting to be summoned to do the queen's bidding. We stood there, while they were seemingly awed by our daring and recklessness.

We showed ourselves. But, we were taken aback by the daunting numbers of their opposing horde.

Those ghouls in back pushed the demons nearest us forward, despite their hissed warnings and outright dread of the crosses we held up in a semi-circular line. The simple wooden icons were our shields. They cast appalling and nightmarish shadows about the hull as our lanterns flickered.

The twinkle and glimmer of our lanterns' small flames was dimmed by the draft pouring down from the open upper decks and rushing through the hold. There were moments of darkness as our lanterns died, the flames fed by oil and candle wax threatening to extinguish.

But, their flames continued, their wicks fed by the oil in the metal vessels of the lantern's cylindrical bases or the wax of the remains of burned down candles. Other unlit lanterns, both candle and oil-fed, hung from about the deck's beams. But, there was no time to light them. We dared not risk the distraction.

In the darkness my small silver cross seemed to glimmer and glow like a beacon. The tiny form's significance was magnified by the light reflecting off its simple arms.

The demons in the foremost ranks strained to keep their feet planted about the deck, trying to halt their slow push towards the heralded religious symbols, stretched out before them. Eyes dropped to the deck and foul mouths uttered blasphemies, their inhuman lips and tongues disguised from us.

But, it was to no avail. Their hellish comrades behind had no compassion. They pushed them closer, ignoring the pained lament of those coming to face the protective talisman of our crosses.

One of our marines could not stand the nearness of his devilish counterpart. As if a bishop offering the dip of his staff in some benediction or blessing, his oversized wooden cross bowed its form, smashing into the fiend an arm's length away along the face.

The demon screamed out in pain, startling and halting the advance of the fiends.

My eyes saw smoke steaming from the side of the creature's

face as if a blacksmith or torturer had taken a hot iron from the coals and pressed it into his flesh.

A burning scar was left along the side of the fiend's right cheek, leaving an indelible imprint of the wood and part of the arms of the cross. He dropped to the deck, rolling about it and clutching himself as if the fire, that had claimed his rotting flesh was harbored inside him.

His screams were unintelligible, rising to reprehensible shrieks.

A second marine followed the action of the first and thrust his cross forward. As if it was a deadly weapon or wicked blade, the fiends bowed or lurched away from it in fear, forced within inches of its incriminating touch by those behind. Several fell into those pressing forward, halting the ghouls advance.

For a moment, it seemed as if our cause and method were invincible, guided and safeguarded by Heaven. I began to order several of the marines carrying the wooden casks of oil forward.

I was intent, on some of them walking forward to the tethered barrels of gunpowder and deluging them with the flammable fluid. I entreated the fanciful illusion, that we might only have to pool the fluid about and leave a trail behind us to ignite, so we could safely reach Vanguard's topsides.

I began to believe the illusion, believing we could destroy our ship and its invading army of demonic fiends and still find some escape, lighting the spilled oil and its trail down into the bowels of our warship and then, jumping overboard.

The burlap bags were dragged forward.

We were too late.

Lieutenant Samuel Isiah Loydd walked forward. A break formed among the creatures filling the deck and gathered the breath of the Vanguard's beam. As if a hallowed commander or royal nobleman had made himself present, they moved aside in supplication and dutiful obedience.

Some almost groveled. Their heads and backs lowered in twisted demonic hunched backs of foul allegiance.

Loydd's eyes fell upon our crosses. But, instead of falling down to the deck or casting their gaze aside, he squinted raising a uniformed sleeve of his royal blue naval jacket to block their holy forms.

His black orbs stared ahead, seeking out the faces of the men holding the revered icons aloft. He avoided looking directly into our crosses' humbling and commanding presence.

His gaze locked on one of our sergeant's marines, a young lad. The youngest of those among our group. He looked as if he was barely of the age to be accepted within our ranks and place his mark within the muster book, signing his life into the servitude of king and country.

He was the weakest among us, a novice, an inexperienced lad, even after the blooding of our ship at Trafalgar. Like an African lion stalking prey from among a grazing herd, Loydd sought out the most vulnerable among us.

Lieutenant Loydd's practiced and hatred-filled eyes spied the weakest member of our ranks. As a lion separating an elderly or sick animal from the rest of herd or alienating a calf from its mother's protection, Loydd was intent on availing himself of our youngest and most vulnerable comrade.

I saw it. Despite the protective aurora afforded us by the crosses and our Spaniard's crucifix, Loydd's eyes ignored their revered images and locked with the fear-laden orbs of the young marine.

Slowly, I saw the young seafaring soldier stand transfixed. He fell into an unmoving daze, bleary-eyed and unaware of his treacherous surroundings. It was as if Loydd's gaze would illicit some foul obedience.

"Sergeant!" I yelled, thrusting my hand out and pointing the silver cross it held towards our susceptible colleague.

Our sergeant turned his gaze. He found the young marine almost swooning about on legs threatening to collapse beneath him. He left his place in our line, brushing along the backs of those holding the semi-circle about the ladders and steps, that had led to the lower gun-deck.

He dropped his open right hand hard atop the young man's shoulder, goading him awake and breaking the trance our second officer's eyes had claimed upon the young marine.

"Keep your wits!" the sergeant's damning voice barked, while he held his own wooden cross high, grasped in the hand burdened with the weight and length of his rifle.

"All of you keep awake! No demon's tricks! Don't look into their eyes!" he hollered.

Lieutenant Loydd lowered his head as if the link between himself and our marine had drained him of some shred of his demonic strength. His eyes closed and head bowed as if physically strained and exhausted from the effort.

Several of the demons surrounding him dared to come nearer, closing the open aisle, they had formed in their ranks.

Loydd sensed their presence and diminished respect for his authority and hellish rank above them. His lips snarled, revealing foul animal-like teeth, before a damning challenge rose from his lungs.

The sound was a horrid mix of a bestial and human tongue. It was savage and monstrous. Those demons nearest to him bent down in crouched subservience. A few to the rear were caught standing upright, caught under the vengeful stare of our second officer for contesting his dominance.

"Move. Move now!" I turned and urged the doctor to take advantage of the moment and carry out our hastily drawn up plan.

"God speed!" our surgeon offered, giving me one last look.

His gaze was filled with forlorn camaraderie and resignation. It showed the respect, I had come to earn in his eyes and it mirrored the insanity, that had led to this . . . the destruction of ourselves and our beloved ship.

One of our two groups would succeed. I was certain of it.

The distraction presented by the contest between Loydd and his devilish minions was unexpected and opportune. We moved.

The surgeon and those, that had been imprisoned in their self-imposed exile in the brig, moved away from the lower gun-deck's landing, near the steps and ladders, seeking the heart of the deck. They sallied forth along the lower gun-deck as the sergeant, Spaniard, and myself claimed the rungs of the ladder to the next deck above.

The sergeant's forceful bulk sprinted up the ladder, flying past several rungs as he claimed them two at a time. Our Spaniard followed closely behind, his small form seeming to match our sergeant's flight upward as if he was afraid to lose sight of the veteran marine and the protection of his rifle's deadly spike.

The Spaniard's effort showed no sign of being burdened by the burlap sack he carried, dangling over his left shoulder and filled with several small casks of lantern oil.

We sought to attack the fiends from two directions. Our slow procession on the decks below had left no doubt among the slow-witted minds of the fiends, that we sought to rise from the bowels of the ship.

Our lingering upon the lower gun-deck had drawn them to us as they sought to outnumber us, before likely swarming over us in an attack we could not suppress, despite the hallowed images of the crosses we bore.

I took one last look below, before the lower gun-deck was lost from my sight.

The last I saw of Radford and his group of marines and tars was a wavering line, basked in the glow of their upheld flickering lanterns. They pushed forward. Their awkward line moved faster, than a walk as Radford and the others sought to use the unpredictability of their movement to surprise the ghouls and keep them off guard.

Radford led, moving towards the stowed barrels of gunpowder. He held his wooden cross and lantern high in one hand, a stake held tightly in his right.

I claimed the deck above.

The vampiresa.

CHAPTER 38

A Final Blow

HMS Vanguard
Nearing the Coast of Portsmouth, England
Day 20-The Moment

Our swift movements had been rewarded. Save for only a few lingering demons, the middle gun-deck was nearly empty.

Our sergeant was already charging down its length, his heavy footsteps echoed over the heavy wooden planks. Our Spanish comrade labored to keep pace, the burlap sack along his back swayed about wildly.

My feet leapt from the ladder's rungs as I sought out the planks of the rolling deck. The waves of the nearing shoreline were beginning to greet our ship, welcoming it back to the Vanguard's homewaters.

I wanted to flee topside. I wanted to glimpse one last look of home, despite the distance and the darkness. But, there was no time. We had been blessed with the advantage of outwitting our opponents, if only temporarily.

The bulk of the demons had gathered on the deck below to meet our threat. They now confronted the remainder of our divided forces, the surgeon and his small band. The others were pressing on, trying to ignite the gunpowder store about the lower-gun-deck, while I and my two companions sought to do the same with the remaining powder stores, that had been laxly left unsecured about the middle gun-deck. I prayed, both our groups might succeed.

Only one group needed to, for our effort to defeat the ghouls and deliver them and our vessel to the depths bordering Portsmouth Harbor.

I watched as two of the ghouls, about the deck, turned around, searching for the purposeful din of our charging sergeant. Our sergeant was atop the first, before the demon's eyes gleamed with the realization of what he saw.

On the run, the sergeant swung the long rifle's barrel wide, its spike finding the demon's neck. The spike's honed edges and the power of the swinging arc were multipled with the force of the charge. The blow tore the rotting flesh of the fiend. Its head fell aside, severed from the thin decaying neck.

Like the chopped off head of a fish, the ghoul's mouth opened and closed in a sickening gape. But, freed from the life and force of its hated body, no sounds or words spilled forth.

There was no warning.

Another demon rose from the cannon, he was seated atop. His first thought was to protect himself as he spied the charging gait of our veteran marine, now nearing the shaft of the main mast running through the middle gun-deck and in the center of the stores of stowed gunpowder.

His hand opened, spiny fingers and long rotting nails spreading like claws. His feet moved several steps, seeking to thrust him out in a forceful leap.

His horrid face took on the appearance of a vengeful banshee as a shriek departed his lips and he took to flight, flinging himself forward.

A loud retort filled the nearly empty deck as our sergeant's rifle discharged. The shot found the chest of the flung demon. But, its impact was not enough to halt the vicious lunge.

The creature impaled itself on our sergeant's spike. Its claws tore at the air as our sergeant struggled, to hold its gyrating form at bay. The end of the barrel's long length seemed too short.

The creature's flailing hands seemed as if they would break the distant bond and protection of the weapon's length. Worse, the sergeant's strength was ebbing. The demon was the most powerful I had seen, next to our second officer.

Despite, the bayonet run through its chest, the demon's contesting struggle continued as if its wound was of no consequence. Slowly, it pushed forward, running down the length of the spike, its hands clasping the barrel of the weapon, it was attached to and threatening to claim the weapon impaling it from the sergeant.

Our sergeant relented, releasing his own grip on the rifle and clasping the wooden cross, he held in both hands. He swung our representation of the holy icon outward. His swing was encumbered by the lantern ring, held in his left hand.

Their struggle was so violent, that our sergeant released his lantern. It dropped to the deck and rolled about.

Some of its oil spilled through the tiny opening, allowing the cloth wick to seat inside. The lantern's open flame ignited the fluid that spilled and burned along the round iron edges and lips of the lamp's surface.

The thick planks, of the wooden deck scorched momentarily, but without more of the flammable fluid following the flame, the sand still covering the deck and spread for our battle at Trafalgar slowly conspired to extinguish the lone flames.

One of its splintered cross's arms, formed by the carving of a bayonet, plunged into the creature's flesh.

The creature, who had been struggling to free itself of the

rifle's spike, freed its hands of the long barrel. Its hands groped for the wooden cross and the buried splintered arm, that had found the hollow flesh beside its right collar bone.

As one, the demon's flesh and the cross's wood began to smolder. Then, as if a recently kindled fire, there was a rush of air as the flames fed by it ignited, engulfing the cross and the creature's chest.

Both burned with a ferocity, that defied belief. The creature's hands flailed wildly about the burning cross, it continued to try to free from its body. Yet, it hands could not bear to touch the flaming hallowed form.

Its mouth parted in a shrill shriek of agony as it fell backwards onto the floor. Its demonic tongue implored mercy as it withered in torment.

The sergeant bent to the rifle, still skewered through the creature's gyrating body. He grasped its stock and placed a firm hold about its flintlock and trigger, before pulling the cherished weapon free.

The finish about its barrel was scorched. Its dark deep-stained color and polish distorted in a myriad of sickly burnt hues. The forward, edge of the long wooden stock smoldered.

The sergeant was joined by the Spaniard, who held his small metal crucifix between himself and the blazing demon.

I joined them as the sergeant began reloading his weapon and the Spaniard pointed the flintlock pistol, I had given him earlier, at the unmoving charred remains of the smoldering fiend laying atop the deck.

I pushed on towards the length of the main mast, running through our ship's hull. I grabbed the burlap bag. I opened it, claiming two of the oil-filled wooden casks and removing the cork stopper from one.

I halted short of the stowed barrels of gunpowder, encircling the main mast and tied securely in cargo-netting, lashed about by rope. I shoved my silver cross deep into a pocket of my jacket. I placed my lantern safely aside, using its dim light to handle the cask I had retrieved. I was just beginning to tip the small cask over on its end, when a sound rose from the deck below.

My heart raced half expecting the gunpowder on the deck below my feet to send me flying into the final oblivion, I knew was to come. I expected the good doctor and his accomplices to mirror the success we were enjoying.

It was not to be.

The shrieks and hollers, that filled my ears were those of men. They belonged to men set upon by a vile evil, whose malfeasance and malignant purpose rejoiced in their torment and demise.

I recognized the doctor's voice, despite the inhuman horror and sorrow released from his frightful lungs. Radford and the others had failed. The screams left no doubt.

I poured the contents of the cask about, splashing it over the netted barrels of gunpowder. The liquid splashed about. But, it failed to empty the cask quickly enough. I raised it above my head, some of the fluid running down my arms or splashing about the deep blue material of my uniform's blue jacket.

I ignored its stain and odor, thrashing my arms down forcefully, before releasing the half full cask to the deck in front of the stowed gunpowder.

The cask's wooden slats and tarred seals broke free, shattering from the two thin iron bands securing their carefully carved shapes. The oil pooled and puddled, even as I picked up the second cask.

The Spaniard claimed another cask, joining me as more demons appeared about the deck in front of us, towards the hatches leading above and below.

He removed the container's cork, stabbing at its resisting closure with the jagged edge of his tiny crucifix. Its opening free, he began pouring out the flammable contents.

But, he faced the same dilemma as I. The opening was purposely and deliberately designed to be small, to lessen the chance of spilling the fluid and its risk of fire aboard our ship. The oil trickled too slowly for our Spaniard's heated temper. He threw the cask, mirroring my own brash action.

He was withdrawing another container from the burlap bag, when I saw the demons approach.

Three, four, five, then more of the creatures began climbing up from the lower gun-deck, using the ladders and steps, we'd used only moments before.

Others tried to enter through the gunports, assaulting us from the outside of the hull. I heard the strain of ropes and the splintering of wood as the gunports and their thick cords' secured strength was tested. To starboard, I saw the gunports' thick covers waver. The covers tugged and pulled, only to fall shut, seated by the ropes lashing them fast.

Then, one pulled outward with unbelievable force. The ropes inside the gun-deck restraining the cover ripped and tore. The hinged cover swung out to sea and upward.

The cover was replaced by a bony limb and a clawing hand, grasping for a hold inside the middle gun-deck. It was followed by the demon's head as he snaked through the narrow gunport and the cannon lashed down behind it.

He had clung to the outside of our rocking ship, despite the unsteady seas and rising waves.

Other creatures hung onto the towering vertical sides of our tall hull. The deck's gunports banged with the desperate pulls and tugs of the demons trying to break in.

The Spaniard and I continued dumping the oil about, finding new containers to open and pour.

Another of the gunports was freed. It was followed in turn by others. The demons' hated shapes filled them.

One gunport, banging incessantly fell quite as the demon was washed away, fallen overboard and claimed by the depths in silence.

But, the assault was underway. We could not repulse it.

Our sergeant fired off a quick shot and began reloading his rifle.

The shot did little. A demon staggered, but still continued. As if realizing the gravity of their plight, those demons, that had reached the middle gun-deck, charged us. They did not wait for the others.

"To the rear . . . the junior officer's cabin!" I shouted, trying to gain our sergeant's attention.

He did not heed me. He stood his ground, reloading his weapon with a speed, I did not think possible.

The Spaniard and I moved off, carrying the small casks. We pointed them upside down and liberally left a trail of oil about the deck, immersing planks and strewn sand alike.

I had abandoned our lantern and our sergeant's lamp. Both rested upon the deck, one overturned, the other resting upright forgotten in our flight. There was no time to retrieve it.

A demon lurched up in our path. He had been laying in wait, after entering through a compromised gunport. I claimed the flintlock pistol from my belt and fired on the run within five paces of the fiend.

The shot had little effect.

I clubbed outward with the heavy pistol's iron and hardwood. My swing pelted the demon in the face. I heard his skull crack and felt bone shatter as the pistol was swallowed up in the creature's putrid flesh.

I released my grasp on it as the demon's mouth snarled and its teeth sought out my flesh. My free hand searched for the small silver cross, secreted inside my jacket's pocket and escaping my trembling grasp to reclaim it.

The fiend's teeth scratched at the flesh of my left hand as I held it in front of me with the emptying cask.

My flesh burned with the infectious bite as if an open flame had touched my skin. My own ears did not hear the scream, emitted from my lips.

The demon's eyes lifted to my own, rejoicing in the victory to come. My right hand was trapped inside the folds of my torn right pocket, searching blindly for the small cross as my eyes saw the creature's menacing mouth grow closer.

In horror, I recognized the fiend or who, he had been in his past life. It was Ensign Higgins. It was my friend and counterpart. In the madness of the moment, I fell into inaction.

Though the creature before me was devoid of life and mercy, I saw past its foul black eyes and the darkness mirrored inside their depths. I saw only a comrade and advocate, a friend sharing the same trials of our initiation into the officer ranks of the HMS Vanguard. I saw an old friend, now lost to me.

The demon shrieked as the Spaniard slammed his palm into its forehead. Hidden in the hand's cupped surface was the Spaniard's small crucifix.

The demon yelled, falling back and dropping to the deck. The small icon was buried in his flesh and skull.

The Spaniard tried to pull the crucifix free, but it was buried, locked in bone and flesh as the demon convulsed about in torment.

More of the demons rushed upon us. Some had bypassed our sergeant, now overwhelmed and taken to swinging his rifle about as a club.

In horror, I regained my footing and wits. I started forward, pulling our Spaniard with me.

He clung to his own spewing cask, abandoning his cherished crucifix, buried in Ensign Higgin's forehead.

We were only mere paces from the cabin in the nearing stern.

Behind us, we heard the loud thud of our brave marine sergeant being felled to the deck. The sound resounded with the spiteful glee of the demons besetting him.

I didn't look back. But, I heard a final curse spat from our sergeant's lips as his fists searched out one of the ghouls befouling his body with their teeth and unholy appetites.

His words were followed with a long exhaled breath. There was no surrender as his body expended its last measure.

The two lanterns left behind extinguished. The one on floor, beside our sergeant's body, died first. It was followed by the one I had set near the main mast. Darkness engulfed the deck.

I pushed our Spaniard through one of the cabin's two doorways so hard, that his flailing feet collapsed and he fell to the floor. I followed behind, tripping over him and releasing the cask in my left hand.

My right hand and arm stretched out in an attempt to break my fall. The small cross, I had searched for only moments before, was clasped tightly in my fingers.

I rose in the darkness. Mercifully, the night sky shined through the tall ornate windows of the cabin's stern. It was enough.

I saw my cask rolling slowly about the yawing deck of the cabin. I was about to turn around to face the door, we had entered and find the soft dampness of the spilled oil, when I saw her haunting image.

The foul maiden, I had witnessed, the cursed mistress, who had befouled and bewitched our ship, hung outside the slanting vertical rise of our stern. Her white gossamer gown flowed as if drifting upon the uplifting currents, caressing the stern and our wake.

Her black mane cascaded about her face and shoulders, lifting and falling with the coming winter winds, driving the Vanguard towards harbor. I spied her slippered feet, hanging lifelessly in the air. They were devoid of perch or movement, merely floating in midair, over two decks high.

Her face searched slowly from side to side, her eyes piercing the darkness of our cabin, through the reflective sheen of stars and moonlight, gleaming off the multi-paned glass of the cabin's windows.

Her head's deliberate movements halted as her dark eyes fell upon me. I felt she was aware of our presence without seeing. She knew where we were. I think she had known all along, that we were moving up from the bowels of the ship. She knew we were moving against her and her minions.

On my knees as if a humbled and beaten supplicant, I twisted my eyes up to look upon her slender seductive form. Her skin was as white and virginal as the gown, that draped and clung about her form.

She had all the features and beauty, so richly envied by the ladies of Europe's most elaborate and exulted courts. Many fanciful and wealthy young women had embraced malnourishment and starvation to gain the soft alluring and gentle pallor the haunting specter's skin bore.

But, contrasting that feminine softness and vulnerability were her dark black eyes. Like, those of our second officer, that had nearly claimed one of our marines under the spell of his own orbs and will, her eyes beckoned and enticed me.

She sought to lure me into inaction. She sought to halt me from the harm, she knew I would bring to her invading vanguarding army of fiends and the ship, we all shared.

We were so close to home. We were so close to carrying out her final plans.

The Spaniard's lips moved in disbelief and wonderment at the beautiful creature before us. Without his crucifix, he seemed susceptible to the beckoning lure of the spectral spirit, dangling off our stern. She was an enticing apparition, floating among the salt and brine, wafting about the night sky.

I thrust the small cross in my hand upwards even as I heard her minions moving towards our cabin along the deck outside.

It was enough. The spell was broken.

Her soft red lips, pouting with feint innocence and offering their embrace, parted in a nefarious snarl. The small cat-like teeth, I had witnessed earlier, grotesquely clenched, then opened in a monstrous growl. Her tongue lashed out, mouthing some demonic curse or command as her lungs expelled a horrid hiss, that shrieked and shook the glass of the windows framing her. She fled, body and haunting specter flying upwards, disappearing from our sight and no doubt seeking the sanctuary of the captain's cabin, harboring her monstrous iron coffin.

I turned for the open doorway, there was no more time.

My right hand withdrew the handful of matches, still lingering about my jacket's torn right pocket. In my haste, one or two fell from my grasp, their thin light forms too frail to my trembling touch.

I claimed one from those remaining, striking its head against the beam near the doorway, the beam containing the hidden pocket carved into its disguised exterior.

The match's head failed. I ran its phosphorus head against the beam, once more, scraping my knuckles with the rash act. I could feel the warmth of the blood running along my fingers.

Its scent seemed only to enrage and excite the demons, lunging ahead.

The match's head flared. In the darkness before me, that small pinprick of light took on the brightness of the world and the light of day. Its diminutive glow lit the faces of the creatures nearest the door. It startled them.

Their unholy mouths dropped in bewilderment. Their black eyes fell to the red-painted planks of the deck they raced across. A few remained uncomprehending. They stared blank-faced at myself and the Spaniard, framed in the dim light of the match and the sheltering doorway.

I lowered my outstretched right hand and the lit match to the deck and the pool of oil, still growing from the remaining contents of the Spaniard's nearby cask.

The deck erupted in a flash of glowing flame, that flared and grew, running in two directions. It nearly set my oil soaked sleeve aflame. One trail of flame ran towards the stern, following the nearly empty cask I had dropped.

The other ran from the door, through which we had entered. The forward running trail darted across sand and deck, neither offering any impediment to its rapid advance. It separated as it retraced the separate paths of the Spaniard's cask and my own.

In the blink of an eye, the two trails racing towards the main mast reached the feet of the nearest ghouls. Fearing its flames, they leapt aside. They dumbly ignored the path of the fire towards the stowed gunpowder.

Behind us, the cabin was beset with a small explosion, that sent the oil cask I had dropped flying. It showered splinters and burning debris from its ruptured form.

Some landed atop the berths, others fell upon the desk or among the books or writing paper, coveted by the junior officers. The bedding and paper smoldered, before leaping into flames.

I stood, knowing our end was near. Yet, I felt no fear or remorse. My hand rested alongside the beam, next to the doorway. It came to place atop the hollow cover of my journal's hiding place.

As if as an insignificant afterthought, I removed the metal case and my vaulted journal from my uniform's jacket. I watched the twin blazing trails dancing over the deck as with a practiced hand, I unseated the disguised cover and dropped the journal and its watertight case inside.

I returned the wooden cover as the two flaming paths edged nearer to the barrels of gunpowder soaked in lantern oil.

My right hand reclaimed the small silver cross.

I no longer bothered to thrust it forward. I had no fear of the nearing demons. Their haunted shapes were outlined by the fiery trail, that had passed behind them. Their shadows loomed out in the semi-darkness, stretched across the deck and hull.

I closed my grasp around the small silver icon. The act was not in fear. That had left me. I clenched the cross, a gift from home, as I tried to return to Portsmouth in my mind's eye.

I sought to find one last glimpse of the simple shop, both store and house, that had been my parents' home.

I could slowly recall my parent's faces. I fondly remembered one of the shared moments, when we had all gathered, after a day's labors, to feast upon a simple supper of hearty soup and freshly baked bread.

I saw the firm softness and forgiveness of a mother's eyes. I saw the resolute determination of a father, intent to contend with the toil of a daily struggle to better the life of his son.

One of the trails dimmed, then blossomed as it ran up against the strewn sand, displaced by the movements of the demons. It faltered again, dimming and finally extinguishing.

The remaining trail sped forth.

Its flames drew the attention of several newly arrived ghouls. Their eyes widened in horror and they flung their powerful unholy forms outward, straining their outstretched limbs to reach its rushing flames.

They were too late.

History recorded the tragic loss of the HMS Vanguard on

November 2, 1805. One of the few recorded witnesses, a night watchman lighting the streetlamps of one of the narrow lanes, bordering the great harbor of Portsmouth, described the loss, "as if hell had opened up in the waters off the harbor and devoured the ship in its fiery inferno."

The ship was taken whole. It was claimed by the sea and night with barely a scrap of wood or debris reaching the shore, save for the smallest pieces.

But, there was no mistaking the great warship, that had nearly reached the mouth of the harbor. The harbor's lookouts, alert sentries, still fearing reprisals from the defeated French, had spied the ship's approach. They had enough time to lift telescopes to their eyes and make out the graceful lines of the hallowed ship, despite the darkness engulfing the harbor.

All of Nelson's Squadron had been accounted for, having made Portsmouth or some other friendly harbor. The HMS Victory had been towed to Gibraltar, the British crown colony and fortress seaport near the tip of Spain and other valiant ships, depending on their damage, either sailed with her or found other safe havens and ports.

The late arrival could only be one vessel, the HMS Vanguard. There was no doubt. Her massive three tiered deck and black and yellow livery, matching the striping of HMS Victory's hull, confirmed her return.

There was no mistaking the elegant spires of her bowsprint, fore mast, main mast, and mizzen mast. The lack of sail from her towering masts was noted by those few observers ashore, watching her procession in the rough waters between the harbor and the Isle of Wight.

There had been time to watch the ship's graceful lines, cutting steadily towards shore in the driving winds and rough waters. Despite, the night's darkness, the moon and stars had broken through the clouds, enough to bask the heroic ship in their luster, turning the waters, she sailed upon, into a sea of shimmering diamonds.

So close to home and a hero's reward, the heralded warship

had met her end with the loss of all. The Vanguard had been claimed by the sea, the mistress, whose fickleness and mischievousness nature had claimed small and great ships alike.

But, the loss was that more tragic with her journey nearly complete. Her crew was so close to the shores, they had labored and fought so valiantly to once more attain.

But, like all seafaring tragedies, the loss of the HMS Vanguard silently retreated into the forgotten pages of history as newer disasters and losses claimed the headlines of their own time.

She had been cloaked in the darkness of the depths surrounding Portsmouth Harbor. Lost from the sight and memories of men, save for the few accounts of her involvement in the battle at Trafalgar or the fanciful renderings in oils and lithographs of Nelson's vaulted squadron.

She was a memory, a ghost of the past. Her men and age forgotten.

CHAPTER 39

The Present

September 17, 2003

SS Reprise
Portsmouth Harbor
September 17, 2003
1437 Hours

Alan Ward awoke to the sounds of doors slamming and diesel engines idling on the docks above. The Reprise's steel and aluminum hull and superstructure had muffled the trucks' and work crews' earlier arrival.

The nearly half-empty bottle of bourbon leaned against Ward's left side, seated in the crumpled up blanket, strewn restlessly about him. Its gold plastic cap was missing, its open neck pointed askew towards the ceiling and the wall behind him.

Slowly, Ward's senses fought to return to the dim brightness, flooding through the narrow room's single porthole.

His head throbbed and his mouth was dry. He rolled his parched tongue around, only to find the lingering bitter taste of the bourbon on its coated surface. His breath was labored, the heater still ran on its singular high setting from when he'd first sought the tiny room's warm refuge, retreating from the cold chill and rain assaulting the dock and salvage barge the day before.

His thoughts were fogged as his eyes stared at the spring-green colored ceiling above. He used its blank sterile surface to focus his thoughts, trying to recall the events of yesterday.

His eyes squinted from the light finding its way in through the lone porthole of the cabin. Ward blinked his eyes, fighting the bourbon's lagging hangover.

He dully looked at his wristwatch, it was after two-thirty in the afternoon.

The book, it was his first groggy thought. He lowered his head to his chest as his nostrils filled with another lungful of the room's dry stuffy air. His fingers searched about the top, of the blanket and his bunk's mattress for the small leather-bound book.

He felt the sharp pointed corner of the small metal box, he had become so fascinated with. His fingers groped for its metal surface, partly hidden beneath his disheveled bedding.

He pulled it free of his bunk's blanket and his own weight. Ward held the small treasure up before his eyes as if seeing it for the first time. He marveled anew at its simple, yet delicate construction, that formed the hinged hollow shell, that had become the repository of Ensign Robert Lewis' journal and warning.

His eyes became transfixed on its ornamentation and design. The container's lattice grid work face and the clasp, that had earlier eluded him entry were the work of a long-forgotten craftsman, whose skills and patience had been lost with the onslaught of the Industrial Age and mass production.

The box was a treasure in itself. It was an antiquity befitting the cherished displays of the finest museums or the private collections of the black market, dealing in the exchange and transfer of lost or stolen treasures.

But, that was not the prize Ward's fingers continued to search for. He rose on his elbows, before rolling on his side and frantically scouring along the narrow length of his bunk for the small leather-bound journal.

His heart raced with the fear, he had dropped or ruined the frail book and its dry decaying pages.

His fingers halted as the comforting feel of the book's small worn leather form met them along his thigh. It was exactly were he had deposited the book, before the exhaustion of the recovery of the HMS Vanguard and his larceny had joined with the bourbon to lure him to sleep.

Ward fingered the pages of the book, opening it slowly, almost reverently. He tried not to further break or damage the journal's cracked and worn spine. It was there.

The story he had read with such interest and disbelief was penned in the flowering tiny words, scribed by a hand, ages ago.

Ward raised his head to the ceiling, his lips laughing in the dim light of the cloudy day, piercing through the porthole high behind him.

Ensign Lewis must have been a remarkable young officer or a very bored one with a fanciful imagination and not enough duties to keep him preoccupied.

Ward marveled at the fanciful tale the young officer had written. It was a whimsical tale or better yarn, incorporating the lore and superstitions of the time, when unexplained calamities and disasters were blamed on demons or God's just reprisal.

It was an extravagant story, its telling was complete, incorporating much of what the young officer had probably witnessed during his short career, blended into a tale of the occult and supernatural. But, it was a tale.

Had it been a precise record of the HMS Vanguard's short life, it would have been invaluable, almost priceless. It was doubtful the ship's log and a record of its history at Trafalgar would be discovered. Any true record had met its demise in the cold waters off Portsmouth.

Only the ensign's good foresight or luck, to have pocketed his literary manuscript inside a watertight vessel, had saved it and his story. But, that was all it was a story, an imaginative tale to pass away a young officer's lonely time at sea. It was not a historical record. It couldn't be. The story was too fantastic, too unreal.

Still, it was not without value. But, it would depend on the collector the piece might be marketed to. There would be a willing market for the small metal box and its intricate, yet functional design and latticework covers. But, Ward had never stooped to theft or trying to profit from pilfering any of the treasures the SS Reprise had recovered.

He had been tempted to collect a souvenir or two on more, than several occasions, but professionalism and a job, he loved, had seen to it, that he'd never succumbed to the lure of money.

No, Ward was more in vein with a collector, than a profiteer. He had nearly salivated at the host of Spanish doubloons, recovered from a sunken Spanish Galleon in the shallow waters and reefs off Florida, only years earlier.

One of the Reprise's few original crew members, he and the others had ample opportunity to palm away one of the encrusted gold coins, if only to covet them as a souvenir.

The find had been made days before they returned ashore and filed a claim with the state, whose laws on recovering antiquities and treasures from its waters and shores, ensured the State of Florida received its cut from the valued and auctioned proceeds.

Except, for the journal and its crafted box, he had never stolen anything in his life. Stolen, the word pained his foggy mind. He had made the discovery by accident.

He had no intention of keeping the journal or its vessel. He wanted only to be the first to examine it. It was his find. He had only preceded the others to it. He intended to place it back among the remains, being cataloged on the giant barge beside the resting bulk of the HMS Vanguard's broken stern.

But, a thief . . . Ward was not that. His fall to larceny had been more of the natural seduction to his own obsession to touch the finds, his ROV's, Remotely Operated Vehicle's, found and returned to the surface.

As his career with the Reprise continued, Ward found himself relegated and pushed aside to the role of technician or technocrat, tasked with the latest software updates for his computer operated sleds and the programs operating their complicated unmanned manipulative arms, cameras, and gadgets.

The joy of the hands-on contact with history or the forgotten treasures of the past were denied him as the Reprise's reputation and his workload grew. Soon, expert archaeologists and oceanographers were added to the salvage and oceanographic vessel's compliment, almost completely denying him any opportunity to handle or dwell on the relics, he coveted.

He'd allowed himself this one small private viewing. So, it wasn't done according to the correct preservation methods or procedures, dealing with antiquities or recovered objects from the floor of the sea.

He could remember other times, when such methods, for lack of knowledge or funding, hadn't been employed. All that mattered was that the treasures returned to the surface were still intact and cherished by the museums or societies, that had staked a claim to them by financing the Reprise's continued operation.

Ward gently returned the journal to the seated confines of the metal box. With two hands, he held the container up to his eyes, savoring the relic and the history of its era.

He closed the lid, bringing both symmetrical halves together and catching its delicate, yet strong clasp. It was time to return the borrowed article back to the HMS Vanguard's inventory, scattered about the water-filled plastic tubs and plastic tarps, turned into makeshift bathtubs for the oversized finds, littering the hulk's interior.

Ward placed the cherished relic atop his bunk as he swung his feet over its side and dropped to the floor. He picked up the dark blue windbreaker, laying where he had dropped it the day before. He claimed his black knit cap and the box, shoving it down inside the right pocket of the windbreaker and keeping his hand safely atop it.

He was more nervous about returning the uncataloged treasure to the barge and HMS Vanguard's stern, than he was in pilfering it before. The tiny view out his porthole, showed that the docks were clad in the low gray skies of another day, that promised more rain.

A low fog encircled the hulls of several nearby tugs and workboats. But, there was far too much light and activity for Ward's likes. He began to doubt, his earlier certainty, that returning the "borrowed" antiquity would be so easy.

He exited the cabin and snaked to its left, closing the door behind him. He treaded the narrow aisle, heading for the door to the rear of the lower superstructure.

Only one of the several watertight latches, secured the door ahead in place, allowing the crew members to enter and leave with ease. Ward exited.

The rain had ceased hours ago, though he hadn't heard its departing silence. Ward silently cowered at the openness surrounding him and the working parties, that had descended upon the remains of the Vanguard.

The sky was dark for mid-afternoon. The harbor and shipping confined to its docks and piers was shrouded by the blanket of thick cloudcover overhead.

The low dark purple and black clouds blocked out the sun, threatening rain and cloaking the recovery effort in a semi-darkness, a strange half-light.

But, the dismal weather did little to dampen the spirits of those taking part in the reclamation of the HMS Vanguard.

With the success of the recovery, a horde of archaeologists and historians had flooded the docks and barge. They ranged from the aging white-haired professors; some displaying heralded manuscripts or journals with drawings of the Napoleonic men-of-war, before enthralled college students to professional relic hunters.

One such professor was attended by a small cadre of students, likely assisting him as interns. They prepared to engage in a small part of the preservation effort to save the water drenched timbers and remaining planks of the Vanguard's framework, before exposure to the surface irreversibly damaged or destroyed them.

The plastic tarps, that had shielded the stern's decaying

framework, had been removed. The hoses and water, continually deluging the remains, had been shutoff.

The professor's students were clad in bright yellow and orange plastic rainsuits. Each carried a plastic pail and a large thick paintbrush with the aim of slapping on a thick coating of a temporary wood preservative.

Ward assumed correctly, that the pails were filled with some sort of chemical, meant to seal the porous rotting wood, that despite the rains and dampness of the harbor, were slowly drying out and rotting with exposure to the salt-laced air.

Other groups were busily cataloging the intact timbers of the hull's framework. Wire or plastic ties were fastened about the wide beams and timbers. Yellow cardboard labels hung from them. The numbered tags were protected inside plastic ticket jackets. They danced on the wind, whipping up from out to sea.

Ward turned to the south, to see the dark clouds gathering, rushing forth on a strong wind, that chopped the waters of the protected harbor. The collar of his windbreaker was whipped up along the side of his face, flapping with the growing wind.

Several voices shouted among the workers, some experienced, others novices, attempting to reclaim the historic ship. An agile youth slipped from about the same perch Ward had nearly fallen from, the day before.

A black magic marker used to number the tag tickets fell to the barge below, as the spectacled youth lashed out with frantic hands, trying to halt his fall. He stood near the same timbers marking the doorway where the secreted panel and repository had been uncovered by Ward's own accidental fall.

The lad's hand thrust out as his fingers clawed for a handhold. His feet lost their footing, despite the rubber boots he wore.

There was a scream as the young man's hand grasped the broken wood of the repository. His hand failed to hold him and the youth slipped past the beam and looked as if he would slide beyond the ripped edge of the deck and the ladder leaning beside it.

His legs slipped off the side as his hands made one last

desperate attempt to halt his plunge over the middle gun-deck. He grasped the top of the ladder, clinging to its extended rectangular aluminum frame.

It looked as if ladder and student would tilt forward and vault for the hard deck of the barge. But, the outward travel of the ladder leaving the middle gun-deck was halted as its lashed frame jerked to an abrupt halt.

His hand bleeding, the student recovered, returning to the precarious loft from which he had slipped. He stood beside the beam and its repository in bewilderment, before announcing his find, a broken and hollowed out hole in the supposedly sturdy beam.

A middle-aged archaeologist halted his own work, the boring task of labelling and keying the different parts of the stern's framework. He left his team of like-minded professionals and willing students. He was joined by a member of the London Historical Society, who was intent on dominating the effort with his presence and authority.

Both climbed the aluminum ladder, their feet echoing along the rungs they scaled.

Slowly, they edged to the dangerous perch of the student and examined damaged beam.

"Did you do this when you fell?" the Historical Society representative heatedly demanded, with the crisp and precise accentuation of a British school master.

"No, sir. I couldn't have cut my hand on it, if it wasn't already broken and jagged," the student's embarrassed reply came as he was shamed before the others gathering below by the official's admonition.

The Historical Society's representative inched his thin frail form closer to the beam. His eyes squinted to examine the damage about the smashed panel and the hollow within.

A gust of wind tore the plastic hood of his rainsuit free and stole the hat beneath on a wild tumbling descent to the churning waters beside the barge. His lips pursed tightly in anger, but true to British reserve, he held his tongue. He could think of nothing to say that would smartly salvage the hat or their situation.

His feet slipped about as he clung to the beam, his eyes searching into the darkness of the cavity and its smooth, almost carved lines.

Beside him, the more agile and younger archaeologist edged along the planks close to the stern, where the HMS Vanguard's ornate windows and sculpted carvings had adorned her aft structure. He ignored the newly found cavity, something else claiming his attention.

He removed a flashlight, from his pocket and shined its negligible illumination up at the beams running above, what had been the junior officer's quarters.

The thick heavy beams, now rotting and water-soaked, were pocked and damaged.

The Historical Society representative drew near, puzzled by the archaeologist's abandonment of the hidden cavity.

"You've found something else?" he questioned his more experienced and learned colleague.

"I'm not sure. Look there, you see the damage?"

There was a pause as the two were joined by the haphazard and fortunate student. They viewed the beams and timbers.

"Its damage. Likely, damage from an explosion as gunpowder threw what was ever near flying," remarked the devotee to the relics of the past as he shined his flashlight's beam about.

The torch's light was weakened by the dim sunlight penetrating through the heavy overcast above.

"There!" the archaeologist blurted out, holding the torch's beam upon a scar in the pocked wood, that had caught his attention. "Someone fetch us up a pair of pliers, needle-nose pliers!" he ordered from among the students and workers gathered on the barge below.

One of his one staff dove his hands into a red plastic tool-chest and withdrew a pair of pliers with yellow vinyl coated handles. He made his way cautiously along the slippery deck as Ward and the others watched.

Like those aloft, he scaled the ladder cautiously and inched his way to the stern along the middle gun-deck.

The archaeologist took the pliers.

"Hold me by my belt," he instructed as he snaked dangerously close to the end of the broken stern and its missing glass panes and ornate panels. He reached outward, nearly on his tiptoes, as he stretched for the small object, that had claimed his attention.

The archaeologist cushioned the grip of the pliers on the object embedded in the beam, stuffing a white handkerchief from his pocket in the teeth of the tool's grip.

The narrow nose of the pliers probed the decaying opening in which a small piece of metal had almost been completely driven inside, centuries ago.

It was buried in the thickness of the beam for decades upon decades. Centuries had hidden it in the murk that had claimed and rotted the wood. But, on the surface, the thick beam had taken on the consistency of wet cardboard.

The beam still held the small piece of metal embedded deep inside it. The tiniest of sliver's of reflected light had caught the attention and trained eye of the archaeologist, despite the rot and encrustation coating the find.

He pulled, tugging at the buried metal several times. Some of the surrounding wood crumpled and flaked off, to the consternation of the Historical Society's expert.

He began to berate the archaeologist, purposefully intent on freeing the small object, less it be lost in the dismantling and shipment of the stern's surviving framework and planks.

It came free.

The four figures aloft huddled around the small item. The object and its discoverers were too high and far away from those on the deck of the barge or SS Reprise to fathom its form or shape.

The eager students below fell silent. Anticipation filled those present as those on the middle gun-deck conducted a closer examination.

"Send up a plastic bag filled with fresh water and some preservative solution!" the Historical Society representative ordered, intent on preserving the newly acquired relic.

"And, a basket and line," the archaeologist added, upstaging the Historical Society's surrogate, to the elder's chagrin.

Another of the archaeologist's subordinates claimed a resealable plastic bag and opened it, filling it with a measure of water from a plastic bottle and adding a small amount of a filmy chemical solution. He sealed it shut and placed it inside a plastic basket with a line attached to its handles.

He moved beneath the deck and men above, tossing the basket's line up to awaiting hands.

The object was secreted inside the plastic bag and sealed, before being placed in the basket and slowly lowered to the barge's deck.

"Label it Catalog Item Zed 01, middle gun-deck, found in beam 364, grid HH2," the archaeologist expertly marked the site of his find.

He returned to the beam and the broken wooden shards, where a cover might have been placed over the cavity hollowed inside. He studied the opening, probing inside with the light of his flashlight. It was empty.

"Richards," he hollered to an assistant, still marking the location of their most recent find on an outline drawing of each deck of the Vanguard, that had been laid out in a series of numbered grids, identifying the locations of the few loose objects still lingering about the historic ship's decks.

"Sir!" came this assistant's voice below.

"We've a non-conformity on the middle gun-deck, starboard entrance to the junior officer's quarters, right door beam. It's a hollowed out opening. Some sort of repository, but unlike anything I've ever seen. Mark it for a follow-up . . . it'll be a good research project for the students."

"Grid?"

"I'd guess Q36 . . . but, I'll check the drawing, when I come down," the archaeologist replied.

The basket and its sole contents were lowered to awaiting hands on the barge's deck. All attention was on it, ignoring the men on the middle gun-deck.

All wanted to know what had been discovered.

"What is it?"

"Yeah, what is it?" some of the students broke out, forming a coaxing chorus.

Ward's curiosity was peaked. He leaned forward on the rail of the Reprise and watched with the others. He kept his right hand atop the small box, secreted deep inside his windbreaker's pocket.

The assistant waiting below, claimed the water-filled bag from the basket and held it aloft above his head.

The workers and students fell silent as all eyes focused on the small object, whose shape was distorted by the fogged plastic and water inside. They strained to discern its shape.

"It's a cross!" one of the students, nearest to the object, called out.

Despite, the crud caking one end of it, everyone could make out the gleaming sheen of its tarnished metal, probably silver. Its arms were bent and twisted by the great force that had driven it into the beam. It was further evidence of the fiery explosion, described by witnesses in 1805.

As if to encourage their enthusiasm and curiosity for his own field of study, the archaeologist's assistant took the bag to a nearby plastic tote and its own solution of fresh water and preservatives. Donning latex gloves, he submerged the bag, opening it under the protective layer of the thick filming solution.

"There's an inscription," he remarked in his normal voice, studying the object in the solution, free of the distortion of the plastic bag and water.

His fingers gently rubbed away at the light coating encasing the etched surface. He picked up a small tool, a tiny brush with soft plastic bristles, no larger than a smoker's pipe cleaner, but finer than a toothbrush.

All eyes awaited him as he methodically cleared away the minute depressions, etched by the hands of a jeweler or metalsmith, ages ago. His movements halted.

His head bent lower to the small tub and its restorative cleansing solution. His mouth opened and his lips silently parted forming the first words, slowly becoming legible for the first time, since they had been entombed in the waters off Portsmouth.

"To Ensign Robert Lewis . . . may God return you safely home," his lips moved slowly to a hushed audience, while he wiped away the grit filling the etched words on the back of the silver cross.

"His beloved mother," the inscription ended.

There was silence as one of the historians had already frantically began leafing through the photocopied reproductions of the ship's muster list. He thumbed through the thick aid, he had reproduced from the copies of the London Historical Society's vast archives.

He halted upon the listing of the HMS Vanguard's officers and traced his index finger alongside the last names.

"It's here!" he raised his head in elation, confirming Ensign Robert Lewis was indeed among the ranks of the Vanguard's officers.

Clapping ensued as the enthused students and workers rejoiced in their small discovery and meager role in unearthing a forgotten legacy.

Ward sunk forward on the rail, his weight pressing against it as his legs weakened. It was true. It had to be!

The cross, that silver relic of Ensign Lewis' nightmarish battle, existed. The cursed iron box, a coffin for the foul maiden he'd seen, had survived.

Ward tried to recall the image upon the coffin's lid as he'd seen it bathed in the fresh water repository set up on the barge earlier. It had been too encrusted or worn to make out. But, he could recall the depiction, Ensign Lewis had described and illustrated in his journal. They had to be the same box.

They had to be.

But, could the maiden Lewis described have survived even in the elongated iron coffin's protection for so long beneath the sea, entombed in its cold lifeless depths?

It couldn't be. It couldn't.

But, he could still examine the coffin. He could see if it matched the description of Lewis' foul monstrosity.

Ward pushed away from the rail and made for the gangplank, linking the barge and the Reprise. He walked past a few of the Reprise's crew members, some clicking their cameras, recording the recent find and the delight of the assisting students and archaeological staff.

Ward halted just short of the massive barge and the crane stowed aside of the Vanguard's remains.

They were gone! The treasures that had been resting in pools of water and plastic totes along with the oversized iron box were gone.

Ward ignored the students, still elated with their colleague's near haphazard and disastrous fall, that had led to the discovery along the middle gun-deck.

He moved to one of the professionals, a full time archaeologist, that had been present at the return of the HMS Vanguard to the surface.

"Excuse me . . . excuse me," he interrupted the man, marking a catalog number into an oversized ledger.

"One moment . . . I don't want to forget this number . . ."

"The items, that were removed from the Vanguard, . . . they were soaking topside on the barge . . . were did they get to?"

"You mean the tools, dinnerware, and that gawdawful iron box?"

"Yes . . . that's it!"

"We moved those out last night or I should say, the London Historical Society did," the member of the archaeologist team answered. "If you wanted to see them or take any photos, I'm afraid you've missed your chance. They won't see the light of a museum or a public display for a year or better, now that the London Historical Society's pinched them."

Ward was silent.

"Damn greedy buggers. We were hoping to have those few items on site, when the students joined us this morning . . . you know, show them a glimpse, of what our job is all about, the preservation process. But, far be it for the likes of us to deny the London historians their claim," the technician paused in silent lament.

"Still, it is their right. They have financed most of the recovery and they're entitled."

"So the iron box, it's now at the London Historical Society?"

"No, more likely they've moved it to one of their auxiliary workshops or warehouses, until they're satisfied, that any deterioration has been chemically halted or retarded, so that it can be displayed in one of their museums in the open air or better a climate-controlled environment."

"Why the interest in that bestial monstrosity?" he added.

"It seemed like a real oddity . . . I was curious, what might be inside it."

"My, you must be a late riser," the technician remarked, recognizing the dark blue windbreaker, that was part of the unofficial uniform of the SS Reprise's crew and support technicians.

He spotted the small logo sewn just under the jacket's collar, a ship recognition silhouette of the oceanographic and salvage vessel with a diminutive dolphin leaping out of the water near its fabric bow.

"I imagine you're still recovering from the recovery effort. Splendid piece of work your lot did. Bringing up the Vanguard's stern intact. That was amazing in itself, let alone finding it, after all these centuries, in the cold muck off the harbor."

"Thanks," Ward shrugged off the praise, which had caught the interest of several bystanders, now intent on eavesdropping on their conversation.

"I'd have thought all your crew were off celebrating and accepting medals and honors from those stuffy Historical Society types," the technician remarked as he added a measured amount of an oily preservative into the plastic container of water and solution, bearing the cross.

The additive left a thin film building up across the surface of the water in the small plastic tub, effectively blocking off the air licking the surface of the water.

"The box . . . ?"

"Yes, the box. As I was starting to say, you must be a late

riser. There was nothing inside it. We found it open, this morning . . ."

"Open? I thought it was locked or corroded shut?"

"Everyone did. A couple of bobbies on patrol atop the dock," he added, pointing to the aging and weathered stone facade of the dock, that had likely been built before Nelson's HMS Victory's keel had been laid, "spotted the thing open from up there. They came down at once."

"Did they see anything? Ward's voice asked excitedly, surprising his British colleague.

"No, nothing. They came down and examined the iron container and stood guard over it, reporting immediately to their counterparts atop the dock and at the barriers blocking the public off."

"But, there was no one around, except for a few of our chaps, who had taken to warming themselves in the shelter of the heated workshed. Their torches and our lads confirmed the box was empty, though there were a few pieces of yellowed cloth or fabric left within its confines and what looked like a flattened pile of packed dirt," he added.

"Hell, the fabric . . . or what remained was too fine and there was too little of it to identify what it was from. I know, they saved the few strands as samples to be analyzed and studied. But, there was nothing there of value for a museum display. There was nothing," he added.

"Remarkable thing, that box. I don't think I've seen anything like it, not even in the history books. The thing had no locks or hinges on the outside, it seemed to open from within. But, nobody's found its release or latch . . . that's for the museum and their lot to mull over and pick apart," he halted, testing the small tub of water and preservatives with a paper test strip, searching to find its ph-level.

"Could anything have gotten out . . . fallen out of the box?" Ward asked.

"Gotten out? You're the bloody oceanographer, you know better, than I the pressure, that metal box was under, hundreds of feet below the surface. The fabric debris and dryness tells us the box had air inside, when she went down with the Vanguard. At that depth, on the bottom and the water's pressure, that lid was sealed like a coffin buried under tons of dirt. There was no way for that thing and the vacuum created inside to open by itself, under the waters off Portsmouth."

"That ugly box was sealed, since the day the HMS Vanguard went down. But, I'd love to find the bastards, that opened it. They left it exposed and naked. The tarp set up, to keep it bathed in solution, was drained and fallen about. There's no telling how much damage was done to that relic, even with such a short amount of exposure."

"Damn, I'd just like to know how they figured out how to unlock the bloody thing. Even topside, out of the water, the thing was encrusted and they still had to break a seal formed over centuries. It wasn't an easy task, I'll tell you that," the archaeologist said, satisfied with the color of the test strip, indicating a low acid level in the solution the cross was submerged in.

"They saw no one?" Ward questioned.

"No one . . . well, one of the policemen topside, thought he glimpsed a young woman heading towards town, walking along the edge of dock."

"Thought?"

"I'm afraid, he was on duty too long and a little too bored. His mind was playing with him. She was dressed in an evening dress, some sort of gown. By the time, he exited his policecar' s warmth to check on her, she was gone."

"She disappeared?"

"Not likely. More, she was probably never there. He claimed she was midway along the stone dock, it runs for a good length, at least one-hundred and fifty meters. For some frail little girl to vanish, out in the open atop the bare dock, she'd have had to jump off into the waters of the harbor.

Anyway, there was nothing there and he heard no splash or cries for help. So, it's likely, she didn't do herself in," the technician said with an amused grin.

"It's the fog, clinging to these low stone docks that plays with one's imagination. You stay out here in the dark long enough and you can pretend to see almost anything. But, why this gawdawful interest in that horrid metal box?"

"It had markings on its cover. They were encrusted, when I saw it last. I wanted to see it, one more time . . . to try to make something of them,"

"Well, I can help you with that," the technician turned away, pulling his hands free of the restraining confinement of his latex gloves. He laid the gloves down atop a tabletop of a portable workstation and bent down towards its drawers, encased in its lower frame.

He pulled out a thin wide drawer, akin to that of a mechanics rolling tool-box. His long thin fingers withdrew a rolled up length of white paper from among several others, matching its rolled shape and bound with rubberbands.

The technician snaked the rubberband along the rolled up paper, until it sprang free of one end. He caught the elastic bond in his palm. He unrolled the paper.

Ward looked at the smeared charcoal against the paper's crinkled white surface.

"It's a rubbing," his English counterpart offered.

"I'll admit, it's not the best. But, the surface of that damn box was pocked and porous with rot, like earth or soil had been cast into its metal. I took a handful of these, official and unofficial, after I cleaned away the worst of the encrustation clinging to its surface. I thought a few of my mates might like a souvenir and we made a few extra for the kiddies here, to feed their interest in our dreary lot. You can have this one," he offered.

"Thanks," Ward returned, accepting the smeared image the rubbing represented.

Ward studied the imprinted rendition. He could make out a crescent moon and stars in the background of the box's lid. His eyes focused on the crossed horns or tusks, like ripping teeth or spikes, enclosing a tiny raised crossed with a short dash to its left.

"It's a strange thing, a real oddity, I'll give you that," the technician remarked, seeing Ward's bewilderment with the image.

"What's it mean?" Ward asked, hiding the truth only he knew, of the iron coffin and the journey of the HMS Vanguard.

"No one here seems to know. The historians will be searching the archives of the museums and libraries for a heraldry look-alike. It's obviously a crest or coat-of-arms . . . but, I've never seen anything like it. But, that's not to say it doesn't exist," he added.

"Europe is full of family crests and military badges and displays. And, with the coming of the Industrial Age, merchants and businessmen, lacking the cherished heraldry and status of nobility's pomp, paid to create their own family symbols and emblems. This find might turn out to be as meaningless as the marketing logo's on today's soda cans," the technician exclaimed as he began going about his work.

"Still, it would be interesting to know how that awful metal crate was opened. It certainly wasn't wrested open by some frail little girl in an evening gown. It took a bloody crane to even budge it and we've more, than enough able-bodied and willing young volunteers among us, who tried to move it about without the aid of a lift and failed."

Ward merely shook his head.

He saw no way to return the small metal box and its secreted and damning contents to the remains of the Vanguard. Besides, with the curious, who had gathered about, he'd have no chance to do so unseen.

More police seemed present on the dock above. Perhaps, because of the opened iron box and the puzzle its tampering presented, additional officers had been called in. They loitered about, suspiciously eyeing the archeological effort below.

He turned around and returned to the Reprise, balancing his upward trek along the narrow gangplank with one hand on its rail.

The clouds had darkened, threatening rain and dampening the spirits of the youthful workers and elderly tutors. The latter continued to guide the students through their small role in the recovery's aftermath.

Ward turned around at the Reprise's rail to find the archaeologists hastening their efforts. They tried to tag the last of the Vanguard's timbers and beams for eventual disassembly and transport to some protected warehouse and the chemical and water baths, which would attempt to halt the corrosive process that had accelerated upon her return to the surface.

The barge's crane operator had returned to his station. He sipped, from a cup of steaming tea, waiting for the historians and technicians to summon his aid in lifting the first pieces up to the special crates and lorries, that were arriving along the dock above.

The whole process seemed to ground to a halt, hampered by the large number of volunteers, who only encumbered and slowed the methodical operation.

With the weather threatening to deteriorate, the head archaeologist, in conjunction with the London Historical Society's representative, approved releasing the volunteers, so the most threatened and haphazard of the Vanguard's beams and planking could be removed.

But, even with the students and their aging professors safely aside and relegated to the role of spectators on the dock above, Ward would have no opportunity to return the pilfered article, still shoved deep inside his windbreaker's pocket.

His hand fingered the edge of the container's latticework on its crafted exterior. He lifted it away, aware of the damage his fingers' oils and sweat could reek on the ancient surface. Incriminatingly leaving his fingerprints was the least of his concerns.

The crane's engine started up as the barge's work crew toiled feverishly to beat the approaching rain. Several hands already labored to climb the ladders, scaling about the stern's remains.

They pulled and tugged the blue plastic sheets up about her exposed hull. The large polymer sheets snagged on the exposed beams and jagged framework of the stern. The workers sought to protect those sections of the stern, that would remain outside, lashed to the barge.

The mist changed to a light rain, that pelleted the waters separating the Reprise and the barge. Workers furiously ran about, covering the pieces of broken wood, that had fallen off of the wreck of their own accord as their weight and rot broke them free of the stern.

Some of the cataloged and numbered pieces were merely covered with plastic tarps. Others were loaded into large baskets and hauled to the dock above on a small derrick, out of the way of the crane, preparing to rescue a larger freed remnant.

Ward retreated from the rain assaulting the Reprise's open deck.

CHAPTER 40

Notions

SS Reprise
Portsmouth Harbor
September 17, 2003
1749 Hours

Ward claimed a cup of coffee from the stainless steel communal coffee urn in the Reprise's galley. He chose a table in the corner of the long room, away from the only other occupants, claiming a late lunch.

He'd visited his cabin, before heading to the galley, secreting away the stolen artifact among his disorderly belongings. The cherished box and its journal now resided in the less, than pristine elastic confines of a pair of dirty white socks, doubled together. They normally housed his bottle of bourbon. But, they had made way for his newest treasure. All were secreted away, in the bottom of his locked locker

But, he kept the charcoal rubbing in his possession, wanting to study its ghost-like tracing further.

Ward cupped his hands about the thick white porcelain cup and its steaming contents. He hadn't taken a single sip of the dark black liquid, moving about with the gentle rocking of the salvage vessel as the ship tugged on its tied moorings.

The chop of the harbor's waters was increasing. Rain pelleted the portholes, lining the white walls of the galley at shoulder height.

Ward exhaled slowly. His fears of getting caught with the artifact in his possession bedeviled his thoughts. He sat in the corner, lost to the few occupants of the galley and the cook, beginning preparations for the evening meal behind a partially closed-off counter.

The cook's head bobbed past the opening in the galley's wall. He moved from the food locker to a large table beside the stoves and ovens. All were crammed into the austere, but functional and efficient kitchen space. Several pots and pans clanked and banged as the cook selected just the right one for his culinary choice.

The two diners collected their used plates and cups and placed them in a plastic tote, whose contents would be collected and destined for the galley's dishwasher. One diner dumped a half-eaten meatloaf sandwich in the trash receptacle nearby. Their silverware rattled and clanked among the other dirty utensils in a smaller plastic container with an open-meshed plastic face.

Virtually alone, Ward dwelled on the last twenty-four hours, since he had secured the controls of his ROV, Remotely Operated Vehicle and undertaken his larcenous treasure-hunting venture.

He was now the sole sage of the history of the HMS Vanguard. It was a position, he had not desired and did not wish to continue to hold. Vanguard had become more, than a recovered time-capsule of history, reeled in from the depths off Portsmouth's shore.

Her final journey was a blend of history, lore, and her recovered debris jaded by the fanciful tale of a junior officer. It was a tale or fabrication, Ward told himself as his right index finger circled the rim of the steaming cup of coffee. He sat there, disbelieving the elaborate, but imaginative deception.

A tale was a story, more rightfully a yarn or ballad, sometimes tied by the most slender threads to the truth. But, more often, it was concocted from the fanciful and entertaining thoughts and imagination of the writer or orator, intent on having his fun or stirring his audience to his own beliefs or orientation.

Ensign Robert Lewis had done just that. He had created a tale, an exaggeration or fable, but nothing more than a lie. His story was a fabrication, defying reality and coming close to blasphemy of the strict religious morals of the young officer's time.

Ward sipped his coffee. His heart had steadied.

He thumbed the rolled up paper, laying atop the small square table, he sat at. Its edges were wrinkled from the haste with which he had headed back to his cabin. A few drops of rain had dampened its thin rolled form, spreading along the paper's fibrous surface as it slowly dried.

Without the rubberband, that had been removed by the technician offering him the copy, the paper curled loosely as its rolled form expanded, free of the bond in the dry heat of the galley.

Ward unrolled it, spreading it out atop the table, after sliding his coffee cup aside. Thunder rumbled lowly, well out to sea. It heralded the approach of the coming storm.

The Reprise lifted and dropped in its tethered berth as the chop of the waves surrounding it increased. Tied among the piles, driven into the floor of the harbor, the salvage vessel bounced about like a cork, despite its taunt lines.

Ward's queasy stomach and hangover-plagued mind wished they were underway and out to sea. The Reprise, with her powerful engines and station-keeping thrusters, had ridden out worse storms in the open ocean with less bucking and bobbing. But, tied up in Portsmouth, her unmoving hull became a humbled captive to the lines holding her fast and the tempest growing inside the harbor.

Rain blew horizontally, pelting the glass of the portholes and making Ward appreciative of the dry warmth and comfort of the galley. He lowered his head, staring at the stretched-out rubbing.

His eyes squinted, straining to make out details in the rubbed surface, that had imprinted the design from atop the iron coffin's face. He wanted to go back to his cabin to retrieve Ensign Lewis' journal, but there was no need.

The markings on the iron box were exactly as the journal had described them. The ghost-like trace of an abused and chipped cross was found amid the center of two crossed horns or tusks.

The image took on the hint of blasphemy against God or church.

The tusks' tips pointed to an imaginary heaven, a field of whimsical stars, and a crescent moon. But, as the young ensign had written and sketched, the most disturbing part of the image was a tiny bar to the left of the small raised cross. It seemed like some ancient mathematician's sullied mark, negating the religious piety and mocking the reverence of the scared cross.

Ward fiddled with the image, recalling the meaning of the cross. The image of the cross was not reserved to the sole domain of Christianity. Other faiths and beliefs had found it a powerful and symbolic image.

Buddhists, Brahmans, and Druids had all utilized the symbol. Its shape dated back to antiquity. Even the Egyptians revered it as a sacred symbol.

Ward fingered the image of the cross with his right index finger, smearing some of the charcoal's rubbing. It caked his fingertip.

It had been the Druids, who had attached a pathway or spiritual journey to its arms. They defined the three arms of the cross as separate conditions of the spirit world, the equivalent of Christianity's heaven, purgatory and hell.

The long arm of the cross symbolized a path or the way of life, the short arms referenced the choices or paths, that one's life could take, leading to one's final destination.

It was a simple image with deep-seated meanings, even few lay Christians were readily aware of, in their daily worship. The cross was a simple and powerful icon, even without the addition of a bas-relief image of the savior nailed to its humbling form, creating the essence of the crucifix.

Ward toyed with the memory of the image reproduced in the journal. The few sketches, that had survived in the small leather-bound book, had contained a likeness of Ensign Lewis' rendition of the top of the iron coffin.

Ward didn't need to have it side-by-side for a comparison to the large full-size rubbing to know they were an identical match. The small dash before the cross, harbored within two horns or tusks, was in the rubbing as it had been in Lewis' drawing.

But, the thought of vampires or some maddening combat between good and evil befalling the warship, bordered on lunacy. No, the tale was just that, a fanciful verbal tryst of a bored and inspired writer.

Ward hefted his coffee cup and took a long sip.

But, there had been the discovery of the silver cross, bearing the inscription, confirming its ownership to the young officer. And, it had been embedded in a timber, a beam along the middle gun-deck, the deck the young ensign had mentioned in his tale as one of two targeted by the band of survivors, intent on ridding their ship of . . . demons and ghouls.

In the light of day, the whole adventure seemed absurd. The journal was a fanciful yarn, nothing more. A thousand different things could have been stored in the awful iron box.

Ships like the HMS Victory and Vanguard were supplied with enough stores to last six months. They left harbor with thirty-five tons of gunpowder and one-hundred and twenty tons of round shot aboard.

They were floating powder-boxes, whose worse bane was fire. And set atop it all, were over one-hundred cannon and over eight-hundred men and officers.

An accident, however minor, could easily claim one of the floating tinderboxes in the blink of an eye. That is what had undoubtedly befallen the HMS Vanguard.

That is what the archaeologists and historians would confirm, when they finished their lengthy and cautious examination of the warship's remains. Its broken stern held the answers. It held the truth.

Thunder woke Ward from his thoughts. He began rolling up the rubbing, ignorant of the charcoal image. His action smeared the paper's trapped image. He had more pressing problems. He had to devise some way of returning the stolen trinket back to its rightful owner, the skeletal remains of the Vanguard.

He was about to rise, when two more of the meager crew, left behind to attend to the daily operations of the salvage vessel, entered the galley. They appeared intent on claiming a cup of hot coffee to take on their next watch.

"Hello, Alan!" one crewman broke the silence with a roaring voice that stabbed at Ward's hangover.

"Morning," Ward returned mutely.

"You're looking ill about the gills. This choppy weather taking its toll on you?" the galley's newest occupant taunted as his partner filled two cups of coffee from the large urn.

"A little, I guess," Ward returned as the boat rocked within the confines of its tethered berth.

"It's gonna get worse! A winter storm is blowing in from the southwest. There's a maritime warning on the radio calling all small boats back into the harbor. It was broadcast about an hour ago. Damn, I'd hate to have to earn a living fishing in these seas . . . it's like open ocean between Portsmouth and the Isle of Wight."

Ward merely nodded.

"We were lucky to get that wreck up and tow the barge into harbor. This storm came out of nowhere," Ward's loud companion added.

"Here's your coffee," his partner offered a cup, that dripped onto the floor as he began to sip his own.

"We were lucky," Ward returned, trying to appear his usual self.

"Hey, did you see the paper?"

"Paper?"

"Hell, you know he didn't. We just got it. Its an afternoon addition, Tim," his buddy interceded.

"Give it to me," Tim ragged.

"We've got to get up to the pilothouse . . . the evening watch is coming up. But, look at this," he said, dropping the damp rolled up and perused paper on the table, almost squashing the rolled up rubbing.

As the paper opened, Tim stabbed a hammy index finger along its front page, already stained with coffee.

"Look at this! We just brought this relic up and already the art thieves and grave-robbers are after it, before the sun even rose. The authorities sat on the story, hoping to get a lead on the thieves. They just released the news, this afternoon," Tim's voice boomed with disgust.

The headline was under the banner proclaiming the paper as the Portsmouth Herald. Beneath, its large title a bold-type face announced, **"Recently Recovered Treasure Stolen."**

Ward bent his head following the text. The story detailed the facts of the early morning robbery, mentioning the recent recovery of the HMS Vanguard's surviving stern and several salvaged artifacts. It detailed the shipment of several items, mostly a sampling of the officer's dinnerware, a collection of ship's tools, and implements along with the iron box.

Ward's eyes narrowed as he scanned through the tiny text, racing to the heart of the story. The trucks transporting the items had arrived at the London Historical Society's east side acquisition warehouse, where newly acquired pieces were placed under guard as preservationists went about the delicate and timely task of restoring and protecting the pieces, before deeming them fit for public display.

The warehouse, despite two armed watchmen, had been robbed of the acquisitions. The museum was left only with the sketches, photographs, and inventoried descriptions of the treasures.

Scotland Yard had been called in and a claim was already being filed with the Historical Society's Insurance carrier. But, despite private and police investigations, there was no clue to how the robbery had occurred.

The defeat of the warehouse security and alarm systems,

without any detection or alert, suggested an inside job, probably detailed with the knowledge and wherewithal of a former or present employee.

Ward noted the details of the articles missing and a small paragraph acknowledging the efforts of the American Oceanographic and Salvage Vessel, the SS Reprise and its crew.

He opened the paper up to the inside, finding the column marked Treasure Theft, page A5. It trailed on, adding little more, than a brief summary of the recovery effort and a scant history of the HMS Vanguard. It was the standard press release made available and used almost in its entirety by harried reporters, who felt blessed not to have to do their own homework and research.

Ward tossed the paper down on the table and reached for the last of his coffee. It had gone cold.

He rose and moved to the large urn, dumping the bitter cold remains of his cup in a waste container and filling the cup fresh.

He returned to his table, noting the onset of evening and a heavy fog fighting to rise against the rain, through the portholes lining the galley. His hangover was just beginning to leave him. With the coming of darkness, his tongue began to anticipate the warmth of the bourbon to carry him through another chilly Portsmouth night.

The robbery had relieved him of his own guilt and complicity in his own small act of larceny. His "theft" had saved Ensign Robert Lewis' journal, fanciful as it, was from the private collection of some relic or antiquities collector.

By his act of selfishness, the small book and its ornate box would be saved for the public. He'd think of a credible way to unveil its existence and ensure it fell into the right hands.

Lighthearted and satisfied with himself, Ward returned to his table and collected the rubbing, rolling it tightly in his left hand. He intended to reclaim his room, taking his coffee with him and perhaps, spicing it up with a shot of bourbon.

He was about to discard the newspaper laying atop the small galley table, when he glimpsed a smaller story and a less obtrusive headline capping it. It read **"Ailment Afflicts Portsmouth."**

The short article consisted of only four brief paragraphs, noting a recent influenza or viral infection, that had taken several residents mysteriously ill. Worse the sickness had confounded the local doctors.

The article warned of the symptoms, a high fever, stupor, and incapacitating fatigue coupled with a loss of appetite and vomiting. It sounded like any one of the large number of Asian and local flus, many worsened by the high number of travelers passing through the British Isles by both air and ship transport.

It also smacked of the affliction mentioned in Ensign Lewis' journal, an illness even the ship's surgeon could not fathom.

Coincidence and foolery, that's what it truly was.

The greatest evil in the world was that harbored in the hearts and minds of men. Evil was embodied in the likes of those, who would steal a nation's newly recovered treasures for profit, robbing the public of its chance to glimpse a token part of its nation's past greatness and naval history. Evil rested in the sins of men. They spawned greed, war, and any number to the ills, that continued to plague mankind with strife.

Evil seldom rested in the lores and tales of the past or the demons and creatures of the imagination. The affliction hampering Portsmouth was nothing. At least, it had nothing to do with Ensign Lewis' creative and whimsical tale.

It was coincidence.

Ward left the paper.

Alan Ward opened the heavy steel door to his dark cabin, instinctively switching on the single overhead light as he did so. The first thing, he was aware of was the cold breeze cutting through the room and the open porthole on the other side.

Rain blew through the round opening. A puddle had formed along the floor, beneath the unsecured porthole. A bolt of lighting glared across the room, brighter, than the solitary overhead light.

It cast a white sheen over the wall-lockers on the right side of the cramped cabin. The lighting was followed by the rolling din of thunder, charging across the harbor as a new deluge of rain pelleted the deck outside the porthole.

He froze in dread, that someone had been in his room. His eyes fell to the two wall-lockers, where he had secreted away the journal in the one belonging to him, labeled with a strip of masking tape and black hand-printed letters bearing his last name. To his relief, the combination-lock running through the locker's handle was still in place.

He felt uneasy. He knew his roommate was away and would not return for days. But, on the close confines of a ship like the Reprise, with its almost open quarters and informal environment, it was common place for its crew to visit and exchange information.

Openness and a close-knit family atmosphere allowed and necessitated sharing materials, documents, gear, and even the vessel's cramped living spaces. That's why there were lockers and locks for the few private materials to be kept out of sight prying eyes or borrowing fingers.

The bulk of such private treasures included each man's own private bottle and a varied collection of men's magazines, meant to pass away the lonely nights at sea.

Ward felt less alarmed, viewing his secured locker and its seated combination-lock. He decided to leave the porthole open, allowing the normally stuffy single-setting of the cabin's thermostat to be refreshed by the fresh sea air cooling the room.

He made the cabin door fast from the inside, using its simple mechanical fastener, after placing his coffee cup and the rolled rubbing upon the small desktop, shared by both room's residents.

His bunkmate was still faraway, enjoying the fanfare and ceremony, accompanying the successs of the Reprise's recovery effort.

In time, Ward would avail himself of the other opportunities to share the limelight. For now, all he wanted was to return to the entrails of the journal, savoring its uniqueness, before it was lost to him forever.

He went to his bunk and dug into the back of its thin

mattress, seeking out the bottle of bourbon hidden there. After pouring a healthy finger or two of the warm golden brown fluid into his black coffee and taking a sip, he went to open his narrow wall locker. He thumbed the combination-lock's dial, the spinning numbers eluding the correct combination setting. It took Ward three tries to open the lock.

The lock opened and he bent to the shelf on the locker's bottom.

A pile of foul laundry awaited him, crammed about a pair of well-worn running shoes, that had seen little use along the docks and streets of Portsmouth. He pulled at the white elastic of a doubled-up pair of tube socks.

He halted, fear filling his stomach. The socks were empty, devoid of the treasure, he'd spirited away in them.

He calmed himself. He had more than one pair of socks in the tangled mess at the bottom of his locker. He dropped to his knees on the hard metal and tiled deck, searching methodically for the metal container and its secreted journal stuffed inside two thick white tube socks.

Several more socks were yanked and tugged out of the rank bunch of footwear and clothing. The fact, that the locker was locked and the mess in its bottom was still as he had left it, goaded Ward into believing he had hidden the journal better, than he had imagined. He almost laughed at his own cleverness.

His fingers clawed through the jumble in the bottom of the locker, dropping each unrewarding item from its interior onto the floor. The small room was in disarray as socks, used towels, and sneakers cluttered the floor.

The bottom of the metal wall-locker was empty.

The treasue was gone.

Furiously, Ward began throwing the clothing, hanging from the locker's hangars and hooks, out of its narrow confines. There was nothing. He poked through the metal tray, atop the clothing rack, only to find it devoid of the prize he sought.

"No! God no!" Ward cursed, slamming his fist into the locker's open door as another thunderclap boomed across the harbor. It was distant as the storm began to trail off, moving northward. The rains slowed, then receded.

A returning fishing trawler's horn blared in the distance, echoing into the cabin on the night's dampness through the open porthole.

Ward slammed the locker's door shut and flung himself to the open porthole, even though he knew it would be too late to spy any thief, that had looted his locker.

But, the lock had been secure. Except for the porthole the room was as he had left it.

He reached the porthole, mounted high in the side of the rear of the superstructure, housing the crews' quarters.

The fishing boat's horn was answered by that of a tug, going about the never-ending business of the harbor. The din disturbed a nearby flock of gulls, roosting for the night.

They squawked as they took to flight. They circled about in the darkness, their white forms glimpsed in the reflected light of the lamps about the dock and topside on the Reprise's decks.

Ward grabbed the thick round rim of the open porthole, pulling himself up to it. Its steel was cold. His hair and face were assaulted by the cold draft gusting through the round opening.

He shivered as his eyes searched about the dock and barge ahead. With the retreat of the storm and rains, a fog was quickly engulfing the docks and ships. It misted upward from the chilled waters.

The HMS Vanguard was not to be seen, it was again entombed in a protective shroud of plastic tarps as it sat forlornly and forgotten in the darkening night. A fog misted and swirled about its shrouded form, eerily haunted by the glaring lights of the stone dock above.

The Reprise rocked, pushed against the piles it was tied up to alongside the salvage barge and its stowed crane. The small flock of gulls loitered about, some floating silently atop the waters beyond the Reprise's hull, others circling the barge or dock, awaiting any refuse dumped overboard by the cook.

The birds images blurred as the fog rose.

Ward blinked as if doing so would push away the thick fog, blanketing the docks and surrounding gangplanks. He saw and heard nothing as darkness and fog filled the night.

He bowed his head in resignation, swallowing the pain of the loss of the treasure, that had fleetingly been his.

Ward raised his head, not knowing why. It was as if something was amiss. It was as if he sensed something, when only darkness was present.

His eyes moved beyond the barge and the entombed stern of the Vanguard. They lifted to the stone and mortar docks above.

There on the precipice of the dock's sharp corner, he saw a figure.

The wind pushing the storm northward blew openings in the gathering fog. The fog slowly swirled as the waters and winds pushed in from seaward. The waves smashed against the dock's worn stones. Slowly, the white mist receded, yet a white image or object still remained atop the edge of the precarious dock's height. It hung atop a corner of the raised stone surface.

Ward strained to see the form, blinking his eyes in disbelief. She was there.

It was the young woman clad in the ghostly flowing gown, Ensign Lewis had recorded. Ward's eyes froze on the sight of the gossamer fabric lifting hauntingly around her frail thin form as her black mane flowed about her head, lifted on the chilling breeze.

The gown's fabric was in haunting shreds, that trailed away from her form. Some of its dulled fabric still held its shimmering luster, despite its age and decay.

As if she was aware of his observations, the figure turned towards the Reprise and the light spilling from the open porthole.

Ward watched the young maiden turn without a limb moving. She rotated about to face towards him. His eyes dropped to her feet and the dock.

Her feet were clad in slippers of the same delicate cloth as the gown's. Their fineness was marred by the yellowing discoloration and disintegration of age. Her feet floated above the dock's harsh stone surface, her toes pointed earthward as if she was a practiced ballerina. They dragged about the surface of the wet dock.

Ward watched as her eyes reflected the light of a nearby lamp and glowed with a damning blackness. Her hands extended from the sides of her body to reveal the small box Ward had come to covet along with the journal inside.

His lips parted, but Ward could say nothing. He was in awe of the beautiful maiden, a stone's throw away.

She seemed to relish his attention and noted the recognition reflected in his eyes. Ward strained to keep upright against the high porthole. His chin rested atop its cold steel rim.

The maiden slowly turned her back on the Reprise, carrying the small lattice framework box regally in her two hands as if a handmaiden or lady in waiting.

The flowing gown trailed about her, lifting on the tide's breeze.

Ward blinked in disbelief as he struggled higher in the porthole.

When next he looked, the haunting image was gone. Only fog swirled about the dock as it thickened and obscured the stone surface from his sight.

She was gone. The journal and his proof vanished into the night.

THE END